I0613900

Gapman

A DragonEye, PI story

Karina Fabian

LASER COW PRESS

Laser Cow Press

MERRITT ISLAND, FL

Laser Cow Press
Merritt Island, FL
https://fabianspace.com

Publisher's Note: This is a work of fiction. Names, characters, places, and incidents are a product of the author's imagination. Locales and public names are sometimes used for atmospheric purposes. Any resemblance to actual people, living or dead, or to businesses, companies, events, institutions, or locales is completely coincidental.

Cover art by Dawn Grimes
DragonEye & Laser Cow Logos by Allen Oaks

Book Layout © 2017 BookDesignTemplates.com

Gapman/Karina Fabian -- 1st ed.
Print ISBN: 978-1-956489-22-4

Dedication

*To all the Vern fans (or "Vernerds," as Cesar Chacon
calls them, himself included). Thanks for keeping this
series alive with all your support. Here's your chance
to fly with Vern.*

When life gives you lemons, make lemonade.
When life gives you toxic waste...make
yourself a superpowered pain-in-my-tail?
Who decided this?

Contents

Chapter One: Call Me Ron

Vern

The thing about being an Eighth-day Creation is that my only true equals are my own kin. We played, conspired together, even fought, and always we came away better for it. My kin were a blessing—one I lost almost nine centuries ago.

Since then, my interactions with anyone approaching my level have been few and far between. In fact, thanks to St. George, even if I find someone who would have been my equal—Quetzalcoatl comes to mind, or, more recently in the foe department, Shogzallie—I'm no longer at my true size or power. Every fight is uneven; every game, a compromise to favor the lesser being. Then, I came to the Mundane where I spend most of my day-to-day with nonmagical, weak humans. I grew weak as well, and the worst of it was, I didn't even realize it.

My eldestkin, Durrehkeh, had tried to warn me. I hate it when he's right.

The fight with Shogzallie made me realize how far I'd fallen, and not just because of St. George's spell. I was out of practice, and for that, I needed a sparring partner.

Who knew that need would be fulfilled by a Mundane with low self-esteem who happened to be in the wrong place at the wrong time?

Enjoy his story—especially the parts with me in it.

Ron

My name is Ronald Logan Engleson. I prefer "Ron," but people have called me Ronnie since I was a baby, and aside from some wonderfully "Ronnie"-free years in college, I've been Ronnie ever since. Until now.

This is the story of my death—and my rebirth as something newer, stronger. Greater. The story of how Ronnie Engleson was burned in the fires of the phoenix and emerged from the ashes as the hero he'd never known he could be.

This is the origin story of Gapman.

I walked up to the counter, set my comic books on it, and dug in my messenger bag for my credit card.

"Hey, Ronnie. How's it going?" Misty, the assistant manager, asked as she rang up my purchase.

"It's Ron," I muttered. I could understand Owen, the owner, calling me "Ronnie," because he'd known me since I was a kid. But Misty was my age and had moved here from Michigan. She hadn't known me in my Ronnie years.

"Oops, sorry! I was thinking about your latest in the *Gazette*'s special issue on Tokneo's destruction," she said.

"Ah." The editor-in-chief, Johnny Redfeathers (and never call him "chief") was another of the Los Lagos generation who knew me as a shy, nerdy kid and still didn't see me as grown-up. He had stuck my childhood name on my byline. The only person who ever stood up to him was Kitty McGrue, his star reporter. Well, Mom, too, but I wasn't going to whine to her about a nickname. So I shrugged. "That article was a lot of fun."

She hummed agreement, then directed her attention to DC aisles where three teens were in a heated discussion with another patron. "Hey! Cool it, over there. If you want it, buy it. If you want to argue about it, go outside."

After satisfying herself that they were going to behave, she turned to me with a shrug. "Sorry."

"No problem." I saw the latest issue of *Fangolia* on the counter behind her and pointed to it. I had an article on the second season of *Vampires Bite*. Mom would want a copy for her collection.

Misty added it to my pile. "So, anyway, great article. All the parallels of Shogzallie's attack to Godzilla movies... I don't think even Vern realized how many there were."

"Power of research," I said, smiling. I was glad the *Los Lagos Gazette* let me write it, even if Kitty called it fluff-stuff.

"Yeah," Owen laughed as he stuck his head out from the back room. He gave the kids a quick glance before turning his attention to me. "How many kaiju movies did you have to watch?"

"I read comics, too, you know," I added, only pretending to be affronted. I loved my job.

"I am surprised you didn't get a quote from Vern," Misty said.

I sighed. I would love to meet the famous Faerie dragon who had made his residence in our city, but even a year since my return, I hadn't had a chance. "Yeah, well, McGrue claimed the exclusive. I guess they have a thing or something."

Misty and Owen laughed outright. What had I said that was so funny? It certainly wasn't funny to me. I would have loved a quote from the famous dragon PI who had saved our city, but Kitty called dibs, and Mr. Redfeathers sided with her. When I protested, Kitty said it was my fault for asking. What did that even mean? I was glad when Mom broke up with Redfeathers, even if he was the most stable man in her long list of boyfriends.

Then Owen said, "Trust me: he'd rather talk to you about movies than Kitty about, well, anything. Vern and I are friends, so if you ever need a quote from him, let me know. I'll hook you up. So what's next for you?"

His interest was more than polite conversation. I'd been visiting the comic shop since I was 10, a lonely kid spending his after-school hours with his nose in the latest issues of DC and Marvel. Even though he was a decade older, we'd been kindred spirits. He'd talked to me about the history of my favorite heroes, and we'd discussed everything from original artists to the latest actors to take on a superhero role.

He was the reason I had a career as an entertainment writer. One of the best parts of returning to Los

Lagos was renewing our friendship. He understood when I geeked out about an assignment.

Like today. I pointed to the flyer by the register for the Gapway Theater's grand opening. "I get to spend the whole day with the cast of *Captain Extraordinary*, doing interviews, learning about the coordination of tech and magic for the creation of the effects, and interviewing the actors. Tonight, I get to see the first dress rehearsal. I already have three assignments lined up, including *Fangolia*, the *Gazette*, and—"

A voice beside me said, "You're really Ronnie Engleson?"

A fan? I turned to the person behind me with a smile on my face.

The first thing I noticed was the number of piercings on their face. My mind counted twelve before coming to the one that held their lip up in a permanent sneer. Their haircut was short, stylish, and neutral, and their face had tattoos instead of makeup. Despite the late autumn heat, they wore layers that hid their figure. Their T-shirt declared, "If you have to ask my pronouns, you aren't aware."

They looked me up and down like something they'd scrape off their shoe.

My smile faded. "Uh, nice to meet you?"

"You? You are Ronnie Engleson who writes for *Total Drama*?" they asked. "How? *Total Drama* is all about celebrating diversity on the screen, but you're so..."

Misty leaned her elbows on the counter. "What? Are you assuming Ronnie's heritage? Or maybe his gender?"

The person turned beet red and started sputtering apologies. "I, I loved your article on origin stories!" they concluded and hurried off before saying which one. I thought I saw their shoulders twitching.

I gaped at their retreating back. Should I go talk to them? But then one of the kids was walking out the door and it would have been awkward to pass him. "Are they okay?"

Owen chuckled. "Don't worry about it."

Misty added, "Pat comes in every couple of weeks and gives us or our customers a hard time about some misogynist comic or underrepresented character or whatever dumb thing an artist or writer said online. It was nice to use their own rhetoric against them for once."

She waved at the other two boys as they also left the shop.

"Besides," Owen teased, "that's what you get for using 'Ronnie' as your byline."

I sighed. I'd wanted to be "Ron Engleson," but Reefer Transformz, the managing editor, had insisted it was "too reminiscent of the oppressive patriarchy that is antithetical to modern entertainment," and since they paid me $500 an article to write about movies, I had let it slide. Of course, Mr. Redfeathers said it was all the more reason to use "Ronnie" in the *Gazette*, too.

"Not to mention the man purse," Owen concluded.

I looked at the leather bag hanging off my shoulder. "A messenger bag. It's waterproof. It's leather. And it's what we all used in Leeds!"

"Yes, yes, how very European of you." He grinned.

He'd helped pay my tuition at Leeds School of Journalism and the Arts. I composed my face into an expression of Classic British Stoicism as I played along. "You do want me to keep your comics safe, don't you?"

"They're yours now." He handed me my bag and card. "Good luck with the interviews. Have fun!"

I left the store and glanced around the plaza. It was late September, and Summer was still fighting Winter for the weather. Gray clouds were threatening rain, driving most people indoors, but I saw my sort-of fan sitting at one of the tables of the coffee shop with a drink and a pastry. That sounded good, but did I really want to risk a confrontation? What if they asked my preferences and I had to admit I was a straight, middle-class white guy?

It wasn't worth the trouble. I turned toward the street.

"Hey, Mister Engleson!"

One of the boys from the comic book shop sped by me on his skateboard, smacking me on the shoulder and causing me to misstep.

"Come here!" he called over his shoulder. "Got a surprise for you."

A surprise? I turned to look at him. He'd joined his two friends. The three were giggling and high-fiving in a way that made my hackles rise. It couldn't be about me, could it?

I sighed and told my inner bullied-child to shut up. They were just kids—comic book store kids, at that. I should be thinking like a mentor, not a victim. I went over, hoping my years of being shoved into lockers didn't somehow show. "What's up, guys?"

"We heard what Pat was saying to you. That's misspelled," the one who had called me said.

It took me a moment to realize they were using Faerie slang and referring to my encounter with Pat. Before I could protest that it was simply a misunderstanding, he continued. "We're going to have a little fun with it. Wanna watch?"

"Them, not it. What do you mean?" I asked, my heart rate rising.

It must have shown on my face, as one said, "Oh! Nothing bad, just funny. Callum convinced it to play in the fountain." He snickered.

Callum added, "And make out with Apollo!"

The others shouted, "No way!" and started laughing outright.

Apollo? "The statue?"

Callum chortled. "Pat's always looking at it real longingly, you know?"

Too many objections ran through my head, compounded with questions. Why would they think this was funny? Why did they think I would find it funny? But more importantly, "How could you convince Pat to do that?"

The ringleader in a Deadpool T-shirt said, "Pat's only going to do it if it secretly wants to. See?"

He opened his palm to show me the pink capsule he held.

"Is that...?"

"It's Athenal," he said, as proud as if he'd invented the drug himself. "See, it..."

"I know what it does!" Athenal was a drug created with Faerie and Mundane science. It made people susceptible to suggestion, as long as it didn't break a person's deep-seated morals. The actual Faerie goddess, the empyre Athena, created it, and it was being used by psychiatrists in controlled studies, although there was already a street version, puck. People used puck at parties to prank their friends—hence the name. It had only been out a few months, and already there were people in Colorado lobbying for its complete legalization while DARE programs made it top of the list to warn kids against.

Maybe I should be glad he had the real stuff and wasn't involved with street drugs. Still, "Where did you get that?"

He shrugged. "My sister's using it to lose weight. When she's got the munchies, she has to take one and look at herself in the mirror and tell herself she's a smart girl who only eats when she's hungry." He sneered that last.

"I'm a pretty girl, so I don't need a donut," Callum sing-songed, batting his eyes, then yelped when Deadpool-shirt smacked him on the head.

"Don't you mock my sister! Callum snuck one in Pat's pumpkin-spiced soy latte chai or whatever..."

"Then I suggested that Apollo is looking hot for smooches."

He started making kissing sounds. Skateboard kid joined him.

Finally, I found my voice. "Are you out of your minds? You go put that...stuff...back in its bottle. First off, you're stealing! Second, I don't care if Pat were so inclined as to kiss a statue, that's just mean. What if someone played that kind of prank on your sister?"

But they weren't listening. Pat had swallowed the last of their latte and was sashaying toward the statue.

Wincing, with my inner child crying out "It's a trap!" in Admiral Ackbar's voice, I left the giggling trio and ran to intercept Pat.

"Pat! Hi. It's Ron—Ronnie Engleson. From the comic book store?"

"Not interested." They tried to move past me.

I sidestepped to get in their way. "Oh, sure, but I, uh..." How did you talk to someone on puck? "Uh, what are you doing?"

Now they stopped looking past me to the statue to grin at me. "I'm going to give Apollo the thrill of his life."

They started unzipping their hoodie. Fortunately, they had three layers on underneath.

"Uh, it's a statue," I said. "Listen, I don't know how to tell you this, but…"

They snorted. "Then, don't."

They jerked left. I jerked left. They jerked right. I jerked right. Finally, I threw my hands wide. "Pat! Stop! You don't want to do this!"

Pat froze and their eyes cleared. For a joyous moment, I thought I'd gotten through, but then their expression darkened into a glower.

"What did you say?"

I felt myself wither as every lecture about diversity and acceptance I'd ever heard played out in my head. "You, uh, you don't want to… I mean, it's a statue, and…"

"Are you telling me who I can and can't love?"

Their ferocity hit me like hammer to the face. My inner child screamed, "I told you!" while all that came out of my mouth was, "Erk!"

"I should have known!" Pat poked a meaty finger at my chest. They stepped forward. I stepped back.

"Are you putting limits on my love?"

"I...no? But it's not real. You've been—"

The advanced again. "Not real? So I've been deceived? Is that it?"

"Yes! Yes, that..."

Pat was getting red in the face. I don't think they meant that the way I did. Behind them, I saw people in the café turning our way. Behind me, I could hear the boys laughing with abandon. "Look, this is a big misunderstanding. It's just—"

"Now you're mansplaining? Mansplaining *love*?" They advanced again.

"What? No! I'm trying to—Yeagh!"

The back of my legs bumped the edge of the fountain, and unready, I lost my balance and toppled backward into the fountain. My legs flung up and one foot caught Pat between his.

Yeah, his. Mystery solved, I guess.

"Serves you right!" Pat shouted down at me at a somewhat higher octave. "I'm going home right now and writing *Total Drama* about your misogynistic value system!"

"Yes!" I shouted to his retreating back. "Go straight home! That's exactly what you want to do! Drive safe!"

I struggled out of the fountain and tried to wring some of water out of my clothes. I saw my bag and breathed a sigh of relief. It had slipped off my shoulder as I fell and had landed outside the fountain. Aside from some splashes of water puddled on the leather, it was fine.

I turned to glare at the kids, but they were putting their phones back into their pockets and mounting their skateboards.

"Thanks for the show!" Callum called.

"Loser," Deadpool added.

I imagined myself running after them, snagging one and demanding he take me to his parents. In a movie, it'd be awesome. In real life, I'd be a soggy guy in squelching shoes and a man purse whacking my side as I chased a couple of kids for half a block before they escaped. Their parents would probably side with them, anyway.

I watched them go.

Just then, thunder boomed, and the heavens opened up. I reached into my "very European" messenger bag and pulled out my very British umbrella. Like I could get wetter. The last few people in the plaza had rushed into the coffee shop. Even if I wanted to face them now, there'd be a line. And I'd wanted a pumpkin-spiced latte, too.

I went to the street where my Rhyde should be arriving soon to take me to the Gap, mentally composing an email to my editor at *Total Drama*.

Chapter Two:
Ronnie Falls Into His Role

Ron

There's nothing like being on a stage before a production: the controlled chaos of actors running through their lines while the stage crew makes adjustments to props or tests the lights and sound system. The building anticipation, spiced with a tinge of anxiety and sweetened with the hope that this production will be remembered for seasons to come. It's a feeling that transcends cultures, universes, even species.

As I stood backstage at the Gapway Theater, a ten-minute walk from the Faerie side of the Gap, I couldn't help but absorb that feeling, coupled with an awe of what this steampunk-and-magic society could produce. *Captain Extraordinary* promised to rival *Phantom of the Opera* in stage design—perhaps not as polished, but with a flare that—

"Oi!" Dorsch, the director, interrupted me. "It's impressive all right, but are you going to stand there grinning like a fool, or do you want to interview?"

"I was just—"

The dwarf snagged my elbow and pulled me toward the snack area. "Come on! You only got two hours to finish this interview. They did warn you Hawgin understands human, but he doesn't speak it very well?"

"Speaking human" meant not just speaking Mundane English but talking concisely—something that was alien to High Elves. I shrugged. Even though I grew up in Los Lagos, I hadn't interacted much with the Faerie folk. I knew about the notorious longwindedness of High Elves but had never had a conversation with one, myself. "Can it be that bad?"

Dorsch looked at me like I'd come from New York, then tossed his head impatiently. "Ach! You'll find out soon enough. Oi! Hawgindespotlite! Come meet Ronnie Engleson from the *Los Lagos Gazette*!"

"It's Ron," I started, but Dorsch shoved me forward. I stumbled but caught myself before falling onto the buffet table. Even so, I rattled the pewter cups and the plastic bottles of Ping Cola.

The High Elf ended his conversation with a rather tired-looking lady in a classic minion silver jumpsuit and approached.

Hawgindespotlite was, of course, playing the villain, Dr. Despicable, but I could tell immediately women (or "those so inclined" as I'd have to say in *Total Drama*) would be falling for the bad boy. He was gorgeous even among High Elves, and the costumer had done an amazing job with his maroon, velvet suit. The classic 70s wide-lapeled jacket and flared pants nonetheless captured his lean, pantherlike form—all without the aid of stretchy, form-fitting materials. It was all very stylish, except for the necklace. They were just plain, brownish beads, like someone had polished clods of dirt. It seemed an odd fashion choice.

But never mind—what really drew the eyes was his hair. It was so silver, it was platinum, and it swayed with the artistic beauty you find in good anime.

He flipped it back over his shoulder in a way that called for a chorus and background stars, then approached, a grin on his smooth, handsome face.

"Such timing, friend dwarf! For I had just 'wrapped up'—as they say in the Mundane Hollywood, that land where—"

"Yeah, yeah. He's all yours, Ronnie. Here." He set a chair behind me and patted the back. "You may need it." He left without offering one to his leading man.

I stayed standing. It was only good manners. "How do you do? I'm Ron—"

"Greetings to you, Ronnie Engleson, born Ronald Logan Engleson, son of Gordon, who left your mother in your early toddlerhood and subsequently died in the tragic porta-potty explosion that was probably not his fault; son of Trixie, who was, no doubt, better off and raised you alone, wrestling on the Colorado Women's circuit and dancing exotically three nights a week. Yes, I greet you, Ronnie, entertainment report of the *Los Lagos Gazette* who recently wrote a most compelling review of the CSU-Los Lagos production of *A Faerie's Tale*...."

How'd he know about Mom and wrestling? That ended when I was like seven. "Wow, you've learned a lot—"

"...reminiscent of your own starring role in *The Curious Savage*..."

"Thanks, but I'm not—"

"...eschewing the stage for the life of a journalist, contemplating the performance of others who bask in the glory of the limelight, so poignant..."

...And so it went. By the time he got to my comic book obsession, I'd sunk into my seat. I glanced at my watch: 20 minutes had passed! Belatedly, I remembered my pocket recorder. Not that it mattered. Hawgin still hadn't said anything about himself.

If I could just get him to pause, I could ask a question.

I grabbed a can of Ping Cola off the snack table. I didn't dare ask if he was thirsty. What if he took ten minutes to say, "Yes?"

I held it out. "Please, help yourself."

"Oh, Most Considerate Ronnie whose courtesy is known among humans and thus among Elves. Verily, it has been noted that you help the elderly with their packages, open doors for ladies, and called his own mother not less than six times last week to let her know where he was and ask if she needed something from the store. Nay, concern yourself not over your beverage choice, although I, being of the Slow To Age and Seldom Senile Race dare not imbibe lest the deleterious effects..."

By the time he'd finished saying, "Thanks, but Ping is gross," I'd finished drinking the can in my hand and was halfway through the second. At least I'd remembered to put the recorder on.

I asked my first question—the standard, "What do you enjoy most about this role?"—and he was half-way—I think halfway—through his answer when Dorsch showed up at his elbow. He listened a moment, then snapped his fingers in front of Hawgin's glazed eyes and made the hand circles that indicated "speed it up" in both Mundane and Faerie stage direction. The elf nodded.

Ten minutes later, he'd finished. "A brief reply, for which I apologize, but I believe it gives, as you Mundanes say, 'the gist of it?'"

I glanced at my tape. I'd flipped it once and was halfway through the next. "Wonderful. Really. Thanks so much. Um, if I have any follow-up questions, perhaps I could email you?"

As Hawgin opened his mouth, Dorsch said, "Email his agent. He speaks Human."

Dorsch pulled me away as Hawgin started a speech that seemed to boil down to "Yes, he does."

"Don't let the interview give you the wrong impression," Dorsch said. "He sticks to the script I wrote. Very professional."

"And what made you decide to grant him the lead?"

Dorsch shrugged and led me up the narrow stairs to the catwalks above the stage. "He's brilliant with the monologue, of course. We'll set that scene up for you. Right now, I want you to meet my stage designer, Snapdragon."

At the sound of his name, a 12-inch fairy (Midsummer Court, if I remembered my middle-school class in Faerie Races) flew down from where he was putting a blue film on a stage light. He wore bib overall painter's pants and a T-shirt, both stained with grease and paint. My smile must have given my delight away because Dorsch snorted.

"Your first time in Faerie, ain't it? Well, enjoy yourself. I'll go set up the scene." He left, and Snapdragon alighted on my shoulder. He wasn't as heavy as I'd expected, but his wings tickled my ear.

Wait 'till I told Mom about my day!

"Mind your step, sir."

I didn't realize fairies were so polite. I wondered how much Mrs. Kingston, my middle school Faerie studies teacher, didn't know about the fairy folk.

"Don't worry. I used to work the lights for the Los Lagos Dinner Theater. I'm very comfortable around scaffoldings." I stepped around a tangle of wires and grabbed hold of a brace as I looked down at the set. "You've done some amazing work."

Snapdragon straightened up proudly, his wing brushing my ear. "I thought the combination of magic and technology would interest you. The lighting and sound systems are Mundane, as you can see, as is the small generator that runs them. To get the Duke's permission for that, we had to promise his cousin, Lady Elena, a part. Fortunately, she's quite good—she's playing Gertie."

I pulled out my camera and photographed the action on the stage. Hawgindespotlite dominated the scene, standing roughly Stage Right and gesturing as silver-clad minions of varying races dragged in the bound and gagged hero. Dorsch was right; given a script, Hawgin delivered a captivating monologue. I let the camera lens roam the stage, catching Hawgin's smug expression, the Elfmaid minions in tight jumpsuits who clasped each other and sighed like fangirls, the way Salerno Tom's (Captain Extraordinary's) chest muscles bulged as he strained to break free. I hoped they'd repeat the scene so I could take photos from ground level, too.

"Oh, I love this part!" Snapdragon pushed off my shoulder and settled on the wood railing, elbows on knees. I didn't know why he didn't topple over, he was leaning so far forward. Not that it would matter. His wings fluttered.

I set my elbows on the railing beside him. The scaffolding creaked at the change in weight, but like I said, I'm used to that.

Tom had delivered the usual lines of "You fiend! You won't get away with this" and received the obligatory punch in the gut from a stocky dwarf minion. I smiled. That would be Kent. He'd written me when I got the assignment and offered to give me an interview ahead of time and maybe take me out to lunch and get my insights on Hollywood. He was hoping this play would get enough publicity to launch his career in the Mundane.

Hawgin threw back his head and laughed. His voice rose. "Show him what awaits his secret beloved!"

The minion fangirls bowed and rushed off, stage left. Moments later, a squad of pixies and other Midsummer Court Fairies flew in.

"Uh, Snapdragon? Are they glowing?"

Snapdragon's sigh was half-groan. "That's the Tweet Troupe. Studied Mundane method acting.

Graduates of the *They Were Discovered Complete Video Course for the Aspiring Thespian*."

Yeah. Kent said he'd taken the course with them. That didn't explain the glow. "Is the glowing magic, then?"

"Uh, no. Radioactivity."

"For real?"

Snapdragon shrugged. "They snuck through the reactor in Los Lagos. Don't ask me how. They take their art very seriously."

My stomach lurched. Below, they flew around the actors without any concern for the radiation they had to be trailing. "I—but—I... Are they *dangerous* now?"

Snapdragon leaned back as if to show his indifference. "Only if they bite you. But be careful. They're all pretty cranky. Goldleaf tried to bite Hork's head off yesterday, but even a leprechaun is too big for a pixie, no matter how grumpy he is. Look! Here it comes!"

Kicking the rail at a steady beat, Snapdragon whispered stage directions: "One, two—where's that curtain? —four, minions part—Come on, Mark, face downstage!—seven, eight—curtains should be parted by now, eleven—here it comes!"

The actors cleared center stage with carefully choreographed steps, making room for a large caldron, full of—

I leaned back, holding my breath.

"Don't you love it?" Snapdragon bounced on the rail. "Our very own industrial waste. Listen to that glopping sound! Winston tweaked that for weeks."

The goo did indeed glop menacingly. The smell, though subtle, whispered malevolence and danger. Parts of it shimmered. I covered my mouth and nose with one hand. "Is it radioactive, too?"

"Of course not! It's magic. Does match the pixies, though, doesn't it? Whoop!" He laughed at something I didn't see. "Imaayerhedbuttikensyng jerks every time it does that. Our first run, one of the bubbles exploded and immersed her in sticky goop. Made her ears grow three sizes. Ha!"

"Uh…"

"We changed the recipe so it doesn't enlarge things, but she keeps flinching! Dorsch made it part of her character."

I leaned over to look at Imaayerhedbuttikensyng. Her ears seemed normal enough. "What's this batch do?"

"What does every vat of toxic industrial waste do? Severely disfigures you, gives you a mental illness and affinity for clown makeup—the usual. Or gives you superpowers."

I backed to the other side of the scaffold, gripping the rail with one hand, the other still over my face.

Snapdragon finally took his eyes off his pride-and-joy prop and looked at me. He laughed. "Come on! It was a joke!"

Joke. Mrs. Kingston had taught us that fairies liked jokes. She'd warned us about the practical jokes they played. Pucks, they called them, like in Shakespeare. Like the name of the drug those kids had used on Pat. I hoped they'd reconsider what I had told them.

Did fairies just do regular jokes, too? "You're sure?" I asked.

"Mostly." Snapdragon smiled to himself.

He's just kidding, I told myself. I can take a joke.

I took a deep breath and made a show of changing the tape in my recorder and securing it in my pocket. It might claim to be waterproof, but I didn't want to risk it falling into the goo. By then, my legs were willing to carry me forward, and I resumed my spot beside him. I pulled out my camera and started snapping more shots.

"This is the fifth batch," Snapdragon continued. "Winston is meticulous. He studied the script and visited several factories featured on the Greenpeace Industrial Wall of Shame..."

"The what?" I spun fast.

The scaffolding broke.

Chapter Three: A Hero Rises

Ron

I tumbled, scrabbling wildly at the air. I saw wings and reached for them. My fist closed around a glowing pixie.

He bit me.

Thus, my mouth was open in a shriek when we hit the vat of magical toxic waste. The impact knocked the wind out of me, but I managed not to inhale as I sunk into the thick cloying liquid, falling deeper into the darkness with interminable slowness. My ears began to ring, yet I was sure I heard something. My ears strained to listen.

"Oi! The vat's only four feet deep, ya drama queen! Stand up!"

Oh.

I set my feet down and stood. Air! Oh, wonderful air! I coughed and gasped as Dorsch asked if I was okay.

The pixie—Goldleaf?—still had his teeth sunk into my hand.

"Yaahhhh!" I yelled and flung my hand hard. The pixie went flying, and not with his own wing power. People screamed and ducked as toxic goo splattered everywhere. He landed on Hawgin's head.

"My hair!" Hawgin shouted in what was probably the shortest sentence he'd ever uttered, then launched into a long diatribe that seemed to be varying forms of "Get off! Get off!" while he ran blindly Stage Left. The pixie was screaming something, too, and I could almost make out the words. Something about being stuck?

Everyone else was shouting, except Snapdragon, who was floating on his back, his arms around his stomach, laughing.

Hawgin screamed. Goldleaf had bitten him on the scalp!

"Help him!" I gasped as I tumbled out of the vat. A fire hose! We needed a fire hose. I could wash myself and him clean and maybe the pressure would be enough to push the violent pixie off. Heaven knows I wasn't going to get near him again.

Who was I kidding? We were in Faerie. There were no fire hoses! I scanned the area, desperate for another solution. Meanwhile, Hawgin, in his panic, had run backstage, slipped on some of the goo, and crashed into the snack table. He sprawled beside it, dazed, while a toppled bottle of Ping poured out over himself and the now-unconscious pixie still attached by his teeth to Hawgin's scalp.

The other pixies were buzzing about like angry hornets. The elves dashed offstage, arms over their heads to protect their hair. Snapdragon had flopped onto the dwarf actor Kent's shoulder. Both were laughing too hard to talk. Dorsch, meanwhile, was alternately yelling for everyone to calm down and to clean up the mess and get back to work.

No one seemed to notice I was still standing there, covered in magical toxic waste and nursing a radioactive bite.

Wait—what? What was I doing standing here? I needed help, fast!

I ran out the door.

The ten-minute walk was a four-minute run in my panicked state. I was panting and nursing a stitch in my side when I arrived. A huge crowd of people waited at the Gap. What happened? Had it closed? Was I going to be stuck here with no modern medical help?

I started to shove my way through the crowds in a way that would have shamed my university mates, but all I could think about was how little time I probably had. My hand throbbed with my every step, and I imagined toxic witches' brew and radioactive saliva coursing through my body with each beat of my heart. I was having a hard time catching my breath. Was that panic or radiation poisoning? With my good hand, I pulled at my hair. It hurt. Thank heavens it wasn't falling out! But what if I got cancer? What if I developed an affinity for clown makeup?

Who would take care of my Mom?

I got to the front of a crowd to find a rickety barrier patrolled by the local constabulary. A bunch of mages stood in front of the Gap.

I blinked. Normally the Gap, for all its incredibleness, was boring to look at, kind of like a circle of burlap hanging in midair. Now, it seemed to shimmer with colors I could not quite identify. Was I hallucinating?

Was it broken?

"What's happening?" I cried.

A uniformed centaur approached me. "Please respect the barrier, sir. The mages need everyone to stay back, on account of the experiment, doncha know."

I didn't know. The centaur seemed to glow, too. What had happened to me? I squinted, as if I could squeeze the effect out my eyeballs. "Experiment?"

The centaur guarding the rickety barrier shrugged shoulders and withers, making his blanket shiver. It bore the Duke's color and symbol; the severed boar's head seemed to laugh at my plight. "Well, people have complained, you see, about how it's always sunny on one side and rainy on the other, and there ain't much protecting we can do, considering the Gap magics won't let us enclose it with walls or magic. They just twist or dissolve any construction within about 20 feet. Quite a thing to see, truth be told. So someone got the bright idea of creating a calm common area..."

"But I have to cross, now!"

He didn't pay any attention to my panic as he nattered on. "You got your mages and your scientists and they're all mucking about with the weather—"

"This is urgent! I have to get to the doctor. I've been bitten! Look!"

I held my injured hand for him to see. He took a step forward and leaned over it, lips pursed. He nodded knowingly. "Got on the wrong side of one of those method actors, didn't ya?"

"Please! I have to cross—immediately! I'm radioactive! I could be dying," Around me, Mundanes shuffled back while Faerie stepped forward to take their places in what counted for lines around here.

He gave me a patronizing smile. "Yer awful active for a dying man, doncha know? Calm down. It ain't all that bad. I'd be more worried 'bout getting a bath. Whatever you fell in smells nastier than a moor when its nymph dies."

"'Not that bad'?" I forced myself to take a breath. He was a Faerie, right? A Magical. What would he know? Behind him, a few feet away from the Gap, a scientist paused whatever he'd been doing on his equipment to go talk to a man in long robes.

I took a breath and tried again. "Maybe you don't understand. Radioactivity is very dangerous to my species. I. Could. Die." I clenched my teeth to fight back the panic.

"I'm sorry, but my hocks are tied. I can escort ya to the front of the line. When they're done, you can be first out of the gate, like they say in your races. Like that? Learned it in the *Faerie Book of Mundane Slang*."

"Very droll," I said. I grabbed at my wrist like a tourniquet. It worked for rattlesnakes, right? Sort of. I could not believe this day! Had Snapdragon really been joking about clown makeup?

I did a mental check: How did I feel about clown makeup? 'Bout same as usual. Ambivalent. That was something—right?

"How much longer?" I asked.

He glanced back. "Not rightly sure they started. Once they do, could be about half an hour."

"Half an hour?" I shrieked. I could not stand there, coated in magically created toxic waste, nursing a bite from a radioactive pixie, while some eggheads dithered with the Gap. I needed serious medical attention.

"What's that?" I shouted and pointed. A peal of thunder obligingly roared at just that moment. When everyone turned to look, I hurdled the barrier and dashed into the Gap. People called for me to stop, but I was too fast for anyone to catch me.

I felt the familiar pull, then a very unfamiliar and very painful jolt as the Gap lit up with brilliant streaks of light.

My eyes dazzled with lights and colors I'd never noticed before, my ears were overwhelmed with sounds, every cell in my body surged. Time, or my sense of it, warped weirdly. Was I moving? Had the world slowed?

Dimly, I heard the centaur say, "Well, lookkit that. They got it all thunder and lightning on this side, too."

My whole body felt like it was sparking. I was still in the Gap. Why was I still in the Gap? I willed myself to run faster, not sure if I was moving.

It seemed only breaths later that I was on my own porch step, the soles of my shoes smoking. I was home...

...forty miles from the Gap. What?

"Mom!"

The door flew open and my mom stared at me, aghast. "Ronnie! What happened?"

Belatedly, I realized I was covered in hazardous chemicals.

"Don't touch me. I'm toxic," I said, and then the world went dark.

Chapter Four:
Gapman's First Rescue

Ron

I woke up to F.A.E. singing, "Heroes Are Made." Normally, I love the song, but today, I just wanted to sleep in. The last thing I wanted to hear was elvish voices harmonizing with cowbells. I slammed my palm against the snooze button.

The clock shattered under my hand. What the...?

I leaned on one elbow and regarded the smashed plastic and circuitry. Despite the damage, F.A.E. continued to sing about the high calling of heroism, their voices at half-volume and tinny. I reached around the nightstand and yanked the cord out of the wall, oddly relieved I didn't take the wall with it. Then I flopped back onto the soft pillows and tried to remember what had happened yesterday.

Breakfast...Mom made waffles... That whole thing at the comic book store... I got to the theater. I interviewed that elf, Hawgindespotlite—

A vision flashed in my mind. Hawgin screaming, covered in toxic waste and trying to pull a radioactive pixie out of his hair. A pixie I'd flung on him after he'd bitten me—

Wait! Radioactive?

I got bitten by a radioactive pixie—after I fell into the vat of toxic waste!

I sat up fast and looked at my bitten hand. At least, I thought it was my bitten hand. The skin was smooth and unbroken. I checked my other hand, just in case, and found it similarly fine. I pulled up my sleeves, then my shirt. Was I covered in boils? Was my skin unnaturally pale? But no, I looked fine.

Had it been a dream? I looked again from my shattered alarm clock, which was now talking about the failed weather experiment at the Gap. I looked at my unscathed palm. That wasn't right, either. What was going on?

Breakfast. Maybe after breakfast and some coffee, this would make sense. Mom's an EMT; she'd know if I had a concussion or was hallucinating or...what?

Maybe I just had a vivid dream.

By the time I got dressed, I'd about talked myself into the dream idea. I felt way too good to have been bitten by something radioactive or to have plummeted into a vat of goo—magical or otherwise—or... Had I been hit by lightning? I remembered lightning, I thought...

I laughed. A dream, brought by the news about the Gap and reading too many superhero origin stories. Can one overwork reading comic books? Maybe it was time I read some nonfiction. Actor biographies. That would cleanse my mental palette.

My stomach growled.

"Hey, Mom!" I hollered as I hurried down the hall. I resisted the urge to run. It was one of Mom's house rules. I did, however, lean over the railing to see if she was in the living room. "How about some crepes? I'm—Mom!"

Mom was changing the lightbulbs in our chandelier. At five-foot-nothing, she was too short even with the 12-foot ladder, and she balanced on the last step as she stretched to get the bulb in its place.

"Mom!" I scolded. "I told you I'd do that this weekend. Get down before you hurt yourself."

"I'm not an invalid," she protested as she managed to get the bulb into the socket. The ladder wobbled as she screwed it in. "You, on the other hand, were struck by lightning—"

Her protest ended in a squeal as the ladder fell out from under her.

I didn't even think. I jumped from the top of the steps to catch her.

And I did! One arm under her shoulders, the other under her knees—Superman couldn't have done it better. Part of me was geeking out, but mostly, I was mad and worried. "Mom, you could have gotten hurt. I thought we agreed never to use that ladder alone."

She stared at me like I was some kind of alien. "How did..? How are you...?"

"What?" I looked down and realized my feet were not on the ground. We were hovering three feet from the floor!

No sooner did I realize this than we dropped. I hit the floor hard, Mom landing on me. At least she only weighed 115 pounds.

She rolled off me and sat beside me. "How did you do that?"

"Yeah, Mom, I'm fine." I sat up, rubbing my back, but stopped when I realized I'd spoken the truth. I was fine. I checked the elbow I'd landed on. Not a bruise. Not even a red spot. "Am I still dreaming?"

Mom set her hand on my cheek. "Honey, I'm sorry. You were so out of it yesterday, babbling about toxic waste and radioactive pixies and clown makeup. I thought you were delirious, but it's true. My baby has superpowers!"

"What?" I laughed. It sounded nervous and slightly hysterical to my ears. "That's ridiculous! It's impossible."

"Says the guy who lives in the town with an inter-dimensional portal and a resident dragon," she responded. She stood up and went to retrieve the fallen ladder.

Oh, no! She was not tempting fate a second time. I sprang to my feet, grabbed the ladder, and finished screwing in the lightbulb myself. Then I put the ladder away. I returned to find her gaping at the light.

"What?" I asked, annoyed. "I told you I'd replace it, and it was half-done already."

"That took... That was like ten seconds!"

I took in her shock and felt my own mouth fall open. "You mean, literally?" It hadn't seemed especially fast to me, but my mind had been on keeping her from climbing the ladder and on... Hm. That was my only thought. I hadn't had time to think about anything more.

"I could barely track you. You were a blur."

"Like the Flash? I have superspeed?" I wanted to squeal. I had superspeed!

"But why did you use the ladder? You can fly."

I paused. "Can I though? Maybe I can only hover?"

She frowned in thought. "Well, we need to find out! And I know just how to do it!"

I heaved a sigh as I looked at the dust-ridden top shelf of our living room bookcases. My first day of superpowers and Mom wants to test it with chores. Figured. Not that superspeed wasn't fun, but after changing five fire alarm batteries and polishing six bookshelves, it got old just as fast.

"You know, Mom, there has to be a better way to test my abilities," I called as I stuck the last dusted book in place. I reached into the handyman belt and pulled the dusting rag and polish from the pocket.

"But as practical?" Mom called from near the kitchen. "It's only been ten minutes, and look on the bright side. Those shelves were way overdue for a dusting. Besides, you were the one who wanted fourteen-foot bookshelves."

That was true. My nose itched. Did Superman's nose ever itch? What happened when Superman sneezed? The comics and shows were contradictory. I rubbed my nose; if I felt one coming on, I'd zip outside, just in case.

"Fine," I agreed, "but when I'm done, I gotta get the articles done for the *Gazette* and *Fangolia*. Since I didn't get to see the dress rehearsal, all I have is an awful interview with Hawgin..."

I stopped. Hawgin! Was he okay? Would the show go on? "Actually, I may have to go back to the theater and see if everyone's alright."

"Fine, fine. Honey, can you stay still just a moment?"

"Like hover?" Had I ruined the show? Just my luck. I sighed, gently, but it still disturbed the remaining dust on the shelves.

"Yes. Hover. Exactly."

The bland tone made my hackles rise. She was up to something; she always used that voice when she was up to something. Of course, I was too distracted by trying not to sneeze that I didn't bother to look. I just wanted to get the stupid shelves done and get some breakfast. I wondered if this had affected my metabolism, too. "Fine. I'm hovering. When are you going to—"

Something small and hard stuck me from behind. The impact and the surprise smashed me into the bookcase. I lost my concentration and fell to the floor in a shower of freshly dusted books.

"Mom!" What did she do?

"Ronnie! Are you alright?" She rushed to my side and started pulling books off. Then, she yanked at my shirt.

I pushed her away, annoyed, and sat up. "What did you do?"

"Well, I shot you, of course. Did it hurt?"

"Of course it— You shot me?"

"Yes, but just with a BB gun. Did it hurt? I don't see any blood. I thought I hit your back—did I hit you lower?" She reached for the back of my pants.

"Mom! You got my shoulder, all right?" I scooted away, then pulled off my shirt. I craned my neck, trying to see the damage. Apparently, I didn't have the super-flexibility of Lady Contortionist.

Mom sighed with relief. She had her EMT kit open and ready. "Good. I thought I'd lost my touch."

"You shot me, Mom! Did you forget all those gun safety classes we took? You're the one who told me my BB gun could break bones and take eyes out."

"It was a calculated risk! I didn't want you to find out you weren't bulletproof when you were in some dark alley facing a thug with a real gun."

"Why would I...?"

The look on her face silenced me. I had superpowers. *Of course*, I'd want to go protect people, which might mean confronting armed thugs in dark alleys.

"Point taken," I muttered.

She pressed a tender spot I couldn't see, and I yelped.

"Don't be such a baby. You said you smashed your alarm clock and didn't get a scratch; I figured it was a safe bet. Besides, you know I'm a good shot. Lenny and I used to go shooting twice a month. Still, I'm glad I didn't use the nine-mil. The wound's a little red, so you're obviously not bulletproof. That's a pity. Well, put those books back dear, while I find the ax."

"Ax?" I jumped up with superspeed and put my back against the bookcase. "Ax?"

She didn't even look up from closing her kit. "Yes, you've been promising for weeks to take care of that dead tree by the shed. You can do it while I make us breakfast. It shouldn't take any time at all, and since we don't know how long your powers will last, I think we should take advantage of them while we can."

I opened my mouth, closed it, opened it again, and realized I didn't have a single thing to say that didn't make me sound like a surly teenager. I had been putting off the tree, and, if I had to find out I wasn't bulletproof, better by my marksman mother with a BB gun than some mugger with a semi-automatic pistol. I sighed, pulled on my shirt, and started gathering up books. My shoulder had already stopped stinging.

"I want crepes when I'm done," I groused.

She paused at the door. "Absolutely, sweetheart!"

"And no more guns!"

"Nope. No more guns."

True to her word, she had the gun stowed and the crepes ready by the time I'd finished the shelves and the tree—which was pretty good, considering I decided to race myself on chopping the tree down and making a neat stack of firewood to cure for the winter.

Our house stood nestled in 40 acres of mountain land, with a narrow road we paved ourselves connecting us to civilization. I especially enjoyed the privacy today, as I could just fly into the kitchen. "Mom, I'm ready for crepes!"

Mom was hanging up the phone as I came to an awkward stop, jamming my stomach against the chair. Guess I needed some practice. She didn't comment; in fact, she hadn't taken her eyes off the bejeweled case of her phone. "Mom?"

She grinned at me, but her eyes had darkened with worry. "Eat fast, honey, and then find something...nondescript. You have your first real superhero mission."

I thought about protesting, but dread and excitement warred in me, and I ended up not saying anything.

"You remember Duncan?"

"The redcap kid you rescued?" Duncan had been an orphaned redcap from Faerie. Redcaps in our fairy tales were murderous goblins who needed to keep their caps bathed in fresh blood. In fact, Faerie redcaps were regular Faerie folk of different species who contracted a kind of scalp fungus that fed on blood. It did compel them to violence, but Mundane antifungals cured them. A group of them had come to Los Lagos for treatment the year I graduated from high school. Duncan, however, had mental disabilities. Mom had met him when he'd gotten hurt walking into traffic on a dare. Mom had actually thought about adopting Duncan herself before Rosalie and Jesus Martinez took him in.

"He's gone missing. Rosalie said Jose was supposed to have been watching him, but she can't find him either, and they live so close to that awful Real Humans subdivision."

Mom spat out the words. I didn't blame her. Just as FlintCorp was building low-income housing in Territory, one of the poorer sides of town where a lot of Faerie humans and Magicals lived, another entrepreneurial group, Homes for the Deserving, started one of its own on the east side. Unfortunately, it wasn't until several dozen of the low-income condos and homes had been sold, had it come to light that the company only considered Mundanes and a few select Faerie humans who adhered to their bigoted policies as "worthy" of a home in their subdivision.

Kitty McGrue had done a series on it for the *Los Lagos Gazette*. It was one of her better exposés, but it came too late. The government wasn't going to kick anyone out of their home, and even though they tried to get more Faerie and Magicals to move in, the builders had infused the insulation with iron filings. That made them unsuitable for Magicals or anyone wanting to host Magicals in their home. Besides, no one wanted to deal with the hostility when there were better choices just down the road.

It's too bad, really. Most of those people were probably just scared. If they'd get to know their neighbors, they'd see we're all just people.

Mom set a plate full of crepes in front of me, and I dug in. Still, I was wondering if this was a job for a superhero. "Why don't we just get in the car and search the neighborhood? I mean, Duncan looks human enough—he is human. And I'm not sure picking him up and flying him home is such a good idea. What if someone sees me?"

Everybody knew what happened to superheroes who revealed their identities—hounded by the press, loved ones constantly in danger, never a moment to themselves. Sure, Iron Man loved it, but he was always a glory hound—besides, he was a comic book character.

There was a reason I didn't follow my original dream of becoming an actor. Well, I wasn't all that good, either, but even if I had been, I don't think I could have taken being in the public eye all the time.

She opened the coat closet and dug around. "I think we should do both. I'll drive around looking in case he's on the streets, and you skulk the backstreets and alleys at superspeed in case some of those awful boys from the school have found him. I'll find you a ski mask."

I didn't like her worried tone. I'd been bullied for several years as a kid. I knew what that was like—and things were even tougher now, with the growing animosity between Faerie and Mundanes. I ate at superspeed, took the mask, and found something to work as a cape—I wanted a change in my silhouette and, after all, I was a superhero. The weather report predicted afternoon rains, so I chose a tarp. An umbrella only worked for Mary Poppins, and a soggy sheet would just be embarrassing. The tarp was bright green, but waterproof.

I was out the door and flying to the east side of Los Lagos before Mom had pulled out of the garage.

Despite the urgency, the ski mask, and the tarp, a laugh escaped my throat. I was flying!

My elation was short-lived.

In typical Colorado fashion, it had been cool but sunny at our house, but started pouring cats and dogs about halfway into town. I'd anticipated that. What I hadn't anticipated was how much the rain would weigh the tarp down, not to mention the knit ski mask.

Instead of a nice, heroic profile sweeping across the sky, I got—well, I don't know what I got, or at least I wouldn't until I saw the picture Mom took while driving.

My ski mask clung to my face in wet folds. The fabric stretched and kept drooping over my lip, but if I pushed it up, I invariably got water up my nose. Finally, I landed and huddled in a less wet corner behind some construction dumpsters and piles of tarp-covered lumber, with my cape over my head to protect my identity and myself from the elements. Since it, too, was a tarp, I fit right in.

I needed a minute to wring out my mask and figure out what I was going to do about the shouts my superhearing had picked up inside one of the buildings.

The townhouses in front of me were still under construction, although most of the exterior had been finished. Even so, construction had stopped as the Homes for the Deserving dealt with lawsuits and accusations of discrimination. The area was abandoned and the rain kept people indoors, so I'd made it there without getting spotted, even after I caught my foot on a bobcat during landing. Hope I didn't leave a dent in it. Obviously, I was going to have to work on this flying thing. Still, no one noticed—small consolation, considering I was drenched and feeling about as un-heroic as a superhero could get...except maybe for Caliber in Issue 29, when he was half-digested by Cel-lulose—

A change in the rain pattern distracted me, and I glanced up—and hurriedly ducked my face and strug-gled to get my damp mask back on. What was that dragon, Vern, doing here—and why did he glow?

My heart pounded as I tried to review my options in a properly heroic manner. Maybe I should go up to him, announce myself—

—as what? Kitty had often mentioned his penchant for giving people insulting nicknames. I'd probably be Soggy Ski Mask Man.

Maybe I could take the mask off, be myself, and tell him about Duncan?

I peeked past the trash can I was huddling behind. He'd landed near the unit where I thought I'd heard the screams. I'd been ready to check it out once I'd taken care of my mask. So maybe he'd heard some-thing, too? Was he on a case? Oh, man—Kitty had plenty to say about how he reacts to someone interfer-ing with his cases. Maybe I should sit this one out?

Sister Grace's car drove up the road, and Vern stuck his head in a window to talk with her. Definitely on a case, then. I should go offer my help, but seriously—Ron Engleson, Entertainment Reporter? In a green tarp and a soggy outfit? They'd probably laugh. If only I'd had time for a more awesome mask!

Vern looked my way, and I huddled under my tarp and relied on my superhearing as they opened a door and quietly entered the building.

As soon as the door opened, I could hear grunts of someone being gut-punched. I knew that sound. I'd made that sound before. I felt a stab of guilt. Some superhero I was.

Fine. Soggy Ski Mask Man, it was. I stood and regarded the building. If I followed Vern and Grace, there'd be explaining to do and I'd probably ruin their element of surprise. There was a second floor. Maybe I could cover them from there? If only I could see through the walls and figure out where they were heading—

Suddenly, I was seeing the interior of the building!

I couldn't believe it. I was looking right through the walls. I could see Duncan, sitting in a chair, a bag over his head, but essentially unharmed. He even seemed to be giggling for some reason. Maybe he thought it was a game? In the next room, a man was hung by his wrists while two others slammed their fists into him again and again. I wanted to rush in, but I'd read enough comics to know the smart hero gets the lay of the land first. What was it Caliber said? "Thirty seconds of recon can save thirty days in the hospital."

Not one of his most eloquent lines, but good advice. I continued my scan.

Farther away, I saw Vern sniffing at a support strut, and Sister Grace with her hands folded. My superhearing picked up her pretty little song; I didn't understand the words, but I felt safer, stronger.

My phone vibrated in my pocket.

I pressed the button and spoke just loud enough to be heard over the rain. "Mom! I have X-ray vision. How cool is that?"

"Every mother's nightmare! What's going on? Are you helping?"

Vern and Sister Grace were skulking into the next room. I thought I saw motion on the second level and rose to get a better look.

"Mom, Vern and Sister Grace are here. I'm doing backup. I'll call you back."

"Backup? You have superpowers, and you are backing up the *nun*? Is that how I raised you?"

I saw a shadow move and squinted. Someone...with a gun.

"Crap!"

"What? What is it?"

"Ambush!" With superspeed, I hung up the phone and flew toward the man planning to shoot Vern or Sister Grace. I really was going to be backup!

I felt a resistance, then a crash of wood and brick. What the...?

Oh, right! X-ray vision! I literally didn't see the wall until I crashed through it. Instead of the awesome flying punch I'd planned, I tumbled and rolled into a ball of tarp and embarrassment.

At least the noise diverted the shooter's attention, and he missed his shot. I heard a yelp of surprise but not pain as the bullet struck the column inches from Vern's nose. I ignored all that, however, as I straightened to my fullest height, hovering over the second floor to appear taller, arms stretched, holding the cape and looking as fierce and avenging as I could. Okay, so it was a tarp, but the lighting was bad and I was shrouded in shadow. I'd look menacing. Please let me look menacing!

The shooter—just a kid, I could see now—gaped, but brought up the pistol—a 9-mil! Fear gave me an adrenaline surge, and before I knew it, I'd slapped the weapon out of his hands and followed up with a shove at superspeed.

I put too much strength into it.

Instead of just knocking him away, I sent him flying through the plastic curtains and into the next room, where he struck a wall and slid to the floor.

My stomach lurched. Did I kill him?

Below me, I heard a confusion of gunshots, roars, and people yelling. No one had noticed the kid. What should I do? Ah, man! Did Superman ever deal with this?

In a panic, I flew instead of ran to him. What if I killed him?

Don't be dead. Don't be dead, I begged in my mind. I checked for a pulse. I felt the beat strong against his neck. Thank heavens! I examined the kid's head. There was some blood—oh, man!—but not a lot, not for a head wound, I mean.

Concussed. He'd live. Already he was groaning.

My phone buzzed again. This time, Mom texted. *I've got Duncan. Get out fast. Meet you at home. <3*

Below me, there was a melee as Vern and Sister Grace took care of the rest of the bad guys. In the distance, I heard sirens. Let them take the credit. I did not want to go down in history as Soggy Ski Mask Tarpman. Maybe since my victim was concussed, he would only remember a shadowy vigilante. I gave my attacker/victim one last check and looked around for a quick and discreet exit.

On the way home, I thought about how hard I'd hit that kid. Did Superman ever feel remorse? Then it struck me—I could really ask that question now, in seriousness. I was a superhero.

I alternated between elation and guilt all the way home.

Chapter Five:
Gapman's Gap-gaffs Revealed

Vern

Detective Oren Vialpando pushed back from the table and slouched even more deeply in his chair as he announced that we'd go over it one more time. He chewed his gum with a half-open mouth and glared at us with amused contempt. He was such a good Bad Cop.

Normally, I'd play his game only to remind him that an immortal dragon can outlast a mortal police-man, but today, I had Grace to consider. One of the gang members had punched her in the throat to stop her spellcasting, and while her charms had protected her, I could see she was still in pain. I wanted to get her home to another healing spell and hot tea with lots of honey. For that matter, we both wanted to get baths; Homes for the Deserving built their houses on a framework of iron to discourage Magicals, and we were both itchy and uncomfortable from the exposure.

However, she caught my eye, shrugged, and raised her eyes upward. She was willing to give her pain to God, probably on behalf of the annoying police detective who was delaying her relief. That was my nun.

Still, I was not going to let her strain her voice talking. "About eight this morning, Puma came to us because his foster brother, Duncan, had gone missing."

"Why didn't his parents come to the police? Don't give me that '24-hours' crap. Duncan's a retard and a redcap. We'd have made an exception."

I shrugged. They probably would have. Redcaps were Faerie humans who were infected with a magical fungus that compelled their victims to wash their hair in blood, which fed the microscopic fungus that gave their scalp and hair a reddish hue—hence the name. Mundane medicines had cured them, but Duncan, being mentally challenged, had a hard time breaking the habit. "Maybe they don't trust you?"

That was as close to the truth as I was going to get. Puma had told us that Los Despredatores had sent Duncan on "an errand" in the RealHumans territory. Puma didn't specify what errand, but I'd guess it involved spray paint and profanity. They'd sent him at night and Puma had come to us even before his parents had discovered Duncan was missing and after the gang had tried to find him themselves. Obviously, they expected involving the police to bring them trouble.

We'd been making good progress reforming the gang until the RealHumans subdivision popped up and Los Despredatores decided it was their new mission to "defend" the honor of their Faerie brethren.

I continued, "We didn't ask; a kid was in trouble. I started a search pattern centered on Territory while Grace was on the ground looking for clues, and we came upon the building you found us in—"

"In the RealHumans section? Why would you even go there?"

"Because we're good at our job? We found signs of a struggle, assumed Duncan had been abducted, and made a logical decision on who might have taken him and where. I'm sure if it had been you, you'd still be in Territory shouting his name in the streets."

He asked the location of the abduction again and I told him again, grateful (again) that Duncan had not made it into the Homes for the Deserving subdivision but was still blocks away when his kidnappers snagged him. I was going to have to mention it to Puma, though; it sounded like someone knew what they were up to, which could mean a mole in Territory.

Oren took up the narrative. "All right, you tracked them to the house, saw he was in trouble, and went crashing through the wall?"

"I told you: we didn't crash through anything. We went in the back door."

"Which wasn't locked?"

I shrugged noncommittally. As if I was going to admit to picking a lock. That was as much a breaking and entering as actual breaking before entering. "We were saving a life. Would you rather I had busted a wall or knocked down the door? We were going for stealth, after all."

He smirked. "Yeah. How'd that work for you?"

"Is that why we're going through this again?" I asked. "So you can perfect your snark?"

"I want to know when you broke down that wall and hit that kid!"

"We didn't!"

"One of those minions you hired, then? They got a bazooka or something?"

I'd been working out with the National Guard. I knew what a bazooka would do. "You're an idiot, Oren."

"Then explain it to me."

"We can't—because the first we knew about the kid upstairs was when Tracy was calling for an ambulance. And, if you'll recall, Grace ran up the stairs to see what she could do to help."

"Right. With your oh-so-awesome dragon senses, you didn't hear the breaking cinderblock or the guy scream or..."

I sighed. "It was raining and the roof was just plywood, plus there was thunder. I was concentrating on what the RealHumans thugs were saying. I may have heard the crash upstairs—"

"May have?"

I'd explained this, too, but kept it simple. "Selective hearing, remember? I tuned out the rain and a crash like that might have registered as thunder. Just like I've tuned out that gum-smacking of yours. Regardless, I may have heard something, but I didn't think anything about it because people started shooting at us. I was drawing fire while Grace untied Duncan, and then someone was attacking her, and we were a little too busy at that moment saving ourselves to wonder if someone was fighting upstairs."

Just then, the door opened, and Police Chief Captain Michael Santry walked in. He had two Styrofoam cups, both steaming. He passed the one with tea to Sister Grace. I could smell the honey from where I sat.

"Thank you, Michael," Grace rasped, and took a grateful sip.

I tilted my head skeptically. "Yes, thank you, Good Cop. What took you so long?"

He pulled up a chair beside Oren and sat. "As a matter of fact, I've spent the past half hour trying to calm down the Homes for the Deserving authorities."

"HOAs are such a pain," I deadpanned, causing Grace to snicker just a little into her cup. See, that's how you snark. I hoped Oren was paying attention.

Santry met my gaze without humor. "They say you were seen blasting through their building."

"Really? And where were these witnesses when not one but two people were being dragged into a half-built building and being tortured?"

"Was Duncan tortured? His parents say he was fine, and a friend brought him home."

Grace answered, speaking quietly and with a conservation of words. "Duncan was tied up with a sack over his head. Mayhaps they planned on releasing him once their other victim was well-bloodied."

Santry took up her line of thought. "And then record him when he washed his hair in the guy's blood? Make it look like the redcaps were back to old tricks?"

"And since Duncan is a Despredatore, it'd look like the gang was in on it," I said. "They'd take out two birds with one stone."

Santry nodded. "Apologies, Sister Grace, I have to ask: Are you sure there's no way you could have done it? One of your defensive spells gone awry, maybe when you got throat-punched?"

Grace shook her head.

"And you're certain one of your minions or a Despredatores didn't follow you and decide to jump in?

I wanted to protest that I'd told Oren 'No' to that three times, but Grace stopped me with a glance. "We'll check, just in case. Maybe someone has the camera?"

I shrugged. I hadn't sensed anyone there, but with all the iron in the townhomes, my senses were not as good as they would be normally. "Our minions know not to run from the police, especially with evidence...but a Despredatores will probably want to brag. Even so, none of them can blast through a wall, especially on a second story."

"No Magicals on your team? Spellcasters?"

We shook our heads.

Santry waved an arm. "Fine. You're free to go."

"One thing—the guy they were beating up. You holding him?"

"He's in the hospital, and why would we hold a victim?"

So he hadn't been listening behind the one-way mirror. "When they were beating him up, they did a lot of talking. Apparently, he's been giving little kids puck."

Santry swore. People liked to fool themselves into thinking puck was harmless because it couldn't make you do something against your conscience, but Mundanes—most fallen species, for that matter—had more imagination than that. Used on little kids who might not know better...

I had to admit, when I heard that—and the guy's confession—I wanted to extract a little justice myself. "I think one of the guys beating him has a little sister who was a victim."

Santry blew out a breath between his lips. "I'll make sure the D.A. knows. Thanks. If you learn anything about our mysterious wall-breaker, let me know."

We stopped at the desk so Grace could pick up her wallet, keys, and various magic-infused medallions.

At least the rain had stopped. The sky had that heavy overcast look that said it was still debating whether or not it had finished. It was still too warm for snow, despite what last week's predictions had said.

"I am so hungry, I could eat everything in the fridge," I told Grace when we got into the car. Fighting off iron poisoning always builds my appetite. "After a long bath."

She nodded. "And under the cover of night return to a certain crime scene and nose around?"

"Don't know how good my nose will be, but that's the general idea."

Unfortunately, we returned to find the place had been swept clean—and I do mean clean—no iron dust in the air, bullet holes neatly repaired, blood and scorch marks scrubbed away... Even the wall had been repaired—and not just patched. You'd never know someone or something had busted through it. If we hadn't been in RealHumans territory, I'd have suspected brownies. I hoped Santry's team took a lot of pictures. Someone wanted to make sure the police—or I—did not find anything more about this little op.

That also meant all clues about our mysterious vigilante had been erased as well.

The next morning, Santry called. The concussed kid had woken up, but he kept insisting, "Batman hit me." Since I was the only Magical in town with anything close to bat wings, I was back on the suspect list.

When I found Wrecking Ball, I and he were going to have a little talk about him knocking out people and leaving Grace and me to take the heat.

Chapter Six:
Gapman Stops a Shooting

Ron

I woke up the next morning surprisingly less sore than I'd expected to be. I looked at my smooth knuckles, bemused. Not even callouses. Wow.

After my disturbing confrontation with the gunman, I'd decided I needed to practice controlling my strength, and Mom (of course) had suggested I do that by punching the dead trees on the property until I could do it without busting through the trunks...which, of course, led to a lot of felled trees that I could then practice control on by setting a number of ax swings to chop through...

On the bright side, we not only had enough wood to last us through the next couple of winters, but also to sell, and I felt more confident that I wouldn't be punching someone through a wall again. At least, not if I didn't panic.

Sigh. Being a superhero was not quite what I'd expected.

"Do they mention the mammoth appetites in your comics?" Mom complained as she made me yet another helping of scrambled eggs. "If this keeps up, we're going to need to get some more chickens and another deep freeze so we can stock up during hunting season."

"Maybe it'll calm down," I said. I hoped. I didn't mind burning the calories, but groceries were expensive, and we only had so much dead wood to sell. "When you go shopping, will you get a couple of boxes of Ding-Dongs?"

She tsked. "Just because you have the metabolism of a twelve-year-old does not mean you're going to eat like one."

"Like you ever let me eat a bunch of Ding-Dongs. I only got to do that at Owen's."

"Not true! Lenny used to bring them."

I grimaced. "Yeah, when he wanted me to go hide in my room."

"At least he bribed you."

I had to give him that. Some of her other boyfriends would just yell at me or squeeze my arm when Mom wasn't looking. At least those never lasted long.

"You still deserved better," I told her as I dug into my eggs.

"And you deserve better than junk food. So, what's on today's schedule? Can you still come with me to the book signing this afternoon, or are you going to have to go back to the Gapway Theater and redo interviews?"

I sighed. I was not looking forward to that, not after the chaos I'd fled. I reminded myself again that, pleasant results aside, I was the victim here. The scaffolding broke way too easily, and I could have been seriously injured.

Why had that scaffolding broken so easily? I'd been leaning on it only minutes before...

Mom tapped my hand. "Earth to Ronnie!"

"Sorry. Thinking about the theater."

"Well, and I was saying, don't they have a phone? Maybe you should call first. No point going all that way if they can give you a few quotes on the phone. You got enough photos, didn't you?"

My phone and tape recorder had miraculously survived being dipped in goo, and my camera had caught on the scaffolding when I'd fallen. Had Snapdragon given it to me before I fled? Events were still kind of blurry. But I did arrive home with it, so now, I went up to my room to retrieve both and check out the shots. They weren't great angles for the play, but a couple were salvageable, and most likely, we'd use headshots from the theater, anyway.

That left calling Dorsch and trying to schedule a redo.

Twenty minutes later, I came back downstairs, my ears still ringing. Superhearing was not fun when trying to have a conversation with an angry director with excellent voice projection.

"That bad?" Mom asked. "He's not forbidding you from the set? I mean, he should be bending over apologizing to you. You could have been seriously hurt if you hadn't gotten superpowers!"

"Actually," I stopped and heaved a sigh. I was feeling really awful about all of it. "The show is postponed. I guess that centaur I talked to listened to me after all, or else some Mundanes complained. The Duke's forcing him to clean up the act, literally. They have to remake the goo so it's not actually toxic in any way, and all the pixies are encased in lead boxes and sucking on pencils until the Geiger counter they borrowed says they're inert. And Hawgin..."

I closed my eyes and shook my head, remembering what Dorsch said:

"He's gone—ran right out of the theater, Goldleaf still attached to his head. That pixie was my best extra, too! Hawgin was moving jerky and talking weird. I caught your name a time or two before the doors shut behind him. Not seen glint nor shine of him since!"

Then his voice lowered to a normal volume. "You might want to watch yerself. Elves got long memories." Somehow, the quieter tone made me shiver.

"That was three articles!" Mom exclaimed. "What are you going to do?"

I shrugged. "I'll email my editors and tell them what happened. The show's delayed, not canceled. I can write the reviews when it opens. In the meantime, I'll see what else can fill in. *Total Drama* wants me to write a story about puck, using my experience stopping Pat at the fountain for the angle. So that's one. Maybe I can get an interview with Alistair Kane... Ah, no. Kitty called dibs."

"'Dibs'? What are you two? Eight years old?"

"Feels like it sometimes." Except for the way Kitty turned my insides into jelly when she smirked. That was more like an awkward fifteen, but like when I was fifteen, I was not letting Mom in on my secret crushes.

I went to the cabinet, pulled out a can of tuna and bag of pita chips, and took them to the table. Was this my life now, too—to always be hungry?

I continued, "But Alistair's book, like *Full Exposure* before it, is especially polarizing, and with the RealHumans movement, Kitty gets to interview him on the anti-Faerie angle. I can try to get an interview for a different magazine, but his agent said he only had time for one this trip, and the *Gazette* got it. Meanwhile, I get to review the book, and regardless of whether I give it good or bad marks, someone's going to complain."

"Well, then you have to come. You can ask him for a few minutes of his time while he signs my book. I'm so excited for this one," Mom said as she buttered some toast. "He writes a great thriller, lots of twists, and his steamy scenes? Mmmm-mmm."

I choked on my tuna. "Mom!"

"I gotta have some excitement. Do you know how long it's been since I've had a date?"

I stuck my fingers in my ears and sang, "Lalalalala..."

She smacked me with her napkin, laughing. "Fine! But what about you? I expect grandkids, you know, and with your superpowers, you could easily build me that little mother-in-law's house we always talked about."

"With my superpowers, how am I going to have a relationship? Never mind. First, I have to figure out how I should use them—aside from chores—and I have to keep my identity secret... In fact, I should give some thought to my supersuit."

"I was thinking about it last night. What if you got one of those scuba suits that's shark-proof? They're like a thousand dollars, but we could splurge."

"I'm already bulletproof."

"*Mostly* bulletproof. We still don't know how you'd fare against something with real power. No sense not taking every precaution."

I thought about it. "It'd seem suspicious if someone ordered a shark-proof scuba suit in the middle of the mountains. If someone recorded me and it went viral, people might put two and two together. I'd have to gradually get the cash, then fly to the coast and buy it. Oh! Do my powers have a distance limit, like Magicals do?"

Most Magicals could not travel too far from the Gap without becoming ill from the lack of ambient magic in the area. Something else we'd have to test out. But another day. I finished my snack then went to my computer to send out emails and finish up some assignments while Mom did dishes. One bennie I didn't expect, though, was how my powers affected my typing skills. I typed two articles in less than an hour and with greater accuracy than usual. Please, if I lose my superpowers, let me at least keep that!

Mom came to my room, and I switched gears as we figured out my superhero look. She loved to sew and had lots of material that was great for costumes—a holdover from her dancing days, so we only had a few things we needed to buy. We ordered individual pieces from different websites and used both her and my credit cards to confuse the trail. At least Halloween was coming soon.

By then, it was time to get in the car and head over to Alistair's book signing.

For all that we're the only border town between two universes, Los Lagos is still a backwater, situated deep in the Rockies hours away from the nearest airport. We didn't get many famous authors coming for book signings. And Kane's books were about a conspiracy by the Faerie to take over the Mundane. So I guess it made sense that there'd be a crowd.

I did not expect it to rival ComiCon in size—or for it to be such a circus.

The bookstore had moved Kane's table outside, and the line ran down the middle of the street. Kane fans from teens to geriatrics jostled impatiently as they waited to get their signed copy of *Rome vs. Washington: Crusade*, the first in a planned trilogy. Vendors paced the line, selling scalped copies of the book and posters and T-shirts with the cover or Kane's smiling face, badly copied from the book jacket. Even so, people bought them, especially girls. The man looked like he could model for his own covers.

RealHumans in jeans and royal blue T-shirts and their supporters dominated one side of the street. They stood with arms crossed and glared past the line across the street, where a menagerie of Faerie creatures chanted protests and slogans. That side of the street seemed to glow in pockets, and I realized it was only around the Magicals.

Great Scott! Was I seeing magic?

"Hey, buddy! Move up!"

I jumped a little as the man's snarl startled me. Great—another new revelation. Crowds now made me nervous.

It's just the sensations, I told myself. So many people. So much noise. The smells! We paused by a centaur officer who stood guard over a knot of Catholics quietly praying the rosary, and I was assaulted by a clean horse-not-horse scent. Seeing magic.

And...something else. Something that was making the hair on the back of my neck stand up. The kind of feeling I'd get in middle school just before a bully would step out from some shadow. Was it paranoia or a sixth sense?

"Dude!" the guy behind me snapped again.

"Sorry!" I took the step-and-a-half that brought me next to my mother, who was craning her neck around a gaggle of teen girls to get a better look at the book-signing table. She didn't seem concerned. Was it my imagination?

Satisfied that I was paying better attention to the line, the man behind me had turned back to his friend: "Look, it's obvious that the centaur's relationship with Sister Cecilia is simply a Freudian metaphor—"

Down the line, I heard a familiar voice: "Get your Alistair Kane items here! T-shirts! *Full Exposure* movie posters! The *RVW Crusade* Pope-on-a-rope!"

He stopped to listen to a customer, then whispered to the teen pulling the cart, "A T-shirt special."

Lenny, Mom's on-again-off-again beau. Currently "off-again," which is how I liked it. Great. Just what we needed. Still, that wasn't what was bugging me. I felt like we were being watched... Not Lenny; he hadn't noticed Mom yet. So who, and where?

"Ronnie, what are you looking at?" Mom asked.

"Nothing," I lied. How could I explain among such a crowd? Plus, I didn't want her to notice Lenny. Maybe he'd stay at the back half of the line? "Can you see Kane yet?"

"No. These Barbies are taking too much room."

The three teens in front of us made very un-Barbie-ish sounds at her before returning to their conversation about who was hotter in *Full Exposure*. They practically had to shout as our shuffling brought us beside a band of pixies fighting over a bullhorn, even as they held it above a woman who was jumping for it and demanding a turn. Mom's best friend and former rival, Matilda. Didn't Mom say she was dating a pixie? Or was it a centaur? I couldn't keep up on Aunt Matida's love life any better than Mom's somedays.

I hadn't realized how pixie curses grated on my ears.

At least Mom's attention was safely deflected away from her ex.

I turned my attention to the protestors on each side of the street, using X-ray vision to see past the first row of people for weapons. Yep. Both sides were armed. The RealHumans side seemed more organized about it; I didn't know if that made me feel better or worse. Still, no one was pointing anything at us...yet.

Or were they?

I leaned down to speak loudly into Mom's ear. "Mom, I just don't feel good about this. Let's go. I'll get you a signed book if I can swing an interview."

"What?" she shouted back.

She may as well have used a bullhorn. I yelped and jerked back. "Mom!"

"I'm sorry, dear! Is this too much for you? I forgot your sensitive hearing."

In fact, the noises were hammering into my brain: the high-pitched squealing of an irate pixie as Aunt Matilda successfully snatched the bullhorn, the computerized ka-ching of the bookstore cash register. The derisive snort of the girl in front of me at Mom's "sensitive hearing" comment...

Something else, under all that, though—something that didn't belong, and it raked on my nerves. I scanned the crowd again, seeking the sound.

Then the "Barbies" squealed, and Mom with them.

"We're almost there!" Mom grabbed my arms and turned me toward the entrance of the store, where we could see Alistair Kane leaning across the table to hug some 12-year-old kid. "Isn't he handsome? You know, I read on his fan site that he and his wife are getting back together, after all. What a pity!"

"I'm serious, Mom," I said, then hissed, "It's not safe."

"Nonsense! I'm perfectly safe with you here!"

Aunt Matilda used the bullhorn to beat off the last of the pixies and shouted into it. "For shame! How dare you insult our Faerie friends! Magicals are people, too!" She smacked a pixie, who had again tried to grab the horn, and repeated her chant. The pixies gave up and started chanting with her.

Mom stopped her goggling to shout back. "Shut up, Matilda! Just 'cause you don't read!"

Her comment drew laughs. Matilda threw her a rude gesture, but I knew it was just a game between them. They'd been best friends since they met as rivals on the amateur women's wrestling circuit when I was a baby.

I forced myself to ignore their banter, seeking the sound that I'd heard.

There was that sound again. Metal on metal—a slide then a click. Like someone putting something together. What, and where? I craned my neck to see over the line, realized my feet had left the ground, and settled back down with a jerk.

"Mo-om..."

"Hey, pretty lady!"

And there was Lenny, in his toupee'd glory, tight leather pants and a RVW Crusade—Fiction or Prediction? T-shirt. His cart had caught up to us. "I know you want what I got!"

Behind him the girls snorted and murmured, "Ew!"

Seriously, now? "Mom, no!"

She waved me away. "Well, Lenny. It's been awhile," she purred.

"Mom!" I grabbed her elbow. "Do we have to go through this again? Don't you remember how he made you cry for an entire weekend?" I didn't care if others heard me. She needed to hear me.

Matilda shrieked into the bullhorn and dropped it as the pixie blew dust into her eyes.

"Faerie and Mundanes Living in Harmony!" the pixie shouted into it.

It was like an ice pick through my eardrum. I winced.

Misunderstanding my pain, Mom patted my shoulder. "I'm an adult, dear. There's no harm in flirting."

She turned to her old beau. "So, whatcha gonna sell me?"

I hissed in frustration—and almost missed the heavier slide and crash of a rifle chamber opening.

Rifle chamber?

I searched the crowds again, ears straining to pick out the direction of the sound of a bullet sliding into the chamber...

"Ronnie, hold this while I pay the nice man." Mom shoved her hardback book at me. My hands instinctively closed on it. It was thick enough that if I dropped it, it could break a toe.

...The sound—the rifle—was across the street...

Matilda again grabbed the horn, snarling about the greedy pixie attention-mongers. People pointed and jeered. The police left their posts to break up the fight.

I fought to ignore the chaos and focus on what I'd heard.

Two low thumps—elbows settling?

"Hey!" the guy in line behind us snarled. "Move forward!"

Lenny snapped back. "Hold your horses! I'm making a sale here! So, baby, you know I think about you a lot..."

"Omigod!" The girl in front of him squealed. "He looked at me! I locked eyes with Alistair Kane!"

Alistair!

I followed the line of sight from Alistair's seat to the building across the street to where the police were struggling to separate the gaggle of small, winged creatures from Matilda's hair. A centaur had snagged the bullhorn and held it over his head like a trophy. Above it, on the fourth floor, I caught a dull circle of a muzzle—

—just as my ears picked up the muffled shot.

Without thinking, I raised my hand holding Alistair's book into the trajectory of the bullet.

The impact made me stagger into the girls in front of us.

"Hey! Wait your turn!" One looked back just enough to sneer.

I clutched the book to my chest. A whiff of friction-burned paper tickled my nose. My hand screamed with pain. Had anyone seen? "Sorry!"

She turned back to her friends. "Loser."

I turned away from her, trying not to cry out. Wow, that hurt! But I had to ignore that. What do I do about the gunman? He'd surely know he missed. Should I leap from the crowd? Run at superspeed and hope no one noticed?

Suddenly, there was a collective shout, and a shadow moved over us. Everyone looked up. Vern! And he was heading right to the window where the shot had come from! I was saved.

Mom was also looking up, one hand protecting her eyes from the glare. "Wonder what that's all about?"

"Psst, Mom," I hissed, and when she turned to look at me, I moved the book off my chest just enough to show her. The bullet had punched through the cover, dotting the I in Vatican, and embedded itself into my hand. By a miracle (or superpowers), it hadn't pierced the skin. She gaped at the hole, then met my eyes.

She mouthed, "Are you okay?"

I grimaced to let her know it hurt, but I'd live. I pressed the book back against my chest, trying to keep my hand as still as possible. Did superhealing ensure the bones knit correctly? This was my dominant hand. I needed this hand!

"You can't meet Alistair like that, not if you're going to get an interview. Here."

She wiped my face with the sleeve of her sweatshirt. I hadn't realized how much I was sweating...or the tears of pain that had leaked from my eyes. Embarrassing! Superheroes don't cry.

"You gotta quit babying the boy," Lenny said. "He's a grown man, you know."

Normally, I'd agree with him, but at the moment, I was glad for the help.

"It's hot out here," she protested. "I'm sweating, too."

"Oh, that's just me." He winked.

I tsked in annoyance, especially after Mom crooned, "Maybe. Why don't you give me a T-shirt? It was my birthday last week."

Lenny dug into his piles. "Oh, I remember. You're twenty-five, right?"

The girl in front of us snorted and muttered, "How many times, you think?" to her friend.

Mom heard her. Dang it. Why did Mom have to hear her?

"Fifteen times, if you must know, Barbie," she responded in her snottiest voice. "And you'll be lucky if at my age you look half this good."

She grabbed the edges of her shirt and pulled it off. From the sidewalk, a RealHuman whistled. Lenny leered. From where the police were dragging her away, Matilda called my mom an attention-craving skank.

"Mom!"

"I have a sports bra on. I'm more covered than Tube Top Barbie here. Hoping to give Kane an eyeful, sweetheart? You can't compete. Lenny: shirt." She snapped her fingers and he slapped a rolled-up T in her hands like a surgical nurse. She pulled on the T-shirt as if she'd done nothing wrong, like, you know, publicly mortifying her son.

At least she had distracted me from my hand enough to give it time to heal some. Now it just throbbed. While people stared at Mom, I used superspeed to tuck the book into my bag, along with the bullet that no longer embedded itself into my flesh.

Mom asked Lenny for a permanent marker. He started to hand one to her, then pulled it away playfully.

"I'll have to come by your house to retrieve it," he said.

I sighed. Here we go, again.

Then it was our turn with Alistair. Quickly, I introduced myself as a reporter and asked if he'd have time for an interview.

He read my card. "Ronnie Engleson? You wrote the review of *Full Exposure* for *Reed Reviews*? Yes, I'd love to talk, especially since you'll ask about my writing and not my politics, right? It might have to be over the phone, but I'll have time after the signing. I'll call you?"

I did not expect him to be so friendly. "That would be amazing! Thanks."

"Anything for a fan!" He half stood and reached across the table. I shook his hand, trying not to wince as he squeezed firmly, recracking still-knitting bones. I hoped my frozen smile looked natural.

"Speaking of anything for a fan," Mom interrupted, and leaning over the table in her new T-shirt, she held out the marker coquettishly.

Chapter Seven:
Gapman's Shooter Escapes

Vern

"Well, at least you didn't break the wall this time," Vialpando snarked. He leaned against the threshold of the empty office as if it weren't a crime scene because he didn't believe a crime had been committed.

"I didn't break that wall!" I snapped. Normally, I wouldn't reward him with my reaction, but I was annoyed and distracted. I knew I'd heard a gunshot, and I was sure it had come from this room. But there was nothing to be seen, just some plastic and cans of paint from the renovations. The cracked-open window could have been left that way for ventilation. Nothing unusual, except for a weird sense of...something...that was making my scales itch.

I didn't bother mentioning that to Vialpando; he'd just brush it off with more snark. "Someone shot something from here," I insisted.

With a superior smirk that said, "I'm humoring you," he sauntered to the window and looked down at the crowd. "They seem pretty calm for having been shot at," he observed.

"Maybe he missed? I didn't see where the bullet went. I was concentrating on the shooter."

"Whom you didn't see."

"The light glared off the windows. This guy chose his spot and time well."

"Right. And you just happened to be facing this building as the alleged shot went off?"

I sighed. "I was sitting on the building opposite this one keeping an eye on the crowd."

"The building on the RealHuman side of the street?" He crossed his arms skeptically.

I rolled my eyes at him like he was an idiot. "If I were on this side of the street, the RealHumans might have seen me, and that would just make trouble. On their side, someone would have to crane his neck to notice me. Besides, I wanted to keep an eye on Grace. She's on the Faerie side with the group praying the rosary."

My explanation seemed to appease him. "You know that implies a Faerie did this—if anything was done, which I still don't believe."

"Come on, Vialpando. When have I ever been wrong?"

Vialpando spread his hands as if to say, "What about today?"

Just then, his partner entered the room. "We searched the building. No sign of forced entry. Other than all those Faerie protestors, the only person around was a homeless guy in a red velvet leisure suit and a weird hat."

"Did you take him in for questioning?" Maybe I could match him to this weird smell/feeling that was getting on my nerves.

But he shrugged. "About the hat? What am I—the fashion police?"

The two laughed and high-fived. Useless. Why did Santry keep them on the force? Right—Vialpando was his buddy from L.A. Wish he'd get tired of snow and go back.

I wanted to tell them to look for clues, but I'd already swept the place and hadn't found so much as a hair. The strangeness I felt was strongest in a line between the door and the window, and even more so at the window, but it didn't feel like a magical weapon. Besides, I'd been working out with the National Guard. I knew the sound of a Mundane rifle.

For that matter, it had taken me less than a minute from the time I heard the shot to the time I'd made it to the window. Who could have grabbed their stuff and gotten out of the building that fast, especially from the fourth floor?

I looked out the window. The fight between Matilda and the pixies had been resolved and Pushpedal was sitting on Matilda's shoulder, nibbling on her ear. I did not get what he saw in her. A female Mundane was pulling her T-shirt away from her body to admire something on it; the author's stupid face, I'd guess. The man with her was face-palming while somehow managing to scan the crowd at the same time. I peered closer.

Oh. Ronnie Engleson of the *Gazette*. McGrue said he was the jumpy type.

Other than him, no one else seemed concerned about anything besides intimidating the other side of the street or getting Alistair's John Hancock.

Could I have imagined it?

"Something's not right," I said to myself, then glared at the Keystone Cops. "Aside from your humor, I mean."

Vialpando shrugged. "Well, if you figure out what it is, you know where we are."

The two left me to figure out the mystery by myself—which, truth to tell, made it easier, even if their disbelief annoyed me.

I shut my eyes and scanned my memory. Once upon a time, I had perfect memory—even better than eidetic memory humans have. One reason I hate emus: They're too close to velociraptors, and whenever I look at one, I can feel the nasty little velociraptor teeth scraping my scales. Shudders. St. George took away most of my memories during our epic battle—except the velociraptors; thanks for that, George—as well as my keen ability. I was gradually getting it back, but sometimes, it took effort.

I made that effort now. As they closed the door behind me, I gave a quick check to make sure things were quiet outside and that Grace and the prayer group were safe, then shut my eyes and thought back. I was on the roof of a building opposite and to the left of this one, scanning the crowd. The police were taking care of the misbehaving pixies and their human compatriot. Some of the RealHumans crowd were laughing at them. That hadn't concerned me, except that someone might use the distraction to cause real trouble...

I was looking farther down the street, focused on the sidewalks. The RealHumans had definitely planned their demonstration; I watched as a shift change of sorts happened, several humans stepping up to take the place of those in front. They then stood with crossed arms and menacing expressions while the relieved shift got water. One went to join her buddies in line...

There was a quiet *pew!* like a bullet from a silencer.

I turned fast, saw a bit of dark metal receding from the window...

I concentrated harder on the window, hoping I might remember seeing a shape from it, but no. The afternoon sun was too bright. Fewmets!

I crouched down to see through the crack in the window. What was the shooter after? I thought back to the bit of the gun I did see, tried to judge the angle as it was pulled back, and turned my head in that direction. They weren't after Faerie; that much was certain. It was closer to the bookstore. Alistair Kane, then? That meant Faerie or Faerie sympathizers, but why use a Mundane weapon? Maybe a RealHuman trying to frame the Faerie, like they were trying to do with Duncan? But then, why not use a spell?

Then again, this was the only empty building on the block. Maybe it was simply convenient.

I sighed. I was speculating in a vacuum.

I turned my attention to the wrongness I felt in the room. It was fading now, but if I directed my attention to the floor, I could still catch a trace. I should have done that first before calling the cops. That's what I get for trying to play nice.

Not that it mattered; once I left the room, the feeling dissipated. I checked the stairs and the elevators. Nothing. I thought I caught something by one of the rooms, but it was locked as were those around it. Had Vialpando's partner checked any rooms?

With a huff of frustration, I went outside, hoping to regain the trail. I looked in the window of the locked room where I thought I'd felt some of the oddness, but the office was empty save a roll of carpet waiting to be laid down. Not even dust on the bare floor to leave incriminating footprints. There was an open dumpster below, full of scraps and broken items, but a four-story drop? Even in the movies, there'd be a convenient awning to break the fall.

Still, I checked—and jerked back with a gasp of disgust. People had been throwing their personal trash in there. It smelled like rotting vegetation and maybe something dead. Maybe I should suggest Vialpando check it personally for bodies? Nah, it wasn't that kind of smell.

I felt a wrongness in the alley, too, like twisted magic. Not evil, necessarily. Just...wrong.

I looked up and down the alley, but the bum was gone. I took to the air, but I didn't see a red outfit or crazy hat anywhere. So much for the only possible witness.

Could it have been Wrecking Ball, out for a little revenge against the RealHumans for kidnapping a redcap kid? If he could break through walls, maybe he had other capabilities. But then, why use a gun now and not the other night?

My phone rang.

"The rally is done," Grace said. "Other than the pixie debacle, it was quiet enough down here. We thought we saw you flying overhead."

"Nothing happened around Alistair?"

"Just the usual jostling in line, and a woman decided to change shirts in front of everyone. Trixie Engleson—remember her?" I could hear the eyeroll in Grace's voice. "Why?"

"I'll explain when we get home. It's probably nothing."

I hung up, not believing my own words. I know what I'd seen and what I'd sensed. If only I had some evidence.

Ron

I set the book with the bullet inside it on the top shelf of our tall bookshelves, then flew out to the back porch where Mom had burgers grilling. I yanked off my shirt and settled into the hot tub with a sigh. I didn't care if I had superhealing; it felt so good as my muscles relaxed in the hot water. Mom had placed a plate with a couple of ice packs on the ledge, and I sandwiched my hand between them.

"Did the interview with Alistair go okay?"

I knew she was worried about my hand rather than the interview. "I recorded it, but I took a few notes. It's not bad. I'll be fine in a few hours, I'll bet."

"Does it still hurt?" she asked.

"A little, and the palm is still yellowy. Maybe a shark suit isn't such a bad idea. Or Kevlar. Think you could sew a Kevlar supersuit?"

She added cheese to the burgers as she thought. "I could try. I did make those Kevlar patches for my motorcycle gear when I was dating Snake. I still have the needles and some scraps. We should start with some other material first and make a pattern. Until then, be more careful!"

"Hey, I did what I could with what I had." I didn't bother bragging about what was, in hindsight, a pretty effective solution. The whole thing had happened so fast, it was an instinctive reaction. I was just lucky the shot was so close to me. "I put the book on the high shelf, by the way. I wish there was a way we could tell the police about it without divulging my superpowers. I did try to hint to Alistair that he might be in danger; he said he's got a security guard and is staying in tonight. Maybe I should keep an eye on him while he's in town, anyway."

"Well, take the night off. You deserve it." She set a plate with two burgers beside me along with a margarita, then settled into the tub with her own. She held her drink high. "To another successful mission!"

We toasted, and I sat on the edge of the tub to down my burgers.

"You know," she said after a sip, "I'm not sure the person wanted to hit Alistair. I mean, that was pretty bad aim. Maybe they were shooting at the crowd, or at the RealHumans?"

"Maybe they jerked at the last minute?" I suggested. "Vern did head straight for them right after.

What if they saw him and choked? I didn't see anything on the news, either. Are they keeping it quiet, or did he get away? I dunno. Maybe I should go to the police."

"And say what? 'Hi. So... I'm a Mundane, but I have superpowers now?...and it's just, I stopped this assassination attempt.'" She did a perfect imitation of me when I felt unsure and awkward. Then she shook her head. "Trust me, I dated a detective on the force. Oren."

"What? When?"

"While you were in Leeds. What a character. It didn't last long; he's too California for me. Anyway, he told me about the police chief and how much he hates Magicals. You tell him you have magical superpowers, and Captain Santry will lose his mind. Besides, he's government. What if he has to report you? The next thing we know, you'll be carted off to Area Fifty-One."

"Mom." I rolled my eyes, but then again, could I take that chance?

"Look, you said Vern was on it. Everyone knows his motto is 'Wisdom of the Ages.' He'll figure it out."

"But I have the evidence...which I can't explain." With a groan, I slid back into the water, all the way to my chin.

"Oh, honey. Think about it: Vern was flying over us like half a minute after you caught that bullet. He must have gotten the shooter. They're just keeping it quiet to avoid a riot. I'll bet that's why Alistair's all snugged up for the night in his hotel room alone. Relax. You did good."

"I suppose." I sighed, releasing tension. "But if anything else happens..."

"Once you have your supersuit, you don't need to explain anything. Let's look in my closet and pick fabrics tonight. I'll start sewing. I haven't done a costume for you since Alice in Wonderland. You were the most adorable caterpillar."

"Please don't make my supersuit look like a caterpillar," I teased.

Chapter Eight:
Gapman Stops a Seduction

Ron

"Alright," Mom called from deep within the walk-in closet of her sewing room, "I think we have some good choices to start with. Find anything in the patterns?"

"Oh, yeah," I called as I pulled out another promising prospect. It was a Flash costume, but Mom had drawn modifications over the design in marker. Funny. I didn't remember her making that one for me. I knew she sometimes sewed for other people, though. She could have been a professional seamstress, but she used to say exotic dancing kept her in shape and paid better, and now she loves being a paramedic.

"Why do you have so many superhero costumes, anyway?" I asked. The pattern envelope felt thicker than the others. Curious, I opened it and saw photos inside. Cool. The first photo was a buff guy I didn't recognize posing in the classic one-knee-one-fist landing position. I started flipping through the others.

"Oh, when the Avengers were such a hot deal, Sidney at The 96 decided we should do a superhero theme. Don't worry. I won't make yours tear-away."

"Yaagh!" I dropped the photos as I came across one of him ripping off his briefs and quickly shoved them all back into the envelope.

"Oh!" Mom said from over my shoulder. "Good choice. That was one of my more successful projects. Well. Come here and look at what I have."

She'd laid out bolts of green, gold, and purple on her sewing table next to the scraps of Kevlar she'd found. I looked from them to her questioningly.

"Some of us were going to NOLA, but then the pandemic hit, and Christie got pregnant, and Darrel went into detox and moved back to Minnesota with his family. Aren't they pretty? And four-way Spandex!"

"I'm not going to be Mardis Gras Man," I told her.

"I didn't say you had to! What if you pick gold or green as the base? The purple is wrong for your skin tone. We can use the other for accent work and buy some neoprene for shoulder pads and your briefs."

"My briefs? I really don't want to wear my underwear on the outside." I still remember all the teasing I'd gotten when I went to school as Superman one Halloween.

"Well, you're wearing a cup, and I'm reinforcing it with Kevlar. I suppose I could make a thong..."

"Mom!"

"It's not hard. I did it for Darrel. I have a photo of him in one of these patterns. Of course, he wasn't wearing an athletic cup—"

"Mom! Please!"

"We can save that for last. Now, about the gloves. I figure you want to have the best use of your fingers. Do you want weightlifting gloves?"

I calmed. Gloves, I could discuss with my mom. "Oh, no. They need to be full. I don't want to leave fingerprints."

"That's right! So I'll probably have to make them fit snugly, then we'll use the Kevlar covered in our accent material to protect the palms and back of the hands. I should have enough. You always had delicate hands."

"These 'delicate hands' punched through trees," I reminded her with a frown.

"Oh, don't be sensitive! Surgeons have delicate hands. But that reminds me; in some ways, your skin will be tougher than your suit. Punch the trees bare-handed, okay? I probably should make you two suits. You'll need one while the other is in the wash. Let's look at the patterns you liked and see if there's enough material for them."

One thing about the classic superhero suit—it's really just a fancy leotard. We settled upon a design and decided what pieces would be green and which gold. Then Mom pulled out some paint chips from the paint store, and we chose a couple of colors that would make a good third. We'd use it for gloves, boots (really covers for my running shoes. I was not going to wreck my feet running in boots), and for the mask.

"A half mask," I said. "Enough to hide my identity and look mysterious."

"Can you use superspeed to grow a five o'clock shadow?"

I laughed. "You don't like me unshaven. You say I look scruffy."

"But with the mask?"

I thought about it. It would hide my identity...and I might actually look hot. Still. "It might be too much trouble, growing then shaving at superspeed multiple times a day. Hey! What if we sewed hair on the back of the mask?"

"Hair?"

"Yeah! I could have long locks that flow in the wind as I fly! Maybe blond waves... or jet black..."

"Your hair color is perfect."

"Sure. For a hamster." I snorted derisively.

"Will you ever get over that? Missus Kingston meant it as a compliment."

"How is 'hamster' a compliment?"

"They're so soft and cuddly."

"The perfect qualities in a superhero," I concluded, my voice dripping sarcasm. I really should get over it, but when your sixth-grade teacher calls you "Hamster," in that faux auntie tone, it sticks with you—especially when Bobby Chow ambushes you during lunch and shoves food in your mouth to see how much your cheeks will hold "in the name of research." Now, he runs a pet store. There's irony for you.

Mom threw back her hands in that "There's no arguing with you, so I won't try—but I win" way of hers. "I'm not sewing hair into your mask so you can pretend to be SuperFabio. What if someone grabs it and pulls off your mask? I will not be responsible for such an embarrassing wardrobe malfunction. Besides, once people know it's you, they'll figure out that I made your costume, and how will I live down an amateur mistake like that?"

"You're right," I said with a sigh. We got down to design, getting my measurements, and making a shopping list. Blue and green neoprene, heavy sewing needles...

"What size athletic cup do you wear?"

"Mom!"

"Well, I haven't bought you one since you went out for baseball in sixth grade. How should I know?"

I rubbed my brows. "I'll order it online, okay?"

"Well, get three, and go up a size in case...you know."

My mouth dropped open, but not even an exasperated "Mom!" came out of it.

"It'll make a better silhouette."

I buried my burning face in my hands. Only my mother would think of that.

She tsked. "Besides, it's practical. A good-looking boy like you and an actual superhero? There will be fangirls. Besides, what if you have to rescue one? She'll probably be clinging to your neck..."

I walked out as Mom described me carrying a beautiful damsel from a burning building. I heard her chuckle and mutter something about raising such a shy boy before she went back to the list.

"That reminds me. We should get some of that fireproofing spray and test it on the fabric."

I ascended the stairs to my studio office. It was really the attic room of our Tudor-style house, which meant the steep slants of the ceiling limited the usable area. That made it perfect for a desk, a comfortable chair, some low shelves, and the only distraction, the amazing view outside. I'd grown up in crappy apartments only to go to college in Leeds where I lived in a side room of my Aunt Lizzy's flat. For study breaks, I'd cruise the real estate listings and dream of having more than 150 square feet to call my own. So glad I had, because we got this place as soon as it went on the market.

I paused at the medieval-style door. It was the details like this that had sold me on the house. Well, and the fact that it was 3,000 square feet on 40 acres. We got it cheap because it was so far from town and needed a lot of work, plus the road was a mess in the winter. I was fine as long as I had Internet, but Mom often spent the night with a friend when snow was bad. We really needed to fix the road, but it was expensive...

Then again, how expensive would it be with a superhero doing the work?

I hurried to my desk, noting that I could repaint the burnt-orange walls pretty quickly, too, and got to work on my article. Once that was done, I researched how to pave a gravel road.

I was sketching out plans and thinking about what materials we had on the land that I could use when Mom called from downstairs. "Sweetie! I got a start, but I need a break. I'm heading into town for supplies. Text me if you need anything."

I texted her for a couple of gallons of paint, then went back to my research on Alistair. A message popped up on my computer from the associate editor at *Total Drama*:

Hey, Ronnie, I must turn you down on the Alistair article. We don't care how popular his books are. At Total Drama, we have a strict policy against anything promoting womanizing cismales. You should know that, but you can be so naïve sometimes. Just check out these links before you write anything for anyone else. I didn't pitch it to Transformerz but be careful next time!

We're planning a 5-year class reunion, BTW;
thought I'd better tell you early so you can save
for plane tickets.

I sent back a quick "Thanks" and that I'd let her
know about the reunion. (Could I fly that far? Like,
superhero fly?) Then I followed the links to articles
and chat rooms about Alistair's affairs and conquests.
He seemed to get a power trip off seducing beautiful
reporters.

Oh, no! Kitty!

I threw on the outfit I'd worn my first night of superheroing—including the tarp—and dashed out of
the house. She was probably meeting him in his hotel
suite right now!

I hurried to the Broadmoor-Los Lagos. I remembered my friends in England teasing me because the
Broadmoor was a famous asylum there. Here the Colorado, the Broadmoors were a high-end hotel chain.
The Los Lagos one was nestled in the mountains
about 10 minutes from town and 20 from my
house...if I were driving. Now, I understood what
Alistair meant when he told me he liked the hotel for

its "opulence and discretion." I'd thought he meant it was harder for fans to get to him. I should have called Kitty ahead of time and warned her—

Yeah, right. How would that have played out? "Seriously? You think I'm like some starry-eyed fangirl like you'd find at ComiCon? I can handle myself."

And then she'd roll her eyes at me, and any rapport I may have with her would be ruined. I needed another way to help her if she needed help.

"What kind of bird is that?" I heard a hiker ask from below me and quickly rose into the clouds.

Once at the Broadmoor, I saw Kitty's car in the lot, its passenger side crowding the dividing line. I found a hiding place in a tree and sat with my back against the trunk, my feet tucked tight around the branch and my green tarp around me as camouflage. Assured I wasn't drawing attention, I used X-ray vision to find Alistair's room. There! And just as his aide was letting Kitty in!

Dang, she looked good. Why did she have to look so good? I knew she was wearing her power suit, but those heels and the pencil skirt showed off her legs. She accepted a glass of wine—wine, really, Kitty?—and watched with amusement as the aide left the room.

A moment later, Alistair emerged from the bedroom, pulling at a cuff. *That dog! If I had heat-ray vision...*

Calm down, Ron. She's a hard-nosed reporter. She can take care of herself. She'd have done enough research to know he's married...

"Ah, Miss McGrue."

"Miz," she corrected. She had a thing about being called "Miss." *How did he not know?*

Or did he? Oh, this guy was good. Dang it!

"Of course, Miz McGrue. Alistair Kane. Call me, 'Alistair'." He took her outstretched hand and raised it to his lips, kissing her knuckles. "Enchanté."

Kitty withdrew her hand, but not quickly enough. "We'll see about that. I'm not some star-struck entertainment reporter...but you already know that."

My racing heart slowed. She's onto him, but what was that crack about entertainment reporters?

But then doubt set in. *Had she pulled away fast enough to discourage him? Did she want to be discouraged? She knew he was married, right? She wouldn't—you know—with a married man, right?*

She looked down at the file bearing her name on the side table, "carelessly" tossed so that some of her articles were peeking out. Not just the ones from the *Gazette*, either.

Alistair laughed. "Miz McGrue. Kitty? Kitty, I always do my research. Surely you are familiar with the writings of Sun Tzu."

Kitty raised an eyebrow. "Know thy enemy? So you consider me an adversary?"

"I do hope not, Miz McGrue, but there's no doubt that you are a dangerous woman."

Their gazes locked and held. After a long moment, Alistair looked away. He let her win! That cad!

I heard a scuffling, and then something crawled on my shoulder. A squirrel pulled at my mask, his little claws catching on the knit fabric. I tried to ignore it.

Meanwhile, Alistair had settled in the chair facing her and poured himself a glass of wine. "I've found that one must not simply understand the enemy. As a businessman, I need to understand our clients and my employees. As an author, I must know the audience I write for. And not just know them but know how to make them understand the respect I hold for them. This room is a good example."

"Yes. You've moved the furniture." She set her glass on the coffee table that now flanked their chairs instead of sitting between them.

"I don't believe in artificial barriers." He smiled an oily smile—and she grinned back.

Not good. Not good.

This time, she broke their gaze first, reaching into her purse to pull out a small recorder, which she set next to her glass. "Let's get down to business. Between *Full Exposure* and the *RVW Crusade*, you've insulted half of the Faerie species and the only religion in their world."

"A challenge from the start! I'd expect nothing less from a Pulitzer nominee."

No! Don't feed her ego!

The squirrel, intent on getting its foreclaws free, slipped on the tarp. It slid down my chest. My mask pulled over my eyes—something I felt rather than saw, since I was still in X-ray mode. It scrabbled wildly. I felt little pinprick scratches on my neck.

"Come on! Stop it!" Blindly, I reached for it, trying to move quickly but gently. The last thing I wanted was to squash the poor thing. It skittered, still attached to my mask, avoiding my grasp.

Meanwhile, Alistair was leaning forward, his hands out entreatingly, talking about how he never intended to offend anyone, that he was writing for the Mundane audience and didn't expect the Faerie reaction.

So much for understanding his readership. McGrue had that skeptical grin of hers, but she was leaning toward him.

My hand closed on something furry. Finally!

It bit me!

"Ow! Geez!" I pulled it off and dropped it onto a neighboring branch. I glanced away from the drama in the hotel room to check my hand. My attacker had gotten me in the skin between thumb and forefinger. It didn't break my skin—yay, superskin! No worries about rabies—but I could see the bruise forming. I just healed from the gunshot, dang it!

I heard Kitty ask something about if he really expected people to believe he was the good guy in all this. The warmth in her smug tone made the hair on my neck stand up.

Alistair had posed himself leaning on one arm of the chair, swirling his drink causally in its glass. It was the mirror image of Kitty's position.

Hey! That was on page 185 of Full Exposure—right before the love scene!

He spoke earnestly. "It was a failing on my part; I write for the Mundane audience, one that thrives on escapism and adventure. I truly did not anticipate the Faerie reaction. Not to belittle them, mind you, but they live among what we consider the fantastic daily, and it has shaped their attitudes and how they look at things. Simply put, they're not as sophisticated as we are."

Alistair sat back and raised his drink to Kitty before taking a sip.

Kitty sipped hers as well.

No, don't mimic his moves. He's drawing you in!

The squirrel chittered at me quizzically and I realized I'd spoken that aloud. "Never mind," I told it and turned back to the scene in the hotel room.

"And what about the RealHumans League? Your books are required reading for members. I'm surprised they don't quote you in their literature."

He blushed. "Fortunately, I can afford good lawyers. We stopped that bit of...unfortunateness...before it could start."

"'Unfortunateness?' The RHL wants to close the Gap and kill all the Magicals stranded on our side."

Alistair set his drink back on the table and rubbed his hands together. He didn't meet her eyes.

"Told you I wouldn't make it easy." She smirked.

Don't make it anything, Kitty!

The squirrel had jumped back onto my branch and was chattering at me angrily. I knew exactly how it felt. I ignored it, listening hard to Alistair's reply, and to Kitty's breathing. Was it getting heavier?

"Kitty, if you did, it wouldn't be nearly as satisfying." He scooted forward in his chair, his knees touching hers. "Let me explain this in terms of writing. In college, I took a single creative writing course—a lark and an easy A, I thought, but I learned some valuable things. One is that writing is not a solitary activity, but a relationship."

He placed his left elbow on his knee, his hand up, palm facing her.

"As a writer, I initiate the relationship. I set the pace, establish the tone. It's my duty to entice you, the reader, into engaging."

Wait a minute! He told me this same story. Were we back to the interview? But no—he reached out to take her hand—and she let him!

"As the reader, you have the power to accept or reject, to trifle with my offering, or to throw yourself fully into the experience."

"He's using the same stupid story to seduce women," I told Squirrely. "What a hack! And she's falling for it. What do I do?"

Squirrely wasn't listening. Instead, he had torn a hole in my tarp and was worrying at the zipper pull of my fanny pack. I picked him up, set him on the branch in front of me, and dug into my pack for a granola bar. My hand brushed against my phone.

That's it!

I tossed Squirely the granola bar, then started scrolling for Kitty's phone number. Meanwhile, Alistair kept playing Happy Fingers while he continued his—did he actually memorize them?—lines about writer-reader intimacy...

"—the desires you bring to the relationship."

"Desires?" She watched as he caressed her hand with his.

Kitty—don't be so gullible!

"New adventures. Exploring things you might never dare to experience in reality. That taste of the forbidden fruit. Kitty, I've read your work. You know exactly what I mean, I think."

Oh, no! He's off-script. He knows she's got a thing for danger, and he's playing into it. Dang it—why didn't I ever try that? Focus, Ron! Where's the number? Come on...

She glanced up, a challenge in her eyes. "I'm not done with my questions yet."

"After we spoke on the phone, I cleared my calendar. I'm yours for the entire evening, Miz McGrue."

"Kitty."

He smiled. "Kitty."

There! I pressed Dial.

Again, they'd faded into silence, save the sound of their fingers sliding against each other. When the cell phone started playing, "Dirty Laundry" they both jumped.

Kitty snatched the phone out of her purse, growling when she saw my name. "What?"

"Listen, Kitty, I know you're interviewing Alistair Kane—"

"Of course I am! Redfeathers gave me the assignment."

"Yeah, I know, but I'm the one who writes for the entertainment section, so I thought—"

"He's front-page news!" She rolled her eyes apologetically at Alistair.

"Two questions! Five minutes. Come on! Put me on speaker—they might help you, too."

With a huff, she tapped her phone and held it between her and Alistair. "I'm sorry for the interruption, Alistair. Meet Ronnie Engleson, our entertainment reporter."

He blinked, surprised. "We've already met. Do I hear a squirrel?"

Ack! Think fast, Ron! "Yeah, I'm, uh, in the backyard. Listen, I appreciated your time yesterday. Reed's Reads loved the interview; they're running it next week. I just need a little different angle for the *Gazette*. I know Kitty will be talking the political aspect with you, so I'm thinking more, uh... Anyway! I just have two questions, and I'm out of your hair."

"Of course, anything for a member of the press." Alistair kept his voice cordial, but I saw him wink at Kitty. She smirked back.

Come on, Engleson! What will set off Kitty's alarms?

"Okay, first question: Your personal assistant is on the RealHumans newsletter list?"

"Why, yes. Of course. To be sure that they are not using any of my words in their propaganda."

Ack! Too easy. "Oh. I thought that your lawyers would have handled that. Always good to have a double check, and since he's your biggest fan and your first editor, he's very familiar with your words, I'm sure."

"That's my angle!" McGrue started to hang up.

"Wait! Your wife—"

Kitty froze, her finger hovering over the button. She didn't know? Never mind—she did care! *Yes!*

"She doesn't like to have a public profile, I know. But she's such a gifted children's writer. My cousin Elise's daughters love her *Gingerbread House Adventures*. Rumor says you were separated for a bit, but made amends and plan to renew your vows. It's wonderful, really. Now that the two of you are getting back together, any chance you two might collaborate in the future?"

I watched as Kitty raised her brows at Alistair, a frown on her face. *Yes! Gotcha, Sleezo!*

He shifted uncomfortably. "Yes, well. As you said, she is a children's writer. Very different writing styles."

"Different writer-reader relationships?" Kitty asked, her voice dripping venom.

"Ooooo-kay," I said, feigning confusion, even as I gave Squirrely a thumbs-up. "Anyway, that's my two questions, so I'll get out of your hair. Pleasure to have met you, Mister Kane. Thanks, Kitty!"

I hung up. Mission accomplished, and I knew better than to push.

Kitty stuck the phone into her purse and pulled out her notebook and pen. She sat back, legs uncrossed, knees together, ankles tucked slightly under the chair.

"So, Mister Kane. What other RealHumans propaganda do you—sorry, your people—subscribe to?"

"We did it, Squirrely!" I said.

Squirrely took the half-eaten granola bar between its teeth and ran up my chest, over my face, and up the tree. I chuckled and leaned back, basking in my second superhero victory as I listened to Kitty grill Kane about the volatile nature of his book. I wonder if I could casually mention his penchant for womanizing the next time I saw Kitty. If I got her mad enough, maybe we could co-author something scathing for *Total Drama*.

Mom texted: *Where are you? I need a fitting*.

I checked the suite again and, reassured by Kitty's icy tone as she fired off questions, I headed home.

Vern

I landed at the back area of the Broadmoor where my contact had told me to meet him. In a moment, Rufio Rodriquez stepped out from the awning. We'd met when he was a security guard at Tokneo, but after Shogzallie wrecked it and Tokneo Corp abandoned it, they went to a skeleton crew. Fortunately, his heroic exploits helped him get a cushy job at the hotel.

Now, however, he looked harassed. "Man, thanks for doing this. This lady is insisting there's a peeping tom, but I ain't finding nothing."

"A peeping tom, here?" I could think of skankier hotels for a show.

"Yeah, usually, they're paparazzi, but this lady said he was just staring at the building and talking to squirrels. Said he was wearing a ski mask and a tarp."

"Sounds like he's nuts," I quipped.

Rodriguez laughed. "That's what I said! Anyway, I've checked around the trees, but I didn't find nothin', not even footprints, but this lady's freaked and ready to complain to management. Can you do me a favor and fly around, see if there are any clues? If nothin' else, I can say you scared him off."

"A favor?" Grace would have scolded me, but I didn't like working for free, especially now that we had to rebuild the mountain lair or get stuck living in the back corner of our warehouse-made-art-studio.

Rodriquez shuffled uncomfortably. "I can't approve no money. I'm just a grunt. But they're remodeling next month—bet I could score you a table and chairs, or a desk or something. Deal?"

I'd been in the Broadmoor. It had some quality stuff. "Deal."

He pointed out the room of the lady who complained. She was on her balcony watching. I flew up to talk to her.

"He was in that tree, over there." She pointed in the general direction of some tall oaks. "I didn't notice him at first because he had a black ski mask on and was wrapped in a green tarp. But then I saw him moving. He was like kissing a squirrel and talking to it, but he kept staring at us. I couldn't see his face because of the mask, but I'm telling you, there were some intense vibes!"

"You see a camera or anything?"

"No, just a phone. But I went in to call the front desk, and when I came back, he was gone."

I promised to check it out and flew over. Like Rodriguez, I didn't find any footprints on the ground or even a disruption of the mulch. I did, however, find a den holding an angry and bloated squirrel, defending a scrap of green tarpaulin and a granola bar wrapper.

Even more, I sensed that kind of weird magical...something...like I'd sensed at the office building where I thought I'd seen a failed assassination attempt. Was he at it again?

I flew down to Rodriguez. "Your caller is right. Someone was there. Who're in the rooms above her?"

He pulled out a pad and consulted it. "Directly above is a family, but they were in the restaurant, cause I went to ask if they'd seen anything. In the penthouse, there's an Alistair Kane. Oh, hey, he's that author."

"Get him moved and keep quiet about it. Somebody might be after him. Someone Magical."

Chapter Nine:
Gapman Gets His Supersuit

Ron

I pulled my "boot"—really, just a Spandex sock
with Kevlar reinforcements on the top and ankle—
over my running shoes, stood, and walked to the
closet door. I was shaking with excitement.

I'm a superhero, I reminded myself sternly. Superheroes don't geek out over their own uniforms.

Or did they? The scene from *The Incredibles*,
where Mr. Incredible was discussing his costume with
Edna Mode, came to mind. In fact, Mom and I had
had our own version of the famous "No Capes!" scene
only to conclude that Edna Mode didn't understand
Velcro.

I swirled my green cape over my shoulders with a
flourish and attached it. Then, I grabbed the door-
knob, and pulled it open to see myself in the mirror on
the inside of the door.

Whoa! I looked amazing!

The yellow-gold fabric gave a subtle shimmer in the afternoon sun that streamed through my window. Large green-and-blue flame-like designs covered the arms and calves. I knew everything fit, but I had not realized how well. All the marathon running and biking were going to pay off now, not to mention the hours chopping wood and working on the house. I turned to the side and struck a muscleman pose. Oh, man! I looked amazing! I went to one knee, fist on the ground, super-landing style.

Mom and I had finally compromised to Kevlar-reinforced shorts. I'd expected them to be uncomfortable, but I could move just fine in them. I tried hard to not think about how Mom got so good sewing men's shorts. We couldn't quite dye the utility belt the right shade of blue, but it was close enough, and I needed something to hold my phone and wallet. The half-mask was enough to hide my identity and give me a dangerous, edgy look. My mouse brown hair was nondescript enough to escape notice. Only a few curls escaped in the back, anyway. Maybe I should grow it longer. Ron could always wear a manbun.

"Well?" Mom called from the hallway. "Don't keep me in suspense!"

I gave myself one last look in the mirror and scrunched up with my fists against my mouth to hold back squeals of joy. Then I took a deep, cleansing breath. *I'm a superhero.*

I strode to my bedroom door, threw it open, and stepped out. I struck a superhero pose, hands on hips. "How may I help you, Citizen?"

Mom gave a little shriek and stepped back.

I immediately dropped my façade. "Mom! What's wrong?"

She waved her hands at me, telling me to wait. "Give me a minute. Wow—you look gorgeous! Wow. No one is going to recognize you."

"Gee, thanks."

"Oh, my baby!" She cupped my cheek in her hand. "You know what I mean. Of course, you're a handsome man, but you don't advertise it, with all those nerd shirts and loose jeans. But this! The girls will go nuts. Speaking of..."

She grabbed my sleeve and pulled hard.

"What are you doing?"

"Just double-checking that it doesn't rip easily. The green hotpants are perfect, too—so much better than briefs."

Hotpants? I felt my face heat up. Mom was right: I always did prefer my pants looser except when biking. But this wasn't me—or rather, wasn't Ron Engleson.

Mom was behind me now, plucking at my suit as only a mother could. "We got the fit just right. Now, I need to know what insignia you want on the chest. What's your superhero name? I could do a monogram like Superman."

I cringed inside on behalf of the Man of Steel. "I don't have a superhero name yet."

"Well, come up with one!"

"It doesn't work that way," I said with an authority born of thousands of hours of reading comics. "It has to come organically from the public to be a true super-hero name. Otherwise, I may as well just brand myself and wear advertising like Captain Corporate."

"Oh! Can you do that? It works for NASCAR."

"Mom!"

Laughing, she struck a superhero pose. "Nikeman running to save you!"

I braced my feet and planted my fists on my hips. "This rescue was sponsored by Haggis-a-Go-Go."

She leaned on the wall, laughing even harder. "Ha! I am...Sheep's Bladder. No-no! Bladder Control!"

It took us a few minutes to catch our breaths.

"Okay, enough," I said when I could catch my breath. "Let me go out on patrol and see if I can do some courageous deed and get my superhero name."

"Just don't let the dragon see you first," she warned. "I've heard he gives terrible nicknames."

Vern

"I'm sure," I said to Grace as we walked up the road leading to the ruins of our mountain lair. "There was that same sense of strangeness to the magic in both the house where we found Duncan and the office where I'm sure there was a gunman. It's Wrecking Ball, and he's a menace."

"Well, we're not going to convince Michael without proof," she said, referring to the Chief of Police. "After this, maybe you should fly a pattern between the two and see if you sense anything?"

I'd already tried while she was finishing up with the rosary team. "It was too faint and coming from several directions."

"So, more than one?"

"Or someone super-fast."

She sighed. "Well, we may have to pray for patience then."

"Speaking of," I said.

Grace and I passed through the front of the house that would one day be our home again but was, right now, still a shell awaiting its interior. The dust from cut lumber and drywall tickled my nose, and I sneezed. Grace patted my flank comfortingly, but her eyes were on the staircase. She didn't want to admit it, but she was as anxious as I was to get our lair back.

"If you want to go check out the upstairs..." I offered.

"No. It'll just be walls and ceilings. Let's go see what Brain has for your lair."

We headed down the hallway. The front area had been built according to more (pardon the pun) Mundane specifications and had taken the brunt of the damage when I'd fought Shogzallie, a gigantic proto-empyre twisted by Mundane beliefs into a Godzilla-like creature. We'd stopped it before it could attack Los Lagos, but not before fire and landslide and some spiteful swipes of Shogzallie's tail had wrecked our house. The grateful town was coming together to help us rebuild, but it was slow work and low budget.

Deeper in, however, had been designed by the dwarves who built the mountain from (pun intended) the ground up. This was more reminiscent of the cave-like lairs I had called home and had taken less damage. Even the might of Shogzallie could not prevail over dwarven craftsmanship.

We walked through the stone hallway, noting that the lights now worked; they must have gotten the wiring replaced. The hall opened up into a huge room, also rock, and now mostly devoid of any features except the now-empty swimming pool and the also-empty recessed shelves. We were storing the few things that survived the fire in Father Rich's garage at the Little Flower rectory. He had to park his car outside and was hoping we'd be able to at least move the stuff before the snow came, but he did admit he'd rather have my stuff in the garage than me.

I agreed. I wasn't happy in our warehouse, which we'd donated to an art commune living and I didn't want to live in the rectory (even if I could now that people were more used to me). I wanted my own space.

Which was why Brian had called us here today.

He stood from where he'd been on hands and knees polishing a bit of the floor and waved. "Look what came in early!"

As we approached, we saw the circular metal-and-plexiglass door that covered the pit that had been my bed. The coins and jewels were tucked away in a chest along the wall—cheap stuff, mostly nickels and pennies and costume jewelry that Grace bespelled to keep from oxidizing or decaying. The transparent circle, cut in half with a metal that matched the dark flooring, looked into an empty pit of polished stone.

"Nice!" Grace said.

"Now, the whole motor for the original spiral design was fried, so this one is simpler and manually operated, but all you have to do is push here and here." He demonstrated and the two doors swung open on pistons. They had track lighting on the edges and along the circumference of the interior, just below the floor level.

"I thought you might like some light for safety, and it looks pretty cool. You can turn it off here." He showed me a button just inside the pit. Then he pointed out me the combination deadlocks that locked the doors shut when I wasn't around.

I was going to miss the cool spiraling of the floor that I'd only enjoyed for a few short weeks, but it was worth getting my bed back. I could almost feel myself luxuriating on my back, all the coins and jewels massaging my scales as I shifted position. A lot of people think dragons hoard treasure out of greed, but really, we just want a comfortable place to sleep.

"This is great," I told him.

"We can put the treasure back in any time. Want to take a walk around and see what else we've done?"

"Why not?" The Tarped Menace could wait.

Chapter Ten:
Gapman's Baby Buggy Rescue

Ron

I didn't want anyone to trace me back to my house, so I ran through the woods until I was near a clearing close to the highway. There, I doffed my regular clothes, put them in a plastic bag to protect against the elements and bugs, and hid them high up in a tree. I figured I'd have to find different spots each time to keep it random, but a small price to pay for privacy and for keeping Mom safe.

At the edge of the clearing, I paused. Excitement and nervousness coursed through me like electricity, more than any opening night I'd ever been in. This was it. This was my true superhero debut!

I took three steps and launched myself into the air with so much force, I shot through the clouds. I looked down at their fluffy whiteness and started laughing...then wheezing. Wow, the air was thin up here!

The point was to be seen, anyway. I dove back down and headed towards Los Lagos, straining my superhearing for signs of trouble, while scenarios played out in my mind. Would I stop a mugging? I could hear my mom scolding me that I needed something more public. So, if I saw one, okay, but I wouldn't go looking for that this time.

Public...public... A bank robbery? An altercation at the comic book store? That would be ironic. Maybe a daring rescue! I could see it now: carrying the victim to safety, their flustered and confused expression as they gasped in surprise:

"What? But, I..."

Fear not, Good Citizen. You're safe now. All in a day's work.

Oh! I should have a little bit of a Yorkshire accent. Even after four years in England, my accent's laughable to my classmates, but I only wanted to sound different from Ron Engleson. Or maybe Mid-Atlantic. I'd seen enough of the old classics movies I could fake that, and since it's a made-up accent, no one could place it. I could toss in some mannerisms to further confuse things.

My superhearing picked up chants and angry shouts in the direction of the Gap. Another protest,

already? Hey! I was a Mundane and magically pow-
ered superhero. Maybe I could become an icon of
peace between our peoples!

I turned toward the Gap, formulating a short
speech about peaceful coexistence and learning from
each other. Could I say, "Infinite Diversity in Infinite
Combinations," or was that trademarked?

I'd expected to find a protest somewhere outside
the Gapport—the parking lot, maybe. I did not expect
to see an angry mob shouting and waving placards
threateningly only yards from the Gap itself. Like on
the Faerie side, the magic of the Gap did not allow for
any enclosing structures, but on our side, the area was
cordoned off with a high fence of electrified chain link
topped with razor wire. I quickly scanned the fence
but didn't see any signs that someone had broken it.
So how had the forty or so humans with signs gotten
in?

Well, the police could figure that out. I was here to
stop the crowd from getting violent and maybe broker
peace. What a great way to make myself known. But
how? The authorities were already getting between
the opposing sides, making a barrier and pulling folks
away.

The two groups were pushing back against the police, snarling insults at them as well as each other. Meanwhile, some of people wanting to cross the Gap had removed the ribbon dividers that made a snaky line to the gate and were pushing against each other to get a better view. A few were videoing with their phones but others had joined in the shouting.

How should I help? Protestors were starting to use their signs as clubs. Maybe I should grab those. Or I could grab the leaders and get them to talk to each other. Or I could take care of the flying ones, like that pixie that had landed on one policeman's hair and was pulling it like Ratatouille.

Too many choices. What would Vern do?

Just pick something! They're starting to riot!

Suddenly, someone screamed, "My baby!"

There was a collective gasp from the crowd as a stroller rolled from the crowd straight toward the rioters.

"Stop that stroller!" the mother cried.

A couple of hands reached out, but it was too late. The security guard at the gate lunged toward it, but at the last moment, it jinked to the left and he landed flat on his face. Meanwhile, a few travelers took advantage of his absence and rushed out the gate and around the pocket of rioters, ignoring the buggy.

The mother screamed again as another policeman reached for the stroller and missed. It jerked inexplicably just as a placard smashed in its path, then accelerated toward the Gap. What nefariousness was this?

Wait! This was a job for me!

I swooped in at superspeed and snagged the stroller in both hands just before it would have entered the Gap. As the mother screamed hysterically, I shouted out reassurances. "It's all right, Ma'am! Your baby's safe."

Just then "baby" leaped from its seat and sunk its teeth into my glove. Ah! Chihuahua!

I flinched in surprise, my hand closing on the tiny dog's belly while the rest of me reared back. I lost my equilibrium. The stroller fell from my gasp and struck me on the leg, sliding until the handle caught on my foot. The stroller swung, connecting with an upraised protest sign and knocking it from the rioter's hands. It smacked a pixie just as she was about to toss some kind of fairy dust on a RealHuman. She flew away, coughing, as she inhaled her own magic.

The dog continued to snarl and munch on my Kevlar glove, scrabbling at my wrist with its back feet. Great. I'd had the suit all of an hour and it's already damaged.

Suddenly, I realized a shocked silence had fallen over the crowd. Even the rioters had stopped to stare.

At me.

I took in my position, hovering over the rioters, a toothy pocket dog attacking my glove while a dog stroller hung off my foot. Great. Great first impression. With as much dignity as I could summon, I took hold of the stroller in my other hand and flew down to the woman who was crying and holding out her hands entreatingly. Her T-shirt said, "Any woman can be a mother, but it takes someone special to be a Chihuahua Mom."

I set the stroller down gently, then held out my hand to her. The dog hung freely by the teeth. "Ma'am?"

"Oh, Timida!" She grabbed the dog and pulled. A rip of fabric, and the dog was hers. As if a spell had been broken, it spun in her arms and started whining and licking her neck.

"You're all right! You're all right! Oh, sir, how can I thank you?"

"All in a day's work, Ma'am," I said in my best heroic voice, then more quietly, "I'll need that back."

I pointed to the fabric. I couldn't leave anything that might lead to my identity, after all.

"Oh, right. Sure." She handed me the scrap of fabric and turned all her attention to cooing reassurances to her dog and straightening her little pink bows.

Mission accomplished, I guess. I turned back toward the rioters, my speech on my lips.

Except the police had used the distraction to separate and arrest the rioters—those that had not fled across the Gap, anyway.

People were staring at me. Some still had their phones out.

Okay, then. I gave them a modified version of the speech I'd planned on giving the rioters, minus the Star Trek quote.

"Who are you?" someone asked.

Shoot! I didn't have a superhero name. "I'm here to protect the good people on both sides of the Gap," I prevaricated.

"So...Gapman?"

I liked that!

With a grin, I gave a thumbs-up to the teen who christened me, then shot off like a rocket. I didn't stop until I'd broken through the clouds, then zoomed away at top speed toward town. What other derring-do could Gapman accomplish today?

Vern

After checking the progress on our lair, we retired to the kitchen—not to eat, mind you, but to use the table, which was one of the few things to survive Shogzallie's attack. Who knew Formica could take such a beating? Then again, it could hardly have looked worse.

Grace pulled out a map of Colorado from her sleeves and spread it on the table. The lakes and several areas had been marked out in red pen. Bishop Aiden had sent mages to help us check the immediate area for any more proto-empyre that might be hiding in the lakes, just waiting for some innocent Mundane to power it through belief.

However, Shogzallie had lain hidden for months before sufficient belief (and misimagining) had warped it into the Godzilla-like monster that wrecked our home before we could stop it. We weren't taking chances that others had traveled further and were lost or biding their time. We'd been systematically checking out areas and laying some detection spells.

We were not interested in a sequel of Vern vs. Shogzallie and were going to do whatever we could to prevent it.

"The weather's beautiful," Grace said. "What if I take my backpack, and we go here, camp for the night, then head back this way?"

She traced a path with her finger deep into the woods near the border of magic's influence in the Mundane. I'd be weakened the closer to the border we got.

"We probably won't have cell service," I noted.

"That sounds heavenly," she said with a wistful smile. Then with a more practical tone, added. "If we run into trouble that we can't handle, we back off. I'll hide and you fly for help."

Neither of us expected to find any miscreant Magicals so far from the source of magic in this world, but we had to check, for our own peace of mind if not the peace of the Mundane. So, a relaxing afternoon of flying a search pattern while Grace hiked a similar pattern below, a late-night dinner around a campfire, a sleep free of city noise, then more of the same before heading back in the afternoon? Sounded heavenly, indeed.

"I'll text Father and let him know we won't be home until tomorrow."

As we headed down the road to our car, I heard one of the construction guys saying, "Hey, Jerry! Look at this guy saving a dog!"

I rolled my eyes. Sure, we save the world, but they're all agog over some guy saving a mutt.

I probably should have concentrated on what they were saying. It might have saved me some trouble when we returned.

"How are you feeling?" Grace asked as I landed beside the car.

"A little off, still," I admitted, stretching my front legs as if that would restore my magic. We'd spent the morning along the edge line of magic's influence, and since it was a gradual decline, I didn't notice until I was feeling weak and called an end to the search. "But getting better the closer we get to the Gap."

She opened the tailgate of our SUV and tossed her backpack in. "Well, hop in. There's no need to over-stress yourself."

"Are you okay?" Grace was part Siren and a mage; she depended on magic, too.

"Also a little off, but not like how you must feel. Besides, while you need magic to fly, I don't to drive."

On the way home, we prayed the Miraculous Mysteries of the Rosary (a Faerie version), then I told her what my Eldestkin, Durrekeh, had told me about Lazarus. I was just getting to the part about Martha insisting he take yet another bath when both our phones started exploding with notifications.

"What in the world?" Grace asked, then followed up with a quick prayer. Just our luck that some disaster only we could handle would hit the town just as we were away trying to prevent another disaster from hitting the town.

But, no, the messages were more excited than terrified: *Vern did you see this?*, *Hey, Vern, got some competition?*, and several links to various videos and news articles.

Not all were delighted, however. One from Detective Vialpando was littered with profanity.

"...but not directed at me, for once. I got a couple from Santry," I told Grace as I checked her phone, "and it looks like you did, too."

"It was too good to last," she sighed, "but I did enjoy the respite. Why don't you figure out what the hubbub is about, and when we get closer to town, we can decide where to go first."

I scrolled until I found Father Rich's message. I could generally trust him to give us straight news. But this time had me wondering. "Father says there's a superhero flying around Los Lagos doing good deeds."

"A what?" Grace laughed.

I clicked on the link, which led to an article on the *Los Lagos Gazette Online:*

> Goodbye, Dragon – Hello, Superhero!
> Gapman Makes His Debut

"Rude!" I exclaimed. "That's low, even for Kitty."

"Keep reading!" Grace urged as she turned onto the highway.

"In a stunning and unforgettable debut—oh, he has a *debut*!" I started sarcastically.

"Vurnerrah," Grace warned, and with a sigh, I read on.

> In a stunning and unforgettable debut, a superhero has made his presence known to the people of Los Lagos.
>
> The breathtaking saga began when a group of 20 RealHumans blocked the Gap, preventing

travelers from crossing into Faerie. Soon, they were met by Faeries—both magical and human—from the other side of the Gap. By the time security arrived, tensions had risen to shouting and blows.

That's when a pet stroller carrying Timida, a longhaired chihuahua, escaped her pet-mom's clutches and rolled into the crowd, somehow avoiding the grasps of anyone trying to stop it. Just before it would have crossed into the Gap and the Faerie universe, Gapman, in a whir of green and gold, intercepted it.

That was not the end of his heroics. Even as he cradled the terrified canine, he knocked away a protest sign just before the RealHuman rioter could hit a policeman with it.

"I thought I was a goner," said Officer Tracy Sterling. "That sign was sturdy, and I had nowhere to duck. But suddenly, Gapman just used the stroller to whack away the sign. I owe him big time."

He also prevented fairies from casting spells, all the while assuring Timida's owner of her pet's safety. Then, sure that the police had the rioting situation in hand, he returned the distressed dog to the security of his mother's arms and launched into an inspiring speech urging peace between Faerie and Mundanes.

"I'm here to protect the good people on both sides of the Gap," he concluded before taking off like a comet into the clouds.

Gapman emerged as a beacon of hope to stop what could have been a violent riot at the Gap, not only protecting police forces and rioters on both sides but saving a beloved pet in the process. With stunning impartiality and wisdom, he reminded spectators and rioters alike that, Faerie or Mundane, we are all part of the wondrous and diverse universe we call home.

"There are 127 comments!" I exclaimed and read a couple.

Gapman is a symbol of unity, justice, and compassion. His extraordinary ability to inspire change through empathy proved that a genuine hero isn't merely defined by their superhuman capabilities, but by the depth of their character.

The power of compassion can unite even the most divided of societies. We are fortunate to have him as our city's guardian.

Omigosh. I'm so in love!

"Pull over. I need to vomit," I said.

Grace tsked. "Be generous. It sounds like he did a lot of good while we were gone."

I'd moved on to the videos. I laughed in disbelief. "He's incompetent! He didn't cradle the dog; it's attacking him. He almost dropped the stroller on people's heads. Look!"

"I'm driving." But her eyes flicked momentarily toward my screen, and I could see in the furrow of her brow that she agreed with me.

"You know what?" I said. "I think this is Wrecking Ball."

Just then, my phone started chanting "You'll regret this"—the ringtone I'd created especially for my least favorite overworked knight-in-tarnished-armor: Police Chief Santry.

"It's about time you answered," he grumbled as soon as I picked up. "Get over here. We need to talk about this menace called Gapman."

"Do-gooder and saver of dogs?" I asked. "How much of a menace can he be?"

"Just get down here."

Grace and I exchanged glances. Whatever this Gapman had done, Santry wasn't going to rant about it over the phone.

"We're about forty minutes away," Grace told him. "We've been up in the mountains."

He grunted understanding, but I knew he was holding back his irritation. He and my nun had built a bond back during the whole Mishmash debacle. He'd been the first to understand she was dealing with PTSD, something he'd seen his own father deal with throughout his childhood. He'd been kind to her, which was about all the credit I'd give him, and he still treated her with the greatest of respect.

Which meant if he had the chance, he'd wait until he could get me alone and probably yell at me for not being in town while this Gapman was doing whatever it was that had him ticked off.

As Grace drove, I read the messages and pulled up the links about Gapman. My-my; he'd been a busy boy: stopped a purse snatching, pushed a stalled car out of the way of an oncoming train; helped some guy move his couch...

"That's all heroic, but innocuous," Grace said. "He seems rather sweet."

"And unfocused. So what'd he do that's got Santry so riled?" I wondered.

Ron

Fighting back a yawn, I poured coffee from the snack room pot into my nearly empty to-go cup and helped myself to three donuts. I'd overdone it on my Coming Out patrol. I was still famished and would have gladly slept in except Redfeathers had called "All Hands on Deck" for the next issue—and since it was about Gapman, how could I not be there?

"What are you grinning about?" Kitty asked as she poured herself a cup and returned the pot, empty, to the maker.

"There's a superhero in town." I could not keep the glee out of my voice.

"He's not a comic book character," she chided. I watched her pour three sugars, hesitate, then add a fourth. She was as tired as I was. "He's the real deal— or he'd better be."

"What are you talking about?" I asked. "You wrote a great article on him."

She stirred her coffee with enough agitation that it slopped over the side. "Which I did based on videos and one quote Fina got. I spent all afternoon and half the night chasing him down and not once did he slow down so I could ask him a question."

"Maybe he was excited about his first day saving people?" I suggested as I grabbed a napkin and cleaned up the spill. It was half true. I'd also been avoiding her. I hadn't known what to say to Kitty as Gapman. You'd think with all the Superman/Lois Lane stories I'd devoured in my life, I'd have this down pat, but none of them involved Superman panting and sweaty from lifting a car off the railroad tracks. Or answering hard-hitting questions about my origin story while carrying some guy's couch up three flights of twisting stairs.

"Maybe he's just being mysterious. Or maybe he just doesn't want to talk to you," Fina Tabaki, the *Gazette*'s Gap reporter said, her nose crinkling with irritation, and not just at the empty coffee pot. I guess I couldn't blame her. She'd been on the scene to write about the riot. Her story ended up below the fold while Kitty got the headline with an article based on third-party evidence—and one of Fina's quotes.

This is why I liked freelance. I didn't have to deal with office politics.

"Oh, it's probably not that," I started. "Maybe..."

"Shut up, Ronnie," they chorused.

Fina turned to Kitty, "You should be more grateful that I gave you that quote. The least you could do was fill the coffee pot."

"Redfeathers ordered you to give me the quote—and making coffee is for interns. I have more important things to do."

That's when Mr. Redfeathers appeared in the doorway.

"What is this, social hour?" Mr. Redfeathers was a yeller. When he and Mom had been together, she'd been a yeller, too. Our apartment had been so noisy.

Now, superhearing amplified that by a hundred. I winced as his words clanged in my skull like church bells before my body adapted. I missed part of what he said but the intent was clear—we were supposed to be in the conference room where he could yell at us some more.

He was in a mood. Even Kitty wasn't standing up to him.

We slunk out like naughty schoolchildren under his glare. He followed us, pausing to point at our current intern. "Lindsey! Get in there and make the coffee!"

The conference room screens all displayed screen-shots from other news sites. CNN, USA Today, HuffPo—they all had articles about me!

Kitty jabbed me hard with her elbow. "Will you quit geeking out like a twelve-year-old? You know what this means, right?"

I'm famous! "Uh..."

"This is why you write about movies," she sneered and claimed the seat at the foot of the table where she could look Mr. Redfeathers directly in the eye. Everyone knew better than to take her spot.

Still absorbing the flattering prose about Gapman (me!), I settled into one of the last seats on the side.

Mr. Redfeathers stormed in and gestured at the screens with an angry sweep of his hand. "Care to explain how we've been scooped on our own turf?"

People looked at the table, at their hands, at Kitty.

Timidly, I raised my hand.

"What is this, high school?" he snarled. "What?"

"It looks like they're taking their information off MeTube and social media—second-hand stuff," I offered. "Kitty was out all night seeking first-hand information."

I thought I'd diffused the situation, but he slammed his hands on the table and glared across it to her. "And where are all those 'first-hand' reports?"

No one quite said, "Oooo," but you could feel it. Obviously, Kitty had been so focused on cornering me—er, Gapman—that she hadn't bothered to take notes or interview anyone I'd helped.

But instead of apologizing, she slapped her hands on the table and stood, a mirror image to him. "What? Is that what you wanted? These are nothing—police reports! Gapman is the real story!"

Which seemed exactly what he wanted to hear. "And we need to get on top of that! I want to know everything there is to know about this Gapman! Where did he come from? Why is he here? Why is he wearing his underwear on the outside?"

"Hotpants," I interrupted. "They're not underwear, they're..."

All eyes were turned on me. What was I saying?

"...hotpants," I concluded in a murmur, my face heating up. It was probably a good thing my super-hero powers didn't include melting into a puddle and oozing out the door because I'd have given away my identity right then.

Mr. Redfeathers pinned me with a glare. "Are you suggesting our local superhero is a stripper?"

"What? No!"

"Maybe his costume was made by a stripper?"

That hit close to home. "Can we forget I said anything?"

...and he already had. "What's the story with the costume? Where does he stand on the whole Faerie vs. RealHuman debate?"

"Uh..." I and several others started, but he shut us down.

"I know about the pretty speech! I want to know about the man. Is he a man?"

"Seemed man enough to me," Fina murmured to Kitty, who smirked in agreement.

I turned my head to hide my grin. Maybe I should have been annoyed that it took yellow spandex (and flying) to get a woman to notice me, but still.

Mr. Redfeathers snarled at our end of the table. "Is this funny to you? Tabaki, you were right there!"

"I was reporting on the riot," she countered.

"Riot!" he sputtered. His face grew crimson with fury. "Riot? There's a riot on this planet every twenty minutes! Gapman is the world's first superhero! He's the biggest news since the Gap."

The biggest news since the Gap.

Mr. Redfeathers continued to alternate between chewing us out and giving instructions, but I'd stopped paying attention, focusing instead on the articles splashed across the whiteboards. I wasn't just a local hero. I wasn't just news. I was the First. The Only. I was—am—history.

Somehow, my stomach felt heavy and my heart, light. Had any superhero in comics or movies had that sudden realization about how big it all was? Uncle Ben's advice to Peter Parker didn't even come close. I had a sudden urge to retreat to the mountains, stare out over the horizon, and grapple with the implications of it all. Gapman was huge. I was Gapman—but me, Ronnie Engleson...making history?

It was too much to take in here in the newsroom. I bit into my donut. Maybe the fluffy sugariness would distract me from the existential gravitas of what I'd dared to do.

"Engleson, time to shine!"

I choked on my donut. "Sir?"

He glared at me with annoyance. "You're our resident superhero geek. You of all people should have some insights."

He didn't know the half of it. "Cool. I'll get started on it now."

I started to rise, but the glares of my coworkers made me sit back down slowly. "I missed something."

"I don't need an article in the entertainment section. Brief us."

A tiny part of me flared with anger. I was the only one here with a clue; why shouldn't I write the story? But no, Gapman was for all of Los Lagos—all the world. How could Ron Engleson be selfish with what he knew?

I took a sip of coffee to stall. I had to talk about myself in third person, couching everything in fictional references. I looked at the articles on the walls. Where to start?

"Okay. So, I think Kitty is right. Gapman was making his debut. Look at all the stuff he did—rescues, stopping crimes—" Wait. None of the articles mentioned those, did they? The police didn't say anything yet? "I mean, he did stop crimes, right?"

"There was a purse snatching," McGrue said. "He returned the purse and let the kid go with a warning." She snorted, unimpressed, but geez, I didn't know the kid's backstory.

Still, good enough. "Okay, and just, you know, being generally helpful. It's like he's still finding his role in Los Lagos."

That earned me some appreciative looks and even a "huh" from Redfeathers. Kitty, however, demanded, "And you deduced this, how?"

Oops. "Uh, Spiderman? When he first realized he had powers, he webslung around the city, just helping out wherever he came across a need."

"So you think he's new to his powers, then?"

Dang it, she was so smart! "Well, considering he just now showed up..." I shrugged. I hoped I looked convincing. She could be so insightful when she put her mind to it, like when she had that look of concentration that made her right cheek dimple.

"So how do I get him to notice me?" she asked.

Oh, he already does...

Snickers erupted around us. For a moment, I thought I'd spoken aloud, but everyone was looking at Kitty.

"To interview!" she protested, but was she blushing?

Then she turned her embarrassment into wrath and directed it at me. "Well, Mister Superhero Expert? How do we get Los Lagos' only superhero to talk to Los Lagos' only newspaper? 'Cause he was ducking me pretty good last night."

"Maybe he wasn't ready. I mean, consider Spiderman: *The Daily Bugle* smeared him every chance it got. Besides, most superheroes—Ironman aside—are not in it for the glory. And really, Tony Stark, being a genius, billionaire, playboy, philanthropist, was already used to the press. Not to mention all the trouble superheroes get into when people start figuring out their secret identities. Maybe he's afraid of giving away information that might put someone he loves in danger."

"So, we make it nonthreatening?" Kitty chewed the side of her lip thoughtfully. "Sympathetic. Gentle, even. I can do that. I can use velvet gloves."

The room exploded into laughter.

"I mean the interview!"

Chapter Eleven:
Gapman's Good Deed Fallout

Vern

By the time we were pulling into police headquarters, the *Gazette* website had updated with a new article about Gapman.

"No actual news," I reported to Grace, "just an editorial by Kitty. Wow, she's desperate! She asked Gapman to dinner."

"She what?" Grace paused to read the article off my phone with me. Kitty waxed poetic about chasing down Gapman into the night to ask him some questions, then realizing how that probably seemed threatening:

> Even the strongest men have weaknesses,
> vulnerable aspects of their lives. It's only fair that
> you want to protect yourself and anyone you
> may love, yet it's obvious how you're compelled
> to share your might with the world. We at the
> *Gazette* understand. I understand. We just want
> to know our new hero better.

When I ask the hard-hitting questions, it's for the good of Los Lagos. I take pride in being a threat to those with something to hide—but not this time.

Let us meet peacefully as colleagues with a common purpose, as friends with a shared goal. No interview, just conversation. Perhaps over a meal, if you eat. On your time, Gapman, find me. K marks the spot.

"This was not one of her better ideas," Grace said as she caught sight of the comments after the article.

I'll mark my spot, Gapman!

Kitty's Hot For Gapman!

I'm hot for Gapman. He don't have to tell me a thing!

"Oh, dear," Grace said as another, more suggestive, comment popped up, only to be removed as we watched, followed by a notice that comments had been turned off. "People think she wants to seduce answers out of him."

"I wouldn't put it past her," I said, then had a truly horrible thought. I pulled out my phone and texted her: *McGrue, you'd better not have any of that perfume left.*

A couple of years ago, she'd been "gifted" with a bottle of Siren Spell, a perfume that promised to make you more influential—which it did, since it was made with illegally gained siren pheromones.

Almost immediately, I got a reply: *You burned it all, and you know it. Don't be gross. I don't need perfume, anyway.*

I sent her back an eye-roll emoji and slipped my phone back into my pouch. We entered the police building.

Officer Tracy Sterling greeted us from behind the bullet-and-magic-proof glass. "Hey, guys! You've missed all the excitement."

"I thought you'd graduated from reception," I said.

"Oh, I'm just filling in for Kampouris until he gets back from lunch. Where you been? Vialpando's almost done yelling. He's getting hoarse."

Detective Vialpando with laryngitis would be a thing to behold. "Do tell!"

She opened her mouth, then hesitated. "You'd better talk to the captain. All I know is Gapman saved me from getting a concussion or worse, so he's okay in my book."

She buzzed us in. The station looked the same as always—like Tracy said, we'd missed the most entertaining drama—but I did notice one group standing around a large whiteboard with GAPMAN across the top and different lists, items connected by red lines. Looks like I wasn't the only one underwhelmed by Wrecking Ball's performance.

Santry's office was in the middle of the large room, a glass pillar of authority, currently with the blinds all down. I could see from the shadows, however, that he was arguing with someone over the phone. Only a low murmur escaped the glass, but I could pick up the strain in his voice.

Vialpando was at his desk, talking intently to some suit I didn't recognize.

He looked up as we passed. "Vern, you'd better get control of your new friend," he rasped.

Wow. He really had yelled himself hoarse. "Why do you think he's my friend?" I demanded.

He gaped at me like I was stupid. "You're both flying do-gooders."

"Oh! And you—you should do something about that voice. Maybe check with the Hispanic yellers in town. You know them all, don't you?"

He curled his lip at me. "That menace wrecked my investigation. Six months of work—and now we have to start over. So you find that *hijo de*—" He caught Grace's raised brow and took a deep breath. "Sorry, Sister. But thanks to our new superhero, my inform-ant just skipped town."

"Gapman blew his cover?" I asked.

"Gapman," Vialpando sneered the name, "stuffed him into a trash can and delivered him to our door-step with a note."

I snorted. "At least he has style."

"Yeah, so funny. My guy was on his way up. We were this close to finding the supplier, maybe even the lab, but no more! Go talk to Santry. I've got damage control to do."

With that, he turned back to the suit, who had waited with silent patience this whole time. He hadn't seemed intimidated by my presence, just not a talker. So, Colorado Bureau of Investigations? Maybe even FBI.

No wonder Vialpando was mad.

Grace set her hand on Vialpando's shoulder and murmured a prayer for him. I could see tension leave his body. She was so good at that. He patted her hand.

That done, we went to meet the Santry.

"'Bout time you showed up," he grumbled at us even as he offered Grace a seat. "Tell me what you know about this caped do-gooder."

"Probably less than you," Grace answered. "We just heard about him on the way here."

"So he appeared out of nowhere?" Santry glared at me like I'd dropped the ball.

Figured. The Mundanes have the police, the sheriff, the Gap Security Agency, and private security, but when some kind of magical person makes an unexpected appearance, it's *my* fault for not being vigilant enough? I shrugged, refusing to take the blame. One thing I'd learned from my fight with Shogzallie—the Gap situation was becoming too much for one person to handle, even if that person was a superior being like myself.

"It sounds like Gapman's not exactly endeared himself with the police," Grace changed the subject.

Santry slapped a file on his desk. As I leafed through the contents, he said, "In the space of a few hours, he destroyed months of police work. He caught

Vialpando's informant right after making contact with his supplier. Scooped him up, plopped him into a trash can, and delivered him to our steps with a note. 'Helping keep Los Lagos clean from dirty dealers.'"

I snorted. "Sounds like a campaign slogan."

"It was a metal trash can. The fire department had to use the jaws of life to pry him free. Now, we have an informant who's freaked out about being caught, and if his supplier finds out, that lead's burned even if we can get him to return. We can't even press charges against the dealer because we have nothing but coincidence to tie him to the drugs in the trash can. Did Vialpando tell you that as soon as we released him, he cleared all his accounts and took a bus out of town? Six months, we've been setting this sting up, and in six minutes, the Green and Gold Menace nearly ruined it."

"Well," Grace said, trying to find a bright side, "at least he stopped a purse snatching."

"Yes—a policewoman's purse, with marked bills and a tracer sewn into the lining. There's a ring of petty thieves—purse snatchers, pickpockets—that seems to stretch from here to Canon City and across the Gap. What do you want to bet Gapman just drove them underground in Los Lagos?"

She flipped to another page. "He stopped a vandalism. That was nice. I read in the *Gazette* that the kids were quite taken with him."

Santry's gave her a strained smile. He pulled up an image on his phone and showed us a stucco wall with the words "Gapmanz GOAT ACAB" in green and yellow.

"Is that your apartment building?" I asked, trying not to laugh.

"This 'hero' is a menace," Santry said.

"He's trying to help," Grace said. Bless my dear nun. She always wanted to see the good in people, even bumbling do-gooders with superpowers.

Santry sighed in exasperation. "Then he should apply for spokesman for DARE or become a counselor or something. Better than messing up our investigations. Delivering one pusher in the trash wasn't enough. He also found a couple of others and left them bound to a flagpole with the evidence tied around one's neck along with a note: 'Just doing my part to make Los Lagos a better, drug-free place to live. Yours, Gapman.'"

"Good intentions." But even Grace was starting to waiver.

"Except that by the time a squad car got there, someone had cut the bag free and made off with about a grand in uncut puck! To add insult to injury, that puck came from our evidence locker, and the 'supplier' was one of mine. Reese was making a deal with a middleman that would have gotten him in with the real guys in charge. He nearly wrecked that sting, too."

"Nearly?" I asked.

He glared at me with an intense look in his eye that said I was in for work. "Reese is setting up a new deal—and you're going to make sure Gapman stays out of it."

Should have known he wasn't calling me in to complain, but at least this time, someone wasn't asking me for Gapman's secret identity. Kind of a relief. "Yeah? How?"

"Not my concern. Set him on fire if you have to. Just keep him away from the drop point, away from my guys—hell, away from the whole East side."

"If he's such a menace, why don't you just arrest him?"

Santry leaned back against his chair and gave me the fish-eye. "Do you know the difference between a hero and a vigilante?"

I grimaced. If I had the right anatomy for it, I'd have slapped my forehead. "Good press."

"Exactly. The press loves Gapman. The people love Gapman. Of more importance to me, the mayor and the city council love Gapman. And..." He flung a hand toward his computer and phone. "...they are quite confident that I can find an equitable, mutually beneficial and most of all, *discrete* solution to this problem."

I sighed. "You're hiring me to be the heavy?"

"He needs to be stopped."

I felt my teeth baring. "Why should I? I seem to recall that not too long ago, I was the vigilante, the 'dangerous dragon'—"

Santry shrugged. "You still are. You've just learned to adapt to the rules, for the most part. And we've set our barriers on where we disagree on methods."

Speaking of barriers and methods. "And you do know the crime rate inside Territory, where I use my methods?" I fixed my gaze on his.

Santry's eyes narrowed. He leaned toward me. "And where did those criminals go?"

One of the rare times in my life, I lowered my gaze.

Santry's voice softened. "Look. I'm grateful for what you do for the people in Territory. I really am. The kids there have a real chance, and the people living there are finally doing so in safety and peace. But you can't be everywhere, and you can't intimidate everyone into obeying. Neither can Gapman. Even worse, he lacks your—"

"Panache?"

"Your stubborn, superior, dragon attitude. He thinks everyone wants to be nice, to be friends, to be good citizens. Maybe he can mold a steel can into a goody bag, but he's not *strong*. Soon, the criminal elements of this city are going to realize that—and then we're all going to be in trouble."

Damsels and Knights, I hated it when Santry had a point.

"He could be a big help if taught," Grace suggested.

Santry rolled his eyes, "And if he wanted to go into law enforcement, he'd have come to us instead of swooping in to make a grand public reveal and then zipping all over town doing odd jobs and messing up investigations. He's a maverick, and I have enough to deal with as it is.

"I want you to find him, and I want you to set him straight. Keep him away from our operations. If he wants to rescue dogs and help little old ladies across the street, that's his prerogative. But if he messes up an investigation again, I'm coming after you." He pointed a finger at my chest.

"You can't do that!"

He snickered. It was an ugly sound. "It's cute how you think you have rights, dragon."

My wings flared—as much as they could in the cramped space—but Grace stood up quickly and stepped between us. "We'll do what we can, but Michael, you should be ashamed of yourself!"

He met her eyes briefly before looking away. "Sorry. It's been a long night of damage control, and we're still trying to pivot. I need this guy contained."

Apologies were rare from Santry, but today, it was not enough. "So what are we getting paid?"

"What?" Santry shouted. Grace asked the same but with more exasperation than anger.

My nun was not turning this one into a charity case, not if my freedom was on the line. "You want us to 'stop him,' which is pretty broad, so how shall we bill this? Hourly? By goals? After all, I don't want to be a maverick do-gooder."

Grace turned to give me her stern nun look, but Santry just sighed and rubbed his eyes with one hand. "Go take it up with accounting—but I want it done, and fast. So far, nobody's been hurt, but I watch superhero movies. I know the cliché."

Grace went to talk to Tracy and the policewoman whose purse had been "stolen." I went to haggle with the accountant. It took a while; Americans don't haggle, and dragons don't compromise easily. Finally, I met Grace at the entrance.

"I hope you went easy on him," Grace scolded as we piled into the car.

"I let up when that vein in his temple started to throb," I replied defensively. "I'm not a villain."

"Speaking of," she said as she backed out, "I don't think Gapman is the same person you sensed at the shooting."

I grunted agreement. At least Grace believed I had witnessed a shooting. "That makes twisted sense. Where there's a superhero, there's a supervillain. How ironic is it that only Gapman is causing trouble with the cops?"

"Why hasn't our villain?"

"He—or she—is in the middle of the inscrutable machinations of their master plan—bwahaha? Or maybe they've been waiting for Gapman to make his big appearance? You don't suppose that shooter wasn't aiming at the crowd, but someone in the crowd?"

"At Gapman?" Grace asked. "That would assume our villain knows who he is. Kind of a stretch."

"I'm feeling flexible," I said. "Let's check out some of the places we know Gapman went to last night, in reverse order, and see if I can pick up the 'scent.' Besides, there aren't any Magicals in human form and size that can fly."

"So an empyre?" Grace said as she turned us toward City Center. The town had built up a lot since I first arrived in Los Lagos. I stuck my head out the window to admire the shop windows full of items for sale.

She answered her own question. "I suppose one could be posing as a superhero for the attention. Sounds like something Apollo might do. I also think we should ask the GSA about any magic that's passed through the Gap in the past couple of weeks. Maybe someone hired a mage in Faerie to give himself powers."

"Now who's stretching?" I rejoined. "I can only think of a few people with that kind of ability, and most would exact a heavy price."

"Like Titania?" Grace had never met the Queen of the Midsummer Court, but I'd told her tales about the mercurial fairy and her twin sister. Fondly told tales, mind you; dragons did have favorites, and exasperating as the twins could be, they commanded a soft spot in my heart and that of my own twin. "I suppose a Mundane could be desperate enough to seek her out—*could* he seek her out?"

"She'd have to want to be found, and right now, she and her kingdom will be preparing for winter. Ti hates doing anything in the cold. Still, I'll talk to her if we come up empty. Maybe I'll take Father Rich along; she's probably due a Confession."

"Give him a day to prepare himself." Grace giggled at the thought. In one of my and Father's adventures together, Father had gotten himself declared her official Confessor, and even though she'd promised to not limit herself to him, she often liked to save the "best" for him.

As we drove past the City Center Plaza, I saw Misty putting up a banner on the front of the comic book store. I caught the letters P M A N when motion caught my attention. Her ladder wobbled.

I made to jump out the window, but someone ran to her and steadied it before I could leap. Phew.

Although, I thought as we drove past, that would have been a job for Gapman.

Ron

I caught hold of the ladder just in time.

"Whoa! Thanks, Ron!" Misty said as she gripped the top step. "That was a close one."

"You really should have someone holding the ladder for you," I scolded as I took on the job myself. What was it with women and ladders?

She took hold of the center grommet of the banner and reached for the hook above the window. "I know, but I sent Nate to Colorado Springs to buy up all the gold T-shirts and green fabric he could find and Oren's inside with customers. Everyone wants superhero comics today! But we're a comic book store—we have to be on top of this."

"On top of what?" I winced as she came on her toes. "Careful!"

She ignored me, adjusting her position to stretch further. She was as bad as Mom. "Seriously, you know what happened yester– Yike!"

She wobbled and caught her balance. I couldn't take it anymore. "Get down and let me," I begged.

"I guess a couple more inches would help." Reluctantly, she descended, and we traded spots. "There's a hook just under—"

"Yeah, I know," I said as I hooked the grommet on it. "I used to do this before I went to college."

"Yeah, in England. Must have been nice."

"It was," I agreed, "but, I mean, it was cheaper, too."

"Cheaper than See-Sull?" She pronounced CSU-LL like someone who'd attended it.

"It is when you live with your aunt," I said as I descended. "It wasn't a very big university, either. So anyway, be on top of what?"

"Gapman fever, of course! I'm already kicking myself for not getting the website before someone else did. OMyGapman is brilliant, and it's already blowing up."

I snorted. "Thanks. I'll let my mom know."

"Your mom?"

"And my Aunt Matilda. Don't get me started."

"Oh! Well, if they want help, have them call me! Anyway, this is a pitiful second, but..." She pointed to the banner, which declared, "We Love You, Gapman!"

"I hope he knows," she said nervously.

My mouth worked a bit before my voice caught up. "I'm sure he does now!"

Chapter Twelve:
Gapman Gets Shadowed

Vern

After a fruitless couple of hours trying to backtrack Gapman or our potential supervillain, I left Grace at the Gap talking to the officials on both the Mundane and Faerie sides. Meanwhile, I started a flying a circuit of the city, prioritizing by population and crime potential. Maybe I'd get lucky.

I wasn't lucky. By one, my stomach was growling, and my wings were tired, so I coasted over toward the City Center to see if Natura would feed me. As I got near, I felt that odd tingle in my scales like I'd felt at the shooting, only stronger.

Figures, I should have followed my stomach all along.

The feeling stayed nebulous, seeming from several places at once, but all around Natura's, so I landed at the front and moseyed in.

Natura's hostess, Cloe, greeted me with an apology. "The Safe Space Lounge is closed for an event, but there's the quad spot if that's okay?"

The "quad spot" was a designated eating area for four-legged creatures. The table had adjustable legs so it rose to accommodate tall centaurs. Natura had gone out of her way from the beginning to make Faerie folk feel welcome. Lately, she'd taken some heat for that. I frowned at the particleboard that covered one window, broken by a brick courtesy of the RealHumans.

Regardless, the diner was filled with patrons, even though it wasn't a buffet day. School must have let out early. In addition to the usual businessmen, I saw parents with children jabbering excitedly about being Gapman for Halloween, teens bent over comic books discussing theories...even some adults also deep in conversation. Gapman, of course, was the topic.

The one outlier was Ronnie Engleson, the entertainment reporter for the *Los Lagos Gazette*, who was chowing down on a burger and working on his laptop. Owen had told me he was a big geek. Maybe he was on a deadline or something.

That feeling of odd magic was stronger, but...weirder. I'd catch a "scent," then, it'd disappear, then get strong. Did my prey have invisibility? Yeah, that would be fun.

I'd think about it after a meal.

"So, what do you think?" Cloe asked as she lowered the table to the floor. Natura and Grace—the only two people in the Mundane who always assumed I'd rather eat like a dragon.

"Whatever Natura can spare is fine."

"No, silly!" She practically bounced on her toes. "Gapman! Do you know him?"

Some of the diners turned their eyes toward me, expectant and eager.

I sighed. "Why does everyone assume I know every flying creature in Los Lagos?"

"Oh," she looked crestfallen. Had she been hoping for an autograph? "I just thought, since you're both protecting the city, he'd introduce himself or something."

I heard the sudden intake of a guilty breath to my side. I pretended to ignore it; it could have been nothing. Meanwhile, Cloe said they had some creole shrimp and jambalaya from yesterday's buffet and left. I waited patiently, feigning disinterest as I kept vigilant for furtive glances. Would Gapman dare make contact in his alter-ego?

Just as Cloe brought me my plate, apologizing because they gave the last of the shrimp to a beggar out back, the front door opened with a chime of bells, and none other than Kitty McGrue, Los Lagos Reporter and Pain in My Tail, stomped past the hostess station and to my table.

"Where is he?" she demanded.

I held back a sigh. I was not going to get to eat my jambalaya while it was warm. I looked up from my tantalizing meal to glare at Kitty McGrue. She must have caught sight of me while exiting the gym; she was in a sports bra and exercise pants. She certainly drew attention—particularly that of a certain entertainment writer two tables over.

I briefly considered chiding her about appropriate attire, but this was Natura's, where shoes were required by law, not by her. Besides, since McGrue sacrificed her safety for mine during the Shogzallie fight, we'd decided to try something new—being nice to each other.

At least, I was going to try. Sort of. "And good afternoon to you, Kitty. Where's who?"

"Who else is this whole city looking for? Gapman, and I want him!"

Two tables over, a certain entertainment writer choked on his burger. Interesting. I mean, he wasn't the only one, but others then followed up with snickers. Days like this, I was glad I had 270-degree vision as well as heightened senses. I kept my eyes on Kitty, but my attention was on Ronnie Engleson.

Kitty rolled her eyes at the diners in general. "For an interview."

"Uh, huh," I said skeptically, and heard her heart beat a little faster.

And not just hers. What was up with Engleson? Couldn't be that soda he was no longer drinking. And the way he was leaning back to listen without looking like he was leaning back to listen?

Wait. Could it be?

Maybe he just had a crush. He did perk up a bit when he first noticed her. But there was something suspicious about how he was listening/not listening.

Well, there was only one way to find out, and I hadn't toyed with a human in a long time. I was going to have fun with this.

"Why does everyone assume I know all the weird humans in this dimension?" I asked innocently.

"Oh, please! He's obviously Faerie."

"Just because the guy wears tights," I started to see if I got a rise out of Ron, but Kitty cut me off immediately.

"Because he can fly! And he's superhumanly strong and that accent and those eyes—"

"Eyes?" If I had ears that perked, they would have. Come to think of it, so would Ronnie's.

Kitty flushed slightly, hid it with annoyance. "I mean the vision! They say he can see through walls."

"Just walls?" Dragons can't lift their eyebrows, but I managed to convey my intent in my voice.

Increased temperature from two humans. Interesting.

Ronnie shifted position and pretended to be reading something on his computer.

"An interview, huh?" I mulled over the thought. "How do I know you won't take this opportunity to vilify him like J. Jonah Jameson does with Spider-man?" Yeah, I knew my superhero clichés.

"Are you kidding? He stands alone, unsullied by politics or prejudice. When he sees injustice or danger, he charges into the fray—"

"How's that so different from me? Except that I don't wear yellow spandex?"

Kitty gave the exasperated sigh that always told me so much. And if that hadn't, the slight straightening in Ronnie's spine as she'd waxed poetic about Gapman's skills had.

"Look, I'm asking as a favor. I got a deadline." She glanced at her watch, but I had the feeling another clock was ticking.

Okay. Time to play nice. "Kitty, I don't have an in with this guy. I'm pretty certain, though, he'll be finding you. You certainly asked nicely enough to meet up—for an interview."

"Fine. This was a big help." She stormed off, passing her co-worker without even noticing he was there. Ronnie made a point of concentrating on his burger, but I saw his head rise slightly to see her from through the window as she crossed the street.

You've no idea, McGrue. You've no idea.

I dug into my meal, watching Engleson with my peripheral vision while looking at nothing in particular. Just a dragon getting sustenance; nothing to see here.

In the kitchen, I heard the cooks discussing the weird bum they'd just fed. "Did you see the turban? He was like a swami or something. Too bad Natura isn't here today."

One of the other cooks was protesting that it looked like a head injury all bandaged up. "He did seem kind of brain damaged, the way he was talking to himself."

Ronnie, meanwhile, finished his burger and left after paying with his card. I saw his waiter smile; Ronnie must be a big tipper. I gave him a head start to see if anyone left the restaurant or emerged from the alley to follow him. Somehow, I got the feeling that, superpowers or no, Ronnie Engleson was not the kind to notice a tail.

I dropped a tip of my own on the table and left, walking past the parking lot just as my supersuspect was putting a key into a battered and mud-splattered Subaru. I didn't know whether to be insulted or pleased that he didn't notice the 12-foot scarlet-and-black dragon ambling past. I was disappointed, though; I'd been hoping for a challenge.

I guess I shouldn't take the easy jobs for granted—and there was the chance, however slim, that I was wrong. I took to the skies, landing on the roof and watching as he drove out of town, and followed him for a long, boring drive into the mountains. He turned on a sideroad, weather-worn and potholed. Guess it led to his house.

Once he'd left the car and entered the house, calling for his mom, I landed and found myself a nice resting spot where I could see the road and sky without being easily seen myself. I figured I'd be there for a while, but was surprised when only a few minutes later, he came back to the road, lugging a boulder almost as big as I was. He hauled it to a pothole and dropped it, stretched his back—and then pounded it with gloved fists.

The rock shattered into pieces.

He kept breaking up the smaller rocks until he had a pile of pebbles, which he then raked at superspeed over the road, filling in the potholes.

I waited until he went for the next boulder and left. On the way to Father Rich's, I called Grace.

"I found him," I reported. "Tell you about it when you get home."

"Wonderful! Did you talk to him?"

"Nah. He was busy doing chores. But I know where to find him later tonight."

Ron

As I reached for the next boulder, I paused. What was that rustling? It sounded big—like an elk or a bear—and near the house.

Rather than run from the quarry, I called Mom to report my suspicions.

"Funny. Bears don't usually come so near the house. I wonder if that Shogzallie incident has them changing their territories," she said. "Want me to get the rifle and cover you?"

"I have superspeed, Mom. I'll be fine. Just be careful if you leave the house." Reluctantly, she agreed, and we hung up. I hefted the biggest rock I could handle and ran – awkwardly—at superspeed to the next spot on the road that needed filling. After a couple of cool, rainy days, the weather had warmed up again. We might be able to fix our road before the snows came.

Mom would love to bag a bear, but the truth was, I wanted to be alone. I needed to think. I was going to have to do this interview with Kitty. I mean, I practically told her how to invite me. But I hadn't meant it to come off as so...romantic.

I could almost pass it off as a strategic move to make herself look less threatening, but the way she blushed when Vern teased her. Was she into me—into Gapman, I mean? Could this be the start of a Lois Lane-Superman relationship?

What she said about my eyes... I know she tried to pretend she was talking about my X-ray vision, but I knew she was lying. She had that crinkle along her nostrils she got when someone called her on her BS. Did she really see my eyes, or was it an eye/mask thing? If she looked into my eyes, would she realize it was me behind the mask?

Boy, I'd love to stare deep into her eyes. She was so beautiful—and strong and fiery, and I hadn't had a date in...

I slammed my hands against the boulder. Break the rocks. I needed to break the rocks and think about the interview. My first interview as Gapman. I had to stay professional...

What should I tell her? What could I tell her? She was so good at her job; she'd know when I was prevaricating. But I could hardly tell her the details of my origin story—not only did they point directly at me, but they were so stupid! I slipped on the railing and fell into toxic waste? I grabbed a radioactive pixie and he bit me? I got hit by lightning because I panicked and ran through the Gap when it was closed for a weather experiment?

Yeah, that would impress her. She wouldn't even need to know I was at the theater to guess it was me. Loser.

I let my dark mood fuel me as I obliterated more rocks, then forced myself to clear my head and work on something constructive. I had to finish before the sun got low, then change into uniform. I had a dinner date—er, interview—with Kitty tonight.

Chapter Thirteen: Gapman Meets His Lois Lane

Ron

The road ready for paving, I went inside and took a long shower, practicing the lines I'd prepared. Then I rewatched the Christopher Reeves Lois Lane/Superman interview scene and did a little research on how to stop blushing. Relax the neck—check. Imagine jumping into an ice-cold lake—check. Imagine people in their underwear? What? How could they think that imaging Kitty in her underwear would...

Deep breath. Relax the neck. Ice-cold lake.

I donned my uniform, pulling on the new gloves Mom had made, and then it was time.

When Kitty had said, "K marks the spot," she'd meant it literally. There was a huge K in reflective sheets taped to her roof. It was kind of thoughtful, especially considering I could have looked up her address if I'd needed to.

As could anyone else.

I arrived to find Kitty standing on her porch shaking a broom threateningly at a crowd of guys all dressed in approximations of my suit. Yellow T-shirts and green or cammo pants. Tablecloths for capes. One portly guy in a Mexican wrestling outfit of blue and gold with a huge eagle on the chest, his bushy mustache peeking out from his mask. They all claimed to be Gapman—except Lucha Libre. He was declaring himself to be a superior lover to "the skinny fairy *gringito*."

I hovered, torn between guilt and the desire to laugh as she cussed and ordered them all off her yard. A few actually tried to protest that they were the real Gapman. Lucha Libre put his foot on her step, hands out entreatingly, and got a slap of plastic bristles for his efforts.

Yeah, maybe when I was Ron again, I should apologize for the trouble my suggestion caused.

Suddenly someone pointed, "Look! Up in the air! It's Gapman!"

My cue! What should I say? Gotta be pleasant but firm... Remember the accent...

I crossed my arms and smiled at the gaping crowd. "They say imitation is a kind of compliment, and while I appreciate it, perhaps you should leave Miz McGrue alone?"

They scattered like birds, running down the sidewalk, climbing into cars. One even jumped the neighbor's fence and got yelled at by the elderly homeowner. She grabbed him by the ear and dragged into the house with him protesting, "But Grandma!"

Meanwhile, Kitty raced roaring down the stairs, swinging at the wrestler who had paused to blow her a kiss. He took off laughing. He was surprisingly swift for his weight.

"Next time, it will be hot lead instead of straw!" she yelled at his retreating back.

"You carry?" I blurted. At least I remembered the accent.

"Gapman!" she yelped as she spun my way, as if she'd forgotten I was there. Her hand went to her hair. Then she realized she was still holding the broom. She made a halfhearted attempt to put it behind her back, then rolled her eyes and sighed. "I'm so sorry you had to see that."

I lowered myself gently to land on the grass in front of her. "Not at all. It can't be easy to have fans."

She shrugged. "Well, you *are* a superhero."

Feeling bold, I took a step forward. "I meant you."

"Oh."

Our eyes locked and held. How many times had I dreamed of this moment? Did she see who I was? I didn't notice any signs of recognition, just that frank admiration. I really wanted her to know it was me. How did superheroes keep their identities secret?

Finally, I broke the silence. "So, do you?"

"Do I want what?" She was almost breathless.

"Own a firearm?" Maybe I could ask her shooting one day. That'd probably be her kind of first date, something casual...

She started to cover her face with her hands, then realized again she held the broom. "Oh, gosh, you must think I'm terrible! But—"

"Not at all, Miz McGrue. The Second Amendment is a fundamental American right."

Like I'd flipped some kind of switch in her, her eyes lost their starriness, and the reporter returned. "You're American, then?"

Oops! "I'd...prefer to think of myself as a citizen of the multiverse—but I respect the laws of the land."

She smirked. "In other words, you don't want to give any hints to your identity."

I nodded. That's when I noticed the neighbors watching from their homes—including one Gapman imposter peeking his phone over his wooden fence. "Perhaps we should continue this interview in private? Unless you want our conversation posted to MeTube."

I jerked my chin toward the fence. The phone went down fast, but not fast enough.

"Gary! Get in your house!" McGrue shouted, then caught herself. "I'm so sorry, Gapman. I'm making a terrible first impression. No wonder you didn't want to talk to me the other night."

"My apologies. I... It was more that I wasn't sure what to say. There must be a lot of questions about me."

We headed toward the house. It was cute and homey—somehow, I'd expected something more, I don't know, minimalist and modern, like you'd expect a big New York City reporter to live. That, or piled high with papers, dirty coffee cups, and food wrappers like her cubicle.

"This is delightful," I said.

"It's just a porch," she said.

Oops! In my excitement, I'd used X-ray vision. "Oh, sorry. I meant inside the house. You know, X-ray vision..."

Did that sound pompous? That sounded pompous. Get it together, Gapman!

Fortunately, Kitty just snickered as she opened the door. "X-ray vision, huh? Should I be concerned? Maybe I should change into my lead corset?"

Deep breath. Relax the shoulders. Ice cold lake. Witty reply—there had to be a witty reply!

Her hands flew to her mouth, and she almost smacked herself with the broom handle again. She tossed it away, flustered. "Gah! I'm so sorry. I did not mean to embarrass you."

"No, it's fine. I... Why would you have a lead corset?"

"I don't...yet."

I wanted to return her sly smile. I wanted to tease her that she'd brought me here to flirt. Instead, I looked away and cleared my throat.

She let out a shaky sigh and motioned for me to enter. "Wow. Sorry. I'm not being especially professional. I—sorry. Look, have a seat, and I'll get us something. I mean, I promised you dinner. Oh, um— you do eat?"

I had intended to quote Christopher Reeves in *Superman*, about eating when I'm hungry, but what came out was. "Definitely. I'm always hungry. Super-fied metabolism. Um, it smells fantastic."

"Oh, that's interesting!" She paused at the dining room table to type that into her laptop, then moved on to the kitchen. I took a seat. Along with the laptop and table settings were candles and a bottle of wine.

"Help yourself to the wine," she called.

"I don't drink and fly." Now I did quote Reeves, but really, I was thinking about the last time I drank when I was nervous. I ended up quoting *The Velveteen Rabbit* and getting on my knees to beg the most beautiful girl in the room to "make me real." Since the girl was not my date, that night had ended badly. Who knew what tipsy me might do in front of Kitty? I didn't know if I could get drunk, but why take a chance?

She came in carrying a tray in each hand. "I hope you like lasagna. I didn't know if you were vegetarian, so..."

My stomach rumbled. Mom and I usually barbe-qued. "I'll take some of both!"

She put two large squares on my plate, and I added a large helping of salad. Gapman's manners, I de-cided, should go with the accent, so I held my fork on the left, tines down.

"Don't you want to take off your gloves?" Kitty asked.

I shook my head. "Fingerprints. Pardon my rudeness, but I have to protect my secret identity."

"What about DNA?" she asked as I sipped my water.

I shrugged. "I doubt mine is on file anywhere, so unless you have the budget to compare it to every man in Los Lagos and the surrounding areas, including Faerie..."

She nodded. "Good point. Do you live in the area, then?"

"Within flying distance." I'd anticipated this question.

She tsked with annoyance. "All right. I'm not asking directions to the Secret Sanctum. So let me guess: you're six-two and weigh... one-sixty?"

"Perceptive!" I was actually six-foot and weighed 145 soaking wet, but I wasn't going to argue about the upgrade.

"Are you married?"

Dang! Had she watched the Lois Lane/Superman interview scene? "No."

"Girlfriend?"

Superman had used this as a chance to flirt, but suddenly, repeating Reeve's lines felt disingenuous. What would Gapman say? I set my silverware down, my hands flat on either side of my plate. "Miz McGrue, if I were in a relationship, I would not be having dinner with you now."

There—honest with a hint of flirty. I was getting better at this.

She grinned, and I wondered if she was thinking about her interview with Alistair. I hoped so. I wanted her to know she was worth true loyalty.

"Bulletproof?"

I thought about the assassination attempt I'd stopped against Alistair. "Mostly."

"Impervious to pain?"

"Reasonably."

"How sensitive are you, then? Can you feel this?"

Her bare foot caressed my calf.

I started to yelp and quickly cleared my throat to hide it. *Relax the neck. Ice cold lake...* "Very much so."

"And this?"

She jabbed her fork at my hand. Only superspeed enabled me to avoid getting speared in the hand.

The tines dug half a centimeter into the wood.

There was no hiding my reaction now. I gaped at the utensil.

"Sorry," she said in a tone that was half-embarrassed but not remorseful. "I'm an investigative reporter. I don't take anyone at their word."

"No kidding." I blinked, struggling for something Gapmanish to say. Then I had a vision of the guy in the Lucah Libre outfit sitting in my place, eyes wide and screaming through his mustache, a fork sticking out of his hand.

I snickered.

"What?"

I ducked my head and waved my hand dismissively. Gapman would never be so mean. Ronnie was never this mean. But Ron was imagining him screaming while Kitty scolded him that it served him right. I couldn't stop chuckling.

"What?"

I knew that tone. She would not let up until I said something. I took a breath. "I was just thinking, those imposters got off easy with the broom."

Now she laughed. "I guess I can be intense."

"Intense is splendid. I'm sorry about your table." I pulled out the fork and handed it back to her. "But most likely, you'd have bent your fork on my glove.

And before you ask: No, I will not let you shoot me. Perhaps this will suffice: Yesterday, I was bitten multiple times by an angry chihuahua."

I pulled off my glove and presented my hand to Kitty for her to examine.

She took it in both of hers and examined it closely. "Not even a bruise. Did it hurt?"

"Enough to notice, but nothing debilitating. I spent the day crushing rocks, too." I regretted the words as soon as I said them. How stupid was I, mentioning chores? What if she went asking around? At least the paving company we'd hired to finish the work wasn't in Los Lagos.

But her hands felt so nice caressing mine. I had to steel myself against caressing hers back.

"That's an unusual workout. Were you preventing a landslide somewhere, then?" When I didn't answer, she said, "Your hands are so soft."

Was that good? "Uh, superhealing, I suppose."

"It's nice." She threaded her fingers between mine. She smiled shyly at me.

I felt my heart race. Look in my eyes, Kitty. Look in my eyes and realize who I really am.

This time, she was the one to clear her throat and pull away. She pushed her empty plate aside and set the laptop in front of her. As she typed, she said, "All right. I believe you—about the healing. So, X-ray vision. Can you tell me the contents of my bathroom counter?"

And so it went: I answered what I could about my abilities, guessing at some, like how fast I could fly, avoiding anything that might hint at my identity, and answering the rest with Gapman's charming honesty. As I finished my second helpings of everything (gloves back on, of course), she said, "Last two questions: Why are you here?"

"Excellent food and delightful company?" I quipped. She responded with a skeptical smirk that went straight through my heart, but I knew she was not going to be satisfied with a flirt. "It's self-explanatory. I've been given a gift, and with that comes a responsibility. I'm here to help. It's that simple."

"No fighting for Truth, Justice, and the American Way?"

I pushed my empty plate away and leaned my crossed arms on the table. "Are you saying my mission statement needs work?" I teased.

She snickered and typed a single word on her computer. I wished I could use X-ray vision to see the words on her screen. "So these powers were a gift? From whom?"

"I meant in the metaphorical sense. The truth is, I'm not sure how I came by these powers. I simply woke up with them."

"What?" she pounced upon my half-truth. "Were you part of an experiment? Have you taken any strange medications or visited some Faerie mage or something?"

I shook my head. "Nothing so extraordinary. I'm a normal lad who was given an amazing gift, and I'm trying to use it in a way that benefits all the good people in our community."

I saw her throat tighten reflexively.

"Look," I said, "I know that sounds cheesy, but that's how I feel. And I think more people feel that way than we realize. It's easy to focus on the negatives in life, on the people that want to do you harm. But I believe most people are simply trying to do their best not just for themselves, but for those around them. It doesn't take superpowers, just a willingness to say, 'Today, I'll do good.'"

She glared at me, skeptically at first, then searchingly. "Holy crap. You really believe that."

I shrugged. "I don't think I'm the only one. I'm just the only one with superpowers right now."

She pushed her laptop aside and rested her chin on her hands. "You know, I think you are pretty intense in your own way. "

"Thank you." I liked the compliment—and the warmth in her voice. A part of me hoped she'd rub my leg again. I could invite her for a flight, take her in my arms... She'd tell me again that I was intense...

And then, that happy thought popped like a balloon. She thought *Gapman* was intense. Me? What had she said about me? Sure, Ronnie is nice. Scrambled eggs are nice, too, and about as exciting.

Did I want a Superman/Lois Lane romance?

I pushed away from the table. "This has been wonderful, Miz McGrue—"

"Kitty."

"Kitty. But I'm sure you have a deadline..."

There was some awkwardness as she escorted me to the door.

"I suppose I'll be seeing you around?" she said.

The hope in her voice called to me. I took her hand and gallantly kissed it. "I'm sure you will," I promised.

Then I bounded off the porch and launched myself into the sky. As I rose past the rooftops, I heard her cuss. She'd forgotten to take photos.

Vern

I thought he'd never leave.

From where I lurked behind a neighbor's chimney, I watched as Gapman gallantly kissed Kitty's hand, signaling the end of one of the most awkward dinner conversations I'd had the misfortune of eavesdropping on. It might have helped if they'd decided ahead of time whether this was an interview or a date. Personally, I'd have preferred the latter; as it was, I learned only slightly more than I could have figured out from all the videos I'd seen.

The yelp was interesting, though. What had Kitty done to make Gapman cry out like that? Then again, maybe I didn't want to know.

He shot up past the clouds, then headed west, casting a rocket-like shadow that would get him shot at if he flew over military airspace. Not that it lasted that long; even super lung capacity could only handle that little oxygen for a short time. I gave him a 5-count then started after him, grumbling to myself.

Keep him away from our sting... If you can convince him to relocate back across the Gap, better.

Santry's words came back to me. "Relocate." Right. Even if he was from Faerie—which the "interview" confirmed for me was not the case—the last time I ran someone out of town on my tail, people came after me with pitchforks.

Well, not pitchforks really. But pitchforks would have been easier. Then it would have been clear self-defense, right?

Besides, Grace had another idea. She wanted to adopt him and train him up. Which meant, I'd train him up.

"It'll be good for us—all of us," she'd wheedled. "Imagine how much faster we could search for other proto-empyre."

I'd reluctantly agreed—if I thought he was trainable and if I could train him my own way. After his talk with Kitty, I had mixed feelings. He seemed sincere, but good intentions were not enough. Santry was right: he had a lot of weaknesses, including insecurity and indecision.

Speaking of... I caught music floating on the wind. "Kryptonite" by 3 Doors Down. Sheesh, could he be more obvious? I turned my nose toward the east side. By the time I caught up to him, Rob Zombie was howling through Gapman's ear pods.

There were so many straightforward ways I could do this, but even half-again pay isn't compensation enough. I was going to have fun. I swooped under him, almost brushing his superbelly with my spikes.

"Yeeargh!" he cried, accent and heroic demeanor forgotten. He jerked upward, arms pinwheeling and legs flailing. Yep. Very heroic.

"What do you call a superhero who loses his balance at 2,000 feet?" I asked.

"What are you doing?" he cried.

I snorted derisively. "That the best you got, Gapman? Where's your accent?"

He glided toward me, hands out placatingly. "Have I done something to offend you?" he asked—with the accent, I might add.

I corkscrewed around him head to feet, then pushed on his boot so that he spun horizontally until he was facing me again. He recovered faster this time, even letting out a very British, "Oi!"

"Offensive? Know what's offensive? A pretender on my turf!"

"'Pretender'? Take it back!" he yelled.

I tried not to laugh. I'd seen the comment "die die die pretender" on one of the MeTube videos of him. It didn't matter that it was signed by some costumed joke named THE Fuchsia Raccoon from Pasadena. I knew the name would hurt.

"Don't like it, Pretender? A pretty new costume doesn't make you a hero, Tarpman. Show me what you've got!"

"As you wish!" he shouted, then sped toward me.

I twisted out of his way and grabbed him with my tail before he went zooming into the sunset. "Quoting *Princess Bride*? Inconceivable! Gotta do better than that!" I teased, then released him and sped away, muscles and magic straining until the buildings were a blur and the highway lines merged into one long streak. I flew low and headed toward the nearest mountains, following the curvy road at top speed.

I had to give him credit; he caught up to me as Rob Zombie gave way to Soulja Boy. I braked hard and swiped his smartphone as he flew past.

"Hey!" He banked and came round for another pass, arm out. A passing semi blared its horn, even though Gapman missed him by feet. Still, I added situational awareness to my list of training objectives.

I flapped to the right while I used my tail to flip through his favorites. "Does your mother know you listen to that?"

Surprise made him stop instead of pressing his advantage. Not that he had an advantage, but still; it's the principle. We'd have to work on that. "What's wrong with 'Superman'?"

"Other than he's using it as a verb? 'Danger Zone!' There's a song worth flying to."

"Give it back!"

I shrugged. "No problem. Ready to catch?"

His face clouded with self-doubt, but he held his hands out like a baseball player.

I let it drop, then shot straight up into the air.

"Gah!" He dove after it.

"Three dimensions! You have to think in three dimensions!" I shouted as I folded my wings and dove after him. Just before we hit the trees, I snagged his phone with my claw and yanked his earbuds off with my tail.

His yelp turned into a cry of pain as he and the local foliage got personal.

Ouch! "Gapman'd that birch," I muttered and snickered.

I wove through the trees, then headed for the river. He wasn't far behind. I splashed him with my tail. He sputtered the first time, but dodged the second time, gaining height. Good. He can be taught.

"What game are you playing?" he demanded.

"Not a game! A dance. Catch!" I threw the phone, hard, toward the trees. This time, Gapman went in low and just as I was about to snag the prize, he puffed hard and blew it out of my reach. I had to twist hard to keep from colliding with the pines.

"Better!" I shouted, but he'd caught the phone and started back to town.

"Oh, no, you don't!" I snagged him with my claws and rose.

"I don't want to hurt you!" he warned.

I just laughed. "Give it your best shot, Yorkshire-Boi!"

He pried himself out of my claws, grabbed my foot and swung.

Or tried to. He completely forgot that in the air he had no leverage. So his knowledge came from movies. Meanwhile, I had a nice long tail with about 800 pounds of dragon bulk to lever against. I demonstrated by grabbing him with my tail and flinging him away.

Oops, too hard. Gapman smacked against the rocky cliff and bounced off. I caught him and set him on the cliff edge, settling myself beside him. He rubbed the back of his head, wincing.

I settled down beside him. "You okay?"

He started to flop his hands, then decided crossing his arms looked more heroic. Actually, it didn't look half bad, except that the cape wound around his legs and he kicked at it impatiently. "Would you please explain what's going on? This isn't like you, Vern—I mean, based on your reputation."

Despite everything, he kept the accent up. He caught on quick. Now that things had calmed, he probably realized how important keeping his identity hidden was, even from me.

May as well take one stress off him. "Oh, this isn't like you either, Ronnie."

Ronnie blanched. "It's Ron—wait! How did you know?"

"Wisdom of the ages, remember? And you could use some. Can you fly?"

"Yeah. I'll be fine. Superhealing. I'll feel it for a couple of hours, though." He rotated his shoulder.

"Grace'll heal you up. Come on. She's waiting for us in our lair." I rose and stretched.

"What? Why?"

"Because the Powers-That-Be have not been impressed by your Super-SNAFUism; and because, my young padawan, my partner has decided it's best for all concerned if we took you under our wing and raised you in the ways of the Force. Or at least how to use your powers for good without messing up everyone else's efforts in the process. Let's go! Grace is making chicken. You may have had a big dinner, but I've missed mine." I gave my tired wings a long flap. It was a good tired. It had been a long time since I danced dragon-style. Maybe Grace didn't have such a bad idea.

Gapman launched himself off the cliff and followed. "I love chicken!"

"Yeah? After the performance you've been giving, we got you ham."

"Funny. And it's aspen."

"What?"

He pointed down at a white-barked tree with rounded leaves. "It's aspen, not birch."

"Oh, did I say that out loud?" I batted my eyes at him. He corkscrewed around me and his cape slapped me in the face.

Nickelback started playing, "Hero."

Chapter Fourteen:
Gapman Gains a Mentor

Ron

I could hardly believe it. Vern wanted to train me?

Vern led me past the ruined and abandoned Tok-neo to the artificial mountain. The destroyed amusement park atop it looked forlorn and a little spooky in the fading light, but he dove down one side to a walled framework of a house that was dug into the mountain itself. We landed on the road in front of it, and he led me in. As soon as he opened the door, I could smell the roasting chicken. I'd controlled my appetite at Kitty's with only two helpings; now, my stomach growled in protest.

Vern cocked his head at me.

"Super metabolism," I said.

He snorted, then entered first. With a shrug, I followed. I felt a shiver wash over me. "Uh. What was that?"

Vern stopped and gave me a funny look. "What was what?"

When I explained, he grunted. "Grace has a protection shield over the lair. I didn't know you could feel magic."

"Maybe see it, too. Kind of." I explained how other Magicals had looked to me. "But I didn't notice it in the house."

"You shouldn't. What good is a shield spell that advertises itself? Come on."

He led me down a narrow stone hallway, calling, "Look what I found. I'm not sure we can afford to keep him, though. His grocery bills are going to be astronomical."

I stopped and gaped, but he kept on walking.

The hallway opened up to an immense room. I'd call it a cave, but it seemed too luxurious. There was a huge rectangular hole to one side and a round circle on the other side. Both were covered, but did they have an inside pool and hot tub? Maybe they were living better than I'd been led to believe.

Grace was sitting on a cushion in front of the fireplace, where two chickens were turning on a spit, the fat dripping onto the cut potatoes below. She stood up and held out both hands in welcome. "Ronnie! Or do you prefer 'Ron'? It's alright. You may speak freely here. And if you'd like, you can remove your mask and relax a little."

I liked her immediately. "Ron, please, and thank you, Sister."

We sat on the floor for a meal of roasted chicken and potatoes with a salad made of what looked like wild greens.

"I picked them while we were away this weekend," she said. "I'm so sorry we missed your coming out. Did Vern explain that your actions had some unexpected consequences?"

I took the plate she handed to me. "He said some people weren't happy about it, but..."

Vern was already tearing at a full chicken with claws and teeth. "I figured we'd share the details here, where we know we won't be overheard. First, though, I want to hear how you got these powers in the first place."

It was so nice to tell someone other than Mom my origin story...at least until Vern started laughing.

"Vurnerrah!" Sister Grace scolded. "I'm sure it was terrifying!"

"Maybe then. But now? Hilarious. Okay, then, Splashman: You woke up the next morning with superpowers. What did you do?"

I winced, anticipating more laughter. "Chores? I mean, we were kind of figuring out what I could do. Oh, we sort of found out I was mostly bulletproof when Mom shot me—"

"What?" Grace cried, and Vern choked on a potato before bursting into renewed laughter.

I hurried ahead, "And I found out I had X-ray vision when I went to rescue Duncan and saw that shooter on the second floor."

"That was you?" Grace said. Vern stopped laughing.

"I didn't mean to hit him that hard!" I exclaimed. I did not want her thinking I was some kind of antihero like Venom. Just the thought of her looking at me with disappointment tore my heart.

Ironically, it was Vern who reassured me, if you could call it that. He set his tail on my shoulders. "That, Wrecking Ball, is why we're going to mentor you—that and teaching you how not to get in the police's way."

And then, the mortifications began. When Vern finished telling me all the investigations I'd ruined by what I'd thought were heroic acts, I'd lost my appetite. "Wrecking Ball" was right. I groaned.

Then again, "On the bright side, I did stop someone from shooting Alistair Kane." I told them about how I'd caught the bullet.

"Are you certain he was aiming for Alistair?" Grace said. "Then why didn't he try again at the hotel?"

"The assassin went to the hotel?" I said. How could I have missed that? I really was bad at this.

"Someone saw a guy hanging out in a tree," Vern explained. "She said he was a crazy guy in a tarp talking to squirrels but... What? Oh, seriously. You?"

My red face said it all. Could this get any worse?

That's when Vern said, "So then the assassin might have been targeting you after all."

"What?" It was my turn to choke. "Target, me?"

But they were continuing the conversation without me. Grace said, "How much sense does that make, though, when Gapman hadn't shown himself yet?"

"Why would someone shoot me?" I racked my brain. Was it a review I wrote? I did call Mortimer Dryer's latest thriller "pedestrian," but would he fly all the way from London to shoot me?

Vern tapped his claws as he thought. "True. Up until yesterday, Gapman didn't exist, just the Tarped Terror."

"Hey!"

"Squirrel Whisperer?"

How could he joke at a time like this? "Can we get back to someone trying to kill me? Why would somebody want me dead? I'm even nice to the guys who used to bully me in school."

"So who knows you're Gapman?"

"You guys. My mom—and she already shot me once, and it was just a BB-gun." Wow—who knew my mom shooting me would become an alibi later?

"Well, what if they weren't trying to kill you?" Grace asked.

Vern cocked his head. "Testing his powers? Or maybe not sure if he *has* powers! I think we need to have a talk with Snapdragon."

"The stage manager?" I said. "But he didn't do this to me. The scaffolding broke..." But I'd been leaning on it only minutes before, and it had seemed sturdy enough. No. "Come on. No one could have predicted everything that happened."

"Don't underestimate a fairy," Vern told me. "Still, maybe he didn't need to have all the other things happen. Maybe he thought the vat was enough. Or maybe he got to wondering."

"Still, a fairy with a sniper rifle?" Grace asked. "It seems more likely he'd simply spy on Ron until he did something super—which you have been doing a lot of lately, even out of uniform."

"Speaking of," Vern said. "There are a few things we're adding to your training regime."

"Vern," Grace chided. "We agreed, no *Karate Kid*-style training. The lair will be finished soon enough. Besides, I think he does enough of that for his mother."

"Mom!" I was supposed to call her after the dinner—er, interview—to tell her how it went. Kitty probably had an article up by now. I dug into my pack to text her. Yep. I already had a half-dozen texts, including a photo.

How about that? Mom shot the bear.

Vern

"What?" I said, not because I hadn't heard, but because I could not believe what I was hearing.

"Yeah," he said as he texted her a reply—a thumbs-up to her photo. "I thought I heard something in the woods by our house, so before I left, I told her—hey!"

I'd snagged his phone out of his hands. Yep. There it was: a photo with her and the bear, followed by some texts about not worrying about coming home to help; she'd already called a friend ("and don't judge me")...

While he glared at me, I said, "You know, when I made the crack about your mom, I didn't think I was hitting that close to the mark."

His frown deepened. "Just because I have a good relationship with my mother..."

Did he think I was mocking him? Wow. Way to miss the point. "Which I know all about now," I said as I dramatically scrolled through his text history. "Aw, look. Your mom wants to know how things went with *Gapman* and Kitty."

I had to give him credit: When the implication hit, he paled.

"I'm an idiot! All this work to hide my identity and I've been carrying it in my belt! Aargh!" He folded over and buried his head in his hands. "I'm so stupid!"

"You're inexperienced," Grace soothed, "and perhaps a little naïve? But we can help with that."

"We'll get you a burner phone," I said. "One for your mom, too, but only if she takes on an alter-ego.

No more personal stuff while you're on duty. Definitely no more emojis."

I held out the phone with the text from earlier. *Hope your interview is going well.* She'd bracketed "interview" between kissing emojis. Maybe I should let her know it was mostly painful innuendo and openings from Kitty that Gapman utterly failed to recognize.

"Okay." He sighed, then brightened. "We can come up with some code phrases, maybe an alert word. Yeah, okay. What else?"

"What do you know about police procedures?" Grace asked.

He shrugged. "I just thought I'd be saving people, stopping crimes before they happen? Guess I'm not that helpful, after all."

"Don't sell yourself short," Grace said. "I'm certain we could have used your help battling Shogzallie."

His eyes widened.

"We can work up to that," she said. "How about we start by finding out exactly what you can do? Flying—"

"Needs practice," I interjected.

Grace scowled at me. "Aye—and do ye remember pacing the length of the warehouse until you were steady on two human feet?"

Since I was no longer in human form, I couldn't cross my arms over my chest. I did the next best thing, wrapping my tail around my legs and pouting. "It was the boots."

"Of course it was," she condescended and turned back to Gapman. "We'll be finding a way for you to practice all your skills; don't worry about that. Can you see magic? Kind of a haze or a color you can't quite define, perhaps? It would be stronger around Vern than me, and even less so with Mundanes."

He just about squealed in delight. "So that's really what that is, then? That is so awesome! I kind of felt something...tickly...when we passed through the shields."

Grace frowned thoughtfully. "You shouldn't have noticed anything at all."

"I think the shields don't like him," I teased.

Grace tsked comfortingly. "More likely, they didn't know what to do about your magic, but if you passed through unscathed, then your intentions are pure."

"And if they weren't?" Ron asked nervously.

"They would have knocked you out cold, and you'd wake up questioning your life choices," I said. "Don't worry about it. You're fine."

"Could be useful, too. X-ray vision: There are several levels to the mountain above us. How many can you see into?"

We were going to have to work on his super-squint, I could tell.

Ron

What a day.

I flew home more tired today than I'd been after dashing around town saving people. I was brain-fried, overwhelmed, and full of mixed feelings. My wildest dreams were coming true—and I was screwing it all up. I could almost feel my phone burning through my belt, my complete identity and a map to everyone I loved just waiting for someone to snag it as easily as Vern had. Twice.

Then again, did any of that matter if someone already suspected me? Could someone have been trying to shoot me to test my superpowers? Did my mom have a doppelganger? It seemed too unreal. I could more easily believe someone was upset about an article or a book review I'd written. Authors could get so protective of their works...

Besides, the only ones who could even suspect I had powers were people from the theater. Grace and Vern had said they'd see if anyone from the cast and crew of Captain Extraordinary had crossed the Gap. In the meantime, I was going to call Dorsch and make a few discreet inquiries of my own. As Ronnie, I could certainly ask for an update on how the cast was doing after the accident and what plans there were for the play. It'd be a good follow-up to Dorsch's cryptic text from earlier.

Investigations. I sighed. I'd messed up two just on my first day. I thought I was helping people, but instead, I'd put more people in danger. I was so stupid—

It's not stupidity. It's ignorance. I could hear Sister Grace's voice in my head. Ignorance can be remedied.

In a string bag under my cape were a book on police procedures and *Private Investigations for Beginners*. I guess I should have thought of that. After all, Batman studied law and criminology at Yale and had investigative lessons from a famous mercenary, too. I guess Vern was my Henri Ducard.

Suddenly, my glum mood was replaced by a flutter of excitement. I was being mentored by a *dragon*! Even better, he would not turn out to be a villain in a surprising plot twist like Ducard.

Okay—so it was an awkward first few days. I made some mistakes, but no one was actually hurt. Well, except that one gang member, but Grace said he was recovering and Vern seemed more annoyed that he was getting the blame than worried about the guy's health. I have people to teach me now. I can learn.

Plus, people were excited about Gapman. When I left the lair (the actual dragon's lair—I got happy chills at the thought), I'd taken a minute to scan Kitty's article. *Strong in conviction as well as physical prowess, with a disarming charm and genuine humility...*

I could do this. I *would* do this. I'd become the hero that Los Lagos—that the Mundane!- deserved.

Good thing I'd changed before approaching the house. My superhearing had picked up her and Aunt Matilda laughing—no, *giggling*—before I'd gotten in sight of the house, and "Oh, my Gapman!" had been cried out time or two.

"Mom! I'm home!" I called loudly so she would have time to cover her tracks. There were just some things a son did not need to know.

Unfortunately, Mom didn't always grasp boundaries.

"We're in the kitchen! We've got something to show you."

"Oh, my Gapman!" Matilda called out and tittered.

My heart leaped into my throat. Had Mom divulged our secret? No. No, she wouldn't do that. Something else was going on. I stowed my backpack containing my supersuit and books in the back of the closet and then made my way to the kitchen.

I found the two at the kitchen table huddled together in front of Mom's laptop, expressions of absolute glee on their faces. Matilda looked mostly recovered from her encounter with the police at the book signing, although I could still see the bruise under her makeup from where she'd gotten into a fight with a RealHuman while in a cell waiting for Mom to bail her out. Mom had said when she got there, Aunt Matilda was sitting on her attacker, and at 215 pounds, she'd had him pinned good even without her wrestling experience.

Now, she overflowed the kitchen chair and was pushed close to Mom, but Mom didn't care.

Mom looked up with a smile. "So? How was your *date*?" She sing-songed the word the way she used to when I was a kid.

I was hardly going to remind her in front of Matilda that Kitty was interviewing Gapman, so I said, "Don't expect grandkids anytime soon."

I opened the fridge. I was starving again. This was going to become a problem, groceries-wise.

"Lenny cooked you a bear steak," Mom said.

"Lenny?" I shut the refrigerator door, catching myself before I slammed with superstrength or bent the handle with my grip.

Even so, Mom noticed. She gave me a sharp look. "Well, you were busy, and you know you can't let bear meat wait. I had to get help, and Lenny hunts. You know that. He took you when you were ten."

"Yeah, and shot his own foot because he'd been drinking. I had to half-drag him out of the woods until we could get cell reception."

"He's still grateful about that, you know. At any rate, I was the one with the rifle tonight. He just helped me get it into his truck, and we took it to the taxidermist. We have a freezer full of meat, and we'll have the most beautiful blanket. I let Lenny have the head as thanks. Now, quit pouting and put that steak in the oven to warm up while you see what we did."

Holding back a sigh, I did as told. Soon, I was standing behind them, a sports drink in hand. I almost spat out my drink all over them when I saw what was on the screen. "OMyGapman.com?"

"Yes!" Matilda said with pride. "We've officially started the first official fan club for Gapman! Isn't it great? We've got a home page, a database for Gapman sightings, a blog, and a forum. What do you think?"

I let her flip through the pages while I tried to craft an appropriate reply. This was great—my first fan club. Founded by my mother and her friend who helped raise me.

Aunt Matilda sensed my hesitation and drew her own conclusions. "I know, it's a little rough, but we had to hurry so we could be the first."

"It's important for keeping our finger on the pulse of public opinion, not to mention controlling the narrative," Mom said wisely. I picked up the double meaning fast.

Matilda pooh-poohed Mom's statement. "You're always so cynical, Trixie. This is going to be fun. We'll have polls and maybe meetups. Maybe we can get Gapman to make an appearance."

"We definitely need better pictures," Mom said. She flipped through the photo gallery, which was mostly action shots of me pulled from people's cell phones. "You're press, honey. Can you do something about that?"

Matilda tsked. "Ron's an entertainment reporter."

"And Gapman is a superhero—the stuff of comics and movies," Mom retorted. Then she looked beseechingly at me. "What do you think, sweetheart?"

I sighed. "I'll see what I can do." I was already having to learn law and investigations like Batman. Now I could add taking pictures of myself like Spiderman. Did Clark Kent have to deal with this?

I said to Mom, "Maybe if Gapman finds out about the club, he'll let you take some photos?"

Matilda bumped shoulders with Mom. "Wouldn't that be amazing? Us, Gapman's official photographers! Oo! Think he'd take his shirt off for us?"

I choked on my drink. "Aunt Matilda!"

Mom quickly vetoed the idea. "We agreed that we're keeping this site family-friendly. It's right here on the homepage."

"I didn't mean for the website." Matilda bumped Mom again.

Mom leaned her head into her friend's ample shoulder and giggled like a schoolgirl, but behind her back, she gave me a one-handed shrug of apology.

I knew better than to argue with them when they got like this. I grabbed my bear steak, wished them well, and excused myself. I had some studying and even more thinking to do. Why would someone want to shoot at me? It wasn't my fault I fell into a vat of toxic waste.

Vern wanted me to check out the building where the shooter had been. Maybe together we'd find something he'd missed.

I felt a happy clutch in my stomach as I again realized I was partnering with a dragon!

Chapter Fifteen:
Gapman Begins His Training

Vern

Grace connected the wire from our laptop to the television sitting on the table of our lair. It wasn't nearly as nice as the one we'd originally had, but I guess I should count our blessings that the store was willing to give us even a partial refund on the one damaged by Shogzallie. After all, the damage was (quite literally) due to an "act of God." The store manager warned us that he was giving us this one in gratitude for saving the city and most of Tokneo, but that it was a one-time deal.

Someone needed to tell the Powers That Made My Life Miserable that.

"Okay, I think we're ready," Grace said. "Want to pull up the videos?"

"Give me a minute," I told her without looking up from my phone. The foreman of our lair repair had texted me. His team was going to be busy for the next

two weeks with another job—one that actually paid—
but he'd sent me a list of the next steps in case I found
someone to help out in their absence. I had someone
in mind, alright.

Grace caught my distracted tone of voice and
peeked over my shoulder at the phone. She sighed.
"Vern, we agreed: no *Karate-Kid* training style."

"Hey, we're giving Gapman valuable training and
keeping him off Santry's radar. He owes us something," I argued as I double-checked the To-Do list
against the materials stacked up in various parts of
our dismantled home. Since fixing our lair was an all-
volunteer effort, our foreman had been glad to make a
detailed list of tasks in order, along with a few warn-
ings. I doubted Gapman (or rather, Ron) had
electrical certifications, but how hard was putting up
drywall? Plus, I needed to get Ryujin out of the elements before the snows came. Who better to help me
cart a broken and inoperative animatronic dragon to
the garage than a superhero?

But Grace crossed her arms at me, so I relented.
"Fine. I'll ask—no pressure. But he's helping with
Ryujin. We may have gotten it on a platform, but we'll
have to take out a lot of trees to drag it up the mountain. He and I can simply lift it and fly it to the shelter.

Besides, J.J.'s shop class is fixing it as a project. Can you imagine how excited they'll be to have Gapman helping?"

"That does sound like something Ron would enjoy, too," Grace relented.

"What would I enjoy?" came a voice from the hallway.

"Sorry I'm late," he said as he entered the room. "A lady was stranded on the highway, so I took her and her car to the gas station."

"You took the car?" I asked. "As in, you picked up the car with the lady in it and flew them to a gas station?"

He shrugged, grinning. "It was on my way?"

I turned to Grace. "He's helping with MechaVern."

At his raised brow—at least, I think he raised a brow; it was hard to tell with the mask—she related our conversation. I guess I should have given him kudos for not having eavesdropped on it as soon as he was in hearing range, but I was laying odds that he'd had his earbuds on and was listening to some anime superhero soundtrack. I held my tongue, however; we'd cover that when I demonstrated the importance of situational awareness. In the meantime, he loved the idea of helping, especially with the kids.

"I never took Shop. I was more of a theater geek. Maybe Gapman could talk to the kids about the importance of learning a vocation—oh, and Mom will want pictures for the website."

"Website?" I asked, eyes narrowed. What had he been doing all night when he should have been studying?

"Uh, yeah. It wasn't my idea. Mom and Aunt Matilda created it yesterday. Kind of a fan site—but it's a good way to keep tabs on what people think of me—er, him." Marketing Mom's Little Superhero blushed slightly, but his grin said he was more pleased than embarrassed. "Someone would have done it, eventually."

I traded glances with Grace.

She shrugged. "Gapman is a public figure," she said, then changed the subject. "Did you bring the book?"

He pulled out a nondescript, homemade string bag in green and gold from under his cape and took the book out of it. The bullet hole had dotted the *i* in Vatican. He also showed us the bullet, a .56-caliber. "It left a bruise for a couple of hours. If Kane wasn't so wordy, it probably would have broken my hand.

That's my writing hand, too. Do you think the police can match it to the gun?"

"Do you want me to tell them how we got the bullet?" I countered.

He sat down on a folding chair and sighed heavily. "I suppose I should, if it will catch the shooter. Is it worth revealing my identity?"

"Much as I dislike keeping things from the police, I'm not sure it is," Grace said. "We've established that whoever this was is not a known criminal. He or she was most likely targeting you and has superpowers— at least superspeed."

"And magic," I said. "I felt it when I entered the room, but it faded too quickly to be the residue of a fading spell. More like the scent of an unwashed body. Kind of like you."

"Hey! I shower!" Gapman protested.

"Accent, Padawan," I warned. "From now on, if you are in uniform, you use the accent, no matter who is talking to you or what they say."

"I beg your pardon: In fact, I shower regularly. Hygiene is important for everyone."

I rolled my eyes. "It's not something you can wash off. It's more that you have a sense of magic that's twisted somehow."

"Probably because of the radioactivity or the experiment in the Gap," Grace said.

Gapman frowned. "Does that mean I stand out to those who can sense magic?"

Good point. My padawan was starting to think. I turned to Grace. As a mage and part-Siren, she had the ability to sense magic, too.

Grace, however, shook her head. "As a dragon, Vern has a keen sensitivity to magic. I can only tell if I concentrate. Plus, I know to look for it, thanks to Vern. It's stronger when you are doing something superhero-ish. Your alter-ego is safe, I think. Still, I'll see what I can design for a dampening spell."

"Okay, so if it's that subtle, the shooter wouldn't have noticed from all the way up here," he said. "Which brings us back to it being someone at the play. But they were all Faerie. Why use a rifle?"

"A good question, Padawan, which we'll pursue once we're sure that you were the target. That's why we're here. We checked, and no one associated with the play has crossed the Gap—at least not under their own identity—and since the Faerie side of the Gap doesn't do ID checks, the only way to know would be to scan days of security footage. However, our contact did share with us some interesting recordings of your big appearance."

I jerked my head toward the TV, and Gapman turned his chair to watch. Grace pulled up the first recording on the laptop and played it. Like most security videos, it was black-and-white, medium quality, and from a single angle: in this case, pointing toward the crowd behind the retractable belt stanchions that separated them from the protest. One lady had her baby carriage on the other side of the line. Maybe the crowds had pressed too hard; maybe she was hoping it'd give her an edge when the protest ended and they were free to cross the Gap. Either way, the guards were preoccupied with the protestors and didn't seem to notice.

Gapman pointed toward her. "That's the dog mom."

"Yes, it is. Now watch."

She turned her head, presumably to snap at someone who was suggesting she pull her baby back behind the line, when suddenly, the carrier started forward.

"What do you see?" I asked my padawan.

"Okay, so it's a dog, but that stroller should have been behind the line."

"Look more closely," I chided, and Grace replayed the last 5 seconds.

"She didn't let go of the handle," he said, confused. "I mean, she wasn't hanging onto it very hard, but it's like someone pulled it from her grip."

"Now, you're getting it. Keep watching."

We watched as DogMom shrieked and reached unsuccessfully for the carriage.

"Did it jerk forward?" Gapman asked as the stroller moved out of range of the camera.

Grace pulled up another tape while I answered. "Yes. Now watch it from this camera."

This had a better view of the side of the protesting crowds where the carriage was. We watched as several people, from guards to Faerie, tried unsuccessfully to grab hold of the wandering stroller.

"It's like it's jerking away on purpose," Gapman said, his confusion growing. "Was it bespelled?"

"That, or someone was using basic telekinesis," Grace told him. "We've been over the recordings several times and can't find the culprit, so they may be where the cameras didn't pick them up. Did you notice anyone hanging back, maybe gesturing oddly?"

He frowned and shook his head. "I was concentrating on catching the stroller and what I'd say when I returned the baby, and then it turned out to be a dog and it bit me and..." He sighed.

"It was your first rescue." Grace patted him on the shoulder reassuringly. "You were hardly expecting someone to be playing tricks. Let's play the recordings and see if you recognize anyone."

My new apprentice had a good memory for faces. He recognized several people from around town and even a few from the protests at the book signing, but no one associated with the play. "And before you ask: I didn't see anyone from the play at the book signing either. I dunno, Vern, Sister: Maybe it's just a coincidence?"

"Like you getting superpowers is a coincidence?" I didn't buy it. Coincidences didn't happen in my experience unless it was somehow to coincidentally make trouble for me. Which, granted, this was, but my dragon senses were tingling. Instincts of a predator honed by years of solving crimes in the Mundane and centuries of dealing with threats against the Faerie told me there was something more we didn't see. I told him as much.

He lifted his hands in defeat—a gesture I was sure was pure Ron Engleson but had no place coming from a superhero. "Okay, then. What do we do?"

"Once is coincidence. Twice, a potentiality. Three times, a problem you are not ready for. So for now, you train. It's a nice day out. Let's work on flying and situational awareness. And let's see what we can figure out for moving my mechasuit."

Grace sighed.

Ron

The next few days were like a montage of training, study, and heroing. I'd get up early, work on my article assignments and do chores, then head out to meet Vern and Sister Grace for my training. Sister Grace drilled me on basic law, while Vern pushed my limits for flying while we searched for traces of more Shogzallie-like monsters. We worked on my other superpowers, seeking their limits, and Sister Grace even made some magical improvements to my costumes, adding a spell to protect them from the elements.

"It's not fireproof," she warned, "but it will afford you some protection. Plus, you'll be warmer flying around when the winter comes."

I had to admit, it was exciting to have a dragon for a trainer, and I knew what Sister Grace was teaching me would only make things better in the long run, but as the end of the week approached, I started feeling restless.

"I know we're doing the thing with the kids next week," I told Mom, referring to moving the animatronic dragon, Ryujin, which Grace had converted into a mechasuit for Vern for fighting Shogzallie. We'd set up the platform with heavy ropes, so Vern and I could carry it to the garage in the side of the mountain, where the Little Flower Catholic School shop class would be able to work on it safe from the weather. "And it is important that we make sure there aren't any more baby empyrie waiting to grow into another Shogzallie. Still, I feel underutilized."

"People are wondering, too," Mom replied as she piled three waffles on my plate. I grimaced at them. I had originally enjoyed my supermetabolism, but after the novelty wore off, having to eat so much was getting to be a drag.

Mistaking my sigh, she patted my shoulder reassuringly.

"You started out strong," Mom said as she dug into her waffle. "Scattered, but a solid start. People loved your combination of strength and compassion. At least at first. Now that there's been no follow up, even your fans are starting to doubt, like you were a publicity stunt or a one-day wonder. You have to get out there. It's time to stop playing with the dragon and go patrol the city or something."

"But what if I screw up again?" There were nights I didn't sleep, thinking about the pushers still on the streets because I interfered with an investigation.

Mom rolled her eyes. "What have I always told you about mistakes?"

I was a 24-year-old superhero getting lectured by his mother. I held back a sigh and poked at my breakfast. "Making mistakes means you're trying. If you're trying, you can learn. If you learn and keep trying, then you can do amazing things."

"Yes!" She pointed a fork loaded dripping with syrup at me. "And you've already done amazing things. I mean, look at this house."

"Yeah," I muttered, turning my attention back to my own meal. "It's certainly clean. Hey!"

A strawberry had bounced off my head.

"I mean before your superpowers, Salty Boy. *We* did this. You know Matilda is still in that crappy trailer, and that duplex Lenny owns is a dump. He can't even rent out the other side."

"Why do you know what Lenny's house looks like?" I demanded suspiciously.

"Not the point! We're talking about you. You graduated from college. You found your talent and are making it pay the bills. You defied all the statistics about single-parent kids growing up in poverty."

"Because I had a good mom who would have kicked my butt otherwise." I grinned fondly.

She tsked. "You were an easy kid. I always knew you'd go far. Now, you're a superhero, and what are you doing with those powers? Helping others. Okay, so the first day, you got in the way of the police. You also stopped a riot, saved a kid from getting run over—"

"Helped some guy move his couch?"

She ignored my sarcasm. "That's the stuff they're still talking about on the website. And the car you carried to the gas station. Kind of overkill, but people ate it up! Still, they are wondering where you've been lately. There's even a fan theory that Kitty McGrue scared you off."

I dropped my fork. "What?"

She pulled out her phone and pulled up the OMyGapman forum and slid it to me. The thread read, "One interview and Gapman's gone? What'd McGrue do?" The suggestions ran from her intimidating me to my somehow getting temporary superpowers to impress her so much that she'd—

"What? That's disgusting!"

"And untrue...right?"

Was that a hint of skepticism in her voice? I slid the phone back, careful not to put superstrength in my push, even though I wanted to send it through a window. "Completely. It was an interview, not a date. Gapman is not after—I mean, he's all business."

"And his business is helping people," Mom concluded. "So go out there and help. Forget about stopping crimes. There are plenty of other things a superhero can do."

"Like give someone a lift to the gas station?" Dang it, why was this so hard? I'm trying to learn to do things right, and instead people think I'm some kind of, of predator? And Kitty—she must be furious. But how would I know? I'm just the entertainment reporter. I hadn't heard from the *Gazette* since she landed the interview. The article I wrote got cut to three paragraphs and buried under an article about the governor getting high at the medical marijuana symposium. Apparently, she kept giggling whenever someone said, "diagnosis" and instead of delivering her speech, made kabuki theater with the shrimp cocktail, which is why it ended up in the Entertainment Section.

"Like save lives!" Mom scolded. "Now stop pouting! You've been a superhero all of a week. It's too early for a long, dark night of the soul. You don't even have an archnemesis yet."

I thought about my conversations with Sister Grace and Vern. They'd not found any leads; their sources told them the theater troupe had split up, everyone going their own ways, and Dorsch hadn't returned any of my calls. I hadn't had any trouble, as Gapman or Ron, and even though Gapman has been off the radar, Ron had still run errands, visited the comic book store, and basically been seen around town.

"And let's hope I never do," I said. "We narrowly avoided having the town destroyed by Shogzallie. The last thing we need is a superbattle."

I'd finished my latest assignment the day before. I needed to do a review of *Forty Years Until Tomorrow* for a series on K-dramas, but the crew was coming to put the top coat on the road and Mom had work. I could binge watch while being available if they needed anything. Sister Grace and Vern weren't expecting me until the afternoon. I could do a morning patrol. It was a Thursday in Los Lagos, so things would probably be quiet. I'd fly around, do some good deeds, then head to the lair for more training. Keep it low-key...

No sooner did I enter the city limits, than I heard the sirens, gunshots, and screeching of tires. I'd spoken too soon.

Chapter Sixteen:
Gapman Gets a Lunch Date

Ron

My heart beat faster. Sirens. That meant police. Dare I interfere? If I messed things up again...

I heard another gunshot, followed by a scream. That decided me. If nothing else, I'd get civilians out of the way, but if I could stop the firefight, I would.

I really hoped this wouldn't hurt.

I put on superspeed and surged toward the sound. Below me, I heard people call my name. "Gapman, you're back!" It felt good to be noticed. Soon, I saw a souped-up Honda speeding from downtown. Bright blue with jacked-up wheels, an air scoop popping out the hood, and a spoiler almost as tall as the roof, it was hard to miss, even without the two police cars in hot pursuit. A quick peek with X-ray vision showed two armed men in masks and bags of money in the back seat. A bank heist? In Los Lagos!

I pushed the novelty of that aside. I knew exactly how to help, without interfering with due process. I'd just stop the robbers' car.

I'll give them the chance to do the right thing first, I decided, and dove down so I was at traffic level. It was exhilarating and a little terrifying to be flying so low, light poles and people flashing past me—not to mention traffic—and I was suddenly glad for the flight training Vern had given me.

Soon, I was pacing the driver of the getaway car. Part of me wanted to geek out, but I pushed it aside as I put on my stern game face. But I couldn't resist; I knocked on the driver's side window with a knuckle.

He glanced my way, and his eyes grew big. He rolled down the window.

"You're only making this worse. Pull over and return the money," I advised.

Instead, he hit the gas and leaned forward. I paced him, then gasped as I saw his buddy bring up a pistol. I jerked back just as he shot at me! Whoa!

"As you wish," I said, and fell back. When I got to his back bumper, I grabbed the spoiler, then landed, planting my feet firmly in the pavement.

The car bucked in my grasp and the front tires started to smoke as the driver floored the gas pedal.

"I can do this all day," I called out. "Give up now, and maybe the courts will be merciful!"

I heard him shift gears. Guess I was going to be picking up another car. I moved to change my grip when I heard the creak and tear of metal, and the spoiler came away in my hands.

The car swerved and sped off.

What the...? I stared stupidly at the U-shaped bend of metal until a blaring horn startled me. I shot ten feet into the air, just like the saying. Embarrassing!

Yet, fortunately, just what I needed to do. Two police cars sped by beneath me. One of the officers waved at me.

Right! I couldn't let a setback stop me. But how did I stop the crooks?

A scream drew my attention toward the car. It was heading straight toward the dog park—and a lady with a stroller was entering the crosswalk!

I didn't even think. I flew to the intersection, landed between the woman and the car, and held the spoiler in front of me like a shield.

Brakes screamed, and the car swerved, but too late. It smacked into my makeshift shield, but by some miracle I could not fathom, we did not slide back and hit the woman or the stroller. Instead, the hind end of the car flipped up before coming back down so hard it popped both front wheels.

My hands and arms stung all the way up to my shoulders. Ow. Ow. I dropped the spoiler and tried to look heroic as I shook them out. I turned to the woman. "Ma'am, are you—"

I paused as Dog Mom stared at me. Today, she wore a T-shirt that said, "Dog Mom Life is Ruff." In the stroller, Timida, now dressed in a sweater and tutu, was barking like Cujo. At least she didn't leap out to bite me.

"Are you alright?" I finished.

"Her?" came a voice from behind me. "What about us? I think I got whiplash, man! I outta sue. This was my cousin's car, you..." He started a string of insults in several languages.

I had a lot of experience ignoring jeers. I indicated for Dog Mom to continue to the other side of the road, suggesting she stick around to give her statement to the police, who were both screeching to a stop. Then I turned back to the criminals, lest they try to get away on foot. Fortunately, the impact had damaged the frame; the front doors would not open.

"I'm pleased to see you both remembered your seatbelts," I said. The passenger suddenly remembered his gun, but I had, too. I snatched it away before he could get off a shot. "Pity you didn't also remember your manners—or the law."

The driver flipped me off, but I heard a giggle behind me. I turned.

A short, buxom police officer was grinning at me with starry eyes. Behind her, the other cops were just getting out of their cars or from where they were crouched behind open car doors.

"Nice work, Gapman!" she said.

I wanted to blush. Instead, I forced my face to a stern, heroy expression and turned my attention to the gun in my hand. With it pointed down and away, I removed the magazine, cleared the chamber, and handed it to the officer, butt first, muzzle down, and slide locked open.

She took it, her eyes even wider. "Oh, my Gapman! You know gun safety."

"Well, Officer..." I glanced quickly at her nametag. "Officer Briggs. Guns don't kill people. People kill people, even inadvertently. One must set a good example for the children."

"You're so right," she breathed, and I couldn't help but smile back at her.

"Hey! If you're done making cow eyes at each other, how about we arrest these punks before they get away?" one of the male officers yelled. In fact, the driver had beaten down his airbag and was trying to crawl out the window.

Miraculously, neither crook seemed to have injuries beyond a few cuts, a bloody nose, and a black eye, so the police and I covered them as they crawled out the window. I'd offered to pull open the doors, but the driver snarled, "Ain't you done enough damage, Superfreak?"

"Hey! Don't you dis Gapman!" Officer Briggs shouted.

"Or a great band, for that matter," another added.

With the paramedics on scene and the police having everything under control, there wasn't a lot for me to do except keep people at a safe distance. That was easy; I simply walked away from the scene, and the crowd followed me. I answered a few questions, shook hands, signed some autographs. (Glad I'd thought about my superhero signature already). The local news crew arrived, so I did a short interview. My fingers itched to text Mom, but we'd set some ground rules for communication between Gapman and GHQ.

Then I heard the roar of a motorcycle and a feminine voice with the hint of a Pittsburgh accent call my name.

I excused myself to talk to Kitty.

"Welcome back. So I guess I didn't scare you off after all?" She blinked at me in a parody of innocence.

Dang it—she followed the website. Of course, she would!

I took a breath. "Yes, I've seen the forums."

"Is that why you're social distancing?" She indicated the space between us. I'd stopped at least four feet from her bike.

I stepped closer. "Kitty, I must apologize—"

She waved her hand dismissively. "Please. Haters gotta hate, right? I'm just glad to see you—back on patrol, that is. Where have you been all week?"

I knew someone was going to ask; Mom and I had workshopped some answers that were truthful and put Gapman in his best light. "Around, just not in town. I've been assisting DragonEye, PI, in searching for any nascent Shogzallie beasts."

She frowned. "Vern's making you do his job?"

I forced myself not to shrug in apology. "Public safety is everyone's responsibility. I have superspeed and excellent vision. Once I knew what to look for, we've been able to cover a large percentage of the area that still needed searching."

She grudgingly agreed, but her expression was still a little sour. Man, she really *did* have a chip on her shoulder about Vern. Or...was she jealous?

Nope. I could not think about that. No, no. Keep things professional.

"Okay, then. Did you find anything?" she asked.

Now, I did shrug. "We thought we had, but it turned out to be a bear. They seem to be moving toward town this year. Probably because Shogzallie had disrupted the ecosystem, and they're looking for food. We've notified the authorities." Actually, I'd done that. Vern had some kind of animosity toward the Department of Fish and Wildlife.

"Yeah, we're doing a puff piece about some lady in the sticks who shot a bear. Mind if we add your comment? So how do you know so much about wildlife?"

"I wouldn't say I know a lot, but I am from this planet, and it's just common sense. Plus, Vern told me about Shogzallie eating all the fish and scaring the local wildlife. It's surprising Los Lagos hadn't seen more animals in the city, but perhaps all the construction drove them away. Rather a tough conundrum for animals, don't you think? A new predator on the one side, encroaching urbanization on the other."

Her eyebrow rose. Dang it! That meant she thought she had a lead. What had I said?

"So you're against new developments?" she asked. "Old growth environmentalism?"

I forced myself not to roll my eyes. "Not at all. I believe there's a balance, and that we should prepare for the effects of our actions. It's not always easy to predict." Deciding I needed to change the subject before she put Gapman in the political section, I gestured toward the car. "For example, I did not expect the spoiler to pop off the car like that. They were certainly determined to escape, and I confess, I didn't know front wheel drive could be so strong. I guess I underestimated the power of the force."

I paused, anticipating a chuckle, but none came. Not a *Star Wars* fan, then? That was disappointing, or maybe I was just too obscure? I'd have to try the joke on Vern; he'd get it. Who knew a dragon would be such a big geek?

As if reading my mind, Kitty asked, "So you and Vern are friends, then?"

Caught off guard, I answered. "I think so. Why?"

She didn't answer directly, merely shook her head. "Some friendly advice: Don't get too friendly. He'll keep you in his shadow, and you deserve to be in the spotlight."

As often happened when I got unexpected advice, my mind shattered into a thousand thoughts. How sweet that Kitty cared. She cared about Gapman, not Ron. How could she think Gapman was in anyone's shadow? But I was gone for a week. Is that what all this training was about—to keep me out of the spotlight? But Vern seemed sincere, and Sister Grace—

Behind me, Officer Briggs cleared her throat, sparing me having to answer Kitty. "Excuse the interruption, but we're about to head out, and I need to get your statement. Also, some of us were wondering..."

Soon I was standing by the squad cars, signing autographs and posing for selfies with the police. They even let one of the bank robbers out of the car for a quick photo.

"What are you doin', man?" his partner, the driver, demanded. "He's the reason we got caught!"

"Your driving's why we got caught!" the other retorted. "Besides, this is epic! We were stopped by a superhero! *I shot at Gapman.* That's gonna get me so much cred in jail! Hey, can you lift me off the ground for one photo, please?"

When the tow truck came and removed the busted getaway car, I saw that I'd created a pothole when I had braced myself to stop the car. After years of dealing with our pothole-laden drive, I felt a surge of guilt at creating one on such a busy street.

I pulled out my burner phone and called the Los Lagos Public Works. "This is Gapman."

"What?" the feminine voice shrieked. "We just saw you on TV. Oh, my Gapman. I—how can we help you?"

"I'm afraid in the course of apprehending some criminals, I did some damage to the road. Would you mind if I made some temporary repairs? It's a rather popular intersection; I'd hate for someone to wreck their suspension."

"I, uh, yeah. Sure."

While Officer Briggs guided traffic, Angelique from Public Works took the information and directed me to a pile of gravel they were using to fill other holes before adding blacktop. I dashed over at superspeed, grabbed a wheelbarrow full, and filled the hole, stomping the gravel down hard to make a firm surface. Then I sent a photo to Angelique.

"Wow. That looks good. Have you done this before?"

Yeah, for like a week, I thought, but aloud, said, "I'm sure a skilled road worker will do much better, but it should last until you can schedule a repair?"

She took the hint. "I'm putting it in right now. Gapman, you are a treasure!"

"Just trying to help, Miss Angelique," I said, eliciting a giggle.

I called out an "All Clear" to Officer Briggs and got honks and cheers from the drivers around us. Man, what a great morning!

If only Kitty had stuck around to watch.

Then, my superhearing picked up her voice.

"Gapman, if you can hear me talking, come on up to the roof of the Flint building. I got lunch. I hope you like club sandwiches."

Kitty—and food? I shot into the air and was on the roof almost before she'd finished talking.

She laughed when I landed and passed me a 12-inch club sub. "So the way to a superhero's heart is also through his stomach?"

"You'd be amazed how much energy I burn doing all this," I said, biting in gratefully. Extra mustard—heaven!

She leaned against the winterized AC unit and regarded me thoughtfully. "That's the most openly candid thing you've ever said to me."

I paused, the sandwich partway to my mouth. What did that mean? Was my acting that bad? Had I become a caricature instead of a hero?

"Do I seem...disingenuous to you?"

"It's not that," she reassured, and I felt my shoulders sag a little in relief. Hopefully, she would not notice under the cape.

She continued, "No. It's just you're so guarded around me. I mean, I get it: You have to protect your secret identity and all. But I wonder how much is identity and how much is hiding behind the mask? In other words: Is Gapman the man you are or the man you want to be?"

Wow. I think that was the first time she's ever thought of me as a man—and of course, it was while I was wearing my underwear on the outside. I took in a breath and let it out slowly. "That's an insightful question."

Her smile was sardonic. "I'm good at my job, and you're avoiding the question."

It was a good question and deserved an insightful answer. I ate my sandwich while I considered my words. Finally, I said, "I'm not sure it could be anything but both. There is something about the mask, the uniform, the mission, that makes one—makes me—want to be a better man, to live up to what a superhero should be. However, to put it in comic book terms, I'm more Superman than Batman."

"You're a mild-mannered reporter with a thing for your coworker?" she quipped.

Do not blush! Relaxed shoulders, breath through the nose...

I explained, "Bruce Wayne is a frivolous playboy billionaire, while Batman is stoic, mission-centric, and violent. Clark Kent and Superman, however, are both all about truth, justice, and a better tomorrow. I may have different mannerisms but at the core, I live by the same values."

"Hmm." She pursed her lips in thought.

I braced myself for another gotcha question, but instead, she just handed me a bottle of water. I reached for it gratefully. Our hands touched, and even though the gloves, I felt a spark.

"You know, I always did like Superman better."

Warmth spread over me. I thought about asking if she ever imagined herself as Lois Lane. I debated asking if she'd like to go on a flight around town.

Then I heard a distant cry of "Gapman! Help me."

"I'm so sorry!" I said and meant it. "Someone needs me."

She pouted but made a shooing motion.

As I was ready to leap from the building, a thought struck me. "What do I owe you for lunch?"

She laughed. "It's on the *Gazette*. Thanks for the *interview*, Gapman."

As I took to the air, I couldn't help but smile. I could grow to love rooftop lunches. But then the woman called out again, and I felt my mood darken to determination, and I pushed my speed the way I'd learned with Vern. I didn't know if she was being mugged or something worse. I had to get to her fast.

I found her in an alley, curled up against a wall. The alley was empty. Dang it! I was too late. Why did I have to ask about the lunch bill?

I approached her gently and crouched beside her. "Miss? Are you all right?"

She turned toward me with a sweet, predatory smile. "Oh, my dear. I'm fine now."

She threw a powder at my face.

I jerked back fast, catching just a whiff of the cloud. Was she thinking? "What the... *Puck?* Ma'am, are you out of your mind?"

She chuckled warmly. "Good reflexes. That will make this so much more fun."

Before I could back up any farther, she spoke some words of magic.

The world went hazy, then black.

Chapter Seventeen: Gapman vs the Queen of the Midsummer Court

Ron

Awareness came with the feeling of lying on a couch, my head in someone's lap, her fingers in my hair.

"Mom," I grumbled sleepily. "Cut it out. I'm not a kid anymore."

The woman yanked my hair. "I am not your dame."

Not Mom? I jerked in surprise and fell off the couch, hit the floor, which was a step, and rolled to the ground. I sprang to my feet, now fully awake. "What? Who?"

I stood at the base of a dais that held a chaise lounge. A woman of unworldly beauty sat upon it, so amazing that for a moment, I only saw her. She looked vaguely like the woman in the alley—the same lush brown hair, eyes so green they could not be real—but everything about her was enhanced. Her figure was...wow. Perfect. She wore a dress made of daisies that covered just enough to be modest and beguiling, and the crown on her head made her seem powerful and adorable. If she'd been anime, *Faninist Magazine* would have ripped her artist to shreds for promoting exploitative and unrealistic expectations.

The thought called me back to myself and I tore my eyes away from her. Her throne—because it didn't matter if it was a couch, she sat on it like royalty—was surrounded by vines and blooming flowers, like literally blooming, opening themselves up and closing again. We were indoors, but the area felt like a park. I looked at my feet, expecting a cultivated lawn, and found a groundcover of small flowering plants instead.

Around me, people were laughing, and I knew they were laughing at me, but there was something so odd about it. It had the uniformity of a soundtrack, like these people practiced laughing or were so used to it, they naturally fell into a general volume and rhythm, like a long-established choir. Somehow, that made me feel better about being the subject of their mirth.

Just like a well-trained choir, when the vision on the throne raised a single, graceful finger, the laughter cut off.

Just as suddenly, something in my brain clicked, taking me back to middle school social studies class.

"Queen Titania?" I gasped out, unbelieving. Why would the Midsummer Court fairies kidnap me?

The benevolent smile she'd been wearing at my antics suddenly darkened, and the entire throne room with it. "I am indeed Queen Titania of the Midsummer Court, and you, Ronald-Logan-Engleson-Known-as-Gapman, will not address me in that tone or posture!"

We'd spent half a lesson in the eighth grade being told not to deal with the fairy courts and especially not to tick off their queens—considering we studied all of the Faerie governments in a semester, that was a lot. I dropped to one knee, bracing an arm against the other bent leg, hoping I looked knightly and obeisant. She'd kidnapped me as Gapman, and I still had my uniform on; some instinct told me I needed to walk a fine line between superhero confidence and subservience. I kept my eyes on the bend between the first step and the floor as I spoke.

"My apologies, Your Majesty of the Summer Warmth. I was...disoriented. May I know why you have brought me here?"

"Better," she purred, and I felt a surge of relief. "You may rise, my champion."

"Your...champion?" I raised one brow in superheroish skepticism, but my mind was racing. Had I agreed to something while she was playing with my hair?

Then she rose and stretched, and my brain disconnected for a moment. Wow, she was gorgeous! She descended the dais toward me, and everywhere she stepped, small flowers bloomed. I tried to look at the flowers and not her amazing figure, but even her ankles had unworldly grace.

It's a trap, Gapman! Deep breaths. Think about snow and cold rain and, and oh! And that Pat person at the comic book store...

She set her hand on my chest. My skin tingled. I met her eyes. I mean, I had to or else I'd be looking down her dress. I tried to imagine Pat's sneering, judgmental face rather than the lovely and admiring smirk of the Queen of the Midsummer Court.

She said, "You were made for me, you know."

Was she hitting on me? That's what I get for letting Mom make my uniform from a stripper's costume pattern. "I, uh... Pardon?"

"Oh, yes."

She started to circle me, her hand trailing over my shoulders and back. I could feel tingles even after her fingers had moved on. For a minute, I thought she might grab my butt, and despite my stance against uninvited touch, I didn't think I'd mind at all.

But instead, she kept walking, her touch moving to my shoulder then flowing along my arm and hand. When we stood an arm's length from each other, she examined me critically.

"You're not who I expected, but I'm not displeased with Snapdragon's change of plans."

"Snapdragon?" The stage manager of *Captain Extraordinary*? What did he have to do with...

Then it hit me.

"Wait! The broken scaffolding—just as I was standing over the vat of toxic waste. So Snapdragon did engineer this?" In my surprise, I dropped my accent. Not that it mattered. She knew exactly who I was and what had happened.

Her shoulders relaxed just a bit with relief. "You are quick. Good. We were a bit concerned."

"I got bit by a radioactive pixie! He planned that, too? Is he here? Snapdragon!" I cried out. I wasn't sure if I wanted to yell at him or thank him, but I deserved something.

Queen Titania cleared her throat—just a tiny sound, but enough to remind me where I was, whom I faced, and how deeply I could get in trouble if I ticked her off. I shut up fast and regained my composure. Regardless of what she knew, I was Gapman!

"Forgive me, Majesty. I'm confused. Why did Snapdragon... Why would you want..." I wasn't sure what question meant the most to me. Finally, I shrugged. "Why?"

"I lost my champion," she said. "He valiantly defended our court and my reign. His brave, brave efforts ensured the heat of the sun, the thriving of living things, the length of days filled with light. But now, he is gone, and my sister, Mad Mab of the Midwinter Court, seeks to take advantage of our weakness."

A low hiss filled the room, and I was reminded that we were not alone. I glanced around and saw perfect bodies in all sizes, from the behemoth in a Speedo ready to react if I displeased Her Highness to a tiny fairy in board shorts and a beaded halter top resting on a daisy and hissing like a cat.

The queen raised one willowy hand. The room fell silent. She returned to her lounge and resumed her explanation. "My ill-tempered sister seeks to gain control of King Oberon, extending the bitter influence of winter into the glory of summer."

This was happening too fast. My brain was still on falling into a vat of toxic waste, and now we were in the frigid prospect of eternal winter? Around me the Midsummer Court began a lament about the chill and the storms. I had visions of the court, frost-covered, all the fairies in attendance, icy statues. I started getting goosebumps just thinking about it.

"But, Your Majesty...why would King Oberon allow it? I mean, he's king, so..." How did I articulate that her husband should have some authority, maybe man up and do his job? I didn't want to tick her off. I did not want to get turned into a newt.

"Oberon is male, and as my twin, Mab shares my considerable...influence."

She leaned back on the chaise lounge fetchingly, one hand "idly" caressing the line of daisy petals edging her dress. I had to turn my gaze away.

Do not react. Decorum! Immasuperhero, Immasuperhero...

I heard a delicate snort that told me she knew she'd made her point. "But for all her beauty, Mab is cold as an iceberg, and like an iceberg, she has hidden depths. Her icy touch will cool his heart, and all the world with it. Gone, the lazy afternoons under brilliant sun, sweat dappling our languid bodies..."

As she continued to paint the rather suggestive picture of laying around, sunbathing, I thought back to all the wood I'd cut for the winter. How much would I need if the cold never left? What about all those poor Faerie who lived in ramshackle homes barely suited for a couple of months of snowy weather, let alone year-round frostmaggedon?

I shivered.

"You understand!" she cried triumphantly and leaped from the dais to float gently before me. Her hands were on my chest, but this time in the attitude of pleading. "This is why I must have a champion. Why I must have you to champion me. We've been watching you, Ronnie-Engleson-known-as-Gapman."

"It's Ron," I said weakly. The back of my mind, General Ackbar was shouting, "It's a trap!" but she was so lovely and smelled like lilacs and sun-kissed wood. She started talking about my strength and compassion and honor. They'd even tracked all the things I'd done for Mom. That was the best thing. They were talking about me! Ronnie—er, Ron—Engleson, as myself and as Gapman. Either way, I was a hero. "Just Gapman's okay, too."

"My Chosen One, you must defeat the Midwinter Court champion in mortal combat!"

"M-mortal?" I couldn't make myself pull away from her, but the word splashed over me like ice water. "*Mortal?*"

She ignored my objection. "You cannot fail. You were made for this. Every event in your dear, short, limited life has led you to this moment. Will you not fight for the glory of clear blue skies and the warmth of the sun caressing your skin?"

Put that way, I wanted to shout, "Yes!" but *dear, short, limited life?*

"Um... Have you tried talking to her? I mean, the earth—Faerie or Mundane—needs the balance of the seasons. One cannot survive without the other..."

She chuckled sadly. "Dear, sweet, naïve little Mundane. How like you to propose a way of peace. Alas, Mad Mab is beyond convincing, beyond negotiation. No, the challenge has been made—and so have you. There is no one like you in two universes. None with your unique attributes. Will you rise to the occasion? Will you be the champion of Summer Bliss?"

My heart swelled with pride.

Suddenly, I heard a roar and a shadow fell over the court. Then with a crash and shattering of glass, the ceiling caved in. Even though Titania's guardsmen wove spells that turned the broken glass into rose petals, the other fairies in the court screamed and fled for cover.

My heart leaped in my throat. Had the Midwinter Court come to fight already?

But, no—it was Vern!

"You didn't agree to anything, did you?" he demanded.

In my shock and confusion, I stammered a "no."

Titania strode toward Vern, and I could feel the blaze of heat coming from her as if Vern had set her afire. "Vurnerrah! You broke my roof!"

"You kidnapped my padawan!"

"Your...?" She shook her head in confusion.

A diminutive fairy in a Princess Leia bikini that matched her wings flew to the queen and whispered in her ear. I moved to where I could see both Titania and Vern. Somehow, that meant I was between them and a step or two back, like a point on a triangle.

Titania's face shifted from understanding to annoyance, and then turned haughty. Somehow, she looked less like a queen and more like a petulant teenager. "I can't kidnap what's already mine. He was made for me."

"He's a sapient, and a Mundane at that. And he was made—" (I could hear the air quotes) "—because Snapdragon wanted to puck you."

"What?" I gasped.

"Salerno Tom, the guy who played Captain Extraordinary? Snapdragon was supposed to turn him. He's already a decorated knight in three kingdoms. Snapdragon just thought it'd be funny if you got powers instead."

I gaped from one to the other. "So I'm the result of a practical joke?"

Vern ignored me. "Titania may be okay with the switch, but because you were not Her Majestic Warmth's intended target, she does not get to control you. So be thankful she needs your consent and you've not given it yet. Otherwise, you'd be stuck fighting her petty squabbles for the rest of your life."

"Petty?" Both Titania and I gasped—her, in indignation; me, in confusion.

"What's so petty about eternal winter? The death of the Midsummer Court?" I demanded.

Vern paused in his arguing with Titania to blink at me. "The what? Mab wants Oberon for a weekend. Which one is it, Ti? Brooding Day?"

He turned back to me, "It's when the penguin females pass their eggs to the males for incubation. It's June fourth this year."

"It's also the weekend the falimials bloom, and I made plans!" Titania stomped her tiny foot. A bouquet of tiny blossoms exploded from the ground like confetti.

I was struggling to wrap my head around it all. "But the storms! The chill!"

Vern responded with all the exasperation of a parent. When he spoke, he addressed Queen Titania, not me, and he had a little bit of a lilt that made me think of Sister Grace.

"Well, that would be Her Grandness of the Summer Squall, wouldn't it? Don't deny it to me, Youngling. Wisdom of the Ages, Experience of Eternity, remember? I know how you get when you're in a funk."

He turned his head, taking in her court. "And the rest of you: Sixty-five degrees is not a deadly chill! Put on a sweater."

I was starting to feel a little less sure of... I didn't know. The situation? My role? The whole reason for my being?

But Queen Titania drew herself up tall, proud, and haughty. When she faced down Vern, I was reminded what Mrs. Kingston said about how we didn't know the extent of the fairy queens' powers. She certainly felt confident enough to take on a dragon. "The circumstances are of no concern to you, Vurnerrah. The challenge has been made. I need a champion. I have chosen."

"The Mundane whom Snapdragon made into a hero as a practical joke?"

"Oi! I'm right here!" I protested. Whatever the situation, I didn't like being talked about as if I couldn't hear them.

However, Titania continued to ignore me as she smiled mischievously at Vern. "That will make it all the sweeter when he wins. Besides, he obviously wears an outfit made with a mother's love. There's protective magic in that."

"You are not using my padawan to solve your jealous tiff. He's not ready for something like that."

"Now, hold on!" I started, but Vern spoke over me.

"Go negotiate with Mab. It's not like you haven't traded weekends before."

"But negotiating with her is so tedious! No. Snapdragon made him to be my champion."

"Humans have free will," Vern countered.

I saw my chance and jumped in. "Yes, we do!" I thundered to be heard. At least, I hope I thundered. I could hardly hear myself over the thundering of my heart. I didn't often shout at anyone, much less two very powerful magical creatures.

But for a wonder, they stopped and gave me their attention.

I took a breath and continued in a calmer voice. I crossed my arms and assumed what I hoped was a strong Gapman countenance. *I'm a superhero. I'm a superhero.* "Yes, I do, and I'll thank you to stop speaking to me as if I were a child."

Titania snickered. "Little mortal, you are a child. Vurnerrah was created on the eighth day, and I began my reign when your species was still arguing the nature of the Trinity."

I didn't know what that meant, but I continued. "Regardless, O Ruler of the Summer Breezes, in human terms, I am of an age to make my own decisions."

I turned my glare to Vern. "You are not my master."

There was a low, "oooooh" from the Faerie around me. Suddenly, I had the impression that I might have gone too far. Too late now. I hoped this outfit hid sweat stains.

Vern crossed the distance between us and sat in front of me. He stretched his neck so that he glared down at me. I had a perfect view of his glowing gold eyes and large, sharp teeth. His breath smelled like burning coals. I gulped.

"Are you challenging me, *Padawan*?"

Titania clapped her hands, "Oh, for the right to be my champion? How brave!"

I knew better than to back down. No matter how painful it might be now, backing down would only make things worse in the long run. "If that's what it takes."

Vern cocked his head at me. I couldn't tell if he was impressed or calculating.

After a long moment during which I wasn't sure I breathed, he stepped back. "Alright, then, but as the challenged, I choose the weapons."

What had I done? "Fine. Let's take this outside," I said. The walk would give me a minute to collect my nerves.

But he flicked his tail dismissively. "We're fine right here."

"Fine! But no fire. Too much here is flammable."

I was really more concerned about myself, but I heard a couple of the female fairies sigh in approval.

Vern snickered, then he stood and stretched, cat-like. I heard a couple of joints pop. His claws extended. They were big claws. How had I not noticed before how big his claws were?

If he was trying to intimidate me by being so casual, it wasn't working. It wasn't. The shakes were perfectly normal. I'd felt them every time I'd confronted a bully in school. It was adrenaline, that's all.

"Wouldn't dream of it," he said, and sat back down, wrapping his tail around his feet. "For our duel, I choose...compliments."

Cheers and jeers rose around us, and immediately, three fairies moved between us, announcing themselves as judges.

"Hold on," I said. "Compliments?"

Vern nodded. "Best two out of three—if Her Majesty of Warm and Languid Afternoons approves?"

She made a warm and languid "carry on" motion with her hand, then retired to her chaise lounge.

"But," I sputtered. "Compliments? How do you duel with compliments?"

Vern shrugged in a way that rippled down his scales. "You'll figure it out. You're a smart guy with an excellent command of language."

"Thanks, but—" My words caught in my throat as the trio of fairy judges turned and presented their wings. The mottled patterns had transformed to numbers: 7.8, 8.2, 7.1.

Another fairy shouted in an official voice: "First shot to Vern, favored dragon of the Midsummer Court."

My jaw dropped. I turned toward Vern, askance.

He regarded me with a guileless expression, but his tail swished back and forth like a cat contemplating a mouse.

All the fairies were watching me expectantly, so I rallied my brains and command of language. Might as well use what he gave me. "Well played, Friend Dragon, although I should have expected no less from one who can be at once so awesome and so terrifying."

I heard a murmur around me, but Vern simply rolled his eyes.

"I am an Eighth Day Creation, Padawan. God designed me to reflect His glory—of course, I am awesome and terrifying. But a good first try. You're learning."

The judges did a quick spin and gave me their scores: 2.7, 2.2, and oh! 8.1!

The judges stared my high score down. The fairy made an expression of surprise and flipped: 1.8.

"Gapman shot—deflected!" the fairy announcer cried.

"What?" I cried. You can deflect compliments? No one said anything about deflecting. "Hang on! This isn't fair! No one's explained the rules."

"And that, O Queen of Heat and Glare," Vern called out triumphantly, "is exactly why Ron is no good for you as a champion. At his core, Ronald Engleson, aka Gapman, is honorable and kind of heart, a man who believes every battle has rules and a fair playing field. In short, he is an excellent superhero for the Mundanes, who believe in justice and compassion, but too ingenuous and full of integrity for the machinations that comprise a fairy fight."

There was a pause as the fairy took in what he said; then, suddenly, they rose to their feet (or at least an upright position) and roared approval.

9.2, 9.7, 6.9—oops! 9.6

"Vurnerrah wins!"

All around me, fairies started exchanging seeds and flower petals. Had they been betting on us? Did any of them bet on me, and was I in trouble as a result? I looked at the dais. Queen Titania was suddenly absorbed in braiding her hair.

Vern came up to me and said quietly, "Let's get out of here, now, Padawan, before anyone gets any ideas."

"I... but... I..." I didn't know what to say. Should I be relieved or insulted? But he was already walking away, and something about how he hurried without seeming to hurry made the hair on the back of my neck stand up. I made a courtly bow to the inattentive Queen, then hastened to catch up.

"Oh, Vurnerrah," Titania purred. "Just one thing?"

Vern stopped short and I saw his eyes flare before again returning to an open and innocent gaze. He turned back to the Queen. "Yes, Oh Queen of Contented Sunny Days?"

"I expect you back on the Feast of Saint Valentine to defend me against my most greedy and despicable sister."

I watched as Vern's great claws sank into the ground and out again, but he spoke with loving patience. "Ti, you know you're my favorite, but I vowed long ago not to get in between your marital squabbles with your sister and Oberon."

She sighed, feigning deep regret. "Then perhaps you should have been more careful about accepting a duel for the right to be my champion. That was what I said the duel was for, didn't I, Gapman, Defender of Rules and Justice?"

"I meant the right to choose!" I protested.

She shrugged. It was pretty in a mean girl sort of way. "But you didn't specify that and you didn't correct me. It was a public duel, valiantly fought and righteously judged. I'm afraid it's quite binding."

"Ti..." Vern growled, but somehow, it was already too late to protest.

I saw whisps of magic swirling around him. They looked blue and green and shimmered like the heat, but I didn't sense anything comforting about them. Holy cow, was this a binding spell? What had I done?

"Wait!" I cried. "What if he finds a substitute?"

"A what?" Titania demanded, and it was hardly a question as much as a command to stop talking nonsense.

Still, I continued. "A substitute, a second. In every duel, the duelists have the right to appoint a second in case for some reason they cannot fight the duel themselves. It's a rule! And Vern's already said he can't do it because of a prior vow to not get involved."

It seemed everyone held their breath—except me. I felt like I couldn't catch mine. I panted as if I'd run a race. Vern, the fairies, and I all watched the queen, waiting to see how she'd react to my impertinent suggestion. Titania looked from Vern to me, then to somewhere inside herself. I got the feeling that somewhere inside was where she hatched her best plans.

Finally, her gaze returned to Vern and me. "So be it. You make an interesting counteroffer, Ron-Engleson-known-as-Gapman, and I do so enjoy encouraging such creativity of conniving thought. Vurnerrah, my dear, dear dragon, you have until year's end to find me a suitable champion, or you will take your place as my defender."

I sighed with relief.

Vern, however, turned to face her directly and regarded her with narrowed eyes. "Let's define 'suitable.'"

Chapter Eighteen:
St. George Sides With Gapman

Vern

I waited until we were well away from the portal leading from the Midsummer Court before expressing my ire.

"I leave you alone for one morning, and you get kidnapped by the Fairy Queen."

"Is that something I should have known to expect?" he countered. I could tell from the surly edge in his voice that even if I said, "Yes," he'd blame me for not having warned him.

He smacked at a low-hanging branch that extended over the trail we were following. I'd arranged for the portal to deposit us in the woods about a mile from the Faerie Gap, on the side "road" that would take us near the Gapway Theater. As long as we were here, Grace and I had decided to do some investigation. I suppose we could have taken to the skies, but I wanted to have a talk with my padawan, and despite his earlier assertions about his free will, he seemed to naturally follow my lead.

I said, "No, that caught me by surprise, too. We'd figured you were taking a couple of days off, except McGrue came by demanding to know where you were."

He brightened at the mention of Kitty McGrue looking for him, but then stopped. "Wait. What do you mean a couple of days?"

"Time moves differently in the fairy courts. You'd been gone almost a day and a half when McGrue charged into my lair demanding that I stop dominating all your time. Like I don't have other things to do with my own day, such as actual cases that pay the bills. But no, apparently, you're a hero of the people, and I needed to stop acting like a greedy tyrant making you my lackey. I told her 'hero of the people' sounded Communist. Things kind of went downhill from there—"

"Never mind that! I need to call my—"

I cleared my throat noisily. It didn't matter if we were in the middle of the woods. You never knew who was listening. In the Mundane, they say "Walls have ears;" in Faerie, trees could literally be listening.

"—headquarters," Gapman finished without a hitch. "They'll be worried that I haven't checked in."

I was impressed. I nodded for him to go ahead and waited quietly while he pulled out the phone I'd given him. Rather than call, he sent a text: *Gapman to GHQ. I'm ok. Encounter with fairy. Explain when I return. ETA: 90 min.*

I felt a little surge of pride. Texting was smart; GHQ (a.k.a. Mom) couldn't as easily freak out and blow cover with a text as she could with voice.

But when he put his phone back in his utility belt, his shoulders slumped, and I knew he wasn't quite as on top of things as I was giving him credit for.

He sighed and slumped against a tree. "What am I doing, Vern? I mean, I was made as a—"

"If you want to have a long, dark, night of the soul," I interrupted, "do it at home."

"Yeah, okay," he grumbled, but for a moment, didn't move.

A chipmunk regarded him curiously from one of the branches, but it smelled like a normal dumb animal. Even so, I bared my teeth at it, and it dashed away. I turned back to the path, hoping my padawan would pull himself out of the doldrums and follow.

Instead, I found the way blocked by an apparition.

St. George stood before me in full armor, arms crossed, the short sword held so that it protected his forearms. He gave me the saintly stink eye, then jerked his head toward Ronnie, who had pulled a leaf from the tree and was tearing it into shreds at human speed.

"Are you taking his side now?" I asked.

"What?" Ron asked.

I ignored him. "I'm not an emotional support dragon."

"I never said..." but his voice trailed off. In my peripheral vision, I saw that he realized I was facing the road and not him. His brows knit.

Meanwhile, George sheathed his sword and held his hands apart, about 10 inches. The size I was after our epic battle all those centuries ago. I got the message: When I was brought low and was full of doubt about myself and my place in the universe, I had people—humans, in particular—who helped me through it.

I snorted. Humans—St. George, to be exact—were why I was brought low in the first place.

"Are you talking to someone?" Ron asked. He peered down the trail in the general direction of St. George, straining to see something with his supervision. If he squinted any harder, he was going to give himself an aneurysm.

George, meanwhile, was giving me a look that said he'd brook no arguments. Apparently, he was on a mission from God. That, of course, made me more nervous than I was going to admit. God had sent St. George after me because he needed a dragon in the direct employ of His Church, and it's been a roller coaster for me ever since. What was coming that He also needed a superhero?

If that was the case, Gapman would need more than an emotional support dragon.

Ron

"Are you talking to someone?" I asked. I set my gaze intently down the path where Vern was looking, willing my eyes to look in spectrums other than visual. I caught glimpses of...was that heat?...in the brush, but whatever was on the path remained hidden.

Who knows? Maybe Vern was talking to himself. Obviously, I did not know enough about Faerie creatures to say one way or another. Would my ignorance get me killed? Better that than someone else, but still.

I wasn't religious. We never went to church. But at that moment, I felt a weird urge to pray.

God, if I'm supposed to be more than some practical joke, could you let me know? Give me a sign or something?

"You got a patron saint, Gapman?"

"I... uh... What? No."

"You do now!" Vern declared brightly. "Saint George, meet Gapman, my protégé, whether he likes it or not. Gapman, Saint George, your patron saint. Good luck."

Suddenly, there was a brilliant flare I felt as much as saw, and standing on the path was a strong, lean man with a boyish face and wavy blonde hair in a pageboy cut. He wore knightly armor and a red cape, and held a pike in one hand and a palm leaf in another. There was an actual glow around his head, like in all the paintings.

My jaw dropped. To my dismay, the only sound that came out of my mouth was a strangled, "erk."

George grinned at me with affection and mirth. I fought for something clever to say, as Ron or Gapman, but all I managed was a "I...uh..."

Vern cut across my sputtering. "You know, it's usually angels that have to say, 'Be not afraid.' Way to make an appearance, George. The pike and palm are a nice touch. Very *iconic*."

"He's a—you're a—that's a…" I stopped to take a breath. "You're a real saint…uh, sir?"

He nodded regally, and then he spoke! "That I am, but by the grace of God. Well met, Ronald Logan Engleson, also known as Gapman. Know that you are loved and called to a higher purpose. It will be my honor to be your patron."

"Hey," Vern said to him, "tell him you'll watch his career with great interest."

George rolled his eyes at him. "That would be in-*sidious*, not in character."

I didn't think my mind could get any more blown. "Did you just make a pun? A *Star Wars* pun? You, you died like a thousand years ago! How do you know Mundane movies?"

"I know many things," George said mysteriously. Then, in a more normal voice, added, "But I do not know how you fit into God's plan. His ways are ineffable. I only know you are who and what you are for a reason, and it is not to fight a fairy's marital squabble. Listen to Vern. He usually knows the right thing to do."

"Oi!" Vern protested. "Eighth Day Creation!"

"Saint," George countered as if showing a winning poker hand.

Then he turned back to me, and suddenly, he was surrounded by a brilliance that I picked up with Mundane- and super-sight. And more than that. I *felt* it, through my heart and with every cell in my body. I had an urge to fall to my knees, but I knew it was the wrong thing to do.

I wasn't sure if I believed in God before. I mean, I did, but more as an abstract. Now, without a doubt, I knew He existed, and I was looking at one of His blessed servants.

"God be with you, Ronald Logan Engleson, also known as Gapman."

And then, he was gone.

I felt like I'd been released from a binding. I could breathe again—when had I stopped breathing?—and I had to catch myself from collapsing.

"Holy!"

"Watch your next word," Vern warned.

I bit off the profanity that had threatened to escape my mouth. Yeah, that would be inappropriate.

I took a couple of steps toward where St. George had stood. Then I stopped. Was that hallowed ground now? Was I supposed to, I don't know, genuflect or something?

Vern must have sensed my confusion. "It's just dirt."

"But..." I understood for the first time the expression "my head exploded." I felt like my thoughts had blasted from my skull. I was having a hard time reeling them all back in. "That, that was Saint George, right? The actual Saint George? As in, Saint George and the Dragon?"

"The bane of my life," Vern agreed, "And now, apparently, the patron saint of accidental superheroes."

How could he be so casual about this? "An actual saint, like came down from heaven, messenger of God. I mean, he's not even alive, right? He died like a thousand years ago, and he, he came back to talk to me!"

"It'll get old after a while."

I asked for a sign. I asked for a sign and *God sent a saint*?

"No," I declared flatly. "This can't be happening. It's not possible. It's...what are you doing?"

Vern had shuffled back from me and was watching me intently.

"Oh, just waiting for God to strike you dumb like Zechariah."

"What?"

"John the Baptist's father? Told an angel something was impossible, and God struck him dumb until after John was born? You really need to learn your Bible stories. We'll work on that. But for now: Yes, that was a bona fide saint, and yes, he's adopting you. Come on."

He started down the trail.

"But why?" I could hear the plaintive wail in my voice, but I didn't care. I'd been kidnapped by one of the most powerful creatures in all Faerie. I'd just met an actual saint. He'd blessed me! Why would he do that?

Vern paused, but only turned his serpentine neck so he could look at me.

"It doesn't make sense, Vern. Okay, I get it. I was a fairy's practical joke. Haha. That actually makes twisted sense, you know. And I'll do whatever I can to make the best of it. I will. But an actual..." I searched for the word. "...visitation?"

I didn't know what to say next. My thoughts were still trying to unscramble, and my stomach churned with emotions I could not name. Vern, still on the path ahead of me, continued to watch me with a cocked head, almost like a dog trying to suss out his person's feelings.

Good luck. I didn't even know my feelings.

"Did he mean what he said?" I asked in a small voice.

Vern sighed. "That you're meant for better than dealing with Titania's marital squabbles? I told you that."

"No. I mean, that all this happened for a reason. That I was meant to be Gapman. That I'm not just a victim of a fairy's puck."

Vern sighed long-sufferingly, but there was something affectionate in the sound, too.

"Come on, kid. Let's get off the road."

I followed him through a small boundary of trees to a meadow. It seemed incongruously bright and cheerful for my mood, and open, too. But then again, I had just admitted on the road that I was something other than a superhero; plus, George had called me by name. If someone was listening, it was too late.

Vern settled himself among the flowers and motioned for me to do the same. I pulled off my cape and sat on it, facing him.

"We can talk freely; George will make sure of that," Vern said, then frowned up and to the side as if telling the saint he'd better.

I could not imagine talking to a superior being that way—but then again, Vern was a *dragon*, and here I was, pouting to him and comparing him to a concerned dog. I guess you just get used to each other with time. Still...

"Listen," I started. "I know you're not an 'emotional support dragon...'"

"Are you telling me what I can and can't do?" he interrupted.

My apology caught in my throat. What had I done wrong now? "I... No! I just... Well, you said it yourself!"

"And a saint told me to stop limiting myself—advice he gave to you as well, you know. He was just nicer about it."

"Why? What did he tell you?"

"None of your—" Vern started. He sounded irritated. But he stopped, took a breath, and started again. He reminded me that, of all the limitations St. George imposed on him during their great battle, "*which he insists he won*," not caring for others was not one of those constraints.

"In fact, those limitations and the new mission foisted upon me should compel me to greater empathy for my fellow sapients. So perhaps I should rephrase. I don't *want* to be your emotional support dragon."

"Oh." I looked down at the ground, at the flowers valiantly trying to push back against the weight of my cape. I felt that weight, too, and somehow, I felt even more alone now. "I guess that makes sense."

"Does it? Do you want to know why, or are you going to let your low self-esteem put its words in my mouth?"

Harsh! On second thought, I didn't want Vern as an emotional support anything. He could be a jerk. I glared at him and crossed my arms. "Fine. Why not, then?"

"Because I need a partner, not a cause."

"What about Sister Grace?"

"Is Grace faster than a speeding bullet?"

"I'm not—" I started, then the scene at the bookstore came back. Actually, I was!

"You know what I mean! Grace can't fly. Grace can't match my physical strength or speed. Sister Grace McCarthy, for all her admirable talents and who's my greatest treasure, cannot match me in ways I need to be matched. No sapient can—but you can come close."

"So…you want a sparring partner?" I wasn't sure if I was being complimented or used.

"I want a *partner*: sparring, flying patrols, fighting alongside me when needed. Keeping both universes safe. And here you are."

"So I'm the answer to your prayer?"

Vern rolled his eyes. "I'd tell you not to flatter yourself if you didn't sound so insecure. What's with that, anyway? This is not the kid that took on four Mains singlehandedly."

My jaw dropped. That was high school. How did he know about that? "You mean the four guys who nearly beat me to death?"

For a moment, I was back in the hospital bed, an IV in my arm, floating and disoriented from the meds yet aware that I should be aching everywhere. Mom crying like I'd almost died, saying it was all her fault. I'd never seen her cry so hard.

Vern scoffed. "You had a couple of broken bones and a concussion. And the stab wound, but they missed all the internal organs. It was hardly a fair fight, and yet you got a couple of good swings in."

"How would you know?"

"You don't remember? I'm insulted. Who do you think drove them off?"

I paused. Vern had been there? "I hadn't really thought about it, I guess. For some reason, I thought they just got bored after I blacked out."

Vern stared at me, blinking. Then he burst out laughing. "'Bored'? The Mains don't get bored of beating someone up, especially when you blacken their leader's eye."

I frowned. "That was earlier, at school. Strike had video of Mom at work. You're not supposed to take pictures at the club. I don't know how he got it, but he was showing it around. I didn't know what everyone was hooting about until he shoved it under my nose."

I paused, remembering how absolutely shocked and sick I'd felt. Sure, I'd known what my mom did for a living; I'd grown up with it. And she never drank or did drugs or hooked up with guys from the club. I always thought of it like the movie *Flashdance*. I hadn't really understood.

"When Strike made a lewd comment about Mom, I lost it. The next thing I remembered, the teachers were tearing us apart. They said I broke his phone on his face. I got detention and he got suspended. They were waiting for me after school let out. I just figured they got it out of their system. Plus, Strike went to juvie for manslaughter. I figured they were too scared to do anything more."

"They were," Vern agreed, "but more because you had a dragon and Los Despredatores watching your back."

Los Despredatores were the rival gang in our school. I'd gotten more than my fair share of swirlies from them.

"I don't understand."

"They're the main gang in Territory, so I adopted them. They're somewhat less criminal now, thanks to Grace and me, but still a work in progress. At any rate, it turned out, you impressed them. They said you had 'hidden badass skilz.'"

"That's why they called me, 'Minefield'? I thought they were mocking me."

"They wanted to recruit you. I put the kibosh on that. Then, Grace had a long talk with your mom about the impact of her career choices."

"That's why she quit the club? I'd always assumed it was because of me." I'd only been in the hospital four days, but by the time I'd gotten out, she'd left her job and was signed up for the next EMT training at CSU-LL. We had some lean months, but I always felt like what bothered her the most was not dancing any-more.

"It was because of you—and don't go feeling guilty about it. She's better off. At any rate, 'Minefield,' the point is, you've always had it in you to be a hero."

"Because I hit a guy in tenth grade?"

"Because you defended your mother, and then yourself, even against the odds. Because when I told Julio they couldn't recruit you, he said, you wouldn't join a gang, anyway—and because there was a grudg-ing admiration in the way he said it."

"There was? He and his posse stuck my head in the toilet before Homecoming!"

"Was it clean?"

The janitor had already closed the locker room down. "I guess? But that's not the point! I was sopping wet. I had to go home. I missed the game."

"I didn't know you were interested in football."

"I'm not! I was interested in Theresa Martin. I told her I was going to be at the game, and I broke my promise. That was worse than the humiliation. At least I was used to that."

"If you want some revenge, I know where Los Despredatores hang out," Vern suggested. "For that matter, Julio works at Fit-For-Fun. Lots of toilets in their locker room."

"What? No!" How had this conversation gotten so off track? "I'm not that petty!"

"Of course not—another reason why you'll make a good superhero. So what have we learned, Padawan?"

I sighed. "That I'm worthy of the Gapman mantle." I said it begrudgingly, even though I didn't feel it. "But how can you believe that? I'm a screwup. First, I ruined police investigations. Then I get kidnapped by the Queen of the Midsummer Court! I'm not cut out for this."

Vern swished his tail dismissively. "You screwed up; that I won't deny. You got powers and decided you could do whatever you liked as long as your intentions were good. You broke rules you didn't know existed, and that made trouble for Police Chief Santry and hence, for me. But screwing up doesn't mean you are a screwup. You're a writer. You should know how words work."

Low blow! I scowled at him. "So what does that make me?"

"*Untrained*, Padawan. That's where I come in— and Sister Grace, and now Saint George."

He paused, and his mouth twisted like he tasted something sour. "However—and never repeat this—McGrue was right about one thing. Gapman serves Los Lagos. You've made yourself the defender of the community, I can't just keep you hidden away until you're better trained."

I had flown off, half-cocked and depending on my comic-book knowledge and a few conversations with Sister Grace. "Sorry."

Vern stood and stretched like a cat, claws out and everything. "Knights out of the armor now. We'll just have to train you on the job. Wisdom of the Ages, Experience of Eternity, and I'm babysitting a fledgling superhero."

Again, he turned his attention to something beside him. "Of course, it's your fault!" he snapped, but with a warm annoyance that indicated a long-running private joke.

Wow, would I someday have private jokes to share with a *saint*?

"Better?" Vern asked me. "Can we get going? We'll have to fly now."

"Uh, sure!" I rose and shook out my cape before settling it over my shoulders. "Where are we going?"

"The Gapway Theater. Grace is waiting there with Snapdragon. He owes you an explanation."

Chapter Nineteen:
The Self-Made Gapman

Vern

I watched as Ron shook out his cape , plucked off ant stickers, and donned it—Velcro. He attached it with Velcro. I didn't know whether to be impressed with his ingenuity or exasperated at the mundaneness of it. Then, he checked again for any sticker seeds or leaves that attached themselves to the fabric. Ah, yes. Fate had bestowed a weighty mantle on him—and he had used it like a picnic blanket.

His second time on patrol, and Titania had magicked him out of the Mundane. That part didn't bother me so much. The fairy folk had been spiriting Mundanes from their realm since Titania's great-greatgrandsire ruled a united fairy court. But even after that, he was willing to be her champion, to jump right in, not knowing the consequences.

I knew Mundanes, even those that grew up post-Gap, were naïve, but Ron Engleson was far too trusting. Gapman had to be savvier. Which meant I had to teach him.

Now, I had to do it while Gapman continued to do public feats of superheroism for Los Lagos and the world to see. Which also meant making sure any hard-won lessons looked like setbacks and not screw-ups, both for the public eye as well as his self-esteem. What a lot of work.

I hated it when McGrue was right. Fortunately, it didn't happen very often.

"What does that mean?" Ron asked as we took to the air.

I hadn't realized I'd spoken aloud. I really needed to stop muttering, especially around someone with superhearing. "Never mind."

"No, seriously. Kitty's one of the smartest people I know. She's really good at digging up the facts of a story—"

"—and at coming to the wrong conclusions, which more often than not means putting me in a bad light. Be glad she's got starry eyes for Gapman."

"Yeah," there was something hopeful and wistful in his voice that set my scales on edge. Really? The superhero crushing on the investigative reporter? Were we going to be that cliché?

I shrugged. Dragons should not get involved in human romances. You'd think I'd have learned that. Back in the day, I had been paid in fat cows to 'kidnap' the maiden so her intended could rescue her. It was all the rage in human courtship. It was great fun until it backfired on me. Kind of like today. How did I not think about what it would mean if I beat Gapman for the right to defend Titania? I was slipping.

"So what's going to happen if we don't find a champion for Titania?" Ron asked, somehow on the same line of thinking as me.

"I get the 'honor' of battling Mab's champion. Then, I'll have a lot of explaining to convince Mab that I'm not taking sides at all."

"Is that going to be a problem?" Ron asked. I could hear the remorse in his voice.

"It's doable. How long it will take and how much kowtowing I have to do will depend on her mood. It helps that I only agreed to the one challenge and not to be Titania's new champion. Which, incidentally, she would have snared you into if you'd won. Then, I'd have had to explain to McGrue why you were no longer Los Lagos' guardian. Trust me—I'd rather talk to Mab."

I expected a protest that Kitty wasn't so bad, or possibly a snort of agreement. Instead, we flew silently. It was a beautiful, clear day, so it must have been his own thoughts Ron was navigating. I left him to it. I'd done enough lecturing for the moment.

"So, what happened to Titania's other champion? She said he was lost. How'd he die?"

"It's not a euphemism. He didn't die—he's literally lost. He crossed the Gap, turned south, and didn't stop until he was out of her range and off the grid. I've heard rumors that he's in Guatemala, doing mercenary work, but no one's paying me to find out." I shrugged. "She was getting bored with him, anyway, and Mab's champion knew all his tricks. He'd been her champion for three hundred years."

"Three hundred years?" Gapman dipped in surprise, overcompensated, and leveled out beside me.

"If you're going to lose control, make it look like you meant it," I chided. I dipped, crossed under him, overcompensated and circled above him before resuming my spot beside him. "Megamind was not wrong when he said it's all about presentation."

"He's a supervillain," Ron protested.

"Applies to heroes, too. But yes, three centuries. One of the perks of being a champion is a long life—as long as the challenges don't kill you."

"Is that why you challenged me to a duel of compliments?"

"Nah. That was just to make a point to Titania. I'm clever, you know, and difficult to compliment since, as an Eighth Day Creation, it's hard to do my awesomeness justice."

The Gateway Theater came into view. It was a big, round theater, with a large staircase leading to an open porch, lined with seats to accommodate all different species. Grace sat in a giant's chair by the double doors, her legs swinging six inches from the ground as she prayed a rosary.

Humans could be so adorable at times. Her, more than most.

As we landed on the porch, she hopped off the chair with the agility of a child and not the 234-year-old half-siren she was. If she noticed anything patronizing in my affectionate grin, it didn't embarrass her. I think she was enjoying being among the non-human elements of our world for a change.

"All taken care of, then?" she asked. "I have to admit, you're here sooner than I expected."

"Gapman made it easy," I replied blandly. I'd explain in detail later when we could laugh in private.

She nodded. "Well, Snapdragon had plenty of time to talk me through the magical details of his puck. I'm really quite impressed."

I saw Ron's shoulders tighten as he bit back a reply.

Grace noticed, too. "We can speak freely here. Ron, dear, do you understand what a puck is?"

"Pretty much. It's a complex practical joke, kind of like putting the principal's car in his office."

She gave him that nod and smile that teachers gave good students who got something almost right. "It's somewhat more complex than that. Like the joke Puck played in *Midsummer Night's Dream*—which is based on an actual incident—a puck needs emotional, psychological, and physical elements and affects more than one person. In this case, you and Queen Titania were the primary targets of a puck Snapdragon spent almost seven months planning."

"But Snapdragon had only met me that day!" Ron protested. "How could..."

His voice trailed off as he remembered that he was not the original target.

Ron

I had to admit, I didn't care about getting an expla-nation from Snapdragon. I wanted an apology for turning my life upside down.

Or did I? Up until Vern had to rescue me from the Midsummer Court, I'd been pretty stoked about being a superhero. Now, I was also the butt of a joke and an accident—but a saint had taken an interest in me, and Kitty had called me the Defender of Los Lagos.

I sighed to myself. This was so confusing.

At any rate, it was apparent that what I wanted at that moment didn't matter. According to the rules of the fairy court, the victim of the joke had the "right" to an explanation, and the perpetrator had the "right" to explain. It sounded to me like a chance for the joker to brag.

Vern and Grace, however, seemed to think it was important that I knew the facts around my transfor-mation, and that they did, too. Did they think it would help us find the guy who was after me?

Vern had told Titania that Salerno Tom was sup-posed to be her champion. Had he found out about the switch and was mad? Had he shot at me at the book signing? Did Faerie knights know how to use guns?

If not him, then who was upset about the change in target? And why take it out on me? I was the victim! Or was it because I'd decided to embrace my new capabilities?

That would mean they'd seen me doing chores. Why would someone shoot me over doing home improvements?

I was chewing on those thoughts when Sister Grace suggested we go in so Vern and I could get a "somewhat less technical explanation" of the puck.

"That would be good," Vern said cheerily and smiled in my direction. "Dragons tend to be liberal arts majors, you know."

Did they? I looked at him, trying to see if he was joking, but his face was innocent and impassive. I looked at Sister Grace.

She shrugged but didn't contradict him. She opened the door, and Vern set a foot against it and swung his neck to invite her to enter first. She wore a fond little grin when she looked at him, like he was an adorable pet or something. I wondered how the two ever became friends. A dragon and a nun made an incongruous match, but they seemed perfectly suited.

Snapdragon waited for us Center Stage. Much as I wanted to get this over with, I resisted the urge to fly to him and walked alongside Sister Grace down the aisle and up the side steps. He yipped and cheered as we approached.

"The man of the hour, as they say in the Mundane! Welcome Ronald Logan Engleson, a.k.a. Gapman. Let me start by saying, you are brilliant!"

"Uh, thanks? I guess you are, too. I mean, that's what Grace said," I ventured, then mentally kicked myself. I really was bad at compliments.

But he wasn't listening, anyway. "Oh, my, yes! Not only did you take my dear Queen Titania, She of Blazing Days and Shimmering Heat, by surprise, but to then assert your right to choose whether or not to fight for her honor? Ha!"

That wasn't quite how I remembered it. "Actually—"

But he was still laughing. "Then when you not only lost a nonviolent contest of kind words—you, the writer known for writing complimentary reviews of even the worst productions!—no, you then suggest that Vern find a replacement even for himself!"

"I was just—"

Snapdragon did a little flip of glee. "My dear Queen of Short Nights and Shorter Tempers is fit to be tied, to use a human phraseology. Yet, even in her anger, she cannot dispute how well and truly she's been pucked."

Even with superhearing, I wasn't sure I'd heard that right. "Hang on. Are you saying she was the victim of the practical joke? So, what? I was the *car*?"

He paused in his mirth, perplexed. "I am not sure what Mundane transportation has to do with this, but yes, my Queen was indeed the intended target and was given the honor of first Explanation as is her right and rank. However, Sister Grace convinced me that since you, too, were an unwitting victim, you also deserve the honor of understanding. So come, let me explain the grand scheme in all its glory!"

For the next few minutes, he walked us through the process, starting with the loss (literally) of Queen Titania's former champion, and her demand that a new one be found. She had insisted that this time, she wanted someone new and unexpected.

"I had heard of Dorsch's desire to create a superhero play and had learned something of the genre when it struck me—what a wonderful, new, and unexpected champion a superpowered human would be!"

He then ingratiated himself with Dorsch, providing subtle hints and casting suggestions until he secured the job as stage director where he could orchestrate his plan without anyone the wiser.

"I didn't know exactly what would result in a superpowered being, so I tried to cover all the bases," he said. "The pixies were ridiculously easy to influence. I had only to appeal to their art."

"Art? They flew through a nuclear reactor! They were radioactive! How does that translate to acting?"

Snapdragon shrugged. "Mundane actors have done many unusual things to mold themselves to a role. Nicole LaShade didn't bathe for eight months to prepare for her role in *Homeless in Houston*. Calcyon Pike grew his fingernail and toenails five inches and had full-body hair implants to 'become' a werewolf. I just kept bringing up examples. When the time was ripe, I mentioned the Los Lagos reactor, and they came to their own conclusions. Then, they got so cranky, I didn't even have to influence the biting."

Vern had wandered over to the vat and was sniffing it suspiciously. "And the toxic waste?"

"That was hardly a challenge. Winston really was that much of a perfectionist. All I had to do was cause a few splashes and watch for the results. It made me a little nervous. I did keep a close eye on the makeup."

I realized I hadn't heard any glopping or smelled even a hint of the potion's vile stench. "What did you do with it, anyway?"

"Oh, I magicked it away."

I didn't like his flippant tone. "Where?" I demanded. If he'd sent it to the Mundane to some superfund site, I wanted him to bring it right back. My world had enough pollution problems on its own.

But Sister Grace set a hand on my shoulder. "It's all right, Ron," she reassured. "It's been neutralized."

Vern, however, continued to sniff around. Maybe it wasn't quite sniffing. He moved slowly around the area, and while he did poke his nose around—in the vat here, along the floor, there—he seemed to be using senses other than his sense of smell.

Snapdragon watched him for a moment. "I wanted to suggest a couple more tweaks, but Dorsch insisted good enough was good enough, and he didn't want any surprises after dress rehearsal. I knew I'd have to run with what we had and hope for the best. So when he told us you were coming to report on the dress rehearsal, I knew the time had come. You would be witness to the greatest puck in an age."

"That was why we were on the scaffolding then?" I asked. "I was just supposed to watch, and the scaffolding broke from sheer bad luck?"

Somehow that made me feel better.

But no.

Snapdragon snorted. "Dust and daisies! Why would you insult me like that? No, that scaffolding was perfectly safe, right up until I spirited the nails out of the wood!

"I'm not even sure why I did it. I had been all set to have the vat tip over when Captain Extraordinary was doing his solo scene. But there was just something about you. How you freaked out about the pixies being radioactive, but then you went right back to taking photos and asking questions. It was such a compelling combination of terror and fearlessness."

"I think you mean 'courage,'" the writer in me corrected.

Snapdragon shook his head earnestly. "That's not it at all. Oh, don't get me wrong. I'm sure you can be brave, but at that moment, it was like you'd forgotten to be afraid. I was struck with how trusting you were, me being a fairy and our having just met. And it struck me, 'How funny would it be if Ronnie fell into the toxic waste and my Queen got him for her champion?'"

"Classic," I muttered darkly. I had a flashback to when I was five and one of Mom's boyfriends had offered me a candy bar, pulled it away at the last minute, offered it again, and laughed as he yanked it out of my reach. Mom had shoved him out the door even as he protested that I was too gullible.

"Classic, indeed," Snapdragon agreed. "Then you grabbed Goldleaf just as I'd hoped."

Vern took to the air under the broken scaffolding. "About here?" he asked.

"Yep! Snagged his leg. I'd never heard such a shriek—from pixie or from human when Goldleaf bit him. Then, splash! And Ronnie was floundering and oh, my wings! When he flung that pixie at Hawgin!"

For the next few minutes, Snapdragon narrated, beat for beat, the fiasco that was the conception of Gapman. My face reddened with embarrassment, but I couldn't help thinking that Snapdragon really had a talent both for stage direction and storytelling. By the time he'd described Hawgin slumped dazed against the upset refreshments table, Ping cola pouring onto his head and soaking Goldleaf whose jaw had apparently locked mid-bite, I, too, was grinning. I felt a little bad about it, but like I said, Snapdragon had a knack for comedic presentation.

Vern, however, got a keen look on his face. "So Hawgindespotlite was also splashed and bitten?"

"Yeah," Snapdragon said. "Salerno'd developed some pretty quick reflexes after the last couple of 'accidents,' as had most of the cast, but Hawgin was in the middle of his monologue."

"Where is he now?"

Snapdragon shrugged, the straps of his coveralls rubbing against his wings. "I don't know. When Ronnie ran out of the theater screaming for decontamination, Dorsch lost his temper. I hadn't heard such words since Titania clipped King Oberon's wings to keep him home. Dwarf voices resonate, too. Some of us thought he'd bring the theater down. By the time he'd calmed down, Hawgin, Goldleaf, and about half the cast had fled. Lady Elena was in tears, and Salerno took her home."

He turned to me apologetically. "There may have been a few cursing your name. Sorry about that."

I sighed. Great. Now we had more suspects.

"Anyone else bitten?" Vern asked, and I remembered that he'd said he'd sensed a twisted magic where my attacker had set up his rifle.

Snapdragon paused. "No. That would have been great fun, though. Oh, you're thinking Hawgin might have powers, too? Worry not, my dragon friend. Ronnie here did not gain his abilities from my handiwork. As with all good pucks, there is a spark of inspiration behind the execution and of the victim being a tool in his own demise, and as you know, Ronnie chose to run through the Gap as lightning struck."

"So you're saying I did this to myself?" I shouted, and Snapdragon took a bow.

Chapter Twenty:
Gapman Squashes a Bug

Ron

"Well, that was mortifying," I grumbled as we made our way up the aisle to exit the theater. Snapdragon had finished his explanation, answered all of our questions, and headed back to his queen. I was ready to go home and have a long, hot shower and process how my life had gotten so complex just so someone could have a laugh.

Sister Grace set a sympathetic hand on my arm. "But informative."

"Maybe. I still don't get how Hawgin would have gotten powers if it took my running through the Gap and getting struck by lightning."

"Maybe it wasn't the lightning so much as the Mundane element," Vern suggested.

"The Ping, then? Possibly. It does have deleterious effects on elves' brains. I think our next step is to find

Hawgin or Goldleaf, preferably both. But that can wait until tomorrow, don't you agree, Vern?"

Vern was peering at the entrance. "I don't think we get a choice. Put on your mask, Gapman. We have company outside."

I tensed. What now?

"Relax," he said. "It's Charlie—Charlie Wilmot, the Duke's herald. Someone must have told Duke Galen we were in town."

We emerged from the theater to find a grand carriage with four white horses waiting for us at the bottom of the stairs. A redheaded young man in a wildly colored herald's uniform lounged against one huge wheel, watching a smartphone. My superhearing caught the lines of a sitcom I recognized: *Rhoda Dakota*, about a teen singer and her father. Kind of an odd choice, but when he looked up, I saw that he was probably about 18, himself.

The herald—Charlie, Vern had called him—snapped to attention, his phone tucked away so fast, I could have thought he had superspeed.

"Vern d'Wyvern, Sister Grace McCarthy, and Gapman, Hero of the Mundane: Duke Galen of Peebles on Tweed and Duchess Elaine of Peebles on Tweed bid you welcome and request the honor of your presence for dinner this evening at the royal estate."

"I'm starved! Accepted!" Vern said and bounded down the steps.

"Could we take a rain check?" I asked.

Herald Wilmot regarded me with narrow eyes. "I assure you the Duke's reign is legitimate."

Shoot! Had I just insulted the Duke? "No! That's not what I meant. It's Mundane for—"

But Vern interrupted me with a guffaw. "Good one, Charlie!"

He raised a paw for the Herald to high-five as he passed.

Sister Grace patted my shoulder. "You'll have to excuse Charlie. He has spent a little too much time with Vern, I fear."

"Hey!" Vern called as he settled on the top of the carriage.

Charlie, however, gave a slight bow. "My apologies. However, to answer your question, sir: My lady sovereign has prepared a feast, and the Duke insists."

"I'm sure you're hungry," Grace said quietly, "and mayhaps a reminder of how amazing you are would be a salve to your psyche? We can leave early if you like."

Then she headed to the carriage. I followed, trying to move with dignity while inwardly I resigned myself to yet more time away from Los Lagos. I was going to have to come up with a cover story to explain my absence. The carriage rocked as Herald Wilmot took a seat by the driver, and we were on the way. Grace smiled at me, reassured me things would be fine, then pulled out some beads and bent her head.

Would I have to learn how to pray like that now that I was talking to a saint?

I glanced out the window, but no apparition on a white horse followed us. Just the trees and fields. It was maybe ten minutes to the Duke's castle. Normally, I'd be stoked, but right now, I was feeling a weird dread I could not define.

Why hadn't Mom—er, GHQ—texted me? I'd promised her an hour and a half, and we'd passed that ten minutes ago. Then again, I was an adult; once she knew I was okay, she'd probably stop worrying.

Naturally, just as I'd relaxed into that thought, my cell chirped. *911!!! Get here now! Wasps!*

I paused, confused. Mom was not one of those people afraid of bugs, even nasty-minded ones like wasps. Had she forgotten where the insecticide was?

Then a photo popped up. A stinger—just the backend with the stinger. How did she get such a closeup?

Then I saw the splintered wood around it.

"Yeaghh!" I shouted in a very unherolike way and dropped my phone.

Grace blinked at me, then set her beads aside and picked up the phone. She stared at the photo, her eyes growing wide. "Gapman, is that...a door?"

"I have to get ho—to HQ now!"

She didn't question me, just pushed open the door. "Go! Take Vern. I'll catch up."

"Vern! With me!" I shouted as I flew out the door. I didn't turn around to look or to apologize about being bossy. Mom was in danger!

Vern

I was reclining on the roof and teasing Charlie about his taste in Mundane TV shows when I heard Ron yelp and suddenly, he was flying out of the carriage.

"Vern! With me!" he shouted and kept right on flying toward the Gap. I had to give him credit; he sounded very heroish, if not especially enlightening.

Grace stuck her head out the window. "Proto-empyre attack," she said.

Fewmets! I was looking forward to a nice, big dinner. I launched from the roof. Grace tossed me Gapman's phone as I passed.

Racing to catch up with Gapman, I looked at the phone. Wow! Based on the stinger, that thing had to be four feet. The colors on the abdomen didn't look like an American/Mundane wasp. Too orange. In all my retained memories, I didn't recall any giant hornet monsters, but we did have giant spiders, so who knows? Regardless, unless there was a swarm, this wouldn't be too hard.

A text came up: *Well?*

I was going to have to talk to Gapman about abandoning his equipment.

This is Vern. On the way. Where to? How many?

HQ. 2? I'm in the interior bathroom, in the shower stall. I spread mint toothpaste on the threshold, but IDK. Hurry!

Smart! Hang tight!

Meanwhile, we'd almost come to the Faerie side of the Gap crossing. People were looking our way and pointing. I guess that made sense; they'd seen me and fairies and all manner of flying creatures, but never a human in a green cape soaring through the air, one arm in front of him like he was punching a hole in the atmosphere.

Gapman ignored them and sped through the Gap.

"Oi, Vern!" the centaur guard called. "Friend of yours, then? I didn't know Mundanes flew."

His partner elbowed him in the withers. "Idjit. He's wearing one of those ultralights they use. I read about them in *Marvelous Mundane Mechanisms*."

Guess it wasn't illustrated. Still, some things take too long to explain, and not-so-ultralight-sized bugs were attacking the Mundane. I bit back a chuckle as I put on some speed and followed Gapman through the Gap.

I emerged on the other side to cheers. That was new! I almost had a moment of pride when I realized people were shouting Gapman's name. Someone by the flower shop grabbed a bouquet and threw it in the air. The orange and white carnations went about three feet over her head before falling back upon it. The little tissue ghost was flung free and floated to the ground.

Figured. It's all pitchforks and screams when the dragon flies by. Gapman gets flowers and adulation. There's no justice, really.

Even so, Gapman zoomed past without acknowledgment. A few people who came to the right conclusion called out encouragement. "Go get 'em, Gapman!" "You got this, Gapman!" "Go, go, Hero!"

No justice. None at all—at least not for a dragon in the Mundane world.

I caught up to Gapman outside the city limits. "So, got a plan for dealing with the WOUSes?"

"Wooses? Is that what they are?"

"Wasps Of Unusual Size, yes. What do you plan to do once we get there?"

He slowed marginally. "Uh... Squash them?"

"With what? A roof? I have a better idea. You lure them toward me, and I'll breathe fire on them. We'll burn them out of the sky. It shouldn't take long. GHQ said there are only two that she saw."

The tension in his shoulders relaxed just a little. "Two? That's a relief. Wait—how do you know?"

I held up his phone, and he groaned. "Yeah, sorry. I kind of panicked."

I decided to give him a break. "WOUSes will do that to anyone, but as far as proto-empyre go, this should be easy enough. So does having the fist in front of you help fly faster?"

"What?" He blinked at his fist, as if noticing it. "Um, yeah. Yeah, I think it does."

"Then lead on, Gapman."

We heard the buzzing even before we got to the house: a low, heavy drone that even I found creepy, and I generally don't have a problem with bugs of any size.

Gapman snatched the phone from my hand and typed. I hovered, looking over his shoulder.

Here. U OK?

☹☺They're upstairs. I think they've forgotten me.

Stay put. We'll take care of them.

My hero!

I snorted. "Singular. Typical."

"What?"

"Just go lure them out here and let me blast them so you can rescue your mom."

"Right."

And he flew to the house, uncaring of the danger and oblivious to my sarcasm.

Ron

I felt like there was something in Vern's tone that I should have picked up on, but to be honest, I was too focused on the WOUSes. Man, that buzzing was creepy, like a beehive taken down an octave and played heavy on the bass. I could feel it in my stomach. Or maybe that was nerves.

Taking on criminals was one thing—but actual monsters?

I flew to the back porch. The barbeque was toppled but fortunately, cold. The hot tub lid was off. Mom must have been having a soak. She loved the contrast of cool air and hot water. The water bubbled, the heater working overtime to warm the water, but no steam rose from it.

I paused at the back porch door, the one Mom took the photo of. There was a two-inch hole and a dent the size of a dinner plate. Then, they'd broken the window instead. Instinct or intelligence? I really hoped they were as stupid as Vern seemed to think they were.

How was I supposed to get them out into the open?

One thing at a time. First, I had to find them. I opened the door and quietly stepped in.

The door opened into our kitchen. It was a shambles: turned-over chairs, broken dishes. A half-carved pumpkin lay shattered on the floor. One of the cabinet doors was half-unhinged and broken, like something slammed into it. I saw our broom discarded by the island. Mom must have dropped it to run. I snatched it up. Smacking them from a distance sounded a lot safer to me.

I moved slowly into the great room, heart pounding and sure something was going to fly into my face even though my hearing told me the wasps were in the attic. Our Jack Skeleton wall hanging now hung in tatters from its thumb tacks. Books scattered around the floor. Mom must have grabbed some from the shelf and flung them behind her as she made her way to the bathroom.

I thought about going there first, checking to be sure she was okay. But we were texting for a reason. If the wasps heard us, they may come back down. I wanted the danger as far from her as possible. At least they were obliging me by being upstairs. Still, why had they gone to my attic study instead of chasing Mom?

Then again, I didn't care. I just wanted them dead. I took a deep breath, reminded myself I was mostly bulletproof and had a Kevlar-reinforced supersuit, and flew to the second story and up the staircase to the attic. My busted door hung askew, supported by a single bent hinge. Why? What was so great about the attic?

I poked my head in.

Two WOUSes, ground-hornet-shaped but orange, and—gulp—big as my desk, were circling the bare light bulb shining in the middle of the ceiling.

"Hey!"

I meant to shout it; I really did, but it came out as a strangled squawk. I swallowed and tried again.

Or was about to. The WOUSes spun toward me as one and shot my way.

I screamed a very unheroic scream and fled.

I zoomed out the door, down the stairwell, and out the still-open kitchen door, two angry wasps-of-unusual-size hot on my tail.

Vern

If that was Gapman's battle cry, we had a lot of work to do.

At least I was ready when he came tearing out of the house, the hornet-shaped proto-empyre in hot pursuit. Still at the porch, he made a sharp turn up, rising above the treeline and angling toward the clear area where a large pile of asphalt waited to be spread on their road. Smart human—that gave the flaming carcasses a safe place to fall.

Speaking of. Once I was sure my vector would not intercept any of the autumn-dry trees and Gapman was out of range, I blasted the WOUSes with incinerating flame.

I was feeling spunky; my flame lit the area like the midday sun. I kept the flame going hot and wide, long enough to burn my victims to ash and then set the ash on fire.

And yet, I didn't see any ashes, flaming or otherwise, dripping from where my intended victims hovered.

Confused, I cut off my flame.

And there they were: two WOUSes, glowing orange and tripled in size.

"But!" I started.

"The heat! They must absorb the heat!" Gapman pointed at the steamless hot tub.

"That's not fair!" I shouted, then dodged quickly to the right as one of the insidious insects made a beeline toward my head. Apparently, my mouth was its new favorite heat source.

"What now?" Gapman cried. He was hovering mid-air, holding a broom like a baseball bat. The other wasp zipped toward him, and he swatted at it. I heard a crack as the broom impacted its thorax. The handle broke, but so did one of the wasp's wings. It flew in crazy swirl, trying to adjust. Gapman threw the broken handle at it like a javelin, but it missed and sunk into the trunk of a neighboring tree.

I didn't have time to answer because my attacker was coming straight at my head again. I shot off a burst of flame to distract it and dove under it. Once under it, I rolled and, claws out, slashed. It curled its stinger at me; I managed to just avoid being stung, but I felt the scrape against one of my back spikes. I did not want to imagine the pain if it had gotten my wings or the softer scales of my belly.

I whipped my tail around and encircled its sternum just above the stinger. It scratched at me with its hind legs, which had claws—did you know wasps had claws? I didn't until that moment. It bit at my head while it kneed me, getting a lucky poke in my belly with one spur. I twisted and rose, trying to get above it and sink my claws into its thorax and abdomen, maybe break all its wings while I was at it.

It didn't like my plan at all. We rolled in the air, dipping and bobbing. I'd like to think we looked like two majestic griffins or maybe hawks locked in mortal combat, but it felt more like an aerial wrestling match, and I could not keep a good grip and stop WOUS-1 from hurting me.

Gapman, meanwhile, was zipping around the yard, looking for another weapon. He tried to pull the broom handle from the tree, but WOUS-2 nearly clipped him before he gave up and fled. It smacked into the tree and was stunned. Gapman reached for its wings to tear them off, but he was too slow. It shook itself and snapped at his outstretched hand. He pulled away just in time and dashed toward his shed. I lost sight of them.

Just as well. WOUS-1 had almost slipped its stinger from my grip. I shoved it away with a foot to the abdomen then bit down hard on its antenna and tore it off. In the distance, I heard the rattling of yard implements. A shovel flew past us. Then a hoe.

"You're missing!" I yelled.

"I know!" he shouted back. But he kept trying. A rake. A post-hole digger.

When the pitchfork came flying close, I took a chance. Keeping its mandibles and stinger at bay with my appendages, I stretched out my neck and caught the pitchfork by the handle, then whipped my head hard toward my foe.

The tines sunk deep into its side. Ichor and heat magic that I could feel spilled out.

WOUS-1 jerked and started to fall, taking me with it. I twisted hard, putting it under me then flung it away with all my strength. I watched it plummet to the ground, legs pawing desperately at the handle while the body jerked spasmodically. It hit the ground with a thud and stayed still.

I dove down and ripped its head off before it could recover.

Then I heard a metallic screech and turned just in time to see Gapman swing a large panel of corrugated steel. It smacked WOUS-2 with a *thwack* I felt as much as heard. The WOUS was flung into a tree and before it could recover, Gapman jammed the panel edge first into it, cutting it in half.

He settled to the ground, hands on his knees, panting. He was covered in dirt, sweat, and ichor, and parts of his supersuit had torn, but I didn't see any blood or puncture marks. Good.

I flew over to him. "Nice job, Gapman. Was that the shed roof?"

"It was your idea," he gasped, then straightened. "I am so hungry now! I thought you said this would be easy."

I sighed ruefully as I examined the wasp—or rather, the half which was still stuck to the tree thanks to the panel. It managed to look surprised and angry and hateful—though "angry" and "hateful" were probably its resting wasp face. "Yeah, I gotta stop saying that. Any idea how to tell if it's male or female? We need to find where they came from and make sure there's no larvae."

He straightened with a shout. "Omigosh! Mom!"

Miss Engleson was picking her way out the destroyed back door. She made it to the porch railing and leaned on it, surveying the wasps and the damage.

"We're buying more Buggone!" she declared.

Chapter Twenty-One:
Gapman Does a Podcast

Ron

Mom checked the camera to make sure she, Matilda, and I were well-centered on the screen and the odd discoloration on the wall was also in the frame. I hadn't even realized murder hornets (which sounded so much more dignified and dangerous than WOUSes) could spit venom. It was a good thing Sister Grace had put protective spells on my supersuit—and that Mom had made a second one.

I was even more grateful that Mom was all right. In fact, once the shock wore off, she'd decided this was the perfect way to connect Gapman to his fan club.

"Ready?" she asked us, an excited lilt in her voice. Beside me, Matilda tittered.

I summoned my inner British stoicism. "Of course, ladies."

Mom adjusted her "Oh My Gapman!" T-shirt to make sure the logo was straight, then turned on the video.

"Hello, Gapfans! Or should we say Gap*fen*, because fen are fans of anything sci-fi or fantasy, and let's face it: a superhero in Los Lagos is straight out of both! Welcome to the first *Oh My Gapman* podcast! And can you believe it? Our first guest is the Hero of Los Lagos, himself..."

"Gapman!" she and Matilda chorused together like a couple of schoolgirls, pointing at me with open hands. I gave what I hoped looked like a courteous nod and humble smile to the audience on the screen.

"Gapman is, of course, my personal hero as well," Mom continued, setting a hand on my shoulder. It was such a Mom statement, I wanted to roll my eyes, but she was talking about the superhero and not her boy. "Anyone who was following the chat yesterday knows my house was attacked by murder hornets and Gapman came to my rescue."

"With Vern, the dragon from DragonEye, PI," I said because my mentor would flame me alive if I took all the credit. "It was a team effort. For that matter, you did a pretty good job defending yourself before I arrived."

"Yes, yes. She's very good with a folding chair," Matilda said, referring to their amateur wrestling days. "Let's talk about the interesting stuff. Do you work out?"

She squeezed my bicep. I bit back a cough of discomfort. Aunt Matilda didn't know it was me. Even so, my mind went blank. How would a superhero answer?

"Hey!" Mom cut across the silence. "I think maybe our listeners would like to know if they should expect murder hornets in their backyard, don't you?"

Matilda blew a raspberry. "The news covered that. You took care of the nest, right, Gapman?"

She batted her eyes at me coquettishly. I had to take control of the narrative, fast. I kept my face to the camera as if addressing the person behind the lens.

"We did, yes. We found it in a disturbed rock pile further up the mountain. It looks like there were only the two adults, and we destroyed the larvae. Or rather, Sister Grace McCarthy, the mage from DragonEye, PI, did. She drained the magic and then we dissolved the rest with acid."

"Oh! The nuclear option!"

Mom and I had planned the joke. I gave her a heroish smirk. "Only way to be sure. The murder hornets were actually proto-empyre, like Shogzallie or the

Mishmash monster from a couple of years back. I've been helping Vern and Sister Grace search for any other monsters still in hiding."

"Is that why we haven't seen much of you lately?" Matilda asked just as we'd expected.

I nodded. "It's been slow work, but now with a third data point, Sister Grace is better able to see the trajectory of the magic that brought them to our realm. We still have a lot of ground to cover, but—"

Mom cut me off. "Gapfen, let's help our hero out! If you notice anything strange of a magical nature, report it on the OMyGapman discussion thread."

"So that's what you've been doing when we don't see you in town?" Matilda asked. "Just searching for potential threats?"

I looked at her. "Prevention is a preferable option, especially when it comes to monsters. Believe me; I'd rather have dealt with the murder hornets before they got so big. One tried to bite my head off!"

"Makes sense," Mom replied. "You were flying and mostly yellow. It must have thought you were a bee."

"An adorable bee," Matilda said, leaning closer. "I'd bite you."

That was so uncomfortable coming from the woman who used to blow raspberries on my belly when I was six. "Madam, if you knew the man behind the mask, you might not be so interested," I said, praying she'd take a hint.

I should have known she wouldn't. "I'm willing to take that chance," she said.

Mom huffed a loud, disparaging sigh and leaned across me to glare at her cohost. "Matilda, stop throwing yourself at our guest. It's embarrassing!"

Matilda set her elbow on her knee and turned to face Mom while having what I *think* she meant as a coquettish pose. "Embarrassing? Like when you took your shirt off at the book signing?"

"It was hot!"

"And you thought it would make things hotter. Right in front of your son, too. What do you think of that, Gapman?"

It took super-willpower not to shrink under Matilda's gaze, or to pinch the bridge of my nose as Ronme would have done. How could I even answer that as Gapman? One way would tick off Mom and start an argument, and another would sound like I was defending her—or worse, was interested in her.

"Perhaps, we could get back to the interview?" I pleaded.

Matilda broke the glaredown with Mom to look at me, and her eyes widened in delight and surprise. "Oh, my Gapman! You're blushing. Surely, this isn't the first time you've had attractive women fight over you!"

As Ron and Gapman battled for an answer that would end this fiasco without hurting Aunt Matilda's feelings, Mom came to my rescue. "He's just shy! And it's really inappropriate to come on to one of our guests. We should move on."

Matilda sighed. "Alright, then. I apologize, Gapman. It's all in good fun. Besides, we all know you have your eye on a certain reporter."

"What?" I yelped. How did they know about my crush on Kitty?

That's Ron, idiot. Besides, you've read the forums. Fortunately, years of reading comic-book superhero romance subplots came to my rescue. With what I hoped was an unnoticeable pause, I said, "Matilda, I hope you can put an end to those rumors. Kitty McGrue is a respected member of the community and a highly capable reporter. Our relationship consists of a couple of interviews for the *Gazette*. Also, I'd prefer not to discuss any relationships I have—romantic, familial, or otherwise. They could expose someone I care about to anyone who has a grudge against me."

"Who could have a grudge against you?" Matilda asked.

"People I put in jail. My nemesis..." Shoot! I hadn't told Mom about Vern's theory that the gunshot was meant for me.

Matilda gasped. "Do you think we'll be in danger as the presidents of your fan club? Do you think that's why the murder hornets came after Trixie?"

"We think the murder hornets were more interested in the heat from the hot tub, and when that was drained, Miss Engleson was the next closest target."

"So just bad luck," Mom concluded.

I nodded, but I still felt bad. The nest had been under the pile of boulders I was pulling from to make rubble for our road. Sister Grace had told me it was actually serendipitous—if I'd not disturbed the nest when I had, we might have faced a huge swarm come Spring—but I still felt awful about putting Mom in danger.

Matilda said with genuine gratitude and no flintiness at all, "Well, I'm glad you were around to rescue her. You'd just gotten back from Faerie, right?"

"Yes. Queen Titania of the Midsummer Court was interested in retaining my services. But she now understands that I'm here to protect Los Lagos." I hoped that was innocuous enough to not get me in trouble with her or her people.

Matilda squealed. "The fairy queen? What's she like?"

She sat straighter and watched me with clasped hands and starry eyes. Aunt Matilda was a big Faerieboo. Maybe if we kept on the subject of Queen Titania, she would stop flirting with me. Besides, it never hurt to compliment the Queen of Sunburns. "Beautiful. Shrewd. Eminently charming, but not someone you want to be on the wrong side of. Time works differently in the court—probably where we got the Rip Van Winkle legends from. I hadn't realized I'd been there two days. I apologize to anyone who had been wondering about my absence."

I forced myself not to look at Mom when I said that, lest my chagrin clue in someone that I was especially sorry for what I'd put her through, personally.

"And speaking of your fans," Mom said, "we have questions in the chat. Let's grab some at random—but remember, we aren't going to ask anything that might lead to Gapman's secret identity. And let's keep it clean. This is a family show. *Matilda*."

Aunt Matilda was batting her eyelashes me. I guess I hadn't discouraged her as much as I'd hoped. Still, at Mom's warning, she sat up more primly and said, "I'll behave, but let me just tell our viewers: Gapman's adorable when he blushes."

I tried not to cringe. She often said the same thing about Ron-me.

Mom reached for a glass of water and waved at Matilda to start the Q&A. Matilda pulled her pad onto her lap where she could read it. "Here's a good one! Gapguest 3561 asks: Do you wear an athletic cup, and if so, what size?"

Mom spat out the water she'd been about to swallow. "Matilda!"

We answered questions until Mom called an end to the podcast saying she had to get to work.

"Not all heroes wear capes," I'd told her. It sounded like a very Gapman thing to say, but I hope she knew I meant it as Ron, too. After my talk with Vern, I'd been wondering if I'd told her how much I appreciated her quitting the club for me. I knew she missed dancing even if she liked being an EMT.

Once we signed off, I said quick goodbyes and headed to the cliffside where I'd agreed to meet Vern. He was already there, relaxing on the sunny plateau, his tail swinging down off the edge while he laughed at something on his phone. It was an incongruous thing, seeing a dragon scrolling on a tiny screen. He had a rubber nib on his pinkie claw.

"How was the podcast, Gapman?" he asked with a lilt in his voice that said he guessed the answer.

I gave it anyway. "Mortifying."

I sat on the cliff edge, letting my feet hang like I was a little kid. I sighed.

"The Q&A or Matilda throwing herself at you?"

"Matilda, mostly, though the questions weren't much better. 'Do I poop at superspeed?' Who thinks that's an okay question?"

"I liked the kid who tried to trick you into doing his math homework—and that you caught him at it."

He'd tried to be subtle about it, inserting Gapman into his word problems, but they hadn't changed since I went to Los Lagos Middle School.

"He *did* want to test how smart I am." I grinned and didn't add that I had really been trying to skirt the question altogether. I hated math.

"Ready for patrol?" Vern stood and stretched. I noticed his phone and rubber nib were gone.

"Where's your phone?"

He looked at me like I was stupid. "In my pouch. What? Did you think dragons carried their treasure in buckets?"

I hadn't thought about it at all. "Given the way you live here, I wasn't sure Faerie dragons were allowed to have treasure."

He sighed wistfully. "In Faerie, I have the most glorious dragon's hoards, which since my encounter with Saint George, I'm only allowed to visit—much less make use of—on the rarest of occasions."

My heart skipped. "Saint George? He's not gonna make me...? I mean, Everything big I own is also my mom's—"

"Don't worry," Vern said as he shook himself head to tail. "I'm conscripted to the Church. You're not. Most likely, George will be watching over you, praying for you. Maybe, giving some advice or helping out, but only when there's dire need. Don't expect to see him much."

"Okay." It was kind of a relief, really. I had no idea what to do with a patron saint, especially one on a first-name basis with a dragon.

I, too, stood and stretched. It felt good after sitting all morning. Flying was really just pointing myself in one direction and staying still. And holding my gut in. One of the callers had asked if I planned on doing more ab exercises. He'd been promptly booed down in the chat, but still. Maybe super-metabolism didn't mean I could eat more Ding Dongs. Still...

I did 200 sit-ups at superspeed while my mentor watched, shaking his head.

Chapter Twenty-Two: Gapman Gets in a Fight

Vern

Once SuperEgo finished catering to his vanity, we took off and headed to Los Lagos.

"So, I was thinking we fly together a couple of days, kind of like an orientation tour," I told him. "If anyone asks, you're getting intel on the city. Then, depending on how that goes, I'll shadow you so it looks like you're on your own, but we'll stay in contact over radio."

I held out an earbud. He looked at me, askance.

"Why didn't you give me this on the ground?"

"Before or after the sit-ups? Besides, can't you handle a pass-off midair? We practiced."

"Yeah—with pinecones!" Nonetheless, he got closer and gingerly took it from my grasp. Almost too gingerly. It nearly slipped from his fingers as he pulled it from my claws, and again as he put it in his ear. He turned to his side, so his ear was facing up to the clouds as he wriggled it in. So dignified.

"Once you have Santry's trust, we'll get him to let you in on any active investigations. For now, I know what everyone on the force smells like, so we can avoid any undercover ops SNAFUs. So don't go haring off on your own," I warned, and he nodded.

Since we were doing the orientation tour, I took him to Territory first to meet some of my "regulars." When I first moved into the broken-down warehouse that an aging parishioner had willed me, I'd made it a point to protect the people in the neighborhood; they, in turn, had gifted me with food and the occasional favor. It was the poor side of town, so most of the time it was leftovers and discards, but I couldn't afford to be picky. As my influence spread, people took pride in having a dragon on their side; hence, the area took on the name "Territory."

I explained this as we landed near the Lickety Split station. I pointed to a long clawed gash in the brick wall. "That's my mark. People know if they see it to leave the place alone."

He gaped. "There's some lady with a Lexus with scratch marks on the back. I thought it was a style thing."

"Nope. She's mine, too." I smirked, remembering the day she had confronted me about the mess in my yard which ended with her asking me to vandalize her expensive car.

"Yo, Vern!" a voice called from the garage, and Andy stepped out, wiping his hands on a dirty rag. "Not seen you in a while. And—oh! Gapman!"

"Gapman, meet Andy Hernandez," I said. "He was my first principle." I trusted Ron's writer vocabulary to know I meant the archaic definition of "someone I protect."

"Yeah, he stopped some thugs from robbing the place, and I gave him a couple of gallons of ethanol in return. Now, I mostly gas Sister Grace's car once in a while," he said as he shook Gapman's hand. "You here for a drink?" he asked me.

I could see Gapman's brows knit under the mask.

"I'm too big for human drinks to do much for me; a couple of gallons of high-octane are good for a buzz." I cocked my head at Gapman. "You going to drive me to drink?"

He put his hands on his hips and said sternly. "While enjoying the occasional beer is fine, excessive drinking is harmful to yourself and those around you."

I had to give him credit; he didn't even blanch at my particular choice of alcohol.

"You really are a flying public service announcement," I teased.

"You want a beer, Gapman?" Andy asked eagerly. I could almost see the stars in his eyes. Not to mention the internet fame. *Dragons and Superheroes get their drinks here!*

Of course, Gapman held up one gloved hand in polite rejection. I saw a smear of engine oil on it. His mom was going to be mad.

"I don't drink while in uniform," he said.

"You sure? I got that fancy imported stuff. Woldbrow or something."

I suppressed a grin. Waldbräu may have come from Germany, but it was really just a darker version of Coors.

From Gapman's grin, I think he knew it, too. "You're very kind, but no, thank you."

He shrugged, then turned to me. "You might want to check on your *hitos*. They were just in here, talking trash about 'getting even' with those RealHumans. Guess they harassed one of their own?"

"Taking advantage of the last warm days of the year. They say where?"

He shook his head. "And I did not ask."

I nodded, understanding. "Well, we didn't hear about it here, did we, Gapman?"

Nonetheless, I thanked him for the tip, and we took to the air. I called Grace as we headed to the trailer park where Los Despredatores hung out.

She sighed. "I guess we should have expected this. I'm at the parish. I'll light a candle and head out. Call me when you see them."

I hung up and let Gapman know.

He looked me over querulously. "How'd you do that? Magic?"

I laughed. "Phone in my pouch and throat mic under the scale. I'm one tricked-out dragon."

I gave him a moment to laugh, then told him what I expected we'd find. In short: best case, we'd catch them before they got into RealHuman territory and he could stand by sternly while I talked my pups down. Worst case: We were heading into a fight that would include knives and guns.

Gapman said something very unheroic and unheroically nervous. I felt the urge to roll my eyes, but I remembered the first time I had to do battle in my new form: an undersized dragon taking on a hoard of Anansi's spiderchildren. I had been shaking under my scales, and I'd fought dinosaurs and titans many times before then.

Stopping a gang war was a lot to ask of a fledgling superhero whose experience with gangs consisted of being hospitalized after a beatdown.

"Listen, no judgment, but if it looks like more than you are ready for, hang back and call the cops."

His eyes shined with gratitude for a moment; then, his expression hardened. "I'm hardly a superhero if I can't defend my city. But if there's fighting, shouldn't we call the police, anyway?"

"We will. And then we get in there and break it up, move the injured, whatever we can."

"Right." He swallowed hard and was quiet the rest of the flight.

When we got near enough to hear the shouting and catcalls, however, it was clear we were arriving during the warmup before the violence.

And that's when Gapman went Rogue.

Ron

Oh, boy.

Despite my brave words to Vern, my body kept pulling up kinesthetic memories of kicks breaking my ribs, fists slamming into my face.

I'm a superhero. I'm a superhero.

To distract myself, I started searching my memory for times when my favorite heroes had to stop gang fights. "Gang Wars" by Marvel...no, too high-level, organized crime, and the villains were all supers... Stupendan! He was great. What was that speech he made to talk them down...?

For that matter, the speech I'd made at the Gap riot went over pretty well. People were still talking about it on the OMyGapman forums...

I could talk them down. I mean, didn't it just make sense? If people could just see past their preconceived notions and the "Us vs. Them" mentality...

Could we get them to do that? No—Vern couldn't. The RealHumans would see him and immediately place him under "Them."

But I was human—and now, thanks to magic, I was something more. I was meant to be something more. Vern had said it. For that matter, God wanted me to be something more. He'd even sent me a saint to prove it.

So when we got near enough to hear the two gangs shouting epithets and threats at each other, I knew: This was a job for Gapman!

"Hang back, Vern. I've got this!"

I zoomed ahead, ignoring Vern's cry to wait. I could do this! I am that hero!

I arrived at the wide alley to find the two gangs squared up against each other, the leaders both stood ahead of their members. The leaders were armed with knives, but not yet in swinging distance. Ha! I was right. They didn't want to fight so much as make themselves heard.

Cool and calm, I told myself. Tempers are high, and if I come in judgmental or pushy, they'll react badly.

A few of the gang members on each side shouted and pointed as I approached. I landed several steps away from the arguing leaders, walking smoothly toward them with my hands out in an inviting, nonthreatening manner. "Gentlemen, what seems to be the problem?"

They both turned on me with eyes so full of fury, I almost missed a step. It's not at me, I reminded myself. They're angry. They want justice. It's not at me...

But the RealHumans leader said, "None of your business, Gapfreak."

"Yeah," the Despredatores leader chimed in. "Unless you wanna take out these *mundagrinos* for us."

"Mundagrinos" was a horrible slang for a Mundane—usually a white person, too. It was just coming into the vernacular when I was in high school. I hadn't liked it then; now, it made my hackles rise.

Accusing them of hate speech would only make things worse. Instead I raised my hand in a Stop signal. "There's no need for name-calling, Citizens."

"You calling those wetbacks and majheads, 'Citizens?'" the RealHuman leader shouted. "So you are one of them! They belong behind a fence! Just like that Redcap Retard."

"I'm not—" I started, but the others RealHumans started shouting, "Behind the fence!"

Meanwhile the Despredatores began a chanting "For Duncan!"

"Despredatores run free!" the Despredatores leader shouted, and his gang took up the chant. "You're the one goin' to get trapped in your little gulag, Nazi!"

The writer part of me cringed at the awful mix of metaphors. Part of me was starting to panic from the angry chanting. Still more of me was screaming, *Get control of the situation, Gapman!*

In my moment of internal conflict, the two charged each other. On instinct, I dashed between them, ready to push them apart.

"Alright. That's enough!" I raised my voice to be heard. "Let's discuss this like civilized—"

I felt something jab my leg and another scrape across my back.

Suddenly, clawed hands grabbed me by the shoulders and lifted me into the air.

"Didn't anyone ever tell you not to get between two fighting dogs?" Vern scolded.

My back burned, but not nearly as bad as my leg. I looked stupidly at the knife hanging loosely from it.

"They stabbed me?" I said stupidly, and suddenly, I saw red. Of all the ungrateful!

I pulled the knife from my leg—ouch!—and bent the blade over itself.

"What is wrong with you people?" I shouted.

No one was listening. The leaders—both without their knives; the RealHuman must have dropped his— were going at each other with fists, while the rest of the gang members were squaring off for fights of their own.

Vern released me. "Good. Stay mad. And start pulling them apart. Stick them on roofs or something. And take away the guns!"

With that, he swooped into the fray. He breathed a narrow line of fire, causing some of the RealHumans to halt and back away before getting to the fight, then did the same on the Despredatores side. I heard him scolding his "pups" to stay back.

I caught sight of someone raising a gun in his direction and swooped in fast to snag it out of his hands before he could line up his sights and pull the trigger.

Vern, in the meantime, had grabbed the leader of Los Despredatores and deposited him on a roof. The RealHumans leader didn't waste any time heading to another opponent. I zoomed over, grabbed him under the armpits, and hauled him away. I thought about putting him on the same roof as the Despredatore, but they'd probably just start fighting. Instead, I set him on the roof next door.

"Talk it out!" I suggested, then ducked as the RealHuman leader threw a brick at me. Fine, then.

Ignoring my aching and bleeding leg, I went back to doing it Vern's way.

I'd gotten a half-dozen gang members on their respective roofs, alternating so I didn't look like I was playing favorites. Vern did the same. Both sides fought us as much as they did each other. In the distance, I heard sirens. Thank heavens! Vern must have called the police while I was utterly failing to reach an accord.

Suddenly, movement at the end of the alley caught my attention. Sister Grace's car pulled up, and she stepped out. I started to shout a warning when she sang out, "Peace be with you!"

I could see the wave of magic burst from her, like the depiction of a soundwave flowing from Reverb's mouth in *Heroed for Sound*. As it rolled over everyone, they calmed and lowered their weapons. It didn't stop them from glaring at each other, and a few people made some half-hearted shoves as if to prove they were stronger than her spell, but soon enough, the fight was done.

Then I heard gunshots.

Chapter Twenty-Three: Gapman Charges Up

Ron

Vern roared as one got him in the flank. A Despredatore screamed as a second bullet struck her. Everyone, Despredatores and RealHumans alike, went ducking for cover—those on the roofs and those still in the alley. The Despredatores were surrounding the girl who was shot, pulling her behind a trash can. Grace ran toward them, forsaking the cover of her car. A RealHuman was shouting obscenities at one of his own as he pressed his palm against his ear. Had he been shot, too?

Was this what would have happened at the book signing if I hadn't stopped that bullet?

"Get the gunman!" Vern shouted, jerking me from my shock.

"Right!" But I didn't see him...

There! Fleeing the scene—or maybe the wrath of both gangs. I zipped down the alley after him, passing him just as he'd exited into the street. I planted myself in front of him and gave him my sternest look.

"You're not getting away. Just come quiet—"

He pointed the gun at my face!

I acted on adrenalin-filled instinct. I swung out my hand, knocking his gun up and away. He screamed, and I was sure I heard bones crunch.

The gun went off.

The bullet flew high, ricocheting off the metal covering of a streetlight and cutting through a powerline.

Time seemed to slow as the freed and sparking line curled gently toward a car where a woman was putting a baby into a car seat.

Or maybe I was simply moving that fast. I heard myself shout to the lady to get away, and then I was grabbing the wire.

The *live* wire. Thousands of volts of energy surged over and threw me. My skin felt like fire. My teeth sparked. I couldn't move, couldn't even scream. A strangled *gerk* escaped my throat, and it felt like a victory. Yet, somehow I noticed the woman running from the car, holding not a baby, but a dog.

Wait—was that Timida?

Fortunately, I still had momentum from my adrenaline-filled superjump. The cable snapped at the junction, and I was freed.

I landed hard in the dry grass of the small plaza and collapsed to sitting. I smelled smoke and realized it was me. I stared at the ground, not sure I could blink. But I was breathing. I was alive. Holy currents, Gapman! I was alive.

My hair felt weird, and I realized it was trying to stand up under my mask. I rubbed it down, trying not to wince at the odd feeling. People were gathering. Were they moving slowly, or was I moving at super-speed still?

My fingers tingled, too. I pulled off my gloves to shake out my hands. They were just the slightest bit red. Wow. Kevlar plus magic worked really well!

Then, a pair of shapely calves in low boots and tight jeans came into my view, and things returned to normal speed.

I heard Kitty's voice. "Gapman! Are you alright?"

I wanted to look up and give her a heroic, reassuring smile. I wanted to say something clever, like I got a real charge out of that rescue. I wanted to ask about the gunman.

Instead, what came out of my mouth was, "I could use a beer."

And food. I was so hungry again. But I was a superhero, and Kitty was watching—as were a whole crowd of folks. How could the gangs be having such a row so close to this populated an area and no one had noticed?

Think about that later. Everyone was noticing me now. I straightened my back and clapped my hands on my legs.

And winced as a shooting pain went up one side. I pulled my hand away fast to see I'd started my leg bleeding again. "Oh, yeah. I'd forgotten about that," I muttered.

"You forgot you were stabbed?" McGrue exclaimed, though I heard the admiration in her voice. I guess it did sound hard core.

She held out a hand, and I took it so she could help me stand.

Our palms met, and sparks flew between us that had nothing to do with the electrical cable I'd grabbed. It was so much nicer.

"Sit back down, Gapman!" cried a voice so full of familiar authority that my butt went back to the grass before I had time to think about it.

What was Mom doing here? I turned my head and saw her jogging toward me, her big EMT bag over her shoulder. Bix, her partner, ran beside her.

"I'm fine!" I called, more to reassure her than because it was true. "There are others—in the alley—"

Behind them, I saw two policemen blocking off the alley with portable barricades and police tape. One stopped to snag and cuff a gang member who tried to run past them. He dragged the struggling and shouting RealHuman back into the alley.

"They're taken care of," Mom said as she knelt beside me, displacing Kitty who, I just realized, had crouched by me, still holding my hand. On my other side, Bix was putting a blood pressure cuff on my right arm.

People were running out of the bar, drinks in their hands. To watch? People were taking videos. Kitty had stepped back and was taking notes. How embarrassing could this get?

That's when someone pushed a glass in front of my face. "I got you a beer, Gapman! It's pumpkin spice."

For a moment, I had no idea what he was talking about. Then I heard Kitty snort, and my words came back to me.

I gave him what I hoped was a gracious smile. "Thank you, my friend, but I was making a small joke. I'm fine, truly."

I held out my hand to shake his, but Bix pushed it back down and started the cuff again.

Mom said, "Let us be the judge of that. How long were you holding the live wire?"

"Uh..."

"Seven seconds!" someone from the crowd shouted. "I got it on my phone. Did you know overhead wires have seven hundred and sixty-five thousand volts?"

"I do now," I said, and the crowd laughed. They thought I was joking again. Okay. Maybe I could save this.

Mom yelled at them to go away and let Bix and her do their jobs. A few people left, but most just backed up. My superhearing caught a lady saying something about Mom wanting to "get in good with Gapman". Meanwhile, Bix called out stats. My blood pressure was a little high (big surprise) and my pulse a little fast, and Mom examined my knife wound while asking me what year it was, who the President was...

"You'll need harder questions than that," I teased.

Kitty asked, "How do you spell 'indefatigable?'"

I met her eyes. Her little smirk made me forget all the pain and mortification of my current state.

"M C G R U E?"

Bix snorted and muttered, "Well, that's working fine, anyway."

Mom had finished washing out the knife wound and making sure none of my torn and singed costume was in it. She applied a loose bandage. "That's healing so fast! You might not need the bandage after an hour, but go easy for a bit? I don't suppose you'll go to a doctor? No? Hold still."

She stuck a needle in my arm. "Antibiotics," she said. "Can't have our superhero catching an infection."

EMTs weren't supposed to administer antibiotics except in emergency situations like sepsis. I hoped she wouldn't get into trouble, but I didn't know how to ask. What would Gapman know about EMT procedures?

Fortunately, Bix asked me about tetanus shots, and I told him I was up-to-date.

Mom passed me a bottle of water, a protein bar, and some ibuprofen. I could see in her eyes that she wanted to fuss more. She may have scolded me for being a baby when she shot me, but that was when she had control over the situation. Now, her baby had had a shock few people could have survived. Her terse expression said she was torn between treating me like a superhero and caring for me like her child.

I'd had enough attention, anyway. "Thank you, Miss Engleson, Mister Bixby, for your expert ministrations. You're a credit to your profession," I said as I stood.

The crowd clapped and cried out approval.

Something stirred in me, and I pointed toward Mom and Bix, directing the applause to them. Then I said, "Everyone, please! Thank you for your support— but I beg you to heed me. All of this could have been avoided if we just had more compassion for our fellow beings—Mundane or Faerie, human or Magical, we are all travelers sharing the adventure of life. It's up to us to build each other up to make both worlds better for all."

As the crowd's cheers rose to a crescendo, I shot into the air with as much dignity and heroicness as my aching muscles and torn suit allowed.

I took the ibuprofen with a couple of swallows of water and wolfed down the protein bar at superspeed. I finished before I got to the police cars at the other end of the alley. Even so, when I landed beside Vern and Sister Grace, the detective they were talking to looked at my water bottle with disgust.

"So good of you to join us," he said.

"The EMTs were checking me out after the electrocution," I said, trying to sound as matter-of-fact and non-defensive as possible. It wasn't my fault Mom and Bix kept me so long! Besides, Vern himself was sporting a bandage on his hind quarters, so he'd gotten doctored up, too.

You know, it was kind of a relief to know that. Maybe people wouldn't be so quick to judge my getting medical attention when even our dragon needed tending now and then.

"Too bad they didn't sew up your suit," the detective said.

Sister Grace tsked scoldingly at him. "I can help with that."

She sang a little tune, and I felt tugs around the tears as the material stretched to knit itself. I watched, delighted.

"That's...amazing!" I gasped, just barely remembering my accent. "Thank you, Sister."

"Now that our hero's presentable," Vern said with a sneer at the detective that said he was mocking his exasperation rather than my scruffiness, "Gapman, meet Captain Michael Santry, Chief of Police. Santry, meet my pa—"

Grace kicked him with her heel, and he smoothly switched gears. "—partner in stopping this fiasco."

Captain Santry did not look impressed. "We need your statement," he said, then glared at the handful of officers who immediately turned his way to volunteer.

"Of course," I said, then asked, "but did someone catch the gunman?"

Vern grinned. "I did while you were all lit up."

The captain took my statement himself. He made it clear he didn't think much of me, but I felt it was more a professional dislike, that he was waiting for me to earn his trust and respect. I'd had a teacher like that in Leeds; as soon as he'd heard my accent, he'd put me in a box labeled "Entitled, Ugly American." It had taken a semester to prove my worth, but then, he turned out to be a great mentor. A couple of my best clients were thanks to his recommendation.

Thus, I answered all of Captain Santry's questions with calm and helpfulness and ignored the sneers and disdainful sniffs. In the end, I'd felt a subtle shift, something in his posture, that said he was starting to see me as something other than a glory-seeking vigilante or whatever box he'd put me in.

By the time we'd finished, the adrenaline rush had worn off, and I was feeling the aches and weariness of my morning. I'd finished my water but was parched and ravenous, and I could only hope the shakiness I felt was not visible. I wanted to lean against the car, but the red Dodge Charger with a portable siren attached to the top had to be someone's private vehicle, maybe even Captain Santry's. It was perfectly kept up; someone cared about that car. I didn't want to risk disrespecting it.

Around me, first responders were cleaning up. The gang members had all been loaded into wagons and taken to jail, except the injured, who had already left in ambulances. Vern, I saw, was flying a pattern where the power line had gone down.

"Somewhere you'd rather be?" Captain Santry asked.

I turned my attention back to him. "Apologies. I was wondering what Vern is looking for."

He glanced back and sighed. Then he leaned toward me. "Listen. I told him to keep you out of my hair—out of trouble is too much to ask, I'm sure. I think you can learn a few things from him—but don't tell him I said that. However, he's always going to have his own agenda. *Capiche?*"

I wasn't sure I did, but I promised to be careful and assured him I wanted to work with the police and not at cross purposes. "You are, after all, the front line for safety and justice."

He snorted. "Glad you see it that way. I'll call if we have any follow-up questions, but you can go. And Gapman? Good work here."

I waited until I was in the air before I broke out into a wide grin.

Chapter Twenty-Four:
Gapman Gets Pucked

Vern

Well, look at Gapman, feeling all smug. Does he really think he and Santry bonded?

"Yo! Zapman!" I called out, "Come here."

He flew over the roof with an odd look on his face that I didn't understand. As he landed, he said, "'Zapman'? Are you feeling mardy because you were shot?"

Oh-ho! He wanted to call me out and was considering the most Gapmanly way to phrase it. I didn't see St. George around, encouraging him. Did this spunk come with the costume?

Well, I'd give him half a point for standing up to me. I ignored the question as I pointed to the roof across the street, which also had an excellent view of the alleyway, the powerlines, and ChijuajuaChicka's car.

"If you're all done making friends with the local constabulary, look over there and tell me what you see. Use your Gappy senses for magic."

I waited, watching him Gapsquint as he examined the area. Then, he straightened a bit, like a hound catching a scent.

"Come on! It's already fading!"

He took off and I followed. Could he sense the malformed magic better than me? It might be understandable given his unusual origins, but it'd be a blow to my pride. I said a brief, begrudging prayer for humility.

But no, he landed in the alleyway where I'd last sensed it, and looked around, stumped.

Grace called to us, "Over here. I found something."

We joined her at a dumpster she'd climbed in to look through. I had to hand it to her; when she looked for clues, she didn't mind getting dirty. Of course, the spell on her habit repelled dirt, and this was the office district; aside from a few half-eaten lunches, it was mostly papers and spent supplies. Nothing unusual—except for the turban Grace was holding up for us to see.

"There's nothing else for a costume, nor any other hats."

Gapman graciously offered to lift her out of the dumpster, and we examined her find.

"That's glowing, faintly," Gapman said. "Vern, do you see that?"

"No, but I sense magic differently. That's definitely the magic. But I don't sense it anywhere else."

I looked up and down the alley. Nothing looked disturbed. If we'd seen scattered trash or knocked over cans, it might indicate someone running away at superspeed, but everything looked like you'd expect from a business district on a busy Thursday afternoon.

Suddenly, we heard a feminine scream. "Gapman! Oh, my Gapman! It's you!"

Her shout was followed by the trampling sound of high heels and ladies' pumps. This was going to get annoying fast. Wait. It already was.

"Call off your fan club," I snarled. "We've got work to do."

"Of course," he said with seriousness, but there was a sparkle in his eyes.

We watched as he approached, arms wide, at once welcoming and keeping them from walking further into the alley. He tried with limited success to explain that we were working and they needed to go.

I turned back to the matter at hand. "He dumped the hat and ducked into a building, without using his superpowers," I guessed. "We've lost him again."

Grace sighed. "I can try a finding spell on this, but my instincts say it won't work."

In the alley, Gapman was taking more time trying not to answer questions than if he just answered them. "Please, friends, we are investigating... Ma'am, I answered that in the podcast... No, no autographs at this time..."

Grace asked me, "And you don't smell anything? I mean, we are expecting a High Elf."

Even if I didn't know Hawgin, High Elves all had a faint scent of petrichor and budding leaves. It was beyond most sapient's capabilities to recognize, but I should have been able to smell it. But in the Mundane, there was too much iron in the steel of the buildings, the dumpsters, even the broken stapler. It interfered with my ability.

I shook my head.

There was a sudden woosh as Gapman, exasperated, signed autographs for everyone and hustled them away. Women huddled close, giggling and rearranging their windblown hair as they finally left.

He ran back to us, and we moved a little further into the alley where we were not seen from the street. Maybe the fortunate fen would want to keep their good luck to themselves and not direct anyone else our way.

"Where were we?" Gapman asked, "Right. Neither of us can sense the magic unless he uses his superpower."

"And now that you've used yours, you've flooded the immediate area," I chided, then sighed. "But I didn't sense anything, anyway."

He took the turban from Grace. "Well, how's your sense of smell?"

He held out the turban. Great. Now, I'm a bloodhound. But he had a point, so I sniffed it.

And got a whiff of puck.

I jerked my head back, sneezing to expel anything I might have accidentally inhaled.

"Keep away from that thing!" I exclaimed.

Grace, bless my smart nun, stepped back immediately, but Gapman was already an idiot without any help. He said, "Why? What's in there?"

He brought the turban to his face.

"No!" I moved to knock the turban out of his hands, but I didn't have superspeed.

There was a *boof!* And a cloud of puck enveloped us both.

Ron

I dropped the turban and backed away, coughing. Sparkly magic dust was everywhere. "What is this? What's happening?"

"You're an idiot! That's what's happening," Vern said between sneezes.

"Vurnerrah," Grace chided. "Be kind."

"But it itches my nostrils!"

"No, no. Vern's right. I am an idiot." That seemed perfectly right to me, and I felt such a wave of affection for the dragon who was so honest about calling out my weaknesses. Plus, it was so endearing how he was pawing at his nose.

"That's so cute," I cooed. "You remind me of a puppy when you do that."

"I'm not a puppy," he protested but then turned to Sister Grace. "But I am cute. Scratch behind my cheek crests, please, please?"

He turned his head toward her, appealing.

She stepped even further away. "Don't get any on me!"

"I'll scratch your cheeks!" I pulled off my glove and rubbed him behind one cheek, digging in and going faster and faster as he leaned harder into my hand. His skin was smooth and... I, dunno, *porpoisy*... there and I told him so.

Sister Grace looked at us, aghast. I felt like I should be worried, but I mean, Vern needed his cheek rubbed, right? Besides, we were at an impasse with the investigation. She sang a quick phrase and the puck dust on us flew into a neat pile out of the way.

"Whoa! Prestidigitation?" I exclaimed. Vern grunted, and I obligingly scratched harder.

"Yes," Sister Grace said and with another short song, put some kind of shield around it and the turban. The puck dust sparked and wisped as if wanting to break free.

Sister Grace said, "Keep away from the pile and the hat. I'm calling Michael."

Vern said, "Why? He's a party pooper. Five more minutes, please?"

His whole body went limp and he flopped onto one side, purring.

From down the alleyway came a voice that made me want to purr. "Gapman? Are you there?"

Vern jerked to his feet. "It's Kitty!"

I picked up his panic and felt it myself. We were in an alleyway, covered in puck. What would she think of me—or Gapman? "What do we do?"

With an exasperated sigh, Sister Grace threw up her hands and went to intercept Lois—I mean my Kitty. I mean, Kitty! McGrue—Ms. McGrue!

She sidestepped the nun.

"Vern?" I pleaded.

"Just...act casual!" he blurted. "And remember your accent."

Casual. Right. How did Gapman look casual? I leaned against a dumpster, crossing my arms and bracing one foot against the metal. I'm sure I'd seen that pose in the comic books.

"You look like a Western," Vern said, but then Kitty was upon us.

"What's going on?"

"Howdy, Miss Kitty," I said.

Vern laughed so hard, he splooted.

Kitty looked at us, the turban and pile of puck dust on the ground, then back at me. Her eyes held the same mix of shock and confusion Sister Grace's had only minutes earlier. "Gapman...are you...high?"

"It's not his fault," Vern said between chuckles. "The turban was boobie trapped."

"Don't say 'boobie' around Miss Ki—Miz McGrue!" I chided. "You can't talk to a lady like that."

Vern raised his head to look at her, tilting his head as he considered my words. His tilt grew deeper and deeper until his head was almost upside-down. I should have known with his long neck that was possible, but even so, I was impressed and fascinated.

Kitty—er, Ms. McGrue—glared at him, waiting.

"Boobie," he told her. He flopped his head back on the ground and laughed.

He was so funny! I snickered.

Kitty scowled at me.

"Sorry, Miss Boobie—Miz McGrue." I shoved my fist against my mouth to stifle my laughs.

"As you can see," Sister Grace said, setting a hand on Kitty to gently draw her away from us, "these two are quite impaired. I've already called for help. I hope we can count on your discretion?"

Kitty pulled out of her grasp. "What kind of...trap? Is someone after you?"

I burst out laughing. She was going to say "boobie," I just knew it. I opened my mouth to answer, but behind her, Sister Grace pointed a finger at me, that kind of finger-point that meant trouble if you disobeyed. What could a magical nun do to me?

I clamped my mouth shut.

Sister Grace told Kitty, "I'd appreciate it if you didn't take advantage of them in this state."

The words were out of my mouth before I realized I'd thought them. "I don't mind. You can take advantage of me anytime."

Vern wheezed as if laughing was too hard, and his tail swished back and forth. It was a happy tail.

The Dodge Charger I hadn't leaned against while talking to Captain Santry was rolling up the alley, a police car following behind.

Vern turned his head to look—just his head. Why had I never noticed how long and agile his neck was? It was so cool!

A whine escaped his throat. "Why'd you call Santry? I'm not going to sober up in his jail cell."

"He's here to clean up the scene. You may go to the lair until you sober up," Sister Grace said sternly.

"Can I call him 'boobie' first?" Vern asked.

"No. Go home now." She pointed in the general direction of Tokneo.

Vern stood and stretched, then regarded his claws, extending then retracting them. "Hey Gapman, do your fingers feel like they're going to float off your hands?"

I wiggled my gloved fingers. "No, but that would be cool."

"It affects dragon physiology differently," Vern said. "Great. That's great."

He launched himself lightly as if expecting his fingers and toes to lift him away. He was so graceful! Was I that graceful? Maybe I should ask Kitty if I was graceful. No, I shouldn't compete with Vern. He's too awesome.

Maybe I could take her on a flight around the city. No, I should not do that while impaired...

I know! I could sing to her from *The Velveteen Rabbit!*

I turned back to her but before I could start, Sister Grace, said, "Gapman, please escort Vern to his lair and remain until I arrive and confirm you're both all right?"

That was a good idea. Sister Grace was so full of good ideas! But Kitty...

Kitty met my gaze with a flirty smirk. "We can continue this discussion when you're sober."

Could we? *We could!* With a yip of happiness, I launched myself into the air. I didn't even need to take three steps. I've always been good at jumping. I hoped Kitty noticed. Could I tell her? I wanted to tell her. I wanted to tell her everything! But first, I had important escort duty.

I easily caught up with Vern. He was almost gliding along, flapping his wings lazily as he extended and retracted his claws.

"I'm on escort duty!" I announced proudly. I loved being useful!

"That's a great idea," Vern said.

"Sister has great ideas."

"Grace is great!"

"Grace is great," I agreed. "You shouldn't have said 'boobie' around her. It's rude."

"It's a funny word! Humans have lots of funny words. It's one of the things I like about humans. But Grace is my favorite. I shouldn't have said 'boobie' around her." He stopped to snicker at the word, then stopped. "Hey! Want to hear a funny word in dragon?"

I jerked to a stop and hovered, too. "Your native language! Yes! Yes!" I clapped at superspeed.

"Okay, Move aside."

I did, and I listened with rapt delight as he made a squelching sound with his cheeks. Then he blew out a wobbly globe of flame and blew it away with smokey breath from his nostrils.

He started laughing.

"That's a word? I said. "What's it mean?"

"Human!" he cried out between belly laughs.

I paused to ponder. "That. Was...*Hilarious*! It's funnier than 'boobie!'"

"Because it's practically the same thing!"

I buckled over with laughter, lost my aerial balance, and dropped a few feet. Vern scooped me up with his tail. "Careful. You don't want to fall on that lady's stroller."

I peered down. "Is that Dog Mom? She's everywhere! Hey—you don't think that she and Hawgin..."

Just then, my superhearing caught Santry's voice: "Yo! Vern! Get back here!"

I bobbed up and out of Vern's grasp. "The police chief wants you!"

Vern snorted and blew out a different puff of flame. I wondered if it was another word. "He just wants to see if he can mess with a dragon on puck—silly and susceptible to suggestion."

I regarded my mentor with wide eyes. "That's so wrong. But don't you want to go?"

"I'm not that impaired," he protested. Then, his expression turned thoughtful. "Still... Could we use being on puck as an excuse to *play* a puck?"

"That's genius! But we can't hurt anyone."

"Of course not!" Vern nodded his head emphatically.

I thought some more. "And it can't be something Mom wouldn't like."

"Can't disappoint Mom," he agreed amiably.

"And it can't hurt Gapman's reputation."

Vern sighed. "That lets out putting Santry's car on the roof. Then he'll know you're impaired, too."

I pouted. "He already knows. Kitty does, too."

Suddenly, Vern met my eyes and we both broke out in grins.

"Here," I said, pulling off my cloak. "We don't want to scratch the paint..."

Vern

By the time we'd returned to the alley, the hazmat team had cleaned up the pile of puck my sweet Sister Grace had thoughtfully put in a containment field. They had left, but Santry was talking to Grace. Neither noticed as we landed quietly in the middle of the closest roof and, giggling, belly-crawled to the edge and peeked over.

"I've always wanted to do something like this," my GapAccomplice whispered. "I never had the guts."

"Time to Gapman up," I murmured. "You get the engine..."

Grace offered to show him where she'd found the turban, and they started back down the alley toward the original dumpster.

I scooched myself into position to leap over the ledge. "Ready... and... Go!"

Together we dove off the roof and had Santry's Dodge Charger six feet in the air before he had a chance to cuss.

"Vurnerrah! Put that down!" Grace demanded.

"Gently!" Santry shouted.

"We will!" I said.

"We will!" GapPuck agreed. "Very gently!"

"On the roof," I added.

"Definitely very gently on the roof!"

I heard Santry threatening to shoot me in my other flank, but to be honest, I was laughing too hard to care.

Chapter Twenty-Five: Gapman Vs Cobra Chickens

Ron

That evening, I returned to the roof of the Los Lagos Credit Union with Vern and Sister Grace. The sun was setting, and a cool wind whipped my cape behind me. I should have been standing at the edge, one foot on the ledge, hands on my hips, staring pensively across Los Lagos, with Vern and Grace flanking me like the cover of a comic book.

Instead, we were staring at Captain Santry's car, parked neatly between the air conditioner and the access hatch. I wanted to scratch my head, but the mask didn't allow it.

"I don't remember doing this at all," I said.

"I do!" Vern said. He sounded gleeful. He wore a moving blanket like a cape. "It was hilarious."

Sister Grace scowled at him. "It was not! It was mean and ridiculous and completely unbecoming of either of you! Now, you are going to return this car to

Captain Santry, cleaned and shined, and apologize. And then you, Vurnerrah." She paused to stab a finger at him. "You are going to go to Confession."

"Yes, Sister," Vern said with so much docility, I'd have thought he was still on puck.

"But Sister Grace," I asked, "why wash it? Can't you just use prestidigi—"

Her hard glare made the protest die in my throat. Okay, I understood Vern's behavior now. I also understood why she had brought buckets and a hose with her.

"Yes, Sister," I murmured.

"Can't we leave it in the alley and have him come get it?" Vern asked.

"No. You have just enough light to get the car pristine, then the two of you can fly it to his house. He'll be waiting for you."

With that, she turned on her heel and strode to the faucet. Soon cold water was flowing from the cold hose. I put soap in the buckets and added the water. Vern picked up a sponge by extending his claws and stabbing it. He dipped it in the water, then pulled it out, looking at it dubiously. Then he started to rub the car, gingerly, as if afraid his claws would push through.

This was going to take forever. I sighed. "By all means, allow me."

With superspeed, I whipped around the car, sudsing it up as fast as the bubbles allowed. Vern hosed it down, then I zoomed through the drying. Grace handed me the wax, which Vern had warmed, and in minutes, I had the car so shiny, it reflected the back of the building's neon sign perfectly.

I paused, rubbing my damp arms, arms sore, teeth chattering.

"Well done, GapLaRusso," Vern said. I should have known a Karate Kid reference was coming.

The sun had set, it was freezing out, and we were on the roof. No one was watching, and if they were, my washing a car was already embarrassing. I covered my fist with one hand and bowed. Vern chuckled.

Then, Grace smiled at me, and held out her arms. "Come here."

I thought she was going to hug me, but instead, she lay her hands on my shoulders and sang. Immediately, I started feeling warmer. Steam wafted off my suit.

"Thank you!"

"We're going to have to do something about your uniform," she said. "It's only going to get colder. For now, that spell will keep you warm. Now, off with you both."

Reluctantly, Vern pulled off the blanket and used it to protect the car while he lifted the back and I, the front. We counted three together but didn't rise at the same speed or rates. The car wobbled and Sister Grace shouted, "Careful!"

"We are!" Vern snapped as we set the car back on the roof. "This was easier when we were on puck."

"I guess we were in sync," I said.

"Me—in sync with a human? This just gets better. Hang on."

He reached into his pouch and pulled out a small case. Lockpicks?

Grace rolled her eyes. He gave her a look of protest. "I'm being helpful! There's a bunch of loose stuff rattling around in there."

Soon, he had the doors open and was reaching under seats and between cracks with his tail, while Sister Grace watched with crossed arms and a crosser expression. I sighed. As long as we had access to the inside...

I grabbed the chamois and wiped down the dash, doors, and leather seats. The car was already crazy clean. The captain really loved this thing.

Meanwhile, Vern was cataloging his finds. "Two quarters, ammo—9-mil—guitar pick, grocery receipt... Oh! Well, I guess he won't be shooting me with this one today."

"Careful!" Grace said as Vern pulled out a SIG-Sauer P320 XCompact. "It's probably loaded."

"That was just loose in his car?" I exclaimed. That felt uncharacteristically careless for our chief of police.

But Vern said, "Nah. I got it from the holster duct-taped under the seat. Guess you can take a cop out of L.A. but you can't take L.A. out of the cop."

I sighed, gaining a greater appreciation for Grace's frustration. "Put it back."

Finally, we were in the air, the car level between us. Grace sang a spell, and I felt a kind of shadow wash over us.

"That should keep you hidden from anyone who isn't actively seeking you," she said. "And Vurner-rah..."

She spoke quickly in a language I didn't understand, but I could have sworn she said, "Kitty."

Vern rolled his eyes. "Fine. I will."

"Off with ye, then." She made shooing motions.

I waited until we were in the air before asking, "What about Kitty?"

Even with superhearing, I could barely make out his sigh. "Listen, Gapman, I know you're crushing on McGrue, but you need to understand: She's only interested in one thing."

"Uh..." I felt my face heat up despite the chilly air.

Now, I heard Vern sigh—a huge gust of annoyance. "*Herself*, Gapman! Herself. You think she'll be your Lois Lane. She thinks she's Lois Lane. But I'm telling you, she'll go from Gapfan to Gapyawn in a New York Times minute if you disappoint her."

Now, I was feeling hot for a different reason. "Oh, so you're saying if she finds out who I am—"

"What?" Vern exclaimed. "Damsels and Knights! Are you really that insecure? I mean when you stop being the story. But for pity's sake, do not tell her who you are! Do you know what a scoop that would be?"

"Come on—she'd never..."

"You didn't read, 'I Dated a Faerie Dragon'?"

"That story she wrote for *Faeaboo*? I didn't want to say anything but... Wait? That was real?" If I hadn't been hanging onto the front of the police chief's car, I'd have spun around in surprise.

"It's a long, disgusting story that still gives me the heebie-jeebies, but yes. I was cursed into human form; it was confusing, and she had enchanted perfume. It was an aberration." His scales rippled as he shuddered head to tail.

For some reason, that made me more determined. "Well, I don't want to be an aberration. I mean, it's not just her hair and her eyes and her calves—"

"She does have great gams," Vern agreed.

"Yeah, great legs! And the way her eyes don't just shine; they flare. But it's not just that! She's got this spirit to her, you know? She knows what she wants and she goes for it! She's tenacious—"

"So are pit bulls."

"And passionate! When she believes in something—"

"—she doesn't let a little thing like conflicting evidence get in the way. McGrue has to put her own dramatic spin on it to match her narrative. So take it from me: If she makes a pass at you..."

But a wide, dark V had caught my attention. "Duck."

"Yes, exactly!"

"No! Vern, look!" With my head, I pointed toward the flock that was making a V-line in our direction. "Ducks—no, geese! And they're heading right for us."

"Oh, no!" Vern said. "We just polished this car. Take over!"

He lifted his end of the car. Taking the hint, I did the same, then flew under to take on its full weight. Oof! When it landed on me, I bobbed. It was heavier than that Kia Electric I'd hauled to the repair shop the other day.

Vern, meanwhile, zoomed off to scatter the flock, roaring threateningly. Rather than scattering in fear, however, they flew around him. What the heck? I mean, I knew what they said about birds and newly cleaned cars, but wasn't this taking the cliché too far?

Vern looked confused, too. He hovered a moment, then rushed to cut them off. As they started to part around him, he blew a wide stream of flame. I heard a strangled squawk as one unlucky gander got roasted. Then Vern yelped and thrashed as several of the geese started to peck at him.

In the meantime, the rest came at me!

It was the hornets all over again.

"Protect that car!" Vern yelled.

Easier said than done. It's not like I could jink and swerve. Dodge Chargers are not exactly aerodynamic, and I was hanging onto it by the struts. I tried to get above the flock. I rose until the air grew thin and cold and I had to drop altitude before I lost consciousness, yet they were still above me. I turned, banking until the car nearly overbalanced; they followed my every move. The wind buffeted the Charger, threatening to tear it from my grasp. Behind me, Vern roared ferociously—probably dragon swear words.

There! Dark clouds. Maybe I could lose them. I put on as much speed as I could. The thick, moist air soaked my suit and formed rivulets on the car's buff job. In the distance, I saw a flash of lighting.

And still, the geese came.

It was dark when we finally set the car down in the driveway of his duplex, but true to Colorado weather, it wasn't raining in this part of town. Not that that helped us. We were both sopping wet. I never wanted to see the inside of a storm cloud again.

Captain Santry must have been watching from the window because no sooner had the wheels touched the cement, than the lights came on and he came out. "Well, it's about time. Where have you be...."

His protest died in his throat as he saw his car, streaked with bird crap, feathers, and even a little blood from Vern's battle against the geese. The rain had only served to dilute everything, creating a drooling mosaic of reds, browns, and whites.

He glared at us.

"It's not our fault!" Vern burst out. He was similarly poop-streaked, and goose feathers poked out from between some of his scales. "We were attacked!"

"By geese?" Santry sneered.

"Not just any geese," I said. "Cobra chickens! Cobra chickens most foul."

"Emus!" Vern added. "Small, flying emus with bad attitude and ridiculous skill!"

As if to prove his point, he pulled a gray webbed foot from between his scales. I hadn't even known geese kicked, much less flying side-kicks to the ribs. Unfortunately for that gander, Vern's answering chop was with his teeth.

"And an unfathomable interest in your car. Sir, we tried to evade and failing that, fought them off."

"I defended that paint job," Vern said. "I was magnificent but outnumbered!"

I nodded. "It's true! You should see the bird guts on Fifth and Pike—"

Santry cleared his throat, and we stopped our protests of bravery in the face of incredible avian
adversaries. He looked pointedly at his car, then
glared at us. His expression was incredibly clear even
in the light of the single porch bulb. He didn't care if
we were tired, wet, and had driven off an angry flock
of murderous cobra chickens.

I tilted my head to the heavens, askance. Maybe if I
had a saint as a guide, I might get some divine inspiration?

Something poked me in the scalp, and I pulled a
feather out from under my mask.

I sighed. "May we borrow a bucket?"

Vern

"I can't believe I had to wash Santry's car. Twice," I
grumbled.

"I beg your pardon!" Even two thousand feet in the
air, past city limits, and with no one around—not even
birds, thank heavens!—Gapman kept his accent. I was
proud and a little surprised, given the night we'd had.
He continued, his Brit-adjacent accent somehow making his annoyance even more obvious. "I washed that
car—twice. And you, for that matter!"

"And I do appreciate that," I said wholeheartedly.
After finishing the car, Gapman had turned the hose

on me. I was finally rid of feathers and feces. Now, if only it weren't so cold! I had half a mind to set a part of the forest on fire just so I could sit in it.

"I'm going to the Little Flower rectory and cozy up in front of Father Rich's fireplace and take a long nap," I told my padawan. Then, I'm going to find that minemesis of yours…"

"My what?"

"Minemesis—'cause he's about as far from an arch-nemesis as he can get. Sending geese after a car."

I scanned the skies, just in case.

"You think he did it?" Gapman asked. He was shivering, too, but from cold.

"How else could those egregious emu emulators see past Sister Grace's spells? This has his signature style all over it—subtle and low-threat."

"Low threat?" Gapman glared at me. If he'd had heat vision to go with that look, I'd have finally been warm. "Low threat? He electrocuted me!"

"Did he? Or did you grab a live wire?"

Gapman sputtered. "Well, he shot me!"

"So did your mom."

He couldn't argue that. "Still, those geese… They were no small threat. They were not natural, the way they were fighting. And those squawks!"

"Like kiaps. Kung fu emu," I agreed.

Suddenly, Gapman started snickering. "Everybody was Kung Goose Fighting..." he sang.

"No," I warned. "You're a superhero, remember? Gravitas, sacred mission?"

But he gave a fowl squawk, followed by "Those geese were fast as lightning..."

Fine. If he wanted to play... I grabbed his cape with my tail and jerked. The Velcro ripped off.

"Hey!"

I zoomed ahead with my prize as, laughing, he dashed after me.

Chapter Twenty-Six:
Gapman's Left Hanging

Ron

I got home sometime after midnight, but it was worth it. Playing keep-away was fun when it was with a friend and not the school bullies—plus, a *dragon*? I was friends with a dragon! Grace listened to our debrief with sympathy and concern, then used prestidigitation to clean my suit.

It didn't totally eradicate the smell, however. I tossed it in the wash first thing, then took a long, hot shower. Even with the spells she put on the fabric to help against the weather, I was freezing when I got home.

I flopped into bed and slept hard until hunger woke me up at 5 a.m. I didn't even have the energy to fly down the stairs, but shuffled my way into the kitchen, stopping to put my uniform in the dryer on the way. Soon, the sizzle of the bacon was making a counterpoint to the soothing rumble of the dryer.

Mom shuffled into the kitchen, pulling the tie on her fleece bathrobe. "You're up early."

"Hungry," I said, adding a couple more eggs to the half dozen I was already scrambling. "It was an exciting night."

I told her the story as we ate. She choked on her eggs once and almost spit out her coffee. "Poor baby!" she said. "Geese are jerks."

"True, but there was something different about this flock, like they were possessed or something. Vern thinks my nemesis did it."

She set down her cup so hard it sloshed coffee onto her bacon. "You have a nemesis?" I couldn't tell if she was worried or excited.

Still, I wasn't going to worry her. I shrugged and chased the last of my eggs around the plate. "Not much of one if all he does is send geese after us. You should have seen the carnage Vern left. Oh, argh!"

I tossed my fork down in disgust.

"What?"

"We left a mess on Fifth and Pike. I should probably go clean it up."

She patted my hand. "You're too good for this city."

Mere minutes later, I was heading to Los Lagos, with a string bag under my cloak holding all our huge trash bags and a pair of old work gloves. I'd been tempted to don some oversized coveralls, but that didn't seem heroic. I'd just have to ask Grace for another spell. She'd probably do it since I was cleaning up after Vern and myself.

Would she be tracking down Hawgindespotlite with Vern? It seemed wrong that they were the ones chasing after my archnemesis—or minemesis. Whatever. I'm the hero. It should be my job. But I didn't know the first thing about finding someone. I mean, maybe if it were a celebrity with a big online presence, but somehow, I didn't expect a High Elf to be posting on his MePage: *Feeling evil. Might go curse some geese. IDK.*

Once again, I was confronted with just how underqualified I was for the role of superhero.

The already gray clouds grew stormy and thunder rumbled in the distance—perfect for my mood. On the bright side, the rain would wash away the bird guts I didn't pick up. Fifth and Pike wasn't a busy part of town; maybe, with superspeed, I could get the job done before anyone noticed.

I should be so lucky. When I got within line of supersight, I saw four guys in coveralls using trash pickers to shove goose bits into trash bags. I guess I should have expected it. This was an old part of town, mostly full of abandoned buildings undergoing renovation. However, it had one historical landmark—the tallest flagpole in the city. The council had someone come to raise and lower the flag every day.

And there, on the sidewalk, was Kitty McGrue interviewing one of the flagmen.

I could just fly past. It was overcast. It was drizzling. Surely no one would know.

"Gapman!" Kitty shouted.

Or I could go talk to the nice reporter and take it like a man.

As I floated toward the sidewalk, the city workers looked up from the bird bits and greeted me with a smile. I fought back a pang of guilt as I nodded back. I told myself that at least this was the most interesting thing they'd be doing today. It might even be a story for the grandkids, right?

Still... "Why don't you boys take a break? I'll have the worst of this done by the time you finish your coffee."

That earned me some appreciative cheers. One handed me his reacher and a half-empty bag before joining the rest in the manager's SUV. As they rode off, Kitty crossed her arms and regarded me with a pitying and slightly annoyed expression.

"You are too kind," she said, "especially since it's Vern who should be cleaning up this mess."

"Vern?" I asked. Oh, man! How did she know? Did someone tell her? Had someone seen us?

I used my tricks to (I hoped!) keep from blushing. The chilly drizzle helped.

Sighing in exasperation, she pulled the reacher from my grip and used it to pick up a lone goose's head. Just the head, and in the bill, one of Vern's scales. I winced, remembering how he'd yelped at that one.

Kitty mistook my expression. "Look, I know you guys are bonding over patrolling the city or whatever, but he can be a real menace when he wants to. He's arrogant and self-centered and..."

Oh, I knew this windup. I'd seen it in meetings. Usually, I'd sit back and wait for Mr. Redfeathers to put a stop to her diatribe on whatever had gotten her ire up—Vern, more often than not, come to think of it—but he wasn't around.

I looked around the plaza. The city workers must have just started—or had been taking their sweet time since they were paid by the hour. Every bag was only partly full, and there were still pieces of goose anatomy everywhere. I even saw one near the flagpole, fully intact. I could almost imagine it sleeping as it waited out the rain.

I did not have that luxury, and I really didn't want to waste time listening to her complain, especially when it wasn't Vern's fault.

"Miz McGrue? Miz McGrue?"

"And he thinks he's all that—"

"*Miz McGrue!* I was there! This is not exactly what it seems!"

"It seems like an avian massacre!" she snapped.

"That's a mite harsh," I hedged.

"Bird bloodbath?" Her glare challenged even my Gapman composure, but I thought I saw movement by the flagpole.

"Well, yes," I replied, distracted. "That's accurate. But these were no ordinary geese. They're—Zombie Goose!"

The gray gander had risen, ruffled its feathers, and was flying our way!

"What?" Kitty cried, but I'd already dashed past her, launching myself into the air. I head-butted the gander below the sternum and tried to wrap my arms around it. Maybe I could capture him and have Sister Grace examine him.

Honking belligerently, it kicked and struggled. One webbed foot caught me in the Adam's apple. His wings beat me about the head and shoulders, and he pecked my scalp. Bravely, I hung on, trying not to crush him while gaining the upper hand.

"What are you doing?" Kitty cried. She sounded more concerned for the gander than me.

"They're bespelled!" I called out. "Weaponized geese. I... Ow!"

The gander pecked me on the forehead, just missing my eye. He jerked, pulling us toward the right. We grazed the flagpole. My foot caught on the rope, but momentum kept us moving forward. I heard the ping of a rivet coming loose and the rope was freed from the bottom.

"Calm down," I grunted at my avian adversary. Who knew geese were so strong? And wiry. He almost slipped my grasp and I hugged him close as I changed my grip.

We'd reached the end of the flagpole rope. Still wound around my ankle, it pulled taught and jerked us back to the flagpole like a bungee cord. The gander squawked a warning, and we twisted together to avoid smashing into the pole.

We sailed past. Immediate threat gone, the gander again tried to escape, wings flapping desperately. My grip slipped, but I managed to snag his leg. With unganderish strength, he pulled us around and up between the ropes. His free foot caught the line. His panic escalated into frenzy.

Several moments of frantic flapping and twists later, we were both near the top of the flagpole, tangled in the rope and the American Flag.

One of his dark eyes blazed fury at mine.

"Calm down," I tried again. "I don't want to hurt you."

Honk! It poked me in the bridge of the nose, then scrambled free of the ropes.

As part of the rope loosened, I started to twist and fall, like something out of Cirque du Soleil, but without the grace.

"Ya-ah-ah! Oof!"

I stopped, thoroughly bound and hanging upside down, my face about five feet from the ground.

And the rain started in earnest.

"Gapman!" Kitty cried, running up to me. "Are you all right?"

"This is rather embarrassing," I said.

She giggled. It was unexpectedly feminine.

Any other time, I'd have loved to hear more, but I was once again getting drenched. I twisted, as much to shake out the water that was getting under my mask as to try to escape my bounds. After a moment, I gave up and let myself hang limp. Rain gathered along the ropes and fell in rivulets over me.

"I don't suppose you could keep this out of your story?" I asked.

"Well, that depends," she said as she stepped closer. "What's in it for me?"

The warm melody of her voice told me she was not asking for a story. Was she thinking what I thought she was thinking? Was this it?

"Uh…" I bullied my brain for something flirty and superheroish to say. All that came out was, "What did you have in mind?" At least the fact that I was hanging upside down made my voice sound husky.

She set her hands on either side of my face, pressing against my half-mask. The water it contained squished toward the middle.

Oblivious, she said, "Well, I do seem to recall this scene in a movie."

Oh, my Gapman! She wanted to recreate the Spiderman-M.J. upside-down kiss scene! With me!

And water was running into my nose.

I tried as subtly as I could to breathe it out.

And just like that, her hands flew from my face to cover her mouth.

"I'm so sorry!" she said from between her fingers.

"It's okay!" I hastened to reassure her. "It's just—"

"I completely overstepped! I'm so embarrassed!"

"No, that's not it. I'm—" I turned my head to sneeze out water.

"No, no. I understand. You're a superhero. Relationships could compromise you."

"Relation—?"

"Please. Don't make this harder. You're right. Maybe we should forget all about this."

She started to walk away, pausing only long enough to pick up the goose head and put it in a plastic baggie. Was she wanting some kind of weird memento of our almost encounter?

Where was she going? I was still tied up! "Miz McGrue! Kitty!"

She held up her hand, like a heroine in some tragic romance trying to forestall a long goodbye. *It's too painful. Just let me go. We'll always have Fifth and Pike.*

Meanwhile, I was being waterboarded thanks to a deranged goose.

I did an inverted sit-up, a part of me geeking out that I could do an inverted sit-up. The water drained out of my mask, but the ropes squeezed into my sides painfully, cutting my breath and my circulation. My hands were pressed against my chest. No way could I untangle myself. Finally, I had to lower myself back down. Great. Now what?

At least the rain was slowing—five minutes too late!

I saw a shadow overhead. My avian adversary coming to finish me off? No—it was Vern! I was saved.

Vern

I slept hard in front of Father's fireplace, and the next morning, dutifully went to Confession as Grace had asked. Father suggested for my penance that I go clean up the mess I'd made on Fifth and Pike.

So as the dawn broke and the storm clouds gathered, I made my way to the site of the cobra chicken carnage, wondering just where I was going to toss all the carcasses. Rotting gooseflesh wasn't exactly hygienic and I'd already had my fill. In fact, I was still coughing up goose feathers. Maybe there was a dumpster I could toss everything into to incinerate.

A flurry of motion caught my attention, and I saw Gapman struggling with a goose while getting tied up in ropes. More important than that, however, was what I sensed about the ropes. Magic.

Minemesis was at work!

Ignoring the squawking goose and equally squawking superhero, I dove toward the source of magic. There he was: a misshapen figure in a badly fitting rain poncho, moving his hands in a spell.

I dove in, claws out to snag him.

I'd cleared the building when, sensing my presence, he looked up, and I realized he had on two ponchos, one over his head like a wimple.

He dropped his spell and rabbited. I landed hard and ran after him. He turned the corner, me right behind. But when I got there the alley was empty. At least, empty of any physical presence. Magic filled the area, and not just any magic—portal magic.

Fewmets. He could be anywhere now.

I heard Gapman from the flagpole, calling Kitty's name. I sighed. I thought I told him to stay away from her. Well, I was going to stay away. With my luck, she had me pegged for this mess and was not going to hear my side of the story.

I heard the *tap-tap* of her boots as she walked away. Then, Gapman's exasperated sighs and some grunts.

I moseyed over to find him tightly bound and slightly swinging upside down from the flagpole.

Don't laugh, I could hear my nun chiding me. And I wouldn't, I promised.

But that didn't mean I wasn't going to have a little fun.

Ron's face brightened with hope as I approached. I stopped and sat just outside helping distance. His face fell from hope to confusion to pleading. I directed my gaze to the top of the flagpole, where the Stars and Stripes tangled in the Rain and Ropes. I followed it down to the twisted mess that held my padawan captive, then back to his annoyed face. I twisted my neck further, further, until my head was upside down and eye level with his.

"Kitty leave you hanging?" I asked.

"Very funny." He paused to gag, cough, and sneeze. "Are you just going to sit there?"

You know, I didn't think I liked my mentee taking that attitude with me. I straightened up and looked down at him. "Actually, Padawan, I think this is what you Mundanes call a 'teachable moment.'"

"'Teachable moment?' Now? What's wrong with you? I could drown, you know!" He cleared his sinuses with a superpowered sneeze. It sent him swinging.

I snickered. He was making this too easy. "You look like a tetherball. Gapball!"

As he swung toward me, I sent him spinning in the other direction with a light slap.

"Are you out of your mind? How is this teaching me anything?"

"Superpowers mean nothing unless you can use them under pressure!" I chided as I sent him in the other direction with a bop of my tail.

"Could you just tell me the lesson before I do some super-hurling?" he begged.

"Accent," I warned, though no one was around. Well, he was—around the flagpole. I bopped him again to send him the other way. "Think, Padawan. What if I hadn't been here? Were you just going to hang around until someone came to rescue you?"

"I'm stuck! My hands are literally tied. What do you think I can do—superchew my way free?"

I shrugged. "How badly do you want to free yourself?"

I bopped him with the back of one paw. He yelped as he circled the flagpole. I tapped him as he came around, sending him in the opposite direction.

"Stop that!" he cried.

"What are you going to do about it?"

"Vern!"

I bopped him again, just a nice easy, rhythm. I had just gone to Confession, after all. "Think, Padawan! Haven't you ever seen videos of people breaking out of duct tape or zip ties?"

"It's not literally my hands."

"Elbows, knees... Besides what do you have that the average Mundane doesn't?"

With a groan of exasperation and realization, he jerked his limbs outward as hard as he could. Loops of rope pulled thin and snapped. He hit the ground hard at my feet.

I looked down at him. "You can also hover," I reminded him.

"Right. Thanks." He held up a hand for me to pull him up, remembered I was a four-legged creature, and got up on his own. He rolled his shoulder, wincing. "So what now? I was hoping that goose would help Sister Grace identify my nemesis for certain."

"Minemesis," I corrected, "and no worries. It's definitely Hawgindespotlite—and he's not alone. I was chasing them down the alley but they disappeared into a portal."

"Where? Let's go! I'm fine!"

I set a tail on his shoulder. "Relax, Padawan. It's not like the Gap. Once you pass through, it's gone. However, it does give us some clues. There are only certain types of Faerie creatures that can create portals into this world."

"Okay. So what's our next step?"

I grimaced. We could talk to the acting troupe, but if a rogue portal-producing pixie was involved, we would probably have to take this to the authority.

And I already owed Titania.

Chapter Twenty-Seven:
Gapman Makes a Decision

Ron

Changing outfits in the middle of the woods was getting to be a real pain.

Even with superspeed and my rain poncho, by the time I got home, I was soaked through with cold rain. Why hadn't we had snow yet? It might be colder, but at least, I'd be drier.

"Don't Threaten Me With a Good Time" was blaring in the house when I got there. For some reason, it wasn't blasting my eardrums like I'd have expected. But I had heard it halfway home. Maybe my body was starting to adapt to my superhearing. I could use something good to happen for a change.

I poked my head into our small home gym and found Mom hanging upside down from her pole.

"Hi, honey!" She let go with one hand and waved at me. "Want a go? I know you have superstrength, but it's great for flexibility!"

I shook my head, carefully as to not spray water all over the floor. "Thanks," I shouted over the music. "But I've had enough of poles for a day. I'll tell you after I get a shower."

"Save some hot water for me!"

I left as she was grabbing the pole with both hands and changing poses—the dragon, I think that one was called. Another thing I'd had enough of for the day.

Vern and I had argued about seeing Titania again. He wanted to go on his own, but it was my nemesis— or minemesis, to hear Vern talk. Was sub-nemesis a better antonym? Either way, my responsibility. And if I didn't know how to talk to the Queen of the Fairies, whose fault was that? It's not like there was a college class. Then again, did CSU-LL have a class? Whatever. I'd just add it to the many things I needed to learn now that I was the Defender of Los Lagos.

Well, at least I'd convinced Vern I should accompany him, even if I had to promise to keep my mouth shut.

I stepped into the shower and let the hot water flow over me. It helped soothe the chills, but not my mood.

I wish he'd keep his mouth shut about Kitty. I get it: They don't like each other. But that doesn't mean she's wrong for me. We have a lot in common: We both love journalism; we both like to shoot—I might even be a better shot than she is. I know she likes thrillers and romcoms. I could get us opening night seats—previews, even. And I know she likes me well enough physically—at least when I'm dressed like a superhero.

Maybe I should wear tighter jeans. Can I really feel self-conscious in denim when I fly around half the time in Spandex?

Hot water and shampoo felt so good. I was glad once again that we'd replaced the original water heater with an 80-gallon one. Even so, once I was clean, warm, and relaxed, I shut off the valve and got dried and dressed. Mom liked long showers after her workout, too. Besides, delectable smells were wafting in from the kitchen.

"Bear burgers," Mom announced as she set a thick juicy patty on the bun in front of my plate. "It's Lenny's secret recipe."

...which meant Lenny had come by. Great. One more thing I didn't need today.

My disapproval must have shown on my face because Mom frowned at me. "Don't give me that look.

He knows he did me wrong in the past. He wants to make up for it. He's trying."

My eyes narrowed. How did she forget all the times he's "tried" before?

"I own half this house. He is not moving in." The words were out of my mouth before I realized they were in my head.

Her mouth fell open. She turned away quickly and set about slicing a tomato with furious motions. "Who said anything about him moving in? I'm just having fun, is all. Besides, this is GHQ and Lenny can't keep a secret for squat. I'd never do that to you—to us."

She all but dropped the plate of vegetables in front of me. I knew I should feel guilty, should apologize. But today, I'd had it. I'd been lectured by a *dragon* about my romantic choices, and at least McGrue wouldn't sponge off me until she got bored. But apparently, I didn't get to have fun, even as Gapman.

No, I could not feel sorry for drawing a line.

Still, it was Mom.

"Alright, then. Thanks," I said as a compromise between what I felt and what I thought I should feel.

"Alright, then," she repeated and took the seat opposite me. We ate in uncomfortable silence, then she said. "I don't think you've ever laid down the law like that before."

I scowled. "I've told you before I don't want him moving in."

"But you've never forbade it. I think Gapman is starting to bleed into my Ron."

You know how your mom says she's proud of you and then there are times you know she's proud of you? This was one of those moments.

I snorted, embarrassed. "As long as I keep the accents separate," I said.

Our silence became more comfortable then, but she did finally break it. "I know he's not Mister Right, but I'm between beaus, and he's fun for a Mister Right Now."

When was the last time I had a Miss Right Anything?

I sighed. "As long as you both understand that."

"Plus," she paused to wipe bear grease off her chin, "he makes a mean burger."

I had to agree on that.

We finished lunch and cleaned the kitchen together. I was telling her about my mortifying morning while we were washing dishes when Mom's phone rang.

"Johnny Redfeathers!" she sing-songed in that way that embarrassed me as a teen. "To what do I owe this pleasure?"

"You got any connection to Gapman?" I heard him say over the line.

She raised her brows at me, askance. I shrugged back. Had Kitty figured it out?

She continued in her flirty voice. "Well, Johnny, I am the president of his fan club and own OMyGapman.com. And of course, we had the best interview with him on our podcast. I think we have a rapport—probably better than that reporter of yours."

I rolled my eyes and flicked suds at her.

I heard his irritated sigh. John Redfeathers was one of the few men who resisted Mom's charms, probably because she broke up with him. Or maybe that was why she ended it?

At any rate, he said, "Could you come by the paper? I've got a ton of crap in the office addressed to Gapman."

"Well," she drawled as if he'd asked her to dinner, "I might be able to get the stuff to him, but I'm busy today with other Gapman duties. You are having someone cover the launch, aren't you? Or should I ask Ron to do it?"

"I assigned an intern."

"Ron's got more talent than your interns."

"I don't have to pay interns. You send that boy of yours here to get the stuff. If I didn't have half my staff rebelling against the idea, I'd have chucked it all in the trash. As it is, I'm dumping everything tonight, even if my people want to embarrass themselves dumpster-diving for Gapgifts. This is an award-winning newspaper, not a superhero's post box."

"Why hasn't your star reporter delivered them?" she asked innocently.

"Would you just send Ronnie?" he grumbled, then added, "Please."

She glanced a question at me, and I nodded. I had a phone interview later this afternoon, but nothing to do until then.

"He'll be there in an hour or so," she told Redfeathers. "But in the future, have the stuff forwarded to my house. If you don't want to pay my son to write your articles, you shouldn't expect him to be your errand boy."

She hung up before he could reply.

I grinned at her, bemused. "Now who's laying down the law? What launch are you going to, anyway?"

"Didn't I tell you?" Mom asked. "Things have been so busy. Misty at the comic book store has joined the fan club committee and she's made the Gapfen app."

The Gapfen app, Mom explained on the drive to the comic book store, was an extension of the website—a place where Gapfen could chat, swap stories and pictures, start fun polls, and report sightings.

"We'll run contests and even have licensed merch. Misty's already prepped some designs and is taking preorders. That reminds me—we'll need Gapman's OK to trademark."

"Mom!"

The rain had stopped so I felt safe enough turning my eyes from the road for a moment to glare at her.

"Oh, calm down. We have a very reasonable proposal in mind: fifteen percent split between the comic book store, Matilda, and me for running the store; ten percent to the fan club; and the rest to charity or charities of Gapman's choice—or we can poll the Gapfen if you prefer, maybe change it up annually."

"Being a superhero keeps getting more and more complicated," I complained.

"Well, suck it up, honey, because this is our life now, and I intend to embrace every opportunity it presents. Misty, by the way, is a genius—completely wasted at the comic book store. She's cute, too."

"Mom..."

"Just an observation!" Mom wisely dropped that line of conversation and instead went into great detail about the launch party and all the events planned. Misty was even bringing in food trucks. It seemed an awful lot of work for what—a couple-dozen people?

We turned the corner to the plaza where the comic book store was. The open area was filled with people, almost all in green and gold. Most of the kids were in some kind of superhero costume; most of them some version of Gapman. There were lines at all three food trucks, and across the way, Natura's Diner had set up a take-out buffet. The comic book store (and a few of the others) had put tables outside with products. I saw people snapping scans of the QR code plastered on the walls or displayed on posts.

"Oh, my Gapman," I muttered. Mom squealed with joy.

There was no parking, so I got as close as I could. Misty caught sight of the car. She left her table with one of their teen assistants and ran up to the passenger side window.

"Isn't it amazing?" she cried. She had to raise her voice to be heard above the hubbub of the crowd. "So many people showed up early, we went ahead and soft launched, and the app's working like gangbusters! Do you think Gapman might make an appearance?"

"I did ask—didn't I, Ron?" She smiled innocently at me.

"I hope he can!" Misty said. "So many people love him—and with everything this town has been put through—with Shogzallie and evil magic users and whatnot... I mean, I think they want something to celebrate."

"What about Vern?" I found myself saying. How would he react when he hears about this? I did not need him thinking I was self-aggrandizing—or even worse, envying me.

"Vern is great," Misty said, "and totally underappreciated. But he's, well, not as accessible as Gapman, you know what I mean? Gapman is human, maybe even Mundane. He's one of us. He makes people feel like..."

"Like they can be heroes, too." I felt a catch in my throat. I hope Misty didn't hear it in my voice. "Hey, Mom? Why don't you get out here? I'll go run some errands and park the car by the Gazette. I gotta get that stuff, anyway."

"The announcement is at three," Misty told me. "Hope you can make it."

"I'll be in the crowd if nothing else," I said. That would make a good alibi when Gapman made his appearance. But I had something important to do first. More important than picking up whatever my fans had sent me. Misty had inspired me.

If people loved Gapman for his humanness, could Kitty love the man behind the mask?

Chapter Twenty-Eight: Gapman's Identity Confession Fail

Ron

Despite being a small-town paper, the Los Lagos Gazette was always full of noise and activity. I'm sure some of it had to do with being the only border town to Faerie, but the judgmental part of me blamed the setup. The building itself was among the oldest in Los Lagos, but had been renovated in "Industrial Chic," which meant exposed ceilings and lots of metal—not the best choice for sound insulation.

Then, they chose an open office plan, with each department having its own long tables with individual spaces marked out by six-inch-tall dividers. Add double computer screens, and people had just enough room for a notepad and maybe a knick-knack or family photo. While people used earbuds or full-on headsets to get some semblance of privacy, there was always a side conversation or an intern dashing between the aisles on an errand.

Every time I came here, I was glad I could make a living freelancing from my own house.

Right now, though, I was more concerned about what all of this meant for having a private conversation with Kitty. Granted her position as star reporter—not to mention her assertive personality—meant she had taken over two "cubicles" for herself. Or rather, one for herself and one for her stuff. At the moment, Lindsey, the intern, was shuffling some of the papers while telling Kitty that the lab didn't find anything weird about the goose.

I held back a snort of derision. What did they know?

"Engleson!" Chief—I mean, Editor-in-Chief—Redfeathers shouted from his office door. "Quit pining for a job you'll never get and do the job you were given. Get in here!"

With an internal roll of my eyes (so no one would see and take it the wrong way), I turned and entered his office. John Redfeathers had a large and, best of all, *private* office which also held a small conference table. Said table was currently piled with letters and small packages.

"Are those for me? I, I mean—to take home for Gapman, for Mom to get to Gapman, I mean?" I winced. Way to keep a secret identity secret.

"Yes, Ronnie, they are for you," he said with a sneer then went back to shouting. "To take to Gapman! I want that stuff out of my office, and then I expect you or Trixie to come by every couple of days until the forwarding order takes this headache off my hands and onto yours!"

Mixing metaphors—he was annoyed, all right, but not spitting mad. I promised to take care of it, and started shoving envelopes into all the empty spaces between the boxes. Satisfied, Mr. Redfeathers returned to his desk.

In amongst fan mail, I saw packages from major brands and a couple of letters with corporate logos. Were they inquiring about sponsorship opportunities? Wow! Mom and I were going to have so much fun going through this. Maybe I should ask Vern for advice about the sponsorships, though. Mom and I joked about it—was it only a month ago?—but on the other hand, if I could superhero full-time! Nah, that would get tiring, and I loved my job. Maybe we could have them donate to a charity...

"What are you doing?" Kitty demanded from the doorway.

I had not been paying attention to what was behind me. I jumped, sending letters flying.

"Careful!" she snarled, rushing to gather them up. "Those belong to Gapman!"

"And Ronnie is going to get them to him—or to his mother, at least, who apparently has a better connection with Gapman than you," Redfeathers retorted.

"What does that mean?" Kitty and I exclaimed as one.

I followed up with, "There's nothing going on between Gapman and my mom! Not romantically!"

My stomach twisted. Was this my life now? Fielding rumors about Gapman and my *mom*? At least Kitty also looked incredulous and disgusted.

Redfeathers snorted. "She's a good-looking woman, and she's only five years older."

"Ten!" Kitty countered.

I gaped at them both. "You think Gapman is in his thirties?" Before I said anything I shouldn't, I crouched down to pick up the spilled letters and parcels.

Kitty tsked at me. "You really need to work on your powers of observation. At any rate, I said I'd get this stuff to him."

She bent down and snatched an envelope out of my hands. It ripped open, and a pair of red, lacy, underwear dropped out.

"Uh..." Distracted by apparent aging-up as Gapman (please let it just be the mask!), I had not noticed the contents of that particular envelope.

"Ugh!" Kitty picked it up with two long fingernails and tossed it into the trash. I couldn't help noting that her nail polish matched the panties.

Redfeathers fished them out and shoved them into a box. "This is exactly why everything is going to Trixie."

"Why? Because it's her size?" Kitty sneered.

Was she jealous—of my mom?

"Is it yours?" The words escaped my mouth.

She looked daggers at me. Redfeathers blinked, mildly impressed. Oh, no! Did they think I was snarking back?

"I mean, you can have them if you want. I don't think Gapman would mind. I mean..." I dribbled to a stop under their now-united glare. Oh, this day is getting better and better. I pointed to the boxes. "I'll just..."

"Whatever!" Kitty flung her hands in the air and stormed out of the room.

I couldn't use superspeed, much as I wanted to, but I did make haste to get the car packed as quickly as humanly possible. Then I sat behind the driver's seat and whacked my head against the steering wheel a couple of times, careful not to hit the horn.

This was great, just wonderful. After the fiasco in the rain this morning, Kitty probably thinks Gapman's rejected her because he's into my mom. (I stopped to shudder.) When I passed through the newsroom, she was scowling at the computer, pounding the keys with greater than normal ferocity, but I also saw the soggy tissues in that little trash can where she normally tossed her receipts. She was crying—over me!

Over Gapman.

Kitty never cried. She just got angry and competitive. So why didn't she get angry and competitive about Mom? Not that I wanted her to think there was anything to be competitive about but... Was she just giving up?

I smacked my thigh with my fist. This was it. I had to tell her, or else I was going to lose her as Ron and as Gapman.

I had to do this. Now. Before I lost my nerve. How hard could it be? As long as my minemesis wasn't around, I had plenty of opportunity. It was just two words. *I'm Gapman. I'm Gapman.*

I can do this. *I'm Gapman!*

I got out of the car, locked it, and strode back into the newsroom.

I got a couple of looks as I made my way to Kitty's desk. Lindsey, the intern, looked up from where she was pouring coffee and mouthed, "Run!" But no. I had to do this before I lost my nerve. Besides, if she was upset because she thought Gapman brushed her off for another woman, how happy would she be to learn it was as opposite as could be? I'd be her hero in more ways than one. Right?

I rubbed my sweaty palms against my jeans, then shoved them into my pockets so she wouldn't notice them shaking.

She was in the middle of describing the scene at Fifth and Pike in gruesome detail when I approached. Her earbuds were in, and she was listening to... I didn't even know what it was, but there was a lot of yelling in some other language and heavy percussion.

"Kitty?" I said quietly. I tapped her shoulder.

She lifted one hand from her keyboard just long enough to wave me off like an offending fly.

She kept typing. Wow, could she describe carnage! After reading that, I would not want to see the scene— and I'd already seen it! Red squiggles covered her page, making the error-filled document as bloody as the scene she described. Each misspelled word was like nails on a chalkboard, adding to my stress.

I should leave her alone now, part of me argued, but no. I was not going to screw this up like Michael Keaton did in *Batman*.

"Kitty!" I pulled an earbud out of her ear.

"What?" she yelled.

The entire newsroom went quiet.

I lost my nerve.

"It's 'from' not form," I found myself saying. I pointed to the keyboard. "Here... and here..."

Behind me, someone sucked in their breath.

But rather than exploding, she spun back to her screen. She pounded the backspace three times, then, with exaggerated care, typed R O M.

"Satisfied?"

"Thank you?" I wasn't sure of the proper response. Behind me, I heard chairs creak and keyboards resume their clacking as people decided the show was over or my death was inevitable. And then it occurred to me that I was going to confess my secret identity—and my love!—in a room full of people.

No. A room full of *reporters*.

"Kitty, I need to talk to you—privately."

"If you're thinking about hitting on me, this is not a good time," she snapped. While one hand worked the mouse, the other reached out for her coffee cup. She started to take a sip, then grimaced.

"Lindsey! Get me a refill!" She held out the cup, typing single-handedly until it was snatched away by the current intern subjected to her despotism, who replaced the cup with a handful of stapled receipts.

"How am I supposed to work in these conditions?" Kitty muttered as she paused long enough to note the top receipt. It was for our lunch—well, hers and Gapman's. She shoved them into the tiny trash can, which I now noticed was sitting on top of a turned-down photo of her and Gapman. "Ever since Carlos got promoted, can't get a decently warm cup of coffee around here."

"Kitty, it's important. But it's...confidential." I glanced around nervously. This was not good. This was so Bruce-Wayne/Batman-Confession-Fail not good. "It has to do with Gapman."

She spun in her chair to face me fully. "What about him?"

"Not here," I said. "How about the roof?"

"McGrue!" Ramon Garcia, the city desk editor, shouted from his end of the long table. Garcia had been with the *Gazette* longer than I'd been alive, and still didn't understand how to use the internal messaging system. Whenever I had to work with him, I had to call or meet him in person. "McGrue! Where's that goose carnage story?"

"I'm running it through spellcheck—if that's alright with Engleson," she shouted back.

"Engleson! Quit interfering with work. Go home and BM her or something."

It was a testimony to how many times he'd gotten that wrong that no one laughed.

"Look, Kitty," I started again. "It will only take a minute..."

But she was back to her computer, accepting all changes without reviewing and hitting Send. "Done!"

"Good! Now, give me an editorial on the latest Gapman poll."

"Gapman poll?" I said.

"Why me?" Kitty demanded.

"Because you just did that piece on liposuction. Thirty minutes—three hundred words. Get on it."

"Lipo..." I saw the poll Kitty had pulled up on OMyGapman: *The Superhero Paunch—So Hot or So Not?*

"Wait a minute—what?" I clamped my lips down hard before I said anything. *I was Ron Engleson. I was Ron Engleson.* I could not protest that Gapman was fine and so what if he had a little bit of belly despite all the biking and the yardwork, not to mention the superheroing...

Besides, Kitty was staring at the comments section with a calculating gleam in her eye. The kind that said she'd found her revenge.

Her cell phone buzzed. She grabbed it. All over the newsroom, others were also looking at their phones.

"Gapman's been sighted over City Park!" Lindsey the intern shouted. "By the duck pond!"

Kitty rose so fast, her chair rolled until it hit the wall. "I'm getting a quote!" she shouted.

"I said thirty minutes!" Garcia protested.

"I'll phone it in!" Kitty retorted, and not a single person snickered.

She brushed past me.

"Kitty!"

She stopped, then turned on her heel and headed back. I sighed with relief.

"How about if I drive you and we can..."

She walked past me to her desk. She grabbed the receipts along with one soggy tissue that had stuck itself to the bottom receipt, wadded them all into a damp ball, and tossed them to Garcia.

"Approve these!" she shouted.

And then she was gone.

That was it. A Bruce-Wayne/Batman-Confession-Fail. Of epic proportions. And my nemesis didn't even need to make an appearance. Michael Keaton couldn't have botched it better.

I released the breath I was holding, let my stomach muscles relax, and headed back to the car. I didn't care what the Gapfen app said. I was not going to the duck pond—but maybe I would change and do a flyby of the Gapfen app launch. It'd be nice to have someone take me seriously today.

Chapter Twenty-Nine:
Gapman Gets the Girl

Ron

"What is she doing here?" Vern demanded as he stuck his head out of the garage of their mountain lair.

I felt my heart sink at his tone, but as casually as I could, I set down the tool rack I was moving to the other side of the wall to make room for MechaVern and went to join him at the entrance. Sister Grace laid her broom aside and also joined us.

We followed Vern's glare down the winding road to where Kitty's car was tailgating a FAEderal Express delivery truck that was taking up the middle of the road and moving at half the speed limit. Whoever was behind the wheel must not be used to mountain roads. Her impatient honking traveled up the still mountain air like the call of an angry ninja goose.

"I guess she's coming to report on the kids helping with MechaVern?" Grace suggested. After all the craziness with Titania—whom we still needed to go see—

Vern had finally decided to force the issue of protecting his precious mechanical avatar and had arranged for Little Flower Catholic School shop class to come help.

"The kids aren't due for another half hour," Vern retorted. "So why is she in such a hurry?"

Then he turned his eyes to me—just as I was straightening the G on my uniform with a tug known as the "Picard maneuver."

"What did you do?" he asked suspiciously.

I forced myself not to wring my hands nervously. "I... may have suggested she come a little early so we can talk?"

A screech and blaring of her horn made us turn back to the drama on the road. The truck had stopped, and from how Kitty's car nearly kissed its bumper, she'd hit the brakes pretty hard. Even over the horns, I could hear her cussing, but that wasn't what caught my attention.

From the sides of the van, toward the top, little windows flapped open, and small wings popped out. Twenty-five wings on each side, all pastel pink and lilac. They started flapping at a hummingbird's pace.

"You're not planning on apologizing, are you, Padawan?" Vern asked. "She's the one who left you hanging—literally—so she could have her dramatic exit."

"It was a misunderstanding," I replied, distracted. The FAE-Ex truck was lifting off the ground. How was that even possible?

"By her!" Vern retorted. "She should apologize to you. Good luck with that."

"Vurnerrah," Grace chided.

"It's true!" he retorted. "She cannot read a situation. Case in point..."

No sooner had the truck risen higher than her roof, she gunned the engine and drove under it. As she passed under, there was a huge *Woosh!* and the tinkling of bells. The entire area under the van was obscured by a cloud of glistening fog.

"What?" I made to leap to her rescue, but Vern clamped his tail on my shoulder. I heard Sister Grace stifle a giggle. That reassured me everything would be fine, but what had happened?

As if in answer, Kitty's car emerged from the cloud—only now it was shaped like a banana.

Vern smacked me hard with his tail and guffawed.

The van started to play "Dance of the Sugar Plum Fairies" as it ascended the mountain.

"Oh!" Grace said, somehow managing to act as if Kitty's car was not transforming into various fruits and vegetables. "I think they must be delivering something to the house. I'll go."

She left me with my... mentor? Partner? He didn't seem much of either as he collapsed with laughter, thumping his tail on the ground. Meanwhile, Kitty continued to ascend, spouting epithets I could hear through the windows as her car morphed from banana to corn to a very tired-looking carrot. Then, it sprouted ears and a pig nose.

"Is she okay to drive that?" I demanded.

"She's fine," Vern wheezed. "It's all cosmetic. And temporary."

"Still...They shouldn't do that. Maybe we should call the police?"

"This is private property, and I'm not ticking Santry off over a prank. Look. It's already wearing off."

It was true: Her car had returned to its normal shape, even if it had sprouted warts. One had a hair in it. Ick.

"Come on," Vern said. "She'll be here in a second. Let's go into the garage."

I thought he wanted to spare her embarrassment and followed, but when we got inside, he turned back to our original conversation. "We had this talk already, Padawan. You can't trust her. This was a perfect example: she doesn't let anything get in her way—not that truck, not the facts, and not you."

Did he know what I had planned? I didn't care. He didn't know her like I did.

I crossed my arms. "I thought we agreed I was an adult and could make my own decisions?"

Vern rolled his eyes at me and sauntered back out of the garage to greet Kitty as her warty car pulled into the side parking space.

"You should probably get a cream for that," Vern said. Of course, the blemishes were already fading, leaving behind messages: *Please don't tailgate* and *How's our spelling? Call 1-800-FAE-EX-HA.*

"Did you put them up to it?" Kitty countered. She stepped out, and we could see that somehow, the spell had gotten inside, too. Her seats were transitioning from pink fur back to the tan fabric. Her hair was electric green. I didn't think she'd noticed, and I hoped she wouldn't look in a mirror for the next few minutes.

She tried to slam her door, but instead of a satisfying slam, it made a raspberry sound.

"Put who up to what?" Vern asked, and if I hadn't been here when he was laughing his tail off, I would have believed that he had no idea what had happened to her car. "I didn't even know you were coming. Plus, you're early. The kids won't be here for another twenty minutes. Besides, isn't a local puff piece below you?"

Kitty straightened at the veiled barb. I could almost imagine her hackles rising. "It's a follow-up on the Shogzallie attacks," she said, although her eyes flicked my way.

"Really?" As a dragon, Vern didn't have eyebrows to raise, but he compensated well with the twist of his tone and a tilt of his head.

Kitty's cheeks pinked, but she rallied fast. "And as long as I'm here, I thought I might get Gapman's opinion on this new app. Do you know how many false sightings there have been? What do you think about that?"

I pulled out the Gapphone and checked. "Fifteen in the past three days, but it is going down as people self-regulate. I'm not especially concerned about it, actually. It makes a good deterrent, would you not agree? Why don't you and I walk down to MechaVern while we discuss it? Vern can fly down to meet us when Sister Grace returns."

"Oh! Um, sure. That's fine."

She seemed flustered. I'd never made a girl flustered before. Usually, I was the flustered one! Seeing her discomfiture made me feel strong and protective, which was funny because it only seemed to make the girls I was interested in annoyed.

Never mind that now. With what I hoped was an inviting grin, I gallantly waved my hand toward the trail that led to where the mangled and damaged mecha lay under tarps awaiting its resurrection.

Kitty ducked her head and tucked a now-puce strand of hair behind one ear as she started ahead of me. Vern's expression remained impassive as Kitty and I made our way down the trail, but once we were out of sight, I heard his exasperated sigh and a ruffle of his wings like a human throwing up their hands in the air.

"So you don't mind all the false sightings?" Kitty asked. Her eyes were on the trail, which was little more than a rough path interrupted by cleared-out zones where Shogzallie and MechaVern had ripped up (or burned) trees and bushes in their battle. I remembered how Mom and I had gotten out the power washer and soaked down the house in case the epic battle wandered in our direction.

"Not at all," I said. "We wouldn't want the criminal element to know where I am every moment of the day, after all."

"Hm," she responded, "but what if someone wanted to hold you—get a hold of you, I mean!" she stammered, then spoke more slowly and distinctly. "What if someone needed to get a hold of you, like to find you for emergencies or questions or..."

"Rooftop lunches?" I suggested. I had no idea how I could sound this cool. My heart was pounding so hard I could feel it in my throat. She was still into me!

"Something like that." She turned a quick smile my way.

I had to tell her. Everything in me wanted to shout, "It's me, Ron Engelson. I've admired you for years and I think I might love you and..." But she had her phone in her hand and I didn't know if it was recording.

"I mean, you can't always yell for Gapman and hope for the best," she said.

I stepped ahead just enough to push a branch out of her way and let her pass first. It gave me a moment to think. "Well, if someone really needed to know where I was, the best way would be to reach out to Trixie Engleson—at the OMyGapman website, I mean."

I might have said that part too quickly because she regarded me with suspicion. "So, the two of you are...close?"

That really was why she thought I had rejected her? The branch slipped and almost whacked me in the face. I ducked just in time. Thank you super-reflexes. "What? No! I mean not like that, not like you're thinking. I mean, if you're thinking..."

She was already striding ahead, every step telling me she didn't believe my protests.

This was ridiculous. She needed to know the truth—and now. I hastened to catch up with her. I reached out and caught her by the wrist. "Miz McGrue..."

She stopped but glared at me. I was being formal, and I knew it, but I had a reason. "Miz McGrue, please turn off your recorder."

Her mouth opened slightly—oh, those lips!—then she pulled out of my grasp. As I watched, she showed me that she turned off the recording and exited the program. She stuck her phone in her back pocket. "So? Off the record?"

"No—no record at all. This isn't about Gapman. I mean, it is, but not Gapman...it's..."

Her brows had started to knit. I was going to mess this up! In a sudden gesture, I pulled off my gloves and threw them to the ground. Then I took her hands in mine. They were soft, and I realized she'd had her nails freshly done. Usually, she had chips, especially on the index fingers.

She gave a little gasp. I wanted to gasp, too, but right now, I had to concentrate on being suave. "Kitty. I want you to know me—all of me. The hero...and the ordinary guy—"

"Oh, Gapman!" she whispered.

"Please," I said, "my name is—"

But at that moment, she pulled her hand from mine and set it over my lips.

"Shhh," she said. "It's not that I don't want to know, but it could be dangerous. Not that I'm afraid! I live for danger! But you've seen the OMyGapman forums. People are 'shipping us. If you tell me who you are now and we suddenly start dating, someone might connect the dots."

"We could—" I started, but she tapped my lips for silence.

"No—this is the wrong way. Tell you what. Let's give this some time. Let people get used to you. And this—this can be our secret. Then, say, next month?, come to me as your alter-ego and ask me out. I'm sure I'll know it's you."

"But I—" I started. I'd already tried that!

I couldn't protest, though, because her lips were suddenly on mine.

I barely had time to pucker back, when she pulled away, flushed and smiling.

"Well," she said, her eyes sparkling. "That happened."

"Yes, it did." And I really wanted it to happen again. I stepped toward her.

The Gapphone rang. The Imperial March—the ringtone I'd set for Vern.

"How did I beat you here?" he demanded. "You weren't doing something stupid with that reporter? Never mind. I don't want to know; I'm in too good a mood to have it ruined. Just get over here. I have something amazing to show you!"

I returned my phone to my pouch and shrugged. "We've been summoned by a happy dragon," I said. I was being flip about my mentor, but I couldn't help it. Kitty had kissed me!

Kitty, however, snorted, her expression sour as it often was when Vern was mentioned. "Why do you put up with that overgrown lizard?"

How did I answer? As Gapman to a reporter? Gapman to sort-of girlfriend Kitty? I decided to err toward caution. "Vern and I get along very well. He has a lot to teach me about the unique challenges of defending Los Lagos, and I'm one of the few beings who can meet him at his level. We're friends."

Kitty accented her "Tuh!" with a roll of her eyes. "He's a dragon—an *Eighth Day Creation*, in case he hasn't reminded you enough. He thinks you're a lesser being. We're more like pets than friends."

"You don't know him like I do," I countered.

She scoffed. "You don't know him like *I* do." And as if that won the argument, she turned and started down the trail.

I snatched up my gloves and hastened to catch up—at human- rather than super-speed. Was that our first fight? It didn't feel like a fight. I didn't think she was mad. But no, when I got beside her, she glanced sideways and grinned fetchingly. I felt my heart skip.

She was going to keep me on my toes—but could I expect anything less from Kitty McGrue?

I reached out with my now-gloved hand and brushed my fingers against hers. She giggled.

"What?" I asked, feeling a wonderful grin stretching my face.

She giggled again. "I feel like I'm twelve, walking in the woods with a boy, wondering if he'll steal a kiss."

"When you were twelve?" My middle-grade years were spent in the comic book store avoiding bullies.

"Well? What did you think about when you were twelve?" she asked.

I thought a moment, then smirked. "Having superpowers?"

"Well, then." She cocked her shoulder at me. "I guess some people got their dream come true."

"You never?" I found it hard to believe, but I knew what I had to do. I moved in at superspeed and planted a gentle kiss on her lips, then dashed back just as fast.

She blinked, then her brain caught up to what had just happened.

"You!" She wagged her finger at me, playfully. "Is that how it's going to be, then?"

I shrugged, feeling playful, myself. "For a month or so, maybe. Are you sure you want to wait a month?"

"At least!" Then, seeing the disappointment in my eyes, she said. "Oh, come on. It's exciting—a secret romance! In private, it's Gapman and Kitty. In public, it's Superhero and Star Reporter."

I supposed stealing kisses at superspeed could be fun. "As you wish. For now."

With that, she dropped my hand and reached for her phone. Guess it was time again for Superhero and Star Reporter.

"So what exactly is your relationship with our resident dragon?"

I sighed. What was this obsession of hers? "It's pretty self-explanatory, actually. I want to do my utmost to protect Los Lagos against threats Mundane and Magical. Vern has been doing it for almost a decade. He has the experience, the knowledge, the connections... He's mentoring me, but we're also partners after a fashion—and I think we're becoming good friends. Sister Grace, too, has been a wonderful font of knowledge and support—not to mention, she's given me some protection spells to augment my powers."

"Like?" she asked, and shivered as a breeze gusted.

"Like protection against the elements. You think I could be walking in this weather in this outfit, much less flying, without it? It's not glamorous or anything, but I'm truly grateful."

"I suppose you would have looked silly flying around in a parka," she admitted. "But speaking of image: The Gapman Muffintop Poll?"

Muffintop? "I beg your pardon?" I feigned ignorance while telling myself not to pull in my stomach too fast. "I thought it was called the Paunch Poll."

"Does it matter?" Her voice was serious, but her eyes sparkled. She was having fun with me.

Fine. "When I received my superpowers, I did not get a body makeover like in *Spiderman*. I don't have six-pack abs, but my stomach does not hang over my belt—the definition of 'muffintop,' Miz McGrue. A reporter should be exact in her words." I winked to show her I was teasing. "As to my relative 'hotness,' or that of anyone, I think attractiveness cannot be restricted to a single attribute like weight or body shape."

"Can you elaborate?"

Could I elaborate? I once wrote a five-part series on body image and characters for *Faninist*! The hardest part now would be to phrase them as Gapman would so no one could tie my quotes back to Ronnie Engleson's articles. It was so tempting to let one phrase slip, though, just so I could show Kitty the article in a month. But no, she wanted to take it slow. I could respect that.

But I was looking forward to another stolen kiss.

And a bear burger. I was starting to feel really drained again.

Chapter Thirty: Gapman's Kryptonite

Vern

How about if we walk down to MechaVern and discuss it? my padawan says. Who was he kidding? He didn't want to talk about his mom's new app. I wanted to warn him not to do anything stupid, but I knew humans too well. Besides, he'd made it very clear that he was an *adult* free to make his *own* choices.

Which meant I was "free" to bail him out when everything went south, as it inevitably would where McGrue was involved.

When I first met Grace, she had placed a compulsion spell on a child to prevent her from singing a spell that would summon monsters. If I asked her to do something similar to stop Gapman from oversharing with McGrue, would she...?

Then, I remembered all the heat she'd gotten—including from me—for that action. Ah, well. I made a request to George to watch over our love-struck charge, then ambled back to the house to see what the delivery truck had brought us.

About halfway there, I caught the scent of something familiar and exciting. Could it be? I broke into a run.

Grace was hurrying my way, and we met on the road. She opened up the bag she was carrying. "Look! A dragonstone!"

It was beautiful—and huge. More than baseball-sized. It swirled with colors only a few magical creatures could see, and I could hear the quiet singing as it rolled against the fibers of her bag. I think I squealed a little in joy.

"Bishop Aiden sent it. We can use it to power MechaVern."

It was ours! And it would be with us *always*. I hadn't had a dragonstone since...

Wait a minute.

I knew the slight tooth-shaped dents! I'd made them from years of worrying at this stone with my mouth when I was stressed. "This came from my hoard!"

"How wonderful! You get some of your treasure back. How thoughtful."

"Sure—one piece of my treasure," I retorted, suddenly annoyed. This was hardly thoughtful. "If he was going to go to all the trouble to send someone to the Iberian peninsula and get through my wards, why didn't he pick up a couple of gems as well so we could pay to get our house finished?"

Grace tutted. "The house will be finished just fine without it, and we have places to stay in the meantime. Jerry called; they're running a little behind. Why don't you go take this to play, and I'll call you when they arrive?"

She was patronizing me, and I knew it, but the dragonstone looked so pretty and I could feel its gentle tug. I wanted to feel its smooth warmth on my paws and roll it round my mouth like a giant gobstopper.

"Gapman and McGrue are heading to MechaVern. I'll meet them there and show Gapman the stone. I wonder how he'll see it?" To most mortals, it just looked like a purply-brown rock. Some Magicals or those with Magical blood could see the play of magics within it. But only dragons could appreciate its full beauty.

I took the stone in my mouth, and with tingles of joy shooting from tongue to scales, I took to the air. I felt like one of the Costa kids at Christmas. *I had a dragonstone! I had a dragonstone!*

I landed in front of the pile of metal and gears that was MechaVern and smiled at it with a renewed sense of optimism. Last summer, mages had bespelled it to enable me to "ride" it like a traditional anime mecha suit. It was as close to being full-sized as I'd been in nearly nine centuries. While we thought we could repair it enough to get it working again, power, especially magical power, had been a concern. Multiple mages had contributed to powering it for the Shogzallie battle. Grace was planning on feeding it a little each day, storing it up for when we might need to use it again.

With a dragonstone, however, we'd have an unending supply. I could fly it around just for fun!

And in the meantime, I could have other fun!

I spat the stone out hard so that it flew into the trees. Then I spun around three times, crouched, and bounded to where it had landed. My stone! Mine!

Ten blissful minutes later, I heard cars coming up the road. Playtime was over. Where was Gapman? He needed to get here soon if I was going to get to show him my pretty new bauble before we got MechaVern in the air to carry to the garage. The idea was to make it a show for the kids.

Oh, hm. What about McGrue? She was down here now.

I shrugged. She would have to walk back up. It shouldn't take long. In fact, it should not have taken this long to walk down. I called.

Soon, I heard them talking and giggling like a couple of pre-teens. I grumbled at St. George, who did not deign to show himself neither to apologize nor snicker, then tossed my dragonstone in the air and breathed fire on it so it would be all clean and glowy to show Gapman when they arrived.

With a rustle of underbrush, they arrived, Kitty in the lead, Gapman following more slowly behind. Seriously, dragging his feet now?

"Hurry up, Gapman!" I demanded. "I've got awesome news. Look what I've got!"

I held out the dragonstone for him to examine. The softly glowing gem began to pulse, and its myriad of colors that only I could see started to swirl in a distorted way. Then, I realized there was a cloud of distortion flowing from it—to Gapman!

My padawan back away until he bumped into a tree.

"Get that away from me!" he rasped.

Damsels and Knights! It was his kryptonite!

Ron

Vern shouted out a dragon word that I assumed was a curse and shot into the air. Immediately, I began to feel better.

Or maybe not quite. I turned my head away from Kitty and vomited onto a pile of dead leaves.

"What's going on?" Kitty demanded.

"Sorry," was all I could manage to gasp out. What a great impression to make on my new girlfriend. I fumbled in my pouch for the small bottle of water I kept there. I rinsed my mouth and spat. I tried to walk away from the mess with confidence, but two steps later, a wave of dizziness hit me, and I grabbed hold of a tree for balance.

Then Kitty was beside me, supporting me as she helped me sit. "Gapman, talk to me. Are you all right? What's going on?"

"What was that?" I asked instead. I was shivering and nauseated, and while I was starting to feel stronger again, I had a killer headache. He'd pointed that rock at me, and it had felt like it was going to rip my face off from the inside.

I wiped my sweaty forehead with my cape and concentrated on my breathing while Kitty peppered me with questions I couldn't answer. I couldn't even lie to tell her I was fine. What was that rock? My Ron eyes said it was just a brownish stone. My Gapvision said it pulsed and flowed with colors I didn't have names for.

A rustle of wings, and Vern landed in front of us. "I hid it on the other side of the mountain. You okay, Padawan?"

"What did you do to him?" Kitty demanded with protective rage. It almost made me smile.

Vern tsked with annoyance. "You think I meant to attack my partner right before we were going to do something for *me*?" Then he dismissed her and crouched down to better talk to me while he examined my face. "Feeling any better now?"

Sister Grace knelt beside me and took my hand in both of hers. How did she get here? She hummed something. I didn't know what it was, but it flowed over me like a wave of feathers. My nausea eased.

"The good news is, the effects were temporary," Sister Grace said.

"What effects?" Kitty demanded. "What happened?"

I felt as much as heard Vern growl, but Sister Grace intervened. "Kitty, dear, could you give us a little space, please?"

When she hesitated, I gave her a reassuring smile. "I'll be alright," I said, because now I *could* finally say it. My stomach had settled, the headache was fading, and I could feel my strength returning.

Kitty frowned in return but marched toward MechaVern and started scrolling on her phone.

Good enough. "What was that?" I asked. I was absurdly pleased that I remembered my accent even after getting whammied so badly.

"A dragonstone—a rare and magical gem in Faerie," Vern said. He spoke quietly and glanced at Kitty, but she continued to stare at her phone.

"And apparently one that does not like your magic," Sister Grace concluded. "Vern, have you heard of it reacting badly to fairy spells?"

He shook his head. He seemed oddly glum. "It must be the Mundane element."

"So I'm like, allergic?" I felt well enough to stand, although Sister Grace kept one hand on my arm to keep me steady, just in case.

"Or maybe it saw the Mundane element as a contagion and was trying to pull it from you," Vern said. "This could be really bad."

"Fortunately, like Superman's kryptonite, the range is limited," I guessed. "I didn't start feeling sick until we were a couple hundred yards from here. And the effects seemed to have worn off."

"You're sure?" Sister Grace asked.

In reply, I leaped into the air, circled the clearing, then landed. I grabbed a sizable rock and crushed it in my palm.

"Good as new," I said to Kitty because she'd looked up from her phone to watch.

"Still," Grace said, "maybe we should put off moving MechaVern for today?"

"And disappoint the kids?" I said. I struck a pose, hand on hip, chest out, biceps flexes. Stomach tucked in. "Absolutely not. Besides, Miz McGrue is here for a story."

"Oh, don't worry about me," Kitty replied. "I'm fine."

If I'd had fantasies about romance at 12, they probably would have played out just like the rest of the afternoon.

Sister Grace had ridden in on Vern's back, and she offered to walk back up the mountain with Kitty, but I suggested Vern take her to the garage and I could take Kitty.

"If you don't mind the cold, Miz McGrue," I'd said. I knew the answer—she'd once gone to Minot, North Dakota, in the middle of January for a story. But the glow in her eyes belied the feelings she tried to hide with a casual shrug.

Vern gave me a look that I could only describe as "murderously annoyed," but at Sister Grace's urging, he agreed, warning me that if I got tired to try to get close to the ground before dropping any reporters.

When they had ascended, Kitty smiled coyly at me. "You wouldn't drop me, would you?"

"You should hold tightly...just in case." I could not believe how excited and protective and flirty I felt. Maybe there was something to secret romances.

I scooped her into my arms like some old-fashioned movie hero and we took to the air. She clung to my neck the whole time.

I hardly remembered the work with the kids, I was so giddy from holding her that close. Still, Vern and I made an impressive display carrying the damaged mecha into the garage, and whatever I said to the kids seemed to impress them well enough. It was Kitty's admiration I was more concerned about.

Then she left her notebook, so of course I had to fly it over to her house, where I stole another kiss at superspeed. She suggested she'd be up late tonight working on her story, so if I happened to be on patrol...

"It's a moonless night tonight," I said. "The stars will be incredible to watch—maybe from the rooftop of the Arts Center?"

"I'll pack some cocoa," she said, then shut the door before I could sneak in another kiss.

That was fine. I had the feeling there'd be a lot more kissing later!

I bounded off the porch and shot straight into the air, waiting until I'd broken through the clouds before letting out a whoop of joy!

The Gapphone rang.

Kitty already? I almost dropped my phone in my haste. Then I paused. *Act cool. I'm a superhero.* "This is Gapman."

"Oh, cut the crap, Ron," my Aunt Matilda's furious and worried voice sounded over the line. "Just get to my house, fast! Your mother needs you."

Chapter Thirty-One: Gapman's Red-Hot Rescue

Ron

I was on Aunt Matilda's back porch before she'd even hung up. I paused, forcing myself to walk in like a normal person. Even though I heard my mother sobbing from inside the house, I had to remember my identity. *I was just coming over to help the presidents of my fan club. No emergency, no mothers involved...*

As soon as I noticed the curtains to the living room were drawn, however, I dropped all pretense, tore off my mask and gloves, and ran to Mom. She was perched on Aunt Matilda's saggy couch, folded over and crying like I'd died. A pile of tissues beside her said this had been going on a while.

I sat on the coffee table across from her and set my hands on her shoulders. "Mom! Mom, what's wrong? What happened?"

"I hate it when you're right!" she burst out, then flung her arms around me, bawling into my shoulder.

"I'm sorry! I should have listened to you. I'm such an idiot."

"What...?" I started, then it hit me.

Lenny.

"What did he do to you?" I pushed her back so I could examine her face for bruises. I used my X-ray vision to check her for broken bones. I realized now that she was wearing one of Aunt Matilda's XXL T-shirts and yoga pants that fit her better than Matilda. If he had hurt my mother, we were going to see Gap-man get very dark, very fast.

"Easy, Tiger," Matilda said. "He didn't do anything violent."

"It's worse!" Mom wailed. "He broke my heart—again!"

And she collapsed back against my shoulder.

In between the sobs and "I thought he'd changed," and with some help from Aunt Matilda, I got the whole story. He'd invited her over to his place because he had something "life-changing" he wanted them to do, and she'd thought he was going to ask her to marry him—

"Or at least shack up—but I would have said 'no.'"

—so she went over expecting to turn down a proposal. After a dinner of bear steaks and a couple of drinks, he'd pulled out his big surprise.

"It was puck!" Matilda said.

"Puck—like the drug?" I pulled my hands away from my mother so I wouldn't crush her with my fists.

Mom was calmer now. She sat back and blew her nose. "Yes, that puck. I don't know where he got it. It's not like it's hard to find. Anyway, he was suggesting we have a couple more drinks, do some puck, and then make lewd suggestions to each other. He even took a snootful first to prove he was 'sincere.' *Sincere!* I thought he wanted a relationship, and he just wanted a, a good time. It's not like I wanted a relationship with him, but I thought he saw me as something better than that. How could I have been such an idiot?"

She flopped back on the couch and stared at the ceiling like it would give her answers.

"You're not the idiot," I said. "He is."

"And you are past being 'a good time,'" Aunt Matilda said. "He's just too stupid to see it."

"You don't think I'm a ho?" Mom asked me.

My mouth dropped. "Of course not! You're a strong, independent woman who deserves a guy who's smart enough to recognize her value. You... just have a bad knack for picking up the wrong guys."

"Well, never again." Mom sat up and shook out her hair. "No more loser Mister Right Nows. I've learned my lesson. In fact, when I left, I told Lenny he could burn in hell... Oh, no!"

"What?"

"I told him to burn—when he was high on puck!"

I told them to call Vern and the fire department. After a stern admonition to be careful from Mom and a warning from Aunt Matilda that we'd be having a discussion about keeping secrets from her, I sped to Lenny's house.

His duplex was in the older part of town, where nearly everyone was too old or too poor to do much more than basic home upkeep. I remembered thinking that it was a pretty nice house when I was a kid. Now, the only thing going for it was that Lenny was obsessed with sealing every nook and cranny against the elements. Which meant that, aside from the smoke coming from the dryer and bathroom vents and the undulating glow of the windows, there was no sign of the fire raging inside.

Fearing the worst, I pulled open the back door.

A blast of heat knocked me off the porch and onto my back. For a moment, I lay there, staring stupidly at the fire. I was too late! What would I tell Mom?

Then I heard a cough and a weak, "Help."

Oh, this was going to hurt. Covering the exposed part of my face with my cape and praying that Sister Grace's spells would protect me, I dashed through the flames.

I'd intended to run through, grab Lenny, and run out all at superspeed, but the first time I took a breath, the smoke burned in my lungs and broke my concentration. I ground to a halt, coughing. Outside, I heard sirens. *Hurry!*

"Gapman!"

The voice was to my right. I could hardly see through the smoke; then my vision changed, and I saw a blob, like through night vision goggles. I didn't bother to geek out but staggered over to him. "Sir?"

"I don't wanna burn in hell!" He threw himself on my ankles.

"Get up!" I told him, but whether it was from smoke inhalation or stupidity, he just clung to my leg, crying. I could see welts on his skin. I had to get him out of there.

I pulled my cape off and draped it over him, then scooped him in my arms. I tried not to think how I'd carried Kitty the same way just a few hours earlier. He wrapped his arms around me, and between coughs, I thought I heard him saying, "Don't let me go" and "My hero!"

I turned my face away from the stench of Fritos and tequila, surprised his breath wasn't setting the air around us on fire.

In the yard, firefighters were shouting instructions.

We were in the living room. The front door was closest. I staggered that way, then barreled shoulder-first through the door.

Oops! Too hard. It tore off its hinges and fell to the ground. Then again, who cared? There was air.

People...cheered?

Through streaming eyes, I saw about 20 people, mostly women with coats thrown over party clothes, jumping and waving at me from across the street. One held up her phone. Letters scrolled: M A R R Y M E G A P M A N.

My shoulders slacked in surprise.

Lenny dug his fingers into the fabric of my super-suit! "Don't let me go!"

Then, I had to hold him more tightly as coughs racked his body and threatened to spill him out of my hold. He belched wetly.

Standing straighter and trying to look like a super-hero and not the pissed-off son of his mom's no-good drunk ex, I carried Lenny off the porch. I felt coughs threatening to bend me double, but I ignored them. If I had to save Mom's stupid ex, I was going to look good doing it! Even so, I didn't notice as my feet hit air and I floated instead of taking the steps to the side-walk. Only when I heard the adoring sighs of the fen did I realize what I'd done.

A fireman ran to me, craning his neck up. "Uh, Gapman?"

"Right. Of course." I lowered myself to ground level, and the fireman reached for Lenny.

He curled himself into a fetal position and tight-ened his arms around my neck. "No! No! Save me, Gap—-hwack!"

He vomited onto my suit.

I extended my arms, trying to push him into the fireman, who in turn, pulled while reassuring Lenny that he was okay and they were going to get him some oxygen. Lenny's fists tightened even more on my suit until a seam gave and it tore, shoulder to chest.

Screams and titters from across the street, and I thought I saw one girl collapse into her friend's arms.

As two firemen led the sobbing Lenny away, another came to me with a towel and a blanket. "Sorry about that, Gapman."

I wiped the worst off my outfit. Thanks to Grace's spell, it didn't stick! "It's fine, fireman. Suits can be repaired. Lives are precious."

"We should check you out," the fireman said, but from the front of the crowd, a female voice cried, "Gapman, you're so wise!" and a press van was pulling up. They were going to expect a few words of wisdom. Should I say something about the dangers of puck?

The reporter and her cameraman had left the van and were starting toward me. Emboldened, the crowd started across the street, completely ignoring the police who had arrived and were trying to keep everyone back.

Maybe a few words would convince them to stay safe.

I straightened and took a breath to address the crowd—and my lungs would no longer be controlled. Racking coughs pounded out of me at superstrength. The fireman staggered back, and even I had to put one foot behind me and brace myself as I struggled to breathe. I was suddenly aware that my face burned worse than any sunburn I'd ever had, patches of my supersuit were burned, and the soles of my feet felt like they were still on fire.

I sat down. I was dimly aware of people rushing toward me, knocking aside the hastily erected police barrier and the policeman keeping them back.

"Gapman's in trouble! Help him! Oh, my Gapman! Help him!"

A pixie in a doll-sized EMT uniform flew to me and tried to shove a mask onto my face. My cough sent him spinning.

"Gapman!" Sarah Chiu from Channel 3 News shoved a microphone into my face. "What's it like, rescuing someone from such a raging fire?"

"Hot? Smoky?" I managed to gasp out. I held up a hand for them to wait while I fought to control my breathing.

"And you're affected by the smoke! What about the heat? Do you have other weaknesses?"

"What?" Was that the theme *du jour* today?

I hated to be rude to a reporter but... Oh, wait, one of my fans did it for me, grabbing her bodily and shoving her behind him. "Leave him alone, sleaze!"

"He needs help!"

"People, get back! Give the man some room!" a policeman called out ineffectively.

"Mouth-to-mouth! Do you need mouth-to-mouth?" A woman clung to my arm.

The pixie wove between the crowds and tried again. "Hey, Gapman! You need oxygen! I got oxygen. I got the mask and the tank and you need the mask—"

This time, I grabbed it from him and pressed it against my face. The oxygen cooled and soothed my smoke-irritated lungs. Plus, the mask stopped any over-eager fans wanting to give me rescue breathing. I inhaled gratefully and ignored the crowds for a moment.

"He's not a man! He's a hero! Oh, Gapman!" Someone pulled at my sleeve, tearing the seam further as the policeman dragged her off.

The reporter had returned. "Gapman, is this your first fire rescue?"

I took one more breath, then pulled the mask from my face. "Please, citizens, get back across the street." Another coughing fit threatened to take me, but I fought it, forcing my breathing to calm. If I could run the Pikes Peak Marathon, I could do this. "I want you to stay safe."

A few sighed and obeyed, but others took selfies.

"Gapman," the fire chief shouldered past the others. "The fire's too much. I've called my men back."

As if to emphasize his point, part of the roof caved in. The last of the fangirls finally backed off with little shrieks.

The fire chief continued, "The guy is babbling about a woman. Do you know if anyone else is in there?"

"No, there's no one," I said. I wanted to groan, myself. Mom was going to feel so guilty, she might even invite him to stay with us until he found another place...and how could I refuse?

Lenny had recovered enough to start shouting. "Worse date ever!"

Date! I was supposed to meet Kitty 20 minutes ago. No way could I go now, not like this. She might actually be into the torn and sooty costume, but even with magic, the stench of Lenny's vomit lingered. What a night.

At least I was feeling better. Thank you, super healing! I passed back the mask and stood. My fans had finally been spooked by the house collapsing and decided to obey the police. They cheered from the other side of the fire truck.

"Is there anything else you need from me, Chief?" I asked.

"Any details about what you saw inside, to help us determine the cause? That guy"–he pointed to Lenny, who was now on his knees throwing his hands up to heaven and crying to God in between retching on his front lawn—"said he got distracted and dropped his cigarette."

Lenny's cries had moved to belated deals with God to give up porn.

"So he didn't do it deliberately?" I'd never felt happier to hear Lenny had been being Lenny.

I turned back to the bonfire that had once been a 1960s duplex.

With a sag and groan, the house collapsed in on itself.

"Why?" Lenny cried out.

Maybe if I'd not been in uniform, I could have given him an answer.

Chapter Thirty-Two:
Gapman Gets Monologued

Ron

The next morning, I was in the middle of a very nice dream of what my date with Kitty would have been like. We were snuggling on her couch, half-watching a romcom. Our eyes met. She lifted my mask...

Then, in my mother's voice, she said, "Ronnie?"

"Ron! Ronald Logan Engleson, wake up!"

In my dream, Kitty's living room suddenly caught fire and she turned into Lenny. I woke up with a jolt.

"Ah! What?"

The mid-morning sun was shining through the windows. Wow. I must have been tired; normally, that would wake me up. My room was the coldest in the house. I had four heavy blankets tangled around me. I was hugging my Mystique plushie pillow with one arm. I dropped it and ran my fingers through my hair.

Even after a long bath last night, it still smelled faintly of smoke. "What's wrong?"

Mom glared at me from the foot of my bed. "Why didn't you tell me about your kryptonite?" she demanded.

"I was kind of busy saving your ex-boyfriend," I retorted, but I was too confused to be annoyed. "How did you...?"

She shoved her tablet at me.

The Chink in Gapman's Armor
Superhero's Weakness Fortunately a Rare Faerie Element

"By Kitty McGrue?" I shouted. This? *This* was the big story she said she was working on when I called to cancel our date?

"How could you tell her that and not your own mother?" Mom demanded.

"I didn't tell her. She was there." I read on. The story started with my quote about Vern being a mentor, partner, and friend...then cut to her declaring he was also my greatest danger. Anyone who didn't know better would think he shoved that dragonstone at me just for fun, like he knew what it would do.

"She really does have it in for Vern," I muttered.

"Vern?" Mom said. "What about you? She just told everyone your greatest weakness—and the TV station has picked it up, too. Now the world knows if they want to incapacitate Gapman, all they need it a lot of smoke and a dragonstone. And electrocution—that one's making the rounds now as well."

"I got over the smoke inhalation and electrocution quickly enough," I said, "and dragonstones are rare."

"But not impossible to find. And it took you down fast, if Kitty is to be believed. For pity's sake! I thought she liked you."

"She does!" Didn't she? Was she that upset about a broken date? I'd seen the wrath she'd unleashed when the new copyeditor took her parking spot. Not that it was marked; everyone else just knew, but HR had forgotten to warn him. After a long fight in which he refused to apologize, she declared she would find his secrets. And she had. He'd left town the next day. Some folks said he left the county.

Was she jealous that I spoke to another reporter?

No. No, maybe Redfeathers put pressure on her and she caved, coming up with the first story she could find to top the fire.

"I need to talk to her. Is my other suit clean?" I'd tossed it in the laundry sink to soak after the goose incident.

"You're lucky you have your mother to help with laundry," Mom said, still irate. "It's in your backpack, and I cleaned your belt—it's on the dresser." She pointed. "And I made you a dozen scrambled eggs and a pound of bacon."

"You're the best," I told her, then leaned over to kiss her cheek. "Uh, can you go, though? It's just, I was so tired I went to bed in my underwear."

She tsked. "I diapered that bottom, you know. I'll see you downstairs. Hurry up. I have to go to work today. Oh, and tonight, we're going to have to apologize to Matilda about keeping this from her. She's mortified that she flirted with you so much."

When she shut the door, I folded over myself and groaned. This was great—Kitty and I had barely had our first kiss and now we were going to have our first fight. I may be a superhero, but I hate confrontation. Why couldn't people just naturally be reasonable?

Maybe she would be. Maybe she'd apologize. She could have had a good reason for writing that article. I didn't know. I needed to talk to her—but how? What should I say? Should I be personal or professional...?

From my dresser, the Gapphone rang. Sheesh—already? I dragged myself to the dresser and grabbed the phone. It was Kitty's number!

A spike of adrenaline surged through me. How should I answer? Was she calling to apologize or to justify—or maybe to ask a follow-up about the fire like she hadn't just betrayed me in the most public way possible? I should be angry—but I didn't want to blow it.

The phone rang for the fourth time.

I finally decided on cool and distant and tapped the screen. "Miz McGrue. We need to talk—"

"Shut up and listen!" she cried out—and not in anger. She sounded scared and desperate. "I'm in danger. But whatever you do, don't—"

I didn't find out what she was warning me against because her sentence ended in a squeal, and a familiar male voice came on the line. "Greetings, Gapman, Hero of Los Lagos, Padawan—as the Mundane saying goes—of Vurnerrah, Great and Currently Only Dragon of the Faerie and Mundane. Gapman, would-be lover of Kitty McGrue, Reporter of the..."

"Hawgindespotlite?" I interrupted. Even if I hadn't recognized the voice, the typical High Elvish introduction would have clued me in.

"That is not our name!" he shouted back in a weirdly non-Elvish way. "We are U."

"You're me?" Had the toxic waste affected his mind?

"No! Not you. U—like the twenty-first letter and fifth vowel of the Latin alphabet, used by Mundane and Faerie English alike. U as in short for Unity—and U as in I told U it was too short!"

"What? When did you tell me—?"

"Not you! U! Me! Us. We are getting off track. This was all too hasty, and it goes against every fiber of my being but U insisted. Our time in the shadows has reached its fruition. Now we triumphantly ascend the stage—or enter Stage Left, as the Spanish word for left is 'sinistra,' and sinister indeed are our machinations. For verily the last piece of the puzzle has fallen into place; our plans ripen to fullness; our research..."

I put the phone on speaker and dressed while he rambled. Something was terribly wrong—and not just that he had Kitty prisoner. I didn't have a lot of experience with High Elves, but I had listened to the entire 40-minute recording I had, and even though Hawgin had rambled, he had had a twisting kind of logic. This just felt like a lot of short phrases strung together, like a bad improv.

In the background, Kitty yelled, "Gapman! Call Vern! Let him handle this!"

Vern again? What was with those two?

I heard a slap and a yelp from Kitty, and a red haze flooded my vision. No one hurts my Mom and no one hits my woman!

"Keep your filthy hands off her!"

"She will be fine if you follow my directions. Come at best speed to the LLF&I mill, that now-defunct testimony to the power of change, for verily…"

While he nattered on about the history of the abandoned steel mill, I threw on my cape and launched myself out the window. As soon as he hung up, I called Vern. Yeah, I wanted to rescue the girl—my girl—but I wasn't stupid, either.

The small steel mill had been closed long before I was born, but no one had wanted to pay for its demolition. It stood, abandoned, graffitied, and rusting, on the west side of the mountain that had provided its ore. Shrouded in shadow, it looked sinister—the perfect spot (as Hawgin—sorry, U—had said) for a superhero-supervillain first encounter.

If U thought I was going to play into his hands, he had another think coming. I was an *entertainment reporter*. I knew all the tropes.

Unlike Superman, I could see perfectly well through iron. I hid in a tree and used my X-ray vision to locate anyone in the mill. I only saw one body—a woman, sitting in a chair, possibly bound from the position of the arms. It must be Kitty. But where was everyone else? Had they found a way to block my vision? Vern had stealth spells, and Hawgin was Faerie. He could be hiding a whole army of minions. Great.

Should I wait for Vern and Sister Grace? In Hawin's long diatribe, he never once told me to come alone, so when he finally hung up, I'd used that loophole and called Vern for reinforcements. Hawgin had, however, given me a deadline. They would not get here in time. I had to at least make an appearance and stall.

Then again, this was Kitty—my girlfriend. Yet, she told me to let Vern handle it. Didn't she think I could rescue her? No, I had to do this. For me. For us.

So what was my next move? Superheroes usually handled it one of two ways: barreling in at top speed and destroying everything in their path, or sneaking in. He'd expect either. How long would it take to tunnel under?

I thought about how long it took me to crush all the rocks for the road. No, too long, and it'd be noisy. Plus, I didn't have a shovel, and this was my only intact suit.

Could I call him out—a one-on-one showdown for the life of Kitty? Nah. If he'd wanted that, he would have suggested it. He's playing Lex Luthor to my Superman.

Create a distraction, then go in? I checked my pouch: phone, small bottle of water, my camping knife, a tiny first-aid kit, granola bar, and a breath mint. No help there. I was so unprepared! I even skipped breakfast. I ate the granola bar and polished off the water while I thought.

There was nothing to do about it. I had to go in and hope for the best. Crash through at superspeed?

A vision of Lenny's house falling in on itself came to my mind, replaced quickly by the mill doing the same.

Okay. Sneaking, it was—but not through the front. U'd expect that. What wouldn't U expect?

I glanced at the ceiling where I saw the outtake for the old ventilation system. That was it! They'd never expect that. Sure, it was a cliché in action movies, but superheroes never bothered. Besides, in real life, crawling through vents made a horrible racket. U would probably count on my knowing that.

But would he count on my flying through them?

For once, I was glad I was born with the narrow body of a bicyclist and not the broad shoulders of a linebacker. Even so, it was taking all my concentration to keep myself hovering at just the perfect spot to not scrape against any of the exposed bolts or sharp edges of the vent. Sound did carry ridiculously well in the vents, and I could hear Kitty talking to U.

"So why are you doing this? Seriously, what motivated you to wake up in the morning and think, 'I'll become a superhero's nemesis today?'"

U chuckled. "My dear Miz McGrue, as your Gapman so fondly calls you, it is not that I made such a decision—yes, U did! U has choice! For the love of Old Growth, could U not lean into the narrative? Just once so I...alright! We made this decision, but this is the role U was made for, forged by the very same process that brought you your own Gapman."

"Process? What process?" Kitty asked, but U kept going on about destiny and being the yin to my yang.

I came to a junction, listened hard, and chose the vent to the right. In the meantime, Kitty asked more questions. Could she know what I was doing and be trying to help? Was she stalling for time?

Then she asked how he spelled "Unity" and it struck me. She was interviewing him.

Suddenly, U dropped his monologue—including a discussion on whether to alter the spelling of his name for trademark purposes—to tsk at something I could not see.

"It appears that your superhero is late."

"He's smarter than you think," she retorted. "He's not coming. But when Vern gets a hold of you..."

Vern? I almost cried out loud. I had to hurry before that oversized lizard stole my thunder and rescued my girl.

The next vent went down in a dogleg curve. I bent. There! I could see the light and the top of her head. I inched forward.

Urk!

The fabric of my stomach caught on a grommet. Curse you, Superhero Muffintop!

I tried to back up, but the caught fabric pulled on the grommet, causing it to squeak.

"Oh!" U said from below. "The vents! Clever! U did not expect that from a superhero. Yet, so convenient for me."

What was he talking about? I had just enough time to wonder when I heard a hissing. Smoke! Maybe knockout gas. I had no idea if knockout gas would work. I took a deep breath, hoping to get clear air. Then, abandoning all efforts at subtlety, I reached down, pulled my suit free, and crashed into Kitty's cell.

There was gas all around, so I didn't bother with a heroic declaration. I grabbed her chair and spun it around, then drew back in horror.

Kitty was wearing Hawgin's necklace—the stones of which I now realized were dragonstone.

"You idiot!" Kitty shouted just before falling unconscious.

I tried to run, but my breath would no longer be held. I fell to my knees, took in a breath of the gas, and knew no more.

Chapter Thirty-Three: Gapman and the Conveyor Belt of Doom

Vern

Grace and I were in the middle of accepting a missing "persons" case when Gapman called. I excused myself and moseyed away from the client's front porch to take it while I sniffed around to catch the pooch's trail. The lady wouldn't stop going on about how stressed her chihuahua had been the past couple of weeks. I hated dog cases, but this one was paying ridiculously good money.

"Vern, he's got Kitty!" His cool British-ish accent didn't hide the desperation in his voice. From the rush of wind in the background he was flying at super-speed, too.

"Who? Hawgin?" I didn't know why I was even asking. Superhero love interest plus nemesis equals kidnapping eventually.

"Of course, Hawgin—only he's acting strange and he kept calling himself U—"

"Me?"

"No, U—like the letter, and his speech was too quick, and he kept referring to himself in the third person."

"'U' would be second person," I quipped, but I did head over to Grace to call the meeting short.

"Vern, not now! He's holding her at the old LLF&I mill. I'm almost there now."

"It'll be a trap. Wait for—"

And he hung up.

Looked like Timida was going to have a couple more hours of doggie adventures. I told Grace we had an emergency and briefed her before taking to the skies. It'd take me seven minutes to get to the mill—plenty of time for a love-struck superhero to get himself into trouble.

Ron

Something jerked me into consciousness and I instinctively tried to stand, only my legs wouldn't cooperate, my balance was off, and a weight behind me pulled me back into a sitting position. A moment later, I had enough sense of mind to realize my feet were bound, my hands were tied behind my back, and coils of rope held me back-to-back with Kitty.

We were on some kind of elevated conveyor belt in the middle of the steel processing section of the factory. One end led to bins that I guessed fed it materials. The other end had vicious-looking pistons and blades. Just past it, I could feel the heat of a smelter.

"What's going on?" It was a stupid question. I could already guess, but it came out of my mouth before I could hold it back.

Kitty answered, anyway. "What's going on? How about you didn't listen to me? I told you—"

She was suddenly silent.

"Miz McGrue?" I tried to turn my head to see her but only caught a glimpse of her hair flowing back and forth as she shook her head in a struggle against something I could not see. "Kitty!"

"She will be fine," a familiar voice said from the shadows. I heard the metallic clang of footsteps ascending a staircase, and then Hawgindespotlite stepped into my view. He wore a full tuxedo with a top hat. "U've simply silenced her for the moment so we could have a more pleasant conversation."

"Why are you dressed like the Penguin?"

Behind me, I heard Kitty's exasperated sigh.

Not that I blamed her. Was every stupid thing I thought going to come out of my mouth today? I must still be drugged. That was it; I was going to blame the drugs. I did feel weirdly crawly everywhere.

Even so, he had the dragonstone necklace around his neck, so why didn't I feel worse? I squinted my eyes and forced myself to look for my own magic. It was vibrating around me like it wanted to escape; that must be why I felt crawly.

Hawgin, meanwhile, had darted his eyes upward and snapped, "I told you this outfit was too Mundane!"

I was about to ask who he was talking to when his eyes moved the other direction. "Nonsense! We are following a long line of archvillain tradition! And this is a special occasion, wouldn't you agree, Gapman? For indeed this is the day of our first meeting as hero and villain; the start of a long and hopefully fulfilling adversarial relationship for the both of us."

"'Fulfilling'? Listen, Hawgin—"

"We are Unity!" he thundered. Somehow he made his voice sound in stereo, as if more than one person were speaking. It reverberated off the rusting steel. Hawgin—Unity—looked up and around, a bemused grin on his face. From his pocket, something yipped, and he patted the fabric reassuringly.

Was Unity him and a dog? Great. The same accident that gave me superpowers turned him cuckoonuts. I wondered if Snapdragon would find that funny, because at the moment, I sure didn't.

"Look, Unity," I said in my most authoritative superhero voice. "This is between you and me. Let Miz McGrue go."

"Where would be the drama in that? Nay, friend Gapman—"

"Friend? You knocked me out and tied me to a conveyor belt!"

"I told U this was a stupid idea!" Unity snapped, followed immediately with, "Nonsense. We will respect the traditions of the genre that has brought forth our being. For yea, though the High Elves are well-renowned for their deep and rich history, a history that has been carried on in verse spoken and written since—" He snored rudely. "—fine! Let it never be known that we could not adapt to new and verily, exciting customs!"

This was Smeagol-level crazy. Not good! I had to keep stalling until Vern got here. Vern! "Unity, listen to me: We can help you. Return you to the former greatness that was Hawgindespotlite, High Elf and actor. This was done to you by—" I stopped myself before I named Snapdragon. "—magic, right? I'm sure Sister Grace knows healers..."

Unity interrupted me with a laugh. "Do not expect help from your dragon and nun allies. I've seen to it that they will stay busy for some time. You see, you are not the only one who will risk everything for someone they love."

To prove his point, he pulled out a meek and trembling Timida out of his pocket.

"And now," he said, stroking the shivering chihuahua between the ears, "let us see what you will do. Oh, and Miz McGrue."

He gave a dramatic twist of his wrist.

Kitty let out a howl of frustration. "Finally! Let us go right now, or I swear, I'll..."

"Write something scathing about me for your paper?" Unity smirked. "You seem to do that to your friends as well. But I do hope to read what you say about your beloved superhero tomorrow. If you survive. And, dear Gapman, I look forward to when we tangle again."

"Again?" I clung to the thought like a lifeline. "Okay. You're on. You won this one! Why don't you let us go, and I'll give you a head start..."

But he laughed and turned to go. Just before he reentered the shadows, he flicked his wrist. Suddenly, I felt weak and sick all over again. I realized he'd been shielding me so we could talk. How polite—in a twisted evil supervillain sort of way.

The conveyor belt started to move.

Vern

I arrived at the mill and did a quick circuit. Yep—magic traps everywhere. Even some fairy portals. It had to be Hawgin, and he had minions. Did he hire the radioactive pixies from the play? Out-of-work actors will do anything to survive, even in Faerie, it seemed. The portals were moving, too. On a hunch, I took one of Grace's charms from my pouch and threw it. A portal immediately swallowed it up. Yet I saw rats scurrying in a junk pile not too far away. So these things were targeting magic.

But not Gapman. I heard him on the other side of the mill, arguing with someone. Sounded sort of High-Elf, but off. Gapman was right; something was wrong with Hawgindespotlite.

I flew over to that side and landed in the trees out of what I hoped was the range of the portals. I saw movement through the dirty second-story windows. There he was, tied up, back to back with someone—McGrue, probably—and arguing with a High Elf in a top hat. Wow. Guess Hawgin thought this was a special occasion. Elves did love formality. The hat was a little much, though.

I turned my attention back to my padawan. I guess I shouldn't have been surprised that he got caught, but why was he sitting there arguing when he could launch himself into the air and escape? Was he being held by a spell as well as the ropes? Maybe he knew about the portals?

Well, I wasn't any help unless I got past these portals. I needed Grace to take them down—and to help if the rope was bespelled. I got on the phone to ask her ETA.

Unknown. Lizzie slashed my tires! She said she'd pay for them once we find her dog, Grace texted back.

I bit back a curse and forced my tail not to slash noisily in annoyance. Some Mundanes and their dogs—

Just then, I heard a yip from the mill. Of course.

Found the dog, I texted back. *Not missing. Kid-napped. Get over here—make her drive you.*

That was going to be 15 minutes at least. Some-how, I didn't think Hawgin—or U, or whatever he called himself now—was going to let their banter drag that long. Especially not if he was going by U. High Elves did not use monograms.

Now Kitty was yelling. The conveyor belt has started?

That clawed all the options out of my decision. I was going to have to go in fast, hope I could avoid all the portals and free him (and McGrue), and *then* cap-ture Hawgin. Why did I have to do everything? Catching Hawgin might have to wait for another day.

Suddenly, a car came screeching into the parking lot. Grace, already? But no, a pile of teenage and twenty-something girls piled out, in Halloween cos-tumes of varying coverage. Was there supposed to be a rave here tonight? That would be convenient.

But no. They all screamed for Gapman. The portals ignored them as they ran toward the nearest door.

I couldn't yell to them or the portals might sense me. I quickly accessed the Gapfen app and sure enough, GHQ had shared his position. I added my own comments about the location and situation. Maybe we could get everything done after all.

Ron

Kitty started to kick and thrash against our bonds. Every movement jostled me, adding to my nausea.

"Would you stop that?" I finally snapped. "You're making me sick!"

"I'm making you sick? Why didn't you do something—snap the ropes, take off flying? Why are you just sitting there?"

In answer, I leaned forward between my knees, half lifting Kitty off the conveyor belt, and vomited over the side.

"Ew!" Kitty said. "What is wrong with you?"

I spat bile and thanked Heaven that I hadn't eaten the big breakfast Mom had made. "It's not my fault. There must be dragonstone somewhere."

"Don't look at me. He pulled that necklace off my neck as soon as he had us tied. Come on. Dig deep. We have to break these ties!"

She started twisting her hands in the rope which also bound my hands. Every rub of the cord on my wrists made my entire arm feel like it was peeling from the muscles out.

"I can't!" I said. "There's dragonstone in the rope!"

"What? Oh, great!" Kitty groaned with despair and tossed her head back. It smacked mine and she yelped.

"Ow!" I complained. "Listen to me. I have a knife in my belt pouch. We can cut ourselves free. Now, would you calm down!"

"We're on the Conveyor Belt of Doom! Have you seen what's waiting at the end?"

I glanced to my left. Yikes! I didn't care how slow this thing was moving. The chompers were coming up too fast. "Okay. On the count of three, we shuffle right—my right! Your left! Away from the chompers!"

"Seriously? That's the best you've got? 'Skootch our butts'?"

I ignored her. We needed time, and we could skootch faster than the belt. "One, two, three! Skootch!"

I dragged her the first time, but then she reluctantly joined me.

My gloves were too thick to get my fingers under my belt to twist it, and no way was I baring my hands near the dragonstone-infused rope. "One, two, three! Skootch! Kitty, grab my belt and slide it. See if you can get the knife. Let's move— One, two, three! Skootch!"

She did a great job scratching the small of my back, but the belt did not want to shift.

"This is ridiculous!" she shouted. "Who thinks to make a cable out of dragonstone?"

Seriously? She had to ask? "I dunno—maybe someone who read your article?"

"Oh, so this is my fault now? One..."

"Now that you mention it. Skootch!"

"Look! I was just doing my job. The public has a right to know."

"Why? Who benefited from that knowledge other than the criminal element? Is that the public you serve? One, two three..."

"Scootch! You don't understand journalism!"

The effort of moving and the pressure of the belt on my waist was making me sick again—or maybe it was just the conversation. Regardless, I felt my stomach heave. I leaned forward—just as Kitty was skootching sideways. She swung right. The rope dug into my side. The world grayed a moment, and then we were tilting toward the edge.

Chapter Thirty-Four: Gapman and the Femmes of Phi Epsilon Phi

Vern

The portals were moving like sentries around the building...which meant they had a pattern. Bad move, U. I waited for the inevitable open spot and dashed through to the door. I pulled out my lockpicks with my tail and picked the lock while I kept an eye out for any surprises. Meanwhile, the party girls were sneaking their way to a side door—or doing their best approximation while wearing high heels and long puffy jackets. They were also noisily shushing each other. One giggled.

"Alicia, shut up or go back to the car!" one hissed and was told to chill.

Maybe leaving a rescue to them wasn't the best idea.

The lock gave, and I pushed my way in, hoping Alicia's squeal as she stepped into a puddle covered the sound of the door creaking.

Once in, I pressed hard against the wall and stayed still, trusting my wide range of vision to take in the situation. I didn't want to do anything to alert the roaming portals before I had their pattern.

There were Gapman and McGrue, arguing with each other while they butt-shuffled down the conveyor belt away from the grinders and the furnace below it. Excellent! Buying themselves some time. The belt was crawling along at a pace that would put a High Elf diplomat to shame, anyway.

Now, where was Hawgin-U?

There! Heading down a staircase. He wasn't going to watch? Laugh an evil laugh? If nothing else, I'd have expected him to have run or portaled away by now, but he was just dawdling and muttering to himself. Plus, I could sense now, he was wearing a dragonstone necklace. Why not leave that with Gapman? What was his game?

I'd done some research on Hawgindespotlite. He was a gentle soul. Crushing your enemies and tossing them into a furnace was extreme for any High Elf or villain-actor-turned-real villain, but him? Could he be that mad?

Or did he expect Gapman to escape?

Even more reason not to let him go. I was not going to be the dragon in a game of cat-and-mouse. I had the timing of the portals. I bunched my muscles and as a route cleared, blasted from my hiding place, and dashed toward U.

These portals were a little more aware than the outside ones. I jinked left to avoid one, then launched myself into the air to avoid the next. Above me I heard Kitty shriek.

I couldn't spare any attention to them—Gapman would have to save her. I slipped around a portal, nearly losing my tail, then tossed another of Grace's charms. It and a second portal rushed to it like dogs after a bacon snap.

U looked up, saw me first, and started to run while his hands moved to create a portal spell. I recognized the motion—it was a derivative from *Doctor Strange*. Years ago, I and some friends had been portaled back in time to an adventure in Faerie. Samwise, a Mundane friend, had been turned into a fairy and had taught them the moves. They were only for show, but everyone had liked them, and they'd stuck through the centuries.

Which meant Hawgin was using a Midsummer Court spell.

An idea brewed, but I didn't have time to think about it. Another portal was heading my way. I threw myself at U, grabbing him in my claws as the portal swallowed us up.

Ron

Kitty shrieked. I felt myself about to topple over the edge. Below us was a 20-foot drop to hard cement. With a yelp and surge of adrenaline, I jerked us back onto the conveyor belt.

For a few moments, we sat panting. Then Kitty griped, "You couldn't have used that energy to float us to the ground gently?"

We heard a crash of metal and glass and footsteps pounding on the floor below us.

"Gapman!" female voices echoed off the walls. "We're here for you! Gapman!"

Kitty's voice was murderous. "You called your fans?"

I sighed. "Yes! Yes, Kitty. I called my fans. With my psychic fencalling powers—like Aquaman, but with women. It was probably the app."

Then I shouted, "Up here! Cut the power!"

Even skootching, the chompers crept closer to us. Below us, the girls grew frantic as they searched for an off switch.

Kitty grew more and more irate. "Where is Vern?"

Vern

The portal ejected us, and we tumbled. I flung myself to the right and rose to my feet, roaring defiance and ready to take on whatever army of minions and spells Unity had set up for me.

My voice rebounded softly off the insulated walls of an empty office.

"Well," I said, sitting. "That's anticlimactic."

The chihuahua (Timida, I presumed), scrambled out of Hawgin-U's pocket and jumped off his lap. She ran from one end of the room to the other, saw me, yapped furiously, then, satisfied, urinated on a fallen OSHA poster.

Hawgin groaned and sat up. His hat flung itself off his head. A pixie in a silver jumpsuit was tangled in his hair, kicking and beating at his scalp in a temper tantrum.

What the...? "You've got a little something in your hair."

Hawgin turned to look at me and I jerked back in surprise and disgust. The pixie had sunk its mouth into his scalp, and Hawgin's skin had grown to envelop its head. It was like he'd developed a boil with arms and legs and two beady eyes filled with hate.

"And now," Hawgin said in a tired voice, "you know the secret that is Unity."

Ron

"I'm sure Vern is busy," I retorted wearily. I was done with yelling. My stomach was a knot of queasiness, and now a train-stopping migraine was making spots appear before my eyes.

"Well, he should be helping us!" she said. "Oh, no. We're getting closer. Come on! Skootch!"

"Kitty," I said. I had to say it twice more before she stopped dragging me along. "There's a way out of this. I lean forward and we fall."

"Are you crazy?'

"You'll be fine. You'll land on my back."

"And you'll land on your face. Forget it. You don't get to be the hero—"

"I am the hero!" I snapped. "We're going. One, two—"

The conveyor belt jerked to a halt.

The girls started jumping up and down and crying out victory cheers. "Phi Epsilon Phi! Rocky Mountain High!"

"Hey, sororo-hos!" Kitty yelled. "A little help?"

"Shut up, skank!" one called back.

"Ladies, please," I begged. I didn't want to die tied up to the woman who betrayed my trust and got me killed. And I really didn't want to pass out in front of sorority girls.

"Oh, my Gapman!" they squealed.

Even the dim light of the mill was too bright. I closed my eyes and tracked the progress of the girls by their footsteps while I took shallow breaths to fight back the nausea. I straightened my back. I may be weak, but I was not going to look weak.

Kitty caught onto what I was doing. "Really?" she asked.

"Shut up."

Twin gasps and a change in footsteps told me two of the girls were making their way along the conveyor belt to us. I opened my eyes. Ow! The light.

"Belt pouch," I said when one got close. I tilted my head toward the correct one, groaning as pain flared up my neck. "Knife. Cut us free."

"And get rid of the rope," Kitty added. "It's infused with dragonstone. It's hurting him!"

Sure. Now, she thinks about that.

The first girl—everything was blurry but I could tell she had short, black hair—pulled off her gloves and dug into my belt. Meanwhile, the blonde behind her said, "Hey! Aren't you Kitty McGrue?"

"That's right!" Kitty said, a slight preen in her voice. I felt her straighten her posture, too. Now who was being proud?

But the girl said, "You're that dirty reporter who told the world about Gapman's weakness! What are you doing here? Did you get caught in your own trap?"

"'Dirty'?" Kitty yelped. "Who you calling, 'dirty'?"

"Please! The press are the puppets of the establishment."

"Listen here, Barbie—"

"It's Alyssun with a Y, two SSes and a U, and you can quote me when I say..."

I let their argument flow over me and concentrated on the black-haired woman cutting my bonds with careful haste. Were my eyes playing tricks on me? "Are you wearing cat ears?"

She hummed an affirmative. "We were filming a NokNok just a mile or so from here when we heard you were in trouble."

Saved by Catwoman? I felt a little delirious—that's why I grinned, I'm sure. "My lucky day."

She paused long enough to meet my eyes before returning to the ropes. "Almost there..."

The last of the fiber snapped, and the ropes fell loose. My heroine immediately yanked them off me and threw them down. "Alicia! Madison! Throw those into the fire—now! There's more coming."

Soon the ropes binding Kitty and me were flying over the edge.

The pulling-me-inside-out feeling immediately left.

"Thank you!" I gasped, and flopped onto my side. Then, because I didn't want to look so pathetic, I rolled onto my back and cocked up one knee. I put one hand behind my head and the other over my eyes. Wrapped in a spandex supersuit, I probably looked like the opening of a Chippendale's act, but it was less embarrassing than being curled in a fetal position.

Someone pressed her hand on the back of my knee.

"What are you doing?" Kitty demanded.

"I'm pre-med. I'm checking his pulse," my rescuer replied. "This is the best I can do since *you're* in the way."

"I'll be okay," I gasped. "Give me a minute."

I lay there quietly, concentrating on my breathing, feeling myself grow stronger as my body reset or rejected the damage or absorbed magic or whatever it was that it was doing. The girls below shouted, "All done, Brit!" and somehow knowing the rope was destroyed made me feel even better.

Brit kept her hand wrapped around my leg, fingers pressed firmly but gently against the artery in the back of my knee. It was kind of comforting, actually. Wish I could say the same for Kitty. She sat beside me and patted my shoulder in an impatient staccato that sent little spikes to my temples.

"Miz McGrue," I finally said through gritted teeth.

With a sigh that was half-huff, she subsided. "Where is Vern, anyway? This is embarrassing—being rescued by sorority girls."

"I'm okay with it," I said. I tilted my head enough to smile at the girls. Brit's jacket collar had bowed open. She did indeed have a sexy cat costume on. Alyssun, who was crouching behind her friend, caught my gaze and tittered. I was too weak to blush—or maybe I'd just been through so much, it didn't seem worth getting embarrassed about. But I did turn my attention and a friendly Gapman grin to Alyssun.

"Your pulse is stronger now," Brit said, oblivious to my quick gaze. "Think you're ready to stand?"

In response, I held out my hand. With Brit pulling and Kitty behind "just in case," I rose to my feet. I ended up very close to my rescuer. Now that things weren't blurry, I could see that she had makeup whiskers and a cute cat nose.

"So, uh...Do you want to fly down?" she asked, and I could tell she was hoping for a ride.

Still, "I'm not sure how well I've recovered. The stairs are fine."

She frowned, then rallied. "Well, then, be part of our NokNok video? I did rescue you."

"All of us!" Alyssun said. "It was a group effort! Come on—Brit! One for Phi and Phi for all!"

They'd seen me woozy, weak, and tied up—and they still liked me? I felt a surge of happiness rise in me, and a laugh escaped my throat. "Of course, ladies. I'll see what can be arranged. But first, I do have to find Vern—and the villain that captured us before he escapes and attempts other nefarious schemes. It would help greatly if you all were safely away from here."

"But we rescued you!" Alyssun stomped her foot. I saw now that they were clad in Wonder Woman boots.

"And I shall not forget your valor," I assured her, "but your presence would be too distracting. I need to do this alone."

As Alyssun's eyes glittered at the implied compliment, I turned to Kitty. "That includes you, Miz McGrue. Please let these ladies return you safely back to the city."

Then, I realized I'd been hearing other cars coming. "And perhaps warn others away?"

When Kitty reluctantly agreed, I led them to the stairs. I, however, stayed at the top. I felt so much better now—not my usual, but enough that I could use my X-ray vision to seek out Vern...or Unity. It'd taken so long to get out of this mess, then recover, that he could be anywhere by now. Especially if he had a portal, he could be...

Wait.

He was in the manager's office?

Chapter Thirty-Five:
Gapman Deals With U

Ron

I didn't want to chance falling flat on my face in front of the ladies, who were waiting for me at the bottom of the stairs, so I ran at superspeed down the staircase and across the building to the office where Vern was (I assumed) being held. As I neared the door, I felt a familiar pull and skidded to a halt.

Dragonstone!

I could not fall for the same trap twice. I backed up until the weird sucking on my...aura? Magical energy field?... was more of a caress, and thought hard. Vern was in there with Hawgin, but neither was moving. At least they weren't fighting. In fact, they seemed to be having a calm, even amiable conversation, although I couldn't understand the language.

Vern laughed.

What was going on? Since he didn't seem in imminent danger, I reached into my belt pouch and pulled out my phone.

"Vern? Are you alright? I'm just outside the door, but there's dragonstone—"

"Oh, right! Hang on. Hey—U? Ditch the bling."

A moment later, the weird pull disappeared. With a shrug, I walked into the room, where I found...

Nothing. Just some office furniture and Vern sitting and talking to Hawgin. The only odd thing was that the High Elf had a pixie reclining on his head, swinging its feet back and forth like a child watching cartoons. Under a desk, Timida was gnawing on a Thanos bobblehead.

"Well," I found myself saying, "this is anticlimactic."

"Manners, Padawan," Vern scolded. "Unity is going to solve a problem that you created."

"Problem?" I asked as I approached—cautiously, in case Vern was under some kind of mind control. "What pro—Yeargh!"

I jerked back in surprise as I caught sight of Hawgin from the front. Where the pixie's face should be was a malformed tumor. With beady little eyes that looked daggers at me.

"What the..." I gulped. "What happened?"

"You got the better end of Snapdragon's puck," Vern said.

Hawgin, misunderstanding, nodded. "Indeed we did. For now I, once a skilled actor of only moderate fame, can wield fairy magics as well as give a concise interview. Goldleaf, in return, has access to the centuries of knowledge and strategic thinking that only High Elves command."

"And dragons," Vern said, "but don't forget attention to detail."

Hawgin bowed in acknowledgment, causing Goldleaf to grab hold of his hair. "Indeed—attention to detail. And if I left dragons out, it is because there can be no comparison between the mortal races and the Eighth Day Creations. But the fact remains, Unity is a new being, unique to this world, a creation at once bizarre and sublime, for verily...."

Five minutes of self-aggrandizement later, Unity wound down, and Vern took up the conversation.

"Unity's problem, of course, was what to do with his newfound primeness. The natural choice, given his origin story and your taking the mantle as a superhero, was to become a supervillain."

"The yin to my yang," I said. It had been a long day, and even without the dragonstone to suck the life out of me, I was tired and hungry. Outside, the crowd was still growing despite my requests. As much as I wanted to sit down and have a cordial conversation, I could not trust Unity to not suddenly go evil. I compromised by leaning against a desk and crossing my arms. "This isn't a play. Miz McGrue and I could have been killed."

Hawgin shrugged apologetically. "I'm afraid U overdid it with the dragonstone powder in the ropes. A miscalculation, we assure you. I'm an actor, not a mathematician, and Goldleaf now admits he was never good at potions."

He really thought this was a game? "But the bookstore—you shot me!"

"I was aiming for your shoulder—a simple test of your bulletproof nature. Alas, the chaos between the pixies and the robust woman who was the girlfriend of the pixie Ivyroot, friend of Goldleaf, distracted U, and we missed. Quite embarrassing, and we made a hasty exit. We'd intended to try again, but keen-eyed Vurnerrah brought the police to the building. Vern told us your mother did the same thing not a day previously?"

"Never mind that," Vern stepped over the protest I was about to make, "I have the perfect role for them—and it solves our Titania problem."

"You want Unity to be the champion of the Midsummer Court?" I asked.

"There is a certain poetry to it," Unity said. "For it was Snapdragon's mission to find the Most Radiant One a new champion, and the design of his puck to create said champion. I would have the role of a lifetime, and Goldleaf would have the respect of his peers—respect, he says, which is long overdue."

The pixie's eyes shined with excitement.

I found myself wanting to argue. Unity wasn't exactly in his right mind. Heck, they couldn't even decide what person to refer to themselves in. Then again, why was I looking a gift horse in the mouth? Surely, the Queen of Heat and Glare would know how to handle a half-mad elf/pixie hybrid. It wasn't like she was especially stable, herself, anyway.

Hey—would this count as a puck on the puckers? Certainly, Snapdragon won't see this coming.

"Okay… So how do we do this?" I asked.

"We don't," Vern said. He stood and stretched, extending his claws. "You leave Faerie dealings to me. Why don't you go outside and do crowd control before

Santry decides to send some paddy wagons and puts all the blame on us? So, U—how about making a portal to the Midsummer Court so I can get this geas off my scales?"

Once they had disappeared through the portal and it closed, I allowed myself to slump. So this had all been a game. Minemesis, indeed. Yet, he'd almost killed me. We had to figure out a workaround to this dragonstone now that anyone could find out about it—thank you, Kitty...

My phone buzzed again. I had 35 alerts on the Gapfen app and 15 texts. I scanned the app. After the first alert from GHQ—how did Mom know I was in trouble?—there were dozens of messages of people saying they were on the way: individuals and groups and...Why was LLPartyBusInc on the app? A post from Brit saying I had sensual knees—thanks, Brit!... There were pictures of people on the scene... There had to be hundreds...

Happiness and responsibility vied in me, making my stomach churn. Too many mixed emotions. Speaking of which... I turned to the seven texts from Kitty. She got a ride from an Uber driver who had come to help. Figured. She wanted me to come to her place to talk. No kidding—we needed to have a conversation.

If you kissed me at superspeed when you left, it was too fast.

I laughed, but it was not a happy sound. Seriously—I was off to fight the villain, and she thought I was thinking about stolen kisses like a 12-year-old?

Then more requests that we talk. She hoped I could understand her position. An update on her location...

I started hearing a chant from outside: *We stand with Gapman! We stand with Gapman!* It seemed like it was coming from everywhere all at once. Was I imagining things?

Only one way to find out. I headed back and out the door through which the girls had come.

The day was cold, but clear and bright, and I had to shield my eyes until they adjusted. There was a crowd stretched from one end of the mill to the other, chanting and shouting and waving whatever weapons they had brought to the fray: tire irons and guns and swords ranging from cheap plastic to what looked like serious blades. In front of me, Alyssun held a mike and was leading the chant.

Suddenly, it dissolved into a roar worthy of the Broncos winning the Superbowl.

The Phi Epsilon Phis ran up to me. "Gapman!" Brit cried. "You're alright! We were going to leave like you asked, but there were so many people here and then the Kappa Delts said what if the villain tried to escape so we surrounded the building—"

Alicia broke in, "—and then Alyssun thought, wouldn't it be intimidating if we all chanted—"

"—like in *The 300*—" Alyssun added.

Madison concluded, "—but now you're here! The villain..?"

My inner Ron wanted to laugh and cry, but I was Gapman. I took the mic. "Citizens! The threat is over!"

More cheers. Someone fired a gun in the air.

"Cease fire! I hope those of you with guns have licenses and will observe proper safety."

The crowd calmed, and I saw several people stuff their weapons away. A few had furtive looks. Figured. Someone yelled, "Sorry, Gapman." The cheers subsided to murmurs.

"Citizens," I began again. "Friends. That you are here—facing unknown danger—for me—is... overwhelming. I don't know how to thank you..."

"Let's party!" a male voice yelled. Immediately, his friends took up the chant: "Party! Party!"

Soon it flowed over the crowd: "Party with Gapman!"

Even the staid superhero me had to laugh at that. "How can I refuse? But no guns and no drugs!"

As if someone had been expecting it, "My Hero" by Foo Fighters suddenly came on at top volume.

The Phi Epsilon Phis encircled me and started to dance.

Vern

Lucky for me, Titania was absolutely delighted with my substitute champion.

She declared Snapdragon Grand Puck for the Age (which meant until she changed her mind), insisted that the "bulb-headed beast" get pampered, and called for a celebration. While her court scurried to fill the hall with music, food, and dancing, she regarded Unity with a thoughtful frown.

"Still... This look. Too disturbing. Perhaps Mad Mab might appreciate it in a champion, but I have fairer standards. Here, now."

She placed her hands on Hawgin's temples. He immediately stiffened, but whether in pain or surprise, I didn't know. His expression looked like Timida's before she'd gotten sick after crossing the portal. A muffled shriek emerged from his clenched teeth as well as from the bulge on his head that was Goldleaf. Then the pixie started to shrink. Goldleaf's limbs and wings began to grow silver and thread-like while silver hair sprouted from the tumorous growth that had enveloped his face.

By the time Titania released Unity from her spell, they were rocking a mullet that would have made Elvis jealous.

She clapped her hands regally. A half dozen pixies flew to her.

"Find our new champion something more appropriate for his role," she commanded.

I'd never seen a happier elf, and from the way his hair bobbed and swayed, Goldleaf was pretty stoked himself.

Titania turned to me and pouted prettily. "Well, my clever dragon. You've managed to elude my trap."

"I told you I wouldn't take sides against your sister. Don't act so surprised."

She ran a finger along my cheek crest, then reached behind and dug her nails in a light scratch. "I'm not. I'm disappointed. I don't see you often enough. The demands of this post-Gap age weigh too heavily on us both."

I leaned into her hand. "So heavily you have time to fight with your sister for weekend husband rights?"

Her mouth dropped into an affronted O. "One must have priorities! Stay for the celebration? I'll return you—and yes, the dog—not long after you'd left."

I stayed for the feast and a pampering that included a thorough scale cleaning, and left with a groomed and calm chihuahua, some faeberries for Grace, and even a present for Gapman. True to her word, Titania deposited me back in the mill about twenty minutes after I'd left.

Apparently, however, that was enough time for a rave to get started. I estimated a hundred and fifty people of varying ages, some in costume, all mingling, dancing, or sharing drinks. There were a couple of policemen milling about, but they seemed completely at ease. No one was causing trouble. I even saw some RealHumans chatting up a centaur.

Damsels and Knights! Did Gapman suddenly get mind-control powers?

I heard Lizzie scream Timida's name, and suddenly, she was snatching her dog out of my hands, kissing her round head and cooing over her bows while the dog licked her face and whined with joy. Grace appeared soon after.

"What happened?" she asked.

"I could ask the same of you," I retorted, swinging my head to indicate the crowd.

Grace shrugged, but her eyes sparkled. "It was amazing. Gapman's done more to bring people together than any of us realized."

I snorted. Figures. An Eighth Day Creation means nothing to the Mundanes, but when one of their own falls into toxic waste and gets hit by lightning, it's a miracle to rally around. But I'd just had a nice long pampering by people who did appreciate me, so I was willing to be magnanimous.

"Vern!"

I turned to see the hero-in-question surrounded by a gaggle of fans. He waved at me, then excused himself, kissing some of the girls' hands valiantly. Oooo. Kitty was gonna hate that. Where was she anyway? I didn't sense her acerbic personality bringing down the mood anywhere.

It took him a while to get to us, what with the high-fives, handshakes, and selfies, but eventually he, and a gaggle of Gapfen, got there. "Vern! Is this not the most incredible outpouring of community spirit? Did you get Unity to his destination?"

I liked that he was being cagey in his question. People had their phones out, recording. "Let's talk up-stairs."

I led him to the highest intact structure of the mill—the top of the farthest blast furnace. We settled on the scaffolding around it. Gapman laughed. "This is familiar."

"Snapdragon isn't here to break it."

"Even so." He settled on the floor, letting his feet swing over the edge. Below, the party raved on. "Did Titania accept U as a substitute?"

"If you mean U, then yes, and U were pleased as punch with their new role. She even gave U a new look. Speaking of..." I handed him the bag. It was barely the size of my claw, but when he reached in, he pulled out a pair of boots in Gapman's colors.

"Um...?"

"They're magical. Try them on."

He obeyed, then chuckled in surprise. "They feel amazing. And--whoa!" His eyes moved from his toes over his body and to his fingers as he tracked the magic working on his suit.

I said, "I think you'll find your suit is much more durable now, as well."

"My gloves even fit better." He wiggled his fingers slowly and rotated his ankles. "Um, I don't owe her anything, do I?"

"No! And don't ever suggest that. She'll either be insulted or see an opening, or both. Write her a nice thank-you note if you must—but let me check it—but otherwise, accept this as a return on investment for finding her a more suitable champion. Now catch me up—what's with the party? And where's McGrue?"

"They refused to leave." It was Ron talking, awe and disbelief in his voice. I let it slide. "They heard I was in trouble, and I swear, they would have stormed the mill if I hadn't come back out. And then, everyone wanted to celebrate."

"And McGrue?"

"Didn't stick around. But she's sent me eleven texts: three flirty suggestions about how I could sweep her off her feet, five 'We should talk's, and three suggestions about how we should deal with the problem that she still won't admit she caused. And not a single apology."

"You expected McGrue to apologize?" I tilted my head skeptically.

He sighed. "I expected to be a better judge of character than my mother. But I guess I am going to have to talk to her—oh, and speak of the devil."

He pulled out his phone. His eyes grew big. I peeked at the text: *Why haven't you answered? Fine. I'm home now. You have 45 minutes to give me a quote before I turn my article in for the web edition.*

"Article?" He leaped to his feet. "Oh, no! She is not lambasting Gapman or the Phi Epsilon Phis or... I have to go. This is war!"

"What are you going to do?" I asked.

"My job!"

He dove off the scaffolding. Mere feet above the crowd, he leveled out. As they cheered, he did a quick circuit around the party then shot straight into the single cloud in an otherwise cool blue sky. The cloud blasted apart in his wake.

It started to snow.

Chapter Thirty-Six:
Gapman Begins

Ron

"McGrue! Get in here!" Spittle flew from Editor-in-Chief Redfeathers' mouth as he shouted.

A moment later, an equally irate Kitty entered his office. She barely gave me a glance. "What, sir? I told Copyedit that Alyssun spelled her name weird—"

He didn't reply, just slapped a printout of my article on the desk. Confused, she picked it up.

"'City Saves Hero'? Cute play off 'Man Bites Dog.' I learned that trick in Journalism 101, too." She gave me a mean-girl smirk.

Redfeathers told her, "Read on, McGrue. This is what's going online—and on the front page tomorrow."

"What? But I was there!"

"And you were obviously too close to the story to stay objective. 'Gapped-Man: Hero's Incompetence Puts Self, Others In Danger'?"

"The people should know he's not infallible!" she protested.

"True," I said with a casualness I'd practiced in front of the mirror before coming into this meeting. "And I covered that."

"What's more," Mr. Redfeathers continued, "Engleson did it in a way that is still positive and makes our community look good. And he has the whole story, from kidnapping to snowfall."

I grinned. I had to thank Vern for that detail.

"You quote Gapman!" Kitty said. "How did you get quotes? Your mom, I suppose?"

I shrugged and answered truthfully. "I was at the party."

Kitty rolled her eyes. "You? You want me to believe you were—what—dancing with sorority girls? You were trying to scoop my story!"

"I didn't have to scoop anything, Kitty. I got everything on my own. Just because mine is more complete..."

"Complete? Listen you, you movie critic—"

Redfeathers cut across us. "All right. That's enough, McGrue. You'd better learn to get along with your new partner."

"What?" Kitty and I both turned to him in surprise.

"McGrue, you're getting stale. Everything out of you is a conspiracy or a secret crime or a cover-up. We blast it on page one, and two weeks later, we're posting corrections on page ten. You've got good instincts, but you're too quick to jump to conclusions. This time almost got you a one-way trip to an incinerator.

"Ronnie, you don't have experience with hard news. But what you have is a methodical nature, and you write good copy. Easy to read. Makes people feel hopeful. Even when you pan a movie, people believe you've given it the benefit of a doubt. You've been gaining confidence lately. I've noticed, and others have, too. Now this. I think you're ready to move up."

Kitty gave an inarticulate but very meaningful "Gah!"

I think that was the nicest thing he'd said to me since I was twelve. I almost hated to shake my head. Almost. "Thanks, Chief—er, Mister Redfeathers—but I don't think so. I'm doing just fine with my freelancing."

Kitty snorted. "Sure. Fine enough to live with your mom. Enjoy your front-page moment. It's probably the only one you'll ever get."

She turned and flounced out of the room.

Relax, I told myself. McGrue is just being McGrue. She's snarky because she sees me as competition now. That's a win.

And it was.

But it wasn't the win I wanted.

I spun on my heel and followed her into the newsroom. "McGrue!"

She whirled around. Heads popped up from computers, and people pulled out earbuds.

I didn't wait for her to ask me, "What?" in that impatient tone of hers that I used to think was cute.

"I live in a three-thousand-square-foot Tudor home on forty acres of mountain land. And, yeah, I share it with my mother because we're saving for the day when we can split that land and build a second home. In the meantime, I'm paying my half of the rent and utilities and everything else—and I'm doing it writing about comic books and movies and the things I love."

I took another step toward her. "If I don't make 'Front Page News,' it's because my work is online, homepage, above the fold. One of my articles gets more clicks in a day than all of yours do in a week."

Someone in Home and Gardens murmured, "Burn!"

Kitty, however, rolled her eyes. "Do you want an award?"

"No." I moved in close. She had flats on today; I could actually look down into her eyes. "I want the respect I deserve—and I want you to lay off my mom."

I stared her down, half-wondering if at last, she'd recognize who I was. If she'd paid half as much attention to Gapman's eyes as I had to hers...

But instead, she gave a rude "*Pfth!* Whatever," and walked away.

I blinked at her retreating back. Unbelievable! She really was as bad as Vern had said. There was no winning with her. And yet, when I saw the surprised and impressed expressions of the others in the newsroom, I realized that I had earned a greater victory.

By the time I got home, the snow was falling in earnest. Mom and Aunt Matilda were on the porch, greeting the first snow in our traditional way—in the hot tub with mulled wine warmed on the barbeque. I changed at superspeed and joined them.

"You're article's already up!" Aunt Matilda said. "Great job. You were way too forgiving of Kitty in it though—as Gapman and Ron. Still, I love it! 'City Saves Hero' by Ron Engleson."

"Ronnie," I corrected automatically.

"Nope!" Mom said and showed me the site on her phone. Sure enough, there was my name: Ron L. Engleson. "Awesome, right?"

"Yes!" I said, feeling it even more than I had expected.

We toasted my name and Gapman's adventures and the Gapfen app and (of course) OMyGapman.com. Then we went silent, enjoying the bubbling of the jets against the utter silence of the forest snowfall.

"So what'd Kitty think?" Aunt Matilda asked.

"Don't know and don't care—as Ron or Gapman. I broke up with her; I gave her the 'It's too dangerous for us' speech, but she knew Gapman was Gap-pissed. No more dating in my superhero persona."

"Good!" Mom said. "You deserve someone who is going to love you and not the mask."

We toasted to that and again sipped in silence.

"I'm glad you're alright," Mom said at last. "I was so worried."

"How did you know I was in trouble? You had my location and the SOS posted on the Gapfen app before we were tied up on the Conveyor Belt of Doom. Unity didn't mention telling you, and I know Kitty sure didn't."

"I just felt it in my very cells. No, truly. It's science: fetomaternal microchimerism. You may be a super-hero now, but that doesn't change the fact that I grew you in my womb. I carry your very cells within me. I'm forever in your heart and you are in mine."

I leaned my head against the deck of the jacuzzi. "You're making it hard for me to find a woman, you know that, right?"

Just then, Mom's GHQ phone pinged with a text.

"It's from Vern," Mom said, then read, "Why doesn't my padawan have his phone on him? There's a blizzard on the way, and the Forest Service wants our help finding some hikers stuck in the woods."

"Tell him I'm suiting up!" I said as I stood.

"Take the winter survival kit!" Mom called as I dashed up the stairs.

Soon I was dressed with the supplies in my Gap-pack. Mom handed me a thermos of hot tea. I checked the coordinates Vern had texted, and I was on my way.

This was a job for Gapman.

Do you love Vern?

Please take a few minutes to leave a review. Channel your inner Ronnie Engleson and share with others what you like and don't like about the book. It helps readers and helps with Amazon ratings which makes author and dragon happy.

If you want to keep up with Vern's and my adventures in person and on print, sign up for my newsletter. You'll get a free ebook with a Vern story in it!

https://fabianspace.substack.com/subscribe

Acknowledgements

Back around, oh, 2010 (maybe?), when Marvel was just gaining momentum on its superhero movie franchise, I decided I wanted a superhero in the Vernverse. His name would be Gapman and he'd twist every cliché in the comic book! I had so much fun coming up with crazy scrapes for him, from rescues gone wrong to romantic SNAFUs. What I could not come up with was an overall story for the framework. So, I set him aside to concentrate on other things.

However, I'd see something in a movie and think "What would Gapman do?" and get interested again—but always with the same result.

Fast forward to 2024. I'm in Book NINE of the DragonEye series and just about ready to revise the two original ones into the new universe. But suddenly, I knew Gapman's time had come.

The book is SO much better than what I could have written 14 years ago. There's just as much fun, but there's more heart. Ronnie—sorry *Ron*—Engleson is more than a caricature. He's a great character with a wonderful story to tell.

Unfortunately, 14 years means I've forgotten a lot of the people who played with me when I was making up his exploits. (If you helped and I forgot you—contact me! I can always add your name to future editions!)

Becca Calloway and the crew at the Writers Chat Room always had fun ideas and loved to brainstorm. Devon Ellington's writing classes were great sources of inspirations—the chaos of the newsroom, while greatly changed, came from one of her exercises. Ann Lewis has been a faithful writing companion for decades!

Thomas Salerno is an entertainment writer and a great geek. He helped inspire Ron's character. However, Ron is his own person, with his own insecurities and crazy background. They do share messenger bags in common, however.

The CWG crit group is always a great help. Thanks to Sarah Crickard, Suzanna Linton, Matthew Schmidt, Cesar Chacon, Barb Graver, Marie Keiser, Nancy Bechel, Alyssa Watson, Shannon Davies, Joshua St.Onge, and Monica Chenet. Sarah pushed for the Save the Pat scene. Suzanna Linton was nitpicky and pushed me to greater humor. (She and Thomas came up with the FAEderal express truck scene. Yes, I found real cars shaped like corn and carrots.) Nikos Lambdin was my enthusiastic beta reader. Vern loves new fans!

I should probably thank Vern for taking the supporting role in this book. It hurt him a little to have all the chapter names about Gapman. Way to take one for the team, Vern!

Finally, thank you, dear readers. I love getting notes saying how much you love Vern. Vern loves them, too. Next book, we're going back to the beginning of the DragonEye, PI stories with a rewrite of *Magic, Mensa, and Mayhem*! Gapman gets a cameo, and there will be even more fun in the new version. (Now that I live in Florida, there will probably be more local color.)

There's More Fun in FabianSpace!

DragonEye Series

Murder Most Picante

If Wishes Were Dragons

Nun of My Business

Christmas Spirits

Greater Treasures

Siren Spell

Good Intentions

Idol Speculations

Plus short stories

Science Fiction

Space Traipse: Hold My Beer Series

The Old Man and the Void

Dex's Way

Discovery

The Rescue Sisters short stories

Neeta Lyffe, Zombie Exterminator

Zombie Death Extreme!

I Left My Brains in San Francisco

Shambling in a Winter Wonderland